TERROR TRANSIT

"Logan Express now boarding on platform seven."

The stocky man with the scar running through his eyebrow studied the curly-haired youth superimposed between the cross hairs of his rifle sight. The target rose from his seat in the bus station terminal and stretched uneasily, scanning the area around him. No matter, the stocky man reflected, his eyes would do him no good. He stood out of sight fifty yards away in the corner of a darkened repair bay.

While witnessing the aftermath of the explosion he had caused, the stocky man had noticed with no small degree of shock Lennagin lurking among the crowd. A chill had gripped his spine. Somehow he had made a crucial mistake that would cost him more than his job if it was not corrected immediately. There hadn't been time to issue a report and call for reinforcements. There had been time only to follow Lennagin from the fraternity and wait for the opportune time to make his amends.

He moved the barrel a fraction to the left, keeping his target locked in the grid. He pawed the trigger.

THE
LUCIFER
DIRECTIVE

JON LAND

ZEBRA BOOKS
KENSINGTON PUBLISHING CORP.

ZEBRA BOOKS

are published by

Kensington Publishing Corp.
475 Park Avenue South
New York, N.Y. 10016

First printing: April, 1984

Printed in the United States of America

For the Brothers of Delta Phi, where it all began,
and
For my parents, who were always there even before

ACKNOWLEDGMENTS

No book is a totally individual work. The time and patience of others is duly tried and generously given. For their contributions at various stages of this one I would like to thank Bob Grattage, Debbie Marshall, Linda Blankstein, Fenton, Michael Seidman, Tom Millard, Len Messinger, Bruce Botvin, Scott Siegel, and the ever brilliant Morty Korn.

Special thanks go to a miraculous editor, Ann Maurer, and a wondrous agent, Toni Mendez, who puts it all together.

THE
LUCIFER
DIRECTIVE

"The purpose of terror is to terrorize."

—Lenin

I

BLOODY SATURDAY

ONE

The van crept down Mountain Terrace Lane at a jogger's pace. Stolen from a central lot just hours before, it wore the legitimate markings of the Fairfax County Gas Company, a regular enough sight on these roads even on a Saturday night. No one would miss it until Monday and by then the people of Alexandria, Virginia would have other things on their minds.

"You're going too slow," the big man in the passenger seat told the van's female driver, fingering the green cap that rested in his lap. "Take a right past the house and circle round the block."

The driver felt her toes twitch involuntarily as she pressed the accelerator downward. The temptation to jam it all the way to the floor and flee rose in her again, suppressed because the move bore all the logic of a mouse sacrificing its neck for a nibble of cheese. She considered several other strategies, chose none, stilled her toes but was helpless against the rhythmic chattering of her teeth.

The van edged past a white house with fronting pillars and rock music blaring from its backyard. She felt the big man's eyes digest the scene.

"How many guards?" she asked, sweeping the wheel

to the right, reconciled to their task.

"Four, just as we suspected. Two with shotguns, two with side arms. Cake."

He pushed his blond hair under his ears and tucked the green cap over it with the plastic visor tilted low over his forehead. Two quick raps on the partition behind him signaled the four men in the van's rear to ready themselves as well.

The driver swung back onto Mountain Terrace Lane.

"Let's go," the big man instructed.

He lifted the Kalishnikov assault rifle casually from the floor. It was a magnificent weapon, capable of tearing one man apart or spraying a dozen others with automatic fire. The thought made the big man shudder. His mouth was dry but a familiar taste filled it. Chalky and hot. Pleasant.

He watched the van's high beams bite into the night, chewing the darkness and spitting it from their path.

Inside the large white house, Alexander Levine stood anxiously by the window of his second floor study, which overlooked the backyard. Below, friends of his son clustered in groups of varying sizes, the boys at this point conspicuously apart from the girls. Music from a rented stereo system was blasting. Two men in white jackets were at work on the refreshment table. Levine tried to pick his son Jason out of the crowd, failed, and became more anxious.

This was the day of his son's Bar Mitzvah, a day that should have seen him relaxed, proud, in a celebratory mood. It had started that way, all right, but one manila envelope delivered to his door had changed everything. And now he wished he hadn't let his son talk him into this party. At the age of fifty, though, he found himself giving in more and more to Jason's whims and desires. He was too old to be the father he desperately wanted to be and young enough to know it. So he compensated by spoiling the boy, aware always of his own short-comings and hoping Jason wasn't aware of them, as well.

Levine dabbed at his brow with his jacket sleeve and gazed over the backyard scene: forty boys and girls, none over fourteen, having traded the suits and dresses of the morning for corduroys or jeans topped by sweaters or light jackets. Children at the magical crossroads of life when concerns amounted to little and cares to even less. How Levine envied them. He glanced at the manila envelope atop his desk, a message from The Doctor.

The Isosceles Project. . . . He had to stop it. The future was at stake. His own, Jason's, everyone's.

His fears were quelled a bit as he watched one of the guards mingling with the kids. There were four of them in all, wearing the uniforms of a nonexistent agency. In fact, they were expertly trained combat soldiers.

A knock came on the study door.

"Come in," Levine said, forcing his eyes from the window.

His wife Susan, fifteen years his junior in age and ten younger than that in appearance, entered. "Going downstairs, Al?"

Levine moved toward her and forced a smile. "I thought I might leave the kids to themselves, Sue. I don't want to embarrass Jase by hanging around."

"What makes you think you'd embarrass him?"

"At the age of thirteen, all parents are embarrassments."

She moved forward and held him. "They grow up so fast."

"Yes."

"You're trembling."

"Am I?"

"What's wrong?"

"It's been a long day."

"That's all?"

Levine sighed, his eyes darting from the manila envelope to the window and back again. "That's all."

The big man peered through the scope attached to his Kalishnikov. One of the four guards was captured between the cross hairs, escaped, and then was captured again. The fact that the van was moving provided but a minor inconvenience. He pawed the trigger, held the target with his eyes, and pulled.

The silenced barrel uttered a soft spit. The guard collapsed, a bullet neatly impacted in his brain. Another guard emerged from the side of the spacious yard drenched in floodlights. The big man squeezed the trigger again only when the second guard had entered a sphere of moderate darkness. The van pulled to a halt. He rapped on the partition.

"Go!"

The back doors opened. Four figures leaped onto the road, all dressed identically in green slacks and olive-drab polyester shirts with a red badge emblem embroidered over the pocket, their caps tipped low to shield their faces. The big man and the van's female driver joined them. They fanned out stealthily over the yard, each with an assigned area and task. Two edged to the sides of the house en route to the backyard. Two more stayed in the front. The final two sprinted for the door, the blond leader shattering it with a burst from his Kalishnikov.

Upstairs, something shook Alexander Levine from his desk and brought him to the window. It wasn't a sound so much as a feeling. Something cold poured through his veins. His bowels loosened.

Below him the scene was no different, nothing out of the ordinary to cause worry.

But Levine was worried. His soldier's eyes scanned the perimeter in search of his Special Forces guards, found two of them and continued on.

Wait! Both men held automatic weapons, clip loading. Minutes before they had been holding shotguns.

The icy grip of fear found Levine's insides and knotted them. The sharp soldier's edges in him tightened, honed. He moved for the desk and pressed a concealed button that triggered an emergency signal at a half-dozen stations across Washington and Virginia. The light next to it didn't flash on.

The line had been cut!

Levine didn't even bother with the phone.

Instead, he lifted his .45 automatic from a drawer and moved for the door. He fought against panic, realizing what had already happened and dreading what might be about to.

The series of soft spits and strangled scream came just as he reached the head of the staircase.

"NOOOOOOOOO . . . !"

Levine realized the wail was his own as he leveled his

15

.45 at the uniformed figure hovering over the crumpled heap that had been Susan. The figure whirled but too late. Levine squeezed the .45 twice, the first finding the figure's throat, the second its chest. Levine had learned his trade in Israel, where he had spent the first forty-two years of his life, had learned to control fear and make it work for him. They had killed his wife. They would not kill his son. He had ten bullets left and unless there were more than ten of them, they didn't stand a chance.

He had started down the steps when the second figure, much larger than the first, appeared out of nowhere. Levine saw it, fired, but then it was gone. Rolling, spinning, a blur before his desperate eyes, the figure moved faster than he thought humanly possible. He fired wildly again, then caught the flash at the end of his killer's barrel and felt the bullets slice through his abdomen and empty his stomach onto the carpet. He tried to fire the .45 but he'd lost it, lost everything except a grinning face framed by blond hair spilling out from a perfect replica of the green caps worn by the men he had hired to protect his family.

The big man moved through the house quickly, proud of his handiwork. He passed through a set of sliding glass doors into the brightly lit but now silent backyard. The members of his team had already herded the young party guests into a tight mass and spread out about them in a semicircle. The big man sensed his victims' terror, felt their desperate sobbing bring a smile to his lips.

His eyes sought out Jason Levine and found the boy standing bravely in the front with trembling fingers squeezed into fists. The big man stepped forward, grinned at him. The boy's mouth dropped. His stance wavered.

The big man drew the bolt of his Kalishnikov all the way back.

The children screamed.

The big man nodded at the other four uniformed figures, coiled his finger and held it against the trigger.

Five barrels blazed until there was nothing left to shoot at.

Nothing left at all.

The limousine pulled to a halt amidst the chaos in front of the house on Mountain Terrace Lane. Revolving blue lights stung the eyes of the man in the backseat, and the sight of news hounds thrusting microphones or notebooks into the faces of anyone with a uniform sickened him. Then again, who could blame them? They were here to do their jobs just as he was here to do his. The massacre was certainly big news, but to the limousine's passenger it meant so much more. He opened the door and stepped out.

His appearance was at best mundane. He stood a handful of inches below six feet and wore a white trench coat over his sagging frame. His hair was gray and thinning. The face it framed, though, was sharp and angular, alert and sensitive. His eyes were steel blue, emotionless, seeming to blink at intervals as regular as the ticking of a clock. He moved toward the backyard without drawing so much as a single glance from the news people, noticed only by a few official types emerging from the back with their stomachs tucked in their mouths.

17

"Good evening, Major."

"Nice to see you again, Major."

"Damn glad you're here, Major."

The remarks were cursory and the man they called "Major" didn't bother to acknowledge them. He reached the backyard, still ablaze with temporary lighting, and froze in his tracks. The carnage found his eyes at the same moment the stench reached his nostrils. He fought most of the bile back down his throat and leaned over to spit the rest up.

"You all right, Major?" asked a man in a tweed sports coat with an FBI badge pinned to his lapel, though he had never worked a day for the Bureau. He was one of the major's men.

"No, Mr. Goldman, I'm not."

Goldman echoed the statement with his eyes. "I've never seen anything like it myself. Not even in Nam."

Beyond him, uniformed men wearing protective masks and suits were lifting the corpses from the bloody pile and loading them into shiny black bags. They didn't seem to be making a dent in the heap.

"Sorry if I appear disinterested in your war stories, Goldman," the major said abruptly. "I just want to know what the hell happened here."

Goldman consulted his notes. "Things are still sketchy at this point but we can fix the time of the raid at approximately nine-thirty. Footprint measurements tell us either six or seven people were involved. Mr. Levine pressed his panic button upstairs but the wire had been cut along with the phone line. Sabotage obviously. Anyway, it probably didn't matter, because the killers were out of here by nine thirty-eight and it's doubtful help could have arrived in sufficient numbers before that time."

"Any security guards?"

"Four. All dead. But we did get one break."

"Oh?"

"It seems Levine was able to nail one of the killers before he bought it. We should have a make on him by morning and a lead to go with it."

"Anything else?"

"Nothing hard."

"Make it soft."

Goldman closed his notebook. "The killers' weapons were high velocity and caliber. Russian, I'd guess, probably in the Kalishnikov family. Not the kind of weapons you can buy at the local pawn shop. They had silencers as well, strictly a professional job all the way, nothing left to chance. Hell, nobody in the neighborhood's been able to tell us a damn thing yet. And the killers must've been top of the line to boot. The four guards Levine hired were from the Special Forces and they were cut up like candy. But I'll be damned if I can find a motive for . . ." Goldman's eyes swept the area around him, ". . . this. I mean from what we can gather they killed Al Levine before—" Goldman watched the major's eyebrows flutter. "You knew him?"

"I knew him."

"Well, he was certainly political enough to be a decent target for terrorist execution, but why kill forty kids who couldn't even tell you the difference between a Democrat and a Republican?"

"Survivors?"

Goldman shook his head. "I told you it was professional."

"So you did."

*   *   *

Back in the limousine, the major ran his hands over his face and wondered how long it would be before sleep would come easily to him again. The memory of the bodies piled one atop another with lifeless eyes and brutal holes punctured in their young flesh stayed with him the more he tried to block it out.

That was justification enough for his next action.

He reached for a red phone that lacked a dial and picked it up. Across the country similar phones rang on bedsides, in drawers, even in briefcases. A coded sequence of computer signals sped through his ear followed by a final beep. He took a deep breath.

"This is Major Bathgate. Clear all lines." A pause. "I am calling a Lucifer alert. . . ."

TWO

The last thing Dan Lennagin needed was to get wakened up in the middle of the night. What with midterms coming and papers piling up, he needed all the sleep he could get even if his waking hours weren't always spent doing the work he was supposed to. So his first reaction was to silence the ringing phone by ripping its plug from the wall. But his second was to answer it out of anxious curiosity, because middle-of-the-night phone calls often signaled an emergency.

Dan fumbled blindly for the receiver before finding it.

"Hello." His digital clock showed 3:07 in bright red letters.

"This is The Doctor," came a muffled, straining voice.

"Huh?"

"No time. Don't talk. Just listen. Levine got the message and they got Levine. I'm next . . . soon."

"What?"

"The massacre—just the beginning." Two raspy, agonized breaths. "Must . . . get . . . word . . . in. All other priorities rescinded. Standard channels by-passed. Sterilize your line."

21

Dan shook himself awake, groped for the light switch. "Look, I—"

"Message follows, top priority. Black is Lucifer and Lucifer is black. Tell Zeus it's Code Oscar. Repeat, Code Oscar. Destroy the Isosceles Project. Request message read back and line expulsion."

Dan cleared his throat, found the light switch. "Hey, is this—"

There was a crash on the other end, then a horrible scream. Or was it a scream? It could have been anything. Dan pressed his ear firmly against the receiver.

"Hello? Hello?"

He heard a shuffling, scratching sound followed by breathing. But it was different breathing than before, long and heavy, turning his blood cold.

Click.

The line went dead.

Dan replaced the receiver and pushed himself out of bed. The spring night had turned cold and he closed the window, shivering slightly. His mouth felt dry and he pulled a quart of orange juice from his small refrigerator and gulped some down. Then he moved across his room and turned on the desk lamp.

The call was a crank. It had to be. Then why did it seem so, well, real? What if—

Dan grabbed a pen and ripped a sheet of paper from a barely used notebook. He started writing, pulling as much of the call from his mind as possible before it drifted away.

Black is Lucifer and Lucifer is black. Tell Zeus it's Code Oscar. Repeat, Code Oscar. Destroy the Isosceles Project.

Gibberish, nothing more. It made no sense, not to

him anyway. But what of the speaker? There had been desperation lacing his voice. No, more than desperation, it was closer to hopeless resignation.

Resignation to what?

Levine got the message and they got Levine. . . .

Who was Levine?

The massacre—just the beginning. . . .

Dan longed for rest but somehow he wasn't tired. What had happened on the other end of that line after The Doctor had spoken his message? Who had picked up the receiver?

Questions without answers. Dan felt himself nodding off and climbed back into bed.

A crank call surely or some twisted fraternity joke.

But what if it wasn't?

The possibility set him trembling as he fell into an uneasy sleep.

THREE

"A most eventful twenty-four hours, Major Bathgate."

The speaker was a man Bathgate had never met. His stern voice sprang from one of the four intercoms resting on a desk before the major. It originated in Houston and passed through a long chain of electrical sterilizing devices on route to Washington.

"There's no denying that, sir."

Bathgate had entered the nondescript brick building on Fulton Street twenty minutes before. The cover was the American Institute for Retired Persons. Typewriters hummed and chimed in the large anteroom. As always, Bathgate had stepped into a closet and inserted a plastic card into a hidden slot. The wall had slid back, revealing a large office with many telephones—some with dials, some without. He sat down and instituted the call to Houston. Now the intercom linked him to a shadowy man whose power rivaled anyone's in the world.

"Alert status requires a most extraordinary situation, Major," the voice warned him.

"This more than qualifies, as my report indicated."

"I read it. I'm afraid some of your conclusions were

difficult to grasp."

"All the more reason for an alert."

"One way or another, you've got one. Lucifer's been called up. I want you to explain why. Let's get to what happened in Alexandria."

Bathgate cleared his throat and straightened his thoughts. "During the luncheon reception for his son's Bar Mitzvah, a messenger arrived with an envelope for Al Levine. Must have spooked him rather badly because he began making phone calls, said little and sounded scared. One of them was to my office here. He made an appointment to see me this morning."

"Interesting. Any idea what was in the envelope?"

"Only who and where it came from and I'll get to that later. First, I thought I'd bring you up to date on the investigation. We got a make on the dead terrorist twenty minutes ago: Ahmed Suwhari, last known residence Beirut. Links with Al Fatah, the Red Brigades, and Baader-Meinhof. Explosives specialist who dabbled in a little bit of everything. Seemed to fancy plane hijackings, especially when he could blow the passengers up at the endgame."

"Lovely character. Whoever got him deserves a medal."

"Or a casket," Bathgate corrected. "Levine got him."

"Figure of speech, Major, figure of speech."

"In any case, his dossier has provided us with a list of associates and others he was known to have worked with over the years. We've got the computers cross-checking now in a probability search for potential other participants in the massacre based on Suwhari's presence."

"Any other variables?"

"Just footprints. We know for sure now that six

terrorists were involved in the hit, and study of the plaster imprints taken at the scene should provide us with their heights and weights before too long. One thing we're already certain of is that one of them was a woman."

"Interesting."

"And enlightening. That fact coupled with Suwhari's participation and the approximate sizes of the other team members gives us a fair jump in determining the identities of the rest of the killers."

"Good. What about the weapons?"

"Kalishnikovs, as we suspected originally. Part of a shipment that disappeared from Prague two months ago. We traced them to a Swiss arms broker, but that's where the trail runs dry."

"And the envelope delivered to Al Levine?"

"If it's still in his house, we can't find it. I've got a team there now tearing the place apart but my experience in these matters has been that if you don't find something in the first two hours, you don't find it at all."

"The obvious conclusion then, Major, is that Levine was killed for that envelope. Simple matter for the regular authorities. Hardly reason for alert status."

"Except that if the envelope was the only reason for the strike, why murder all those kids?" Bathgate paused to let his point sink in. It was never easy to gauge the man from Houston's reaction. His tone never varied, his words remaining forever noncommittal. "And Alexander Levine was no slouch," Bathgate went on. "He was a pro all the way, a man who took precautions. He's had a thing for security ever since he came over from Israel eight years ago. Hell, the guards at his house last night were Special Forces commandos and the terrorists went through them like they weren't even there. So I called the alert because I'm convinced that Alexandria is the first in a long line of terrorist strikes here to be perpetrated by the same group. And whoever the group is, in one five-minute span last night they totally disrupted the orderly flow of American life. 'Bloody Saturday,' the papers are calling it, and somebody must be reading them. Check the streets. Look how few kids are playing outside. The whole country's running scared. Forty percent of all airline reservations for today have been canceled because people are afraid that's where the terrorists are going to strike next. Calls to local police departments are up a thousand percent because people are seeing suspicious figures lurking on every corner and that, I daresay, is precisely what last night's massacre was supposed to accomplish. A climate of fear—the ultimate atmosphere for terrorists to strike and melt away again."

"Simply stated, Major, you don't think we've seen the last of them."

"Far from it."

The man from Houston hesitated. "Well, since it was important enough for them to take that envelope from Levine, perhaps you should tell me what was inside."

"A message from The Doctor."

"The Doctor? I thought he retired."

"Tried to a couple times but never quite made it. I've had him in my network for three years now. Pushing fifty but he was still the best damn field operative I had. Handled strictly top cover assignments. I sent him to Los Angeles a few weeks ago to poke around some reported Chicano terrorist group with links to the BLA and the Weather Underground to see if alert status was called for. Quite by chance he must have stumbled upon something else, bypassed traditional channels, and sent the material directly to Al Levine."

"I don't like the implications of that," the man from Houston said deliberately.

"Nor I. It's safe to assume that whatever The Doctor uncovered was of a magnitude to make him void standard procedures even when those procedures should have been the safest steps for him to take."

"Apparently he had reason to believe otherwise."

"So he made contact with Levine instead. Levine had built a hell of a rep in Washington for not owing anybody favors and remaining as clean and unattached as possible. He was an outsider in our system, which gave him unique status along with free access to everyone in Washington, including those who aren't present on anyone's rolodex—a man to go to in a pinch. I think we can conclude that later yesterday The Doctor learned of the massacre and knew his cover was blown. He tried to make it out of L.A., failed, and ended up in a phone booth at twelve-oh-six A.M. West Coast time, where he tried to dial the emergency routing exchange and ended up with a wrong number."

"Wrong number?"

"Dialed the 401 area code instead of the 101 prefix. Ended up giving his message to a college fraternity president in Rhode Island. A file on him just came through."

"And what about The Doctor?"

"We got to the phone booth the call was made from three hours later. It had been mashed to hell. The Doctor's body turned up in a garbage can a few blocks away." The major hesitated. "His throat had been crushed."

"Crushed? Good God! You know as well as I who fits

that MO."

"Unfortunately."

"And if he's involved, there's no telling what we might be facing here."

"We know one thing," Bathgate said dolefully. "The Doctor was killed for the same reason Levine was and it all ties in with a phone call that ended up in Providence, Rhode Island."

"Christ." A pause. "Tell me about this college boy, Bathgate."

Bathgate opened a manila folder before him on the desk. "Daniel Peter Lennagin. Age twenty-two. Birthplace: Minersville, Pennsylvania. Father died eleven years ago. Mother works in a sewing shop, gross adjusted income seventy-two hundred per year. Lennagin entered Brown University in Rhode Island three and a half years ago and has depended on financial aid and student loans to keep him there. Mostly the latter. At last count, he owed the university twenty-three thousand. Tests well but has seldom worked up to his potential while at Brown. Joined Delta Phi Omega fraternity spring of freshman year and presently serves that organization as president. Lennagin's older brother, a Vietnam veteran now thirty-three, lives in Allentown, Pennsylvania where he serves on the police force. His younger brother, now fifteen, lives with his mother. Lennagin has no membership in subversive groups, no police record, no history of drug abuse other than infrequent use of marijuana, no evidence of homosexuality."

"In short, the all-American college male," concluded the man from Houston.

"Not exactly. I left one point of his background out because I felt it deserves special mention. His father didn't just die, he was murdered by terrorists."

"Hmmmmmmmmm . . ."

"It seems Lennagin's parents were taking their first real vacation ever, a group tour of Europe. One of those typical put-your-pennies-aside-for-ten-years-for-two-weeks-of-bliss trips. Except their plane was hijacked en route to Paris and forced to land in South Africa."

"I recall the incident. Pre-Lucifer."

"Unfortunately, because the terrorists started executing hostages the minute authorities exceeded the deadline for meeting their demands. Passengers were chosen by a seat number lottery. Lennagin's father's number was the first to come up."

"Good God!"

"It wasn't pretty," Bathgate continued. "And its effect on Dan Lennagin was to provide him with an obsession with terrorism. He came to Brown as a political science major determined to learn everything books could teach him about terrorism." The major paused. "I doubt they prepared him for last night."

"Hardly."

Bathgate switched the receiver to his left ear.

"And," continued the man from Houston, "of course if we know where The Doctor's phone call ended up, it's a safe bet that the people he was fleeing from know, as well."

"Absolutely."

"Which raises several interesting questions. How long did The Doctor speak to Lennagin?"

"The line was open for thirty-one seconds, ample time for him to relay a message. Remember, The Doctor thought he was talking to a sterile emergency

30

exchange. He would've spared nothing so long as time allowed."

"So right now, Major, this young man is the only person in the country who knows what The Doctor was trying to tell us."

"If he remembers it. The call came through past three A.M. Providence time. He might've thought it was a crank."

"We have drugs that will certainly spur his mind."

"I'm not sure we have the right to use them."

"Or the right not to, Bathgate. What would you suggest as an alternative?"

"That we get there before they, whoever they are, do. Then we get the kid out, learn what he knows, and resettle him far away with a new identity, a lot of money, and a bit of plastic surgery."

"Ambitious but expensive."

"I'm sure we can find the funds somewhere in our budget."

"That's not the point, Bathgate, and you know it. Two-thirds of your strategy is right on target. We've got to get to this boy before they do and find out what he knows. As for resettlement, well, it's simply out of the question at this point. Lennagin holds the only link, however slight, to whatever The Doctor uncovered. We've got to set him up as bait, flush the enemy out into the open."

"I can't allow that."

"You don't have a choice, Major."

Bathgate glanced down at the eight by ten photo of Dan Lennagin. Just under six feet tall. Well built. The face not handsome but strong and warm. The chestnut hair curly, hastily combed if at all, hanging in ringlets this way and that. Bathgate liked him immediately.

"I have two kids about his same age," he told the man from Houston. "You—we—can't set him up as a pigeon."

"Why?"

"Because he's an amateur."

"An amateur with a unique interest in our problem. A personal stake in the action, if you will."

"I won't."

"Come now, Bathgate, we're both professionals. Call it fate, coincidence, or whatever you like but Dan Lennagin—thanks to his own experience with terrorism—is the perfect innocent to involve in a high-risk situation. 'Highly motivative' is the term our psychology specialists call it. This is a game of advantages, Bathgate. You only get so many and certainly not enough to squander even one. I'm willing to take the chance. Why, Lennagin might even welcome our offer."

"Only if we avoided telling him what the situation will be like once things get dirty."

"He'll have your protection, Major. That's good enough for me. Worried you can't handle it?"

"Frankly, yes."

"You're a strange man, Major."

"I can't abide using innocent people in our games."

"Those forty kids last night were innocent too."

"That's no reason to make it forty-one," Bathgate said wearily.

"You haven't been to sleep yet, have you?"

"I tried a couple times. You didn't see Levine's backyard."

"I saw the pictures."

"You can't smell pictures."

"It'll happen again, Major, you said so yourself, unless we flush them out. We need Lennagin to accomplish that."

"I'll find another way."

"You'll do it *my* way. Otherwise, I'll get someone else to coordinate this affair who in all probability will lack your compassion and the boy will be all the worse for it. He won't turn us down, Major. You can tell that from his file as clearly as I can. The only remaining question is who presents him with the offer."

"You make it sound like we're doing him a favor."

"Maybe we are."

Bathgate searched for an argument that didn't exist. They had to use the boy; there was no getting around it. As a company man, he saw that but still resisted the sight.

"I'll be on the next plane to Providence," the major offered in frustration.

"Anything I can do at this end, Bathgate?"

"Just keep your gold pen handy."

"Why?"

"You've written this boy's death certificate. You might as well sign it."

II

LUCIFER

FOUR

For a day and a half, Dan Lennagin had run Saturday night's phone call through his mind over and over again. It had become an obsession for him, infringing first on his waking time and then keeping him from sleep—after he'd seen the Sunday late edition of the *New York Times,* which told the story of a brutal terrorist massacre in Alexandria, Virginia.

The massacre—just the beginning. . . .

The Doctor's words.

The article had shocked him so much that he almost missed the name of the family at whose home it occurred—Levine.

Levine got the message and they got Levine. . . .

More of the shadowy conversation.

Certainly a sophisticated prankster might have based the call on a late night news report, but why bother? And if the call was legitimate the question remained what to do about it. Dan had tossed several options through his mind, rejecting them all. He could call the police or local FBI, but what could he tell them? He might ask advice from a professor he trusted, except there wasn't any. Ignoring the phone call altogether was a possibility, though one he found it increasingly difficult to live with. What, then?

Dan felt confused, helpless, a little frightened. And his schoolwork was showing a strain it could ill afford. He needed to pass five courses to graduate and was towing the mark in barely three of them. So he had set this day aside to catch up on his reading and term papers. Only his mind had wandered away most of the day and the prospects for the rest seemed little better. His advanced seminar on the American Intelligence Community was a snap. Work couldn't come easier. But Political Economics was something else again. And the Philosophy of Radicalism, well. . . .

The simple fact for Dan was that college had played itself out long before the mysterious phone call had come. Maybe they should make it three years long instead of four. He had come looking for direction and had found little, if any. People these days kept asking what he was going to do when he left Brown. His reply had evolved into a simple shrug.

I'm going to hunt down the terrorists that killed my father, he wanted to say. But that would be giving away his innermost drive, something he kept alive for those days when his past chewed at him. Dan's flesh crawled every time a terrorism story hit the news. They were always hijacking a plane or blowing up a building, claiming the lives of innocent people as sacrifices to their cause.

I'm going to hunt down the terrorists that killed my father.

A pipe dream surely, but one that gave the frustrations in him a channel. Kind of like when the schoolyard bully kicks your ass and your revenge comes in the form of fantasizing about kicking his. Maybe someday you will. Who's to say?

Dan felt himself slump in his desk chair. His mind pulled away from his grasp, lurched toward the past. Truth was he loved his old man. Loved him for spending twelve hours a day in the coal mines of Pennsylvania so the family could make ends meet and then taking on a weekend job so they could do a little better. Loved him for dressing up as Santa Claus and making the rounds to all the local orphanages and group homes on Christmas Eve, even though he was dead tired. Loved him for always having a smile and a hug.

Peter Lennagin had left no insurance and no pension. The airline had sent one modest check for $10,000, which lasted only long enough for the family to miss it. Dan's mother had gone to work sewing in what amounted to little more than a sweatshop. She liked it because they let her bring work home with her on the forty-five-minute bus ride after a day that left her too tired for anything but sleep. Still she worked into the early morning hours every day but Sunday and never complained.

Dan, meanwhile, had first vented his misery over his father's death by striving to be exactly like him. If the old man could work two jobs, then he could, at the very least, handle a double paper route. So he rose every morning of the week at four-thirty to blanket houses up to three miles away with copies of the *Scranton Times*. Sundays were the worst because of the papers' extra bulk. He rigged up a wagon to the back of his bike, which worked fine until winter set in and ice painted the roads. Going downhill one dismal Sunday morning, his bike wheels struck ruts, spun crazily and sent him flying. Worse, the papers went flying as well, into a pool of slush. Dan fought back tears, rose to his feet, and limped toward them. His jeans were ripped at the knees, exposing jagged cuts to the biting wind. He hoped his mother could mend the pants because there was simply no money to buy a replacement pair. He put the papers back together as best he could, drying them with his jacket, and delivered the salvageable ones on foot. By the time he'd finished, the flesh around his exposed knees had frozen blue and he'd lost whatever hope there might have been of saving his jeans. The people who didn't get their papers complained. Dan lost the routes.

And it was about then that he started dreaming about hunting down the terrorists who murdered his father.

There was a knock on the door.

"Come in."

Obviously someone from outside the fraternity, because a D-Phi brother would've spared his knuckles the trouble and just walked right in.

The door swung open and Tommy Lee Hudson entered, his black afro looking like something chiseled by a sculptor.

"What's happenin', Dan?"

"The usual."

"Got a few minutes?"

"I think I can squeeze you in."

Tommy Lee shut the door behind him. His eyes wandered to Dan's bookshelf, crammed with books relating to all spheres of terrorism, the spines of a few holding the whole collection in uneasy array.

"Shit, man, you plannin' to start a library?"

"No, just a revolution. Interested?"

Tommy Lee chuckled. The two of them had been friends since freshman year when both had been starters on the JV football team, Dan at tailback and Tommy Lee at flanker. And their friendship had weathered the years well, even when the radical black community threatened to ostracize Tommy Lee for keeping time with the whites. But Hudson was hearing none of it because he owed Dan more than he owed any other living soul. And only the two of them knew it.

"Just got some news, Danny boy. Wanted you to be the first to hear." Hudson's face had the look of a volcano about to explode.

"Wouldn't have anything to do with the NFL draft, would it?"

"Just that yours truly was picked on the fourth round by the Detroit Lions." Hudson's face erupted into a smile.

Dan leaped from his chair and grabbed Tommy's hand, pumping it furiously. "That's great!" he beamed. "I mean it's fantastic! And in the fourth round yet. . . ."

"Yup, that surprised everybody. Guess I must be better than I thought I was."

"Either that or some Lions scout had too much to drink at the Yale game."

Hudson slapped Dan's shoulder and flopped down on the bed. "I haven't even called the folks yet. You deserved to be the first."

"Tommy—"

"Don't stop me now, man, I'm gettin' ready to tell you something that's needed sayin' for the longest time." Hudson sat up. "I got a debt with you I'll probably never be able to pay, 'specially now. But if you need anything, I mean *anything* ever, you come to me first."

Dan smiled uneasily, embarrassed by his friend's words. His mind drifted back to the fall of sophomore

41

year, when Tommy Lee had been entrenched as starting flanker on the varsity, while Dan was relegated to third team defensive back. One afternoon after practice Dan had overheard Tommy in conversation with two cigar-smoking, well-dressed men. He'd picked up only bits and pieces, but the essence was clear: point shaving. A pivotal game was coming up Saturday against Harvard and Tommy Lee's financial aid had been cut to the bone. The well-dressed men were offering him their own brand of aid in return for a few dropped passes at crucial times. Tommy had reluctantly agreed.

"I might've just done the dumbest shit thing of my life," he had confided to Dan later, not realizing he already knew. "And I got no way out," he moaned, "no goddamn way out!"

Dan found him one.

Practice on Thursdays before games was reserved for mild contact with pads. The first time Dan got onto the field the quarterback called a flanker Z-route pass to Tommy. Dan had sprinted across the field and crashed into him as he was leaping for the catch, taking him totally unprepared. The trainer heard Tommy's ribs snap from a field length away. Dan was thrown off the team. Tommy sat out the rest of the season with his injury.

Something passed between them as Dan had helped carry Tommy Lee into the locker room. No words were spoken. They didn't have to be. Both understood.

"I'll never forget that I owe you, Dan, owe you for the rest of my life," Tommy Lee said, sitting on the edge of Lennagin's bed with visions of the silver Lions uniform dancing through his mind. "You threw your football career away because I was about to do something stupid."

"I was gonna quit anyway."

"Bullshit, Danny boy! You never quit anything in your life. You would've stuck it out even if they made you water boy. You're weird, man. You don't give in to people and you don't give up, either. What you did for me, that was really something. Took the kinda guts I only dream about having. The suits never came back and I made all-Ivy junior year and all-East this year. If I make it in Detroit, it's because of you. *You,* man!"

Dan forced a smile. "Remember that when you sign your contract."

"I remember it now. That's why I'm here."

"You don't owe me a damn thing, Tommy," Dan told him. "You already paid it all back. When your black friends said it was me or them, you chose me. I know what that must've done to you inside and it took more guts than *I* ever dreamed of having."

"Sorry, Danny boy, but I can't buy that. See, it'd be great if I could tell you I'd have done the same for you. Only I wouldn't have, *couldn't* have."

"Nobody was exactly trying to get me to shave points anyway. They didn't even spell my name right in the program!"

Tommy Lee laughed. Dan joined him. The digital clock moved to twelve-fifty.

"Gotta run, Tommy," Dan announced. "Got an appointment with the dean at one."

"What for?"

"Beats the hell outta me."

FIVE

When Dan reached the Dean's office, he was surprised to find the secretary absent from her desk. Giving the matter no further consideration, he crossed the anteroom and knocked on the heavy door leading into the court of Brown's dean of academic affairs.

"Come in."

The voice from inside was not the dean's but Dan obeyed it anyway and found himself facing a hunched, graying man in a pale trench coat. By his side stood a tall, slender Japanese woman.

"Make sure we're not disturbed, Keiko," the graying man instructed her. Obediently she filed past Dan and closed the door behind her. The graying man stepped forward and extended his hand.

"The name's Bathgate, Dan, Major William Bathgate."

"I'm supposed to meet the dean," Dan said, taking the hand cursorily.

"He set up this appointment because I asked him to. You and I have something to talk about."

Bathgate extracted an ID wallet from his trench coat and presented it for Dan's inspection.

"Department of State," Lennagin noted with no

small degree of shock. "I don't suppose you've come here to offer me a job."

"In a sense, I suppose I have."

"I don't understand."

"There's no way you could. That's why I'm here. Let's sit down and I'll try to explain."

The dean's office was comfortably furnished with leather chairs and rich mahogany bookshelves. His desk was cluttered with current business and in front of it stood a table jammed with future concerns in the form of assorted recommendations, reports, and applications. The room was used, not sterile; warm, not formal. Dan sat down and watched Bathgate remove his trench coat and place it on the back of his chair. He started to sit, reversed his motion, and moved to the window resting adjacent to their chairs.

"Old habits die hard," he said and proceeded to draw the blinds, removing a hefty measure of the room's light. For a long moment silence dominated the room, broken only by a cranky radiator in the corner stubbornly refusing to accept the onset of spring. "Precautions, Dan. You don't mind me calling you Dan, do you?"

"So long as I can call you major."

Bathgate chuckled. He found himself liking this boy right from the start, and with that came a touch of sadness because no matter what steps he took to insure otherwise, there seemed little hope that Lennagin would be alive to see his June graduation.

"I know you're wondering what I have to do with you," Bathgate began. "The answers aren't simple but they'll come in time. I don't believe in forcing things and the beginning is always the best place to start. For you it came Saturday night."

"Saturday night?"

"A phone call, exactly thirty-one seconds in length, that more than likely woke you from a sound sleep."

"The phone call! You're here about the phone call!"

"Then you remember it."

"You bet. I've been running everything The Doctor said through my head for a couple days now."

"The Doctor?" Bathgate felt chilled. "We'll get to his message later."

"So it wasn't a crank, after all. . . ."

"Nor was it meant for you. But since you received it, your involvement is fundamental."

"Involvement?"

"To use a well-worn phrase, it's a matter of national security."

Dan rolled his eyes, not believing what he heard. "And I guess that oriental beauty you sent to guard the door is your bodyguard, right?"

"As a matter of fact, yes."

Dan smothered a smirk. "The Department of State picks pretty strange watchdogs."

Bathgate reached behind him and pulled a styrofoam cup of coffee from the dean's desk. It was still steaming. "They didn't pick Keiko, because I don't work for them."

"But the ID you showed me . . ."

"A convenient introduction, nothing more. The people I really work for aren't in the habit of passing out badges." Bathgate took a sip of his coffee. "The State Department does sign my rather healthy paycheck, but that's where my association with them officially ends. How much do you know about the American intelligence network, Dan?"

"I've taken a few courses, read a few books."

"Enough of both, I trust, to get a feeling for the fact that those charged with safeguarding the interests of our country don't always get along with each other. The CIA and the FBI talk little, and the NSA has nothing to say to either of them. The Secret Service, meanwhile, has virtually no idea what it's supposed to be doing, so it does little and says less. Quite a mess."

"So it seems."

"In any case, since they don't talk to each other, it's too much to expect that they'd be able to settle on their own which one of them gets jurisdiction in a certain affair—fancy word for case. So my office was created to make things easier. The codes and procedures are enough to drive you crazy, but briefly stated when an event or crime with national and/or international implications occurs, I or one of my staff goes to the scene and decides which group to hand the investigation over to."

"Sounds real cloak-and-daggerish."

"Actually, it's rather banal and trite. Most of the time, anyway. There are exceptions." Bathgate's stare grasped Dan's. "Like Saturday night in Alexandria, Virginia."

"The massacre," Lennagin muttered, recalling mention of it in the phone call.

"I was on the scene personally and made my decision as always. Only this time I gave jurisdiction to an intelligence group you've never heard of."

"I'm sure there's a whole bundle I've never heard of."

"This one's different." Bathgate sighed. Something tightened in his stomach. With his next words, Dan Lennagin's life would change forever. "You're about to be taken into a very small circle, Dan, the circle of Lucifer."

"Lucifer? That word was in the message. Twice."

"Lucifer as in Satan, Dan," Bathgate went on, "so named not for his evil but for his being an outcast who lurks in the underground. The same definition applies for the organization which bears one of his anonyms. As a student at a respected Ivy League institution, I'm sure you get your fill of lectures, so please excuse one more. We live in a funny world, Dan, a world that hangs delicately in what journalists like to call a balance of terror. Around my office, a more popular way of phrasing it is a balance of hate. Nobody wants to be the one to push the final big red button, but that doesn't stop them from pushing a lot of little ones." Bathgate leaned back. "World War III doesn't lie in the future, Dan. It's happening now. We call it terrorism."

Bathgate watched Lennagin's features stiffen at his mention of the term. He held his coffee but didn't sip it. "I won't lecture you on terrorism, Dan. God knows I don't have to. But I will say that each country has its own little bastion, and they're all pretty much the same. In Germany, it's Baader-Meinhof; in the Mideast, it's the PLO and a dozen more radical groups; Ireland has the IRA; Italian terrorists call themselves the Red Brigades; in Spain, they're known as ETA-Militar. No country is unaffected . . ." Bathgate reached into his jacket pocket. ". . . and no person."

The major produced a photostatic copy of a newspaper article and placed it on the table before him. Dan's eyes watered at the headline.

PENNSYLVANIA MAN MURDERED
BY TERRORISTS IN SOUTH AFRICA

Bathgate studied Lennagin's reaction. His face had

reddened. His hands had coiled into fists so tight that the blood was squeezed from his knuckles. His mouth was held in an angry stare, one side rising steadily to reveal a glimpse of teeth. It was a cruel move and Bathgate knew it. But once resigned to involving Lennagin he could spare no means in convincing him of the necessity of the assignment. He owed the boy that much. The article had inflamed him. Lennagin needed to be inflamed.

"What if," the major went on with Lennagin's eyes still frozen hypnotically on the headline, "I told you the same terrorists who killed your father were responsible for Bloody Saturday?"

Dan looked up, had almost started to respond when Bathgate continued.

"They weren't—I can promise you that. But they might as well have been, because all terrorists of this sort are generally the same. Their nationalities and cultures, their means and weapons, are interchangeable. Their lives are defined solely in terms of the senseless deeds they perpetrate. They share a common bond that transcends country and cause, chaining them together in what has recently been dubbed the international terrorist network."

"Why are you telling me all this?" Dan wondered distantly, eyes darting back and forth between the headline and the major.

Bathgate returned the article to his jacket. He had the boy hooked and he knew it. "Because we need you to help us."

"And just who is 'us'?"

Bathgate folded his arms. "Up until a decade ago, the World War III I described for you was a one-sided affair. *We* changed that. We decided to beat terrorists at their own game or at the very least hold them in check. And that, Dan, is it."

"Is what?"

"The Lucifer Directive. 'To subvert the subversives and kill those who seek to kill others.' You'll never see that written anywhere but it's as close as I can come to Lucifer's charter. The organization exists well below the mainstream of the intelligence community. Lucifer is international in scope, although its base of operations lies here in America because that's where the technology and manpower are. Its agents travel around the world seeking out terrorists who have committed strikes or are planning them."

"And what means do these agents use?"

"Often the same ones as the terrorists themselves."

"Fight fire with fire?"

"Frequently enough. But it stretches far beyond that. Lucifer doesn't rely so much on bullets as it does on computer software. The organization has built a catalogue of every known and suspected terrorist in the world, a list that is constantly being updated, available to agents at the touch of a button. The same computer also contains information on all terrorist safe houses and properties, so that when someone protected by the network is kidnapped, Lucifer is able to swing immediately into action. They have contingency plans for every conceivable hostage-taking situation. Guns are important, make no mistake about that. But Lucifer's greatest strength lies in its intelligence data and resources. Together they represent the international equalizer in the fight against international terrorism. The point is that until Lucifer came about, the great powers of the free world tended to drag their feet and hold their hands in the air whenever a terrorist pulled a gun. We were all hostages and we paid the price every day. Terrorists have been striving to put forth a unified front, and for the rest of us—their victims—not to respond accordingly would be suicide. Lucifer is our according response." Bathgate paused. "The fact of the matter is, Dan, that if the organization had been around when your parents decided to take their vacation, your father would very likely still be alive now."

Bathgate watched Lennagin's eyes close painfully and then open again. Another low blow. *I'm sorry,* he wanted to say, *but I have to do this. It's for your own good.*

"Where do you come in?" Lennagin wondered.

"Once a Lucifer alert is called in America, my network serves as a liaison between Lucifer and the traditional tiers of the intelligence community and the government. Communication channels are smoothed. Information is made available to the right people. Remember, since Lucifer doesn't exist officially, we have to be careful of who gets what and how. That's our primary responsibility in addition to insuring that Lucifer stays within the lines of its somewhat vague directive. Sounds fancy and elaborate, I know, but during the course of an affair we seldom amount to anything more than overpaid errand boys. I have a direct link with the head of Lucifer. Once the investigation gets under way, though, I'm obliged by position to follow his orders and basically little else. Do you follow me?"

Dan nodded, though he didn't fully.

"All of this usually functions in very neat and precise fashion," the major went on. "There are people who have spent the better parts of their lives putting all the channels together, but once in a while a breakdown still results, some more serious than others." Bathgate finished his coffee. "A few weeks ago I sent the top man in my network, known as The Doctor, out to Los Angeles to investigate some trouble centering around a rising Chicano terrorist group. He was in the process of flushing out their identities for further action when something else caught his attention. He broke off communication for forty-eight hours and went underground, which meant his cover wasn't deep enough to do him any good above the surface. When he re-emerged it was with information important enough for him to violate all traditional channels in relaying it. Since too many circuits had to be crossed to get the message to me, The Doctor improvised and sent it direct to Alexander Levine." A pause. "The terrorists got it after they murdered him Saturday night, which makes you the only person in the country who knows what was inside."

"Jesus . . ."

"He meant to dial an emergency routing exchange and came up with your number instead. How much of what he said can you recall?"

"I jotted down the end part. The beginning's a little hazy. There was something like 'Levine got the message and they got Levine.' Then, 'I'm next' and 'The massacre—just the beginning.' After that, a lot of mumbo jumbo that didn't make any sense. Finally, there was the message." Dan thought briefly. "'Lucifer is black and black is Lucifer.' Maybe the other way around. Then, 'Tell Zeus it's Code Oscar.' He said that twice, and the last thing he said was 'Destroy the Isosceles Project.'"

Bathgate looked away momentarily. He seemed

unsure. "You're certain he said Isosceles?"

"It was in the part I wrote down. Is that important?"

Bathgate avoided Dan's eyes. "It might be."

"What about the rest of the message?"

The major pushed Isosceles into the corners of his mind and elected to hold nothing else back. "To begin with, Zeus is me—my code name, that is. The first part of the message, 'Lucifer is black,' implies that something is about to happen that the organization's network is totally in the dark about. It's a fairly common idiom in our profession, and I'd guess The Doctor must have been referring to Code Oscar, whatever that may be. He must've assumed I know something I don't, because his mention of it ended without any attempt at elaboration."

"So where does the Isosceles Project fit in?"

"It doesn't. That's the problem."

"I'd still like to know more about it."

"It doesn't concern you."

"It did Saturday night."

"Trust me on this one, Dan. There are some things you're better off not knowing," Bathgate said grimly.

"But there are a few others I'd like to know. How you tracked me down, for instance."

"Simple process of elimination. If The Doctor didn't call us, the question was who did he call? Your number stood at the top of the list, just one digit off the emergency exchange. A four instead of a one in the area code—quite a simple mistake to make in a darkened phone booth even for a professional, and one that was confirmed by a computer check of all long distance calls originating in the Los Angeles area between midnight and one A.M." Bathgate's eyes lengthened. "And, of course, if we were able to make the connection, it stands to reason that whoever killed The Doctor will, too."

"And these same people happen to be responsible for the massacre Saturday night."

"Almost certainly. And The Doctor's final message you were unlucky enough to be the recipient of is the only clue we have to something even more catastrophic about to happen. The only way we can find out precisely what will be to uncover who's behind it. That's where you come in. The opposition has no way of knowing how much The Doctor said to you. They've got to find out, in order to determine the level of damage that's been done to their operation. Without that information, they can't proceed. So they'll have to surface to obtain it, and when they do we'll be there."

"You're going to use me as bait," Dan concluded.

"That's the size of it, yes," Bathgate confirmed, hating himself for the words.

So much was at stake, though. Isosceles had been mentioned. That made his task bearable.

"But the bad guys must know you're here and what your plans are."

"Undoubtedly."

"So why bother?"

"They think they're better than us; we think we're better than them. That's the way it always is in this game. The difference is we're right and we've got the advantage, to boot. We know how much The Doctor had to say and they don't. The pressure's on them and my guess is that time's not exactly on their side, either."

"So you get to use me as bait and in return I get to stay alive. Is that the deal?"

Bathgate stuffed his hands into the pockets of his brown sports jacket. "No, there's more. There's a lot of anger in you, Dan, a lot of rage. It's been bottled up inside since your father won a lottery that cost him his life eleven years ago. I'm offering you a vent for that rage. I can't give you the terrorists who killed your father but I can give you the next best thing. And I can also make sure your debt is paid to the hallowed halls of this institution with a substantial bonus thrown in for good measure. I might even be able to do something about a more permanent job when you graduate."

"How do you know about the debt?"

"Your file."

"University?"

"Government. You got one when you turned eighteen. Call it a birthday present from Uncle Sam."

"So everyone really does have a file. . . ."

On another day Bathgate would have smiled but today he failed even to part his lips. This kind of work was new to him despite all his years of experience. He was not a front-line field man, feeling far more at ease in the background. Let the other guys dirty their hands with blood; he preferred ink.

"You know something, Major?" Bathgate looked up. "You might be right about this offer. Since my father was . . . killed, I've spent more time dreaming about gunning down the terrorists who did it than I have studying for midterms. It's like there's this big hole in me that keeps getting bigger and bigger. Maybe you're giving me the chance to fill it in."

"Maybe," Bathgate said, looking away again. "Maybe."

SIX

The man in the soiled khaki suit pulled his jeep off the road and onto the hardened tundra that would lead him to the kibbutz. It was an isolated commune, five miles in every direction from any trace of civilization, which, in the small state of Israel, is a good distance.

The jeep rolled over a bump and the man shoved his hand across to the passenger side to keep the *New York Times* he was delivering from flying out. Sparrow had asked him to bring the paper and Sparrow never did anything without good reason. The man had heard the resolve and fury brewing in his old friend's voice. What he didn't know was why.

The man downshifted and turned onto a dirt road muddied by the previous evening's rainfall. The jeep hit a rock and lurched, found a hole and dropped. The road was bush-lined on both sides, good camouflage for whoever might be on guard duty. The man couldn't see them now, nor could he ever. Enemies approaching would be cut down well before they made it to the kibbutz. The man caught the stone fence out of the corner of his eye and knew he was near. Then the entrance appeared and he pulled up before a guard with a double-barrel shotgun slung over his shoulder so naturally that it might have been an extra extremity. The guard checked his face, inspected the back of the jeep, and signaled him to pass through.

A dozen men and women were at work in the surrounding fields, the women firm and fit, the men bronzed, shirtless, powerfully built. Children of varying ages ran and played, cackled and laughed in the shadow of the kibbutz schoolhouse, which rested at the edge of the dense orange orchards where the man knew two dozen kibbutz members, at least, were nursing the crop. A tractor appeared from a spacious barn that had once been an airplane hangar, once long ago when he and Sparrow had fought the battle of Israel's freedom and the kibbutz had been a secret Haganah airstrip they operated. Where a camouflaged weapons hold had rested, there now stood a large dining hall that doubled as a center for kibbutz meetings. Around it nearly forty smaller houses and dorms had been constructed for residents, wood the same color as the rich earth, looking like fertile extensions.

An older, graying man, his body having the look of something once great, limped forward from the main, two-story house that sat in the center of it all, withdrawn just a bit. Some sort of square-backed pistol was conspicuously protruding from his belt. It was the first time in a number of years that the man in the khaki suit had seen him armed.

"Did you bring it, Yakov?" Sparrow yelled as soon as the jeep had come to a halt.

Yakov met him halfway up the walkway and handed him the *New York Times*. "I suspect what you're looking for can be found right on the front page. Right above the article on the Academy Awards' being postponed again because of a cameramen's strike.

Paradoxical people, these Americans."

Sparrow took the newspaper and studied it briefly. "You know what this means."

"No."

"It's started," Sparrow said distantly. "Something I've always feared. It must be stopped."

"By you?"

"If necessary."

"All because of this massacre?"

"It is much more than a massacre, I assure you."

"The Americans can handle things on their own."

"They don't know enough to even get started."

"You're an angry man, Sparrow."

"Do you blame me?"

"For not offering me a glass of your fantastic ice tea after such a long drive, yes."

Sparrow almost smiled. "I've forgotten my manners, Yakov. I hope you have it in your heart to forgive me."

"Consider yourself forgiven. But I'm still thirsty."

"Come."

Sparrow led his friend up a grassy walkway toward a veranda where a shade-shrouded table rested on the porch in front of the main house. Both men took seats, Sparrow gingerly easing his limp leg underneath.

"How is the pain?" Yakov asked.

"Comes and goes."

"But mostly stays."

"I'm nearly sixty years old. Make believe it's arthritis, Yakov."

It wasn't, of course, and both men knew it. The limp dated back beyond forty years to Germany and the beginnings of the Nazi horror, when Sparrow was still known by the name of Joshua Cohen, a name he had discarded almost as long ago. His family had been walking home one night from the theater, not knowing that while they had been inside watching a new play a violent purge of Germany's Jewry had swept terror through the streets.

In later years Josh would look back on that night as the first time he'd felt his sixth sense for danger activate. Before he listened to it, though, the three figures had sprung from the blackness of an alley, one with the night. Josh's father had caught their presence and responded immediately, throwing his body in front of his wife's while shouting a command to his sons.

"Run!"

Josh had hesitated at first, mesmerized by the action and feeling there was something else he should do. The first volley of bullets shook him from his trance. His father went down and then his mother. He found their eyes one last time, already sprinting away dragging his brother behind him. There was a sharp crack and the younger boy collapsed, scarlet flowing from the back of his neck. Josh let him fall, screamed just once, and tore onward. He might have given in to tears but the bullet that ripped through the back of his thigh had turned his grief to agony. He pressed on miraculously without losing a step, aware of the hot pain searing through him, but wanting very much to live. He heard the frantic footsteps of his family's killers behind him and felt the heat of their bullets surging past, splitting the air.

Somehow, after hiding for hours in a garbage heap, he had made it to the home of close friends of his parents, the Erdharts. A doctor was sent for, Josh's leg patched up to a semblance of its former structure. The

Erdharts hid him for a week in their attic, never betraying him to the house-to-house searches for Jews and keeping him reasonably comfortable. It was during these days that a sixteen-year-old boy with golden locks that made him seem still younger grew into a man, an angry man. His hate for the Nazis had festered, swelled. He was glad when Mr. Erdhart brought news that he had arranged for his escape from Germany, glad because someday he'd come back and take his revenge.

One morning, just after dawn, he had dressed in clothes belonging to the Erdharts' oldest son. They fit him too snugly and the high rise of the pants enunciated his limp. But he was outside for the first time since he'd come seeking refuge and the air felt good and clean. Mr. Erdhart had taken him to the train station, where he would begin his journey to France.

The train made a magnificent sight, snorting and hissing like a bull in the ring. Steam bellowed. Josh's heart had leaped forward in his chest. Mr. Erdhart led him toward the train. Then two men in uniform had appeared suddenly before him, each grasping a shoulder.

"I'm sorry," Erdhart said.

Josh had tried to struggle but his strength was minimal and his leg betrayed him with each sudden move, betrayed him just as Erdhart had. Josh would take what he could from this, a lesson if nothing else. There could be no trust in his life, not anymore. He was alone. The two Nazis pushed him on board the train.

It was a baggage car, crammed so solid with people that one man's motions affected a dozen others. No one could sweat without the person next to him being aware of it. Josh had tried to close his nostrils to the car's stench. After six hours of rambling through some unknown countryside, it was unbearable. The bitter stink of fear and hopelessness. He had pulled as much of his curly hair as he could over his face. Unwashed for a week, its oily scent provided a welcome change from that of the car, but the relief had lasted only a short while.

The only light came from the many cracks in the sides and roof of the car, and thus had revealed a scene of utter futility. Josh helped a man lying next to him get comfortable. The man heaved and rasped, a death cough. Josh did the best he could for him. The man, too weak to speak, smiled and pressed something into the boy's hand. Josh had held it up to the meager light and seen that it was an engraved penknife, a potential weapon.

Josh had never been a violent sort. Now, holding the penknife tightly in his hand till his flesh cracked, he had known that had to change. The weapon had been given to him for a reason, and he had to make use of it.

For the next twenty minutes, he had pushed gradually through the mass of humanity till he gained a perch right in front of the sliding doors. He'd had no concrete plan in mind, for he had no idea what would be outside when the Nazis finally let them out. He had only the shadow of a feeling that he couldn't let himself stay on the train.

The brakes squealed, stinging his ears. The overloaded train had begun to vibrate madly. He flipped open the small blade and made sure it was locked in place. He smelled steam. The train crawled to a stop. A minute passed and voices approached. Josh edged his back against the plane of wall where the doors would finish their slide. Those around him shrank back as far as they could, aware of his intentions and eager to disassociate themselves from them. Didn't they know what was in store? A soft pop met his ears and then he heard the grinding of metal against wood as the lock was removed. The doors started to creak open.

Josh had moved fast, faster than he'd thought himself capable of. The sudden light bothered his eyes but not enough to blur the two gray-uniformed figures before him. He went for the one on the right first, not because he was the closest but because he held a machine gun while the other was still occupied with the door. Josh shot out with the penknife even before his feet touched the ground. The blade ripped into the soft flesh of the soldier's throat. A cascade of crimson shot out.

Josh had turned to the other soldier and gone at him in the same manner, realizing too late he had left the penknife in the dead man's throat. But he kept the motion going, curling his fingers into a tight ball and ramming them home once, twice, three times, maybe more. Enough to make the second soldier slump backwards, clutching for his neck, which meant he wasn't clutching for his gun. Then Josh was on his knees; diving, spinning, rolling under the train to the freedom promised by the other side. Beyond lay an open field, after which was forest.

He wasn't sure how long they chased him or how close their bullets came, or how he had managed to escape with one leg that was practically useless. He knew only that some hours later the train started up again and the soldiers were gone. He was safe, but he was also lost, with no idea where he was or how to get anywhere else. He was hungry, thirsty, and frightened; he couldn't tell which was worse and figured they took turns. Just when he thought he was getting somewhere, he realized he was back where he started, meaning he had been going in a circle the whole time. Then a family of small, dark birds with a peculiar melodic chant had caught his attention. Sparrows. . . .

He had followed their airborne path out of desperation, or maybe instinct, and incredibly they led him to a small town where he could begin his escape from Germany. His blond curly hair and light features made him look more Aryan than Jew—the greatest disguise of any. The person he had been for sixteen years vanished behind it forever, as though Joshua Cohen had never existed at all. A new being was created in his place, named after the birds that had led him to safety . . . Sparrow.

"You're thinking of going out again, aren't you?" Yakov asked him.

An old woman approached the veranda with a tray holding a pitcher and two glasses. She set it down on the table and filled both with sparkling tea. Ice cubes slid forward, dropping into the glasses. Yakov drained his tea quickly and poured himself another as the old woman shuffled away.

"Do I have a choice?"

"Let others handle it, Sparrow."

"Others already have."

"It could be a one-time strike."

"Terrorists don't believe in one-time strikes, especially these." Sparrow turned his eyes to the front gate where the milk truck had appeared with its semiweekly ration. As usual, the isolated kibbutz would be its last stop. The gate guard was checking the driver's papers.

"Forty children were murdered, Yakov," Sparrow went on. "Don't you see? I must get to America before the killers strike again."

"What I see is you abandoning the dream you've held for a quarter-century of living your life peacefully on a kibbutz away from cares and worries and killing and death. You have all of that now and you want to give it up."

The milk truck lurched up the dirt road toward the house, spinning its back wheels. They sank in the mud, spun more, finally pulled themselves out. The truck rolled on.

"You're wrong there, Yakov; I never had it. At times I pretended I did, but the past was always there to haunt me, remind me. I guess I wanted it that way. Why else would I have chosen this parcel of land to retire on, land where forty years ago we smuggled weapons into a tiny nation no one wanted to survive? Sometimes I think I can still see the ruts made by those small transport planes when they landed. Just tractor marks now, but out of habit I always start filling them in before I remember. Men don't change; they only hide from the people they once were."

"That says nothing for—"

Yakov found his words broken off by the icy look that suddenly filled Sparrow's eyes, now focused on the milk truck whining to a halt. Something had activated his ancient defenses. The weariness passed out of his bones. His bad leg throbbed.

The milk truck had almost finished its climb. Mud caked its rear tires three-quarters of the way up.

That was it! The truck always came to the kibbutz last, its lightest load of the day certainly insufficient to cause such sinking into the wet turf.

Sparrow drew his pistol and sprang from the veranda. The motion forced Yakov to jerk back, shocked by the quickness his old friend had moved with. But his eyes caught the milk truck's rear doors bursting open and the sight of two, no three, riflemen leaping out.

Two of the invaders were dead the moment they landed on the ground. The third was able to avoid Sparrow's first bullet, roll once and get off a harmless volley of shots before the old man's second bullet made a shambles of his face.

Sparrow was immediately surrounded by the men of the kibbutz. The women and children had fled instinctively at the first sign of shooting, the children for cover—the women for weapons. It was the way Sparrow had taught them. Now he issued instructions to those around him clearly, precisely, with no hint of indecision. The old warrior back on the battlefield. When he had finished, he returned to the veranda and stood over the trembling Yakov.

"Have some more tea, my friend."

Yakov looked up with glassy eyes. "You didn't even break out a sweat."

"I told told you men don't change." There was vitality in Sparrow's voice, color in his face. "But sometimes they forget. Like you forgot your lessons as a soldier. You stayed in clear view during the shooting, never moved an inch toward cover."

"I . . . froze."

"Yes, and I'm sure you were surprised when I didn't react the same way. That's it, isn't it? You judge me through your own lens, a lens blurred by the papers that clutter your desk. I'm six years older than you but the difference between us is that I haven't forgotten. I haven't forgotten anything."

"Then you *are* going out."

"Five minutes ago, that matter might have been up for argument. Not anymore. They've made their second mistake."

"Second?"

"What happened in Virginia was the first."

"You believe there's a connection?"

"I'm sure there is."

"But you have no proof."

"Nor do I need any." Sparrow glanced over at the bodies being wrapped in canvas and carried away as their blood soaked into the fertile earth. "However, what kind of weapons were used in the American massacre?"

"Kalishnikovs."

"The very same ones our three dead friends brought with them in the milk truck."

"Come now, Sparrow, Kalishnikovs are more readily available in this part of the world than water pistols. You know that."

"And I also know that what I've been expecting for eight years has finally come about." Sparrow paused significantly. "They made a mistake activating this operation in my lifetime. I know enough to stop them, and I will."

"But certainly you can't work alone."

Sparrow chuckled. "Oh, you're right about that. I'm not exactly cut out for this sort of work anymore," he added with an eye on his stiff leg. "They tried to kill me once. They'll try again."

"Why?"

"Because they need me dead. The success of their

66

plan calls for it. So I have to get to them first. But I can't very well cover much ground sitting here drinking tea with you, old friend. They'll stalk me wherever I go. I need a man who can lead me where they won't look—a combination guide, bodyguard, and killer. Can you think of anyone?"

Yakov nodded tautly. "Only one. Felix."

"I thought he was dead."

"Not even close. Last I heard he was in Libya playing hell with Kaddafi's terrorist training camps."

"Can you track him down?"

Yakov sighed and held the chilled glass up to his cheek for comfort. "It won't be easy. There is a long relay system used to get Felix his messages and he rarely answers them. Many channels must be crossed. But many favors are owed me. I'll do what I can and contact you here."

"Don't bother. I'll be gone. Whoever sent the men in the milk truck will have reinforcements here by tomorrow or sooner. I was lucky this time. Caught them off guard. Next time, well, the best solution is to make sure there isn't a next time. I'll close down the kibbutz and scatter my people throughout the countryside. It's all arranged. Has been for some time."

"You've expected this."

"And prayed it wouldn't come. I'll take two of my best men and head south. I'll call you at the usual number in twenty-four hours' time. Then you can give me the news about Felix."

"It might not be good."

"I have faith in you, old friend." Sparrow rose and stretched his bad leg. His back muscles spasmed. Pain shot through his head in rapid jolts. For a few brief minutes he had eluded age and disability. Now they had both caught up with him again, as well as something else more painful than either.

Yakov eyed him worriedly. "You look like a man with the weight of the world on his shoulders."

Sparrow said nothing. Yakov didn't realize how right he was.

SEVEN

Dan Lennagin sat at his desk, history book open but unread. He kept replaying in his head his conversation with Bathgate, struck not so much by fear and foreboding as by excitement and anticipation. The major had come to supply him with the missing piece to his life, the one fragment that made him feel forever incomplete. When his father had been murdered, his eleven-year-old reaction had been to withdraw into fantasies. And when the fantasies didn't wash anymore, he had turned to football. The anger in him was all stopped up. It needed a vent. He had made all-country his last two years of high school. Coaches marveled at the way he hit.

Then he'd moved on to college and the release provided by football had vanished long before he cracked Tommy Lee Hudson's ribs in practice and was kicked off the team, vanished because the lie didn't wash any better than the fantasies. The hitting, the screaming, the pounding—all a mask, a cover-up. He had to face up. But to what? His problems lacked substance. An emptiness, that was all. Like someone had dug a hole in his gut and forgot to fill it in.

"Dan? . . . Dan?"

Someone was calling his name. He turned slowly to his right toward the door of his room. Peter Brent stood there halfway in.

"I knocked. You didn't answer," he said. "Got a few minutes?"

"Sure."

Peter was as close to a best friend as Dan had in the fraternity, a sensitive youth from a wealthy California family who'd had serious troubles making it his pledge year. The ordeals of pledging, while not even approaching what they had been twenty years before, remained a physical and emotional grind. And there were always a few brothers who took the indoctrination task too seriously and lost perspective. Dan had been Peter's pledge master and on more than one occasion had saved him from the berating and abuse when it appeared he'd reached his limit.

"Did you call Appropriations?" Peter asked him.

"What?" Distantly.

"Appropriations. Remember? The thirty-two-hundred-dollar refund the university owes us for that lousy furniture we returned."

"No," Dan told D-Phi's treasurer for this semester. "Never got around to it."

Peter raised his hands theatrically. "No problem, Mr. President. Your noble fraternity is up to its eyeballs in debts and the liquor store won't deliver a single can of beer until we've made good on our balance. And *you* forgot to call Appropriations."

Brent smiled. Dan didn't.

"That was a joke, Dan. You're supposed to laugh."

"I'm not in the mood."

"Ah, so at last we switch roles. After all the times you've talked me out of the dumps, I can finally do the same for you."

"Not this time."

"What's eating you?"

Lennagin managed a smile. "Just got a lot on my mind."

"Like what?"

"You don't want to know."

"And if I did?"

"I couldn't tell you."

"Wow! Sounds like you really got yourself into something this time!"

Dan just shrugged.

"Your regular report's come at a good time, Major. There's good news," the man from Houston reported. "We've sanctioned three of those terrorists involved in Bloody Saturday."

Bathgate did some quick figuring. "That still leaves two at large."

"The lone woman and the man we guess was the leader. We'll have them both before the week's out. . . . But not the people who put them up to it. That's your end at this point."

Bathgate tightened his grip on the phone in the backseat of his limousine. "With that in mind, Lennagin has become our willing agent-in-place."

"Splendid," the man from Houston beamed. "I'm glad you came to see things my way."

"I didn't. But if I'm going to keep this boy alive I need a hundred percent commitment from him. As you suspected, it wasn't hard to obtain it."

"And the message he accidentally received from The Doctor, Bathgate, was any of it helpful?"

"Not directly. But it does raise certain . . . problems."

"I don't like the sound of your voice," the man from Houston snapped.

"Has Isosceles been reactivated?" Bathgate demanded.

A pause.

"That doesn't concern you, Major."

"Doesn't it?"

"Clearly out of your jurisdiction."

"I'll ask you again. Has Isosceles been reactivated?"

"Of course not. What makes you ask?" The voice was tense, thick.

"The Doctor's message included a warning to destroy it. That would seem superfluous if it doesn't exist anymore to begin with."

"Better give me the whole message."

"I'd like an answer to my question first. . . ."

"You've already got the answer. Don't press things, Bathgate," the man from Houston warned.

"Then don't press me. When that boy mentioned Isosceles, it was all I could do to keep from pissing my pants. There were reasons why it was dismantled, deactivated. If it's operational again, I should have been told."

"I told you, it's not."

"The Doctor wouldn't be one to waste words, especially his last ones. Look, I'm not much more than a fancy bureaucrat with a classified job. This cloak-and-dagger stuff is strictly for agents with prepaid life insurance premiums. I don't really give a shit what your overpaid planners come up with on the drawing board. But I do know that this whole thing is a helluva lot bigger than we originally thought if it's got anything to do with Isosceles. The project was abandoned because it was a goddamn Medusa. And now I find out that people are turning to stone again, starting with The Doctor."

"The message, Bathgate, tell me the message!" the man from Houston demanded.

"Tell me about Isosceles."

"I have."

"Then you'll get the message after I do some checking on my own."

"You're talking like a madman."

"Because I'm scared as hell. I'm scared for the world and I'm scared for the boy you insisted we involve in this. I can't do much about the world but I can do something about the boy. I'm pulling him out."

"You haven't got the authority."

"Try me."

"Don't push things, Bathgate. You're expendable."

A thin smile crept across the major's lips. "Aren't we all?"

EIGHT

"What have you to tell me, Yakov?"

"Sparrow, you sound far away. Where are you?"

"Cairo."

"Good God! There's not a safe phone in the whole city."

"I'm not worried. Tell me about Felix."

Ninety minutes after killing the milk truck's occupants, Sparrow was on his way, having scattered his kibbutz family ten miles in every direction. It was with a sense of great loss that he had stood at the gate of his deserted home, the dream he was now forced to abandon for the time being. In a world of symbology it represented peace—everything beyond it, chaos. But the chaos called to him, beckoned him to return. Eight years before he had put this world aside but never away. His returning was inevitable, always had been. Now there were scores to settle, more than he had expected and one that tore at his soul.

"I couldn't reach him directly," Yakov was saying. "But the message has been put out. If he's still alive, he'll get it. That doesn't mean he'll listen. Felix has the reputation for being a man who lets no one pull his strings."

"Where is he?"

"Libya, just as I suspected. Somewhere in the southeast. My message states that you will be in a small township seven miles outside of Al-Jauf by midnight tonight. Seventeen hours. I hope I'm not rushing you."

"I want to keep moving anyway. Makes me forget my age."

"But not the risk, I hope. You're talking about negotiating five hundred miles through unfriendly or downright hostile territory. And once you enter Libya you'll be totally on your own. The roads there are—"

"Thank you, Yakov. I'll call you again soon."

His friend had not told him anything he didn't already know. The risk was extreme, the possibility of reaching the Al-Jauf area safe and on time very low indeed. He had a jeep, two good men, provisions, and plenty of weapons, none of which could do anything against snipers. What was more, he had no idea how far the plot that had reached his kibbutz the preceding afternoon stretched. Conceivably they knew exactly where he was and where he was heading. Evasive maneuvers were a possibility but they took time, and right now time was the crucial commodity.

Sparrow wiped his brow and moved back toward the jeep. His limp leg was worse than usual. It was all he could do to keep it in step, never mind take quick action if that was mandated. Back at the jeep he went over a map with his two men, Joel and David—each among the best soldiers Israel had to offer. In Egypt their route was simple. They would stay on the main road for the two-hundred-mile stretch between Cairo and Al-Kharga, then transfer onto a seldom traveled desert route that would lead them to the Libyan border. Although it would be more time consuming,

Sparrow had elected to cross into Sudan's northwestern corner first to facilitate entry into Libya. Once inside the target country, they'd travel the 175-mile desolate, unpaved road known as "Damnation Alley" with the help of official Kaddafi government stickers to be placed on the jeep's side.

That much decided, Joel took the wheel of the jeep and headed south. David kept a watchful eye, scanning the area with an Uzi machine gun gripped perpetually in his hand. Both men were brave, tireless, strong. Sparrow had handpicked them for work on the kibbutz.

As the road wore on, Sparrow occupied himself with thoughts of the legendary Felix, more myth than man. They had never met, crossing paths only by reputation, so Sparrow could rely only on conjecture in putting a profile of Felix together. It was said he was a giant of a man, proficient in the use of every weapon imaginable including his bare hands.

The legend of Felix had its origins in a small, forgotten town just over the Israeli-Jordanian border, a town of peaceful Arabs who prided themselves on good relations with their Jewish neighbors. One day a band of terrorist guerrillas had stormed the town seeking to make it a refuge post. Such raids were not uncommon. More than one small Arab village had fallen to rampaging terrorists who looted, burned, murdered, and generally left nothing as it had been before. The population of this town, which numbered all of forty-four, had resisted. Three men were gunned down on the street, their bodies later burned in public view. Women were pulled into the town meeting hall and raped repeatedly. A young boy who landed a kick in one of the terrorist's groins had had his testicles sliced off with a hunting knife and then had been hung from a pole in the square, his body left suspended in the air swaying and stinking with the breeze.

That night the invaders had turned the meeting hall into a bar with the prettiest of the town's females serving as entertainment. Somewhere past midnight the doors opened and a giant of a man had swaggered in. The terrorists felt for their weapons but withdrew their hands when it became obvious the man was nothing but a vagabond. He was unarmed and kept the invaders entertained till early in the morning with stories of his many travels. He gained their confidence, participated in the gang rape of a woman, and offered to help them gain access to Israel. The terrorists were receptive. His stories were amusing, as were his constant apologies for the weak bladder that forced him to take his leave often throughout the night.

At first light, one of the terrorists went outside to the houses where the others in their group were sleeping. He returned screaming not a minute later, screaming that half their troop had had their throats cut while they slept. All on-duty guards were dead as well, their necks snapped and heads twisted obscenely around. The eight terrorists still inside the hall turned immediately toward the giant stranger. His flashing grin was the last thing they saw before the machine guns he held in either hand, appropriated from two dead guards, spit fire. Two more terrorists he had somehow missed during the night crashed through the door with guns drawn. The giant somehow ended up behind them, took a head in each arm and jerked till the heads hung limply in the wake of two horrible snaps.

Minutes later, the giant was gone, never to be seen in the town again.

How much of this and the entire legend of Felix was true, Sparrow didn't know. But he did know that, all things considered, Felix was the only man who could see him safely out of the Mideast and to America, because America was where the end was beginning.

"Where are we?" Sparrow asked, awakening suddenly.

"Just crossed into Sudan," answered David who was now driving.

Sparrow checked his watch: just past nine o'clock. The sun was all but gone. The Libyan border would be coming up any minute. This was a safe entry point, used frequently by Kaddafi's terrorist henchmen to move into Sudan. Thus it was never patrolled by Libya and was patrolled poorly by the militarily inept Sudanese.

"We're right on schedule," David reassured.

"Not until we reach Al-Jauf, we're not," corrected Sparrow.

"There's the border," said Joel.

The jeep's lights sliced through the desert night. A hundred yards up ahead stood a series of poles that stretched to the horizon forming a makeshift border. David killed the lights and drove on. He flipped the switch again a quarter-mile later.

"We're in."

Sparrow remained silent.

They had turned onto Damnation Alley, paved only by the army trucks that flattened an irregular section of desert land sparsely decorated with flora. The greenery increased gradually as they drove further north. The breeze picked up, blowing Sparrow's still thick gray hair across his face. He was nervous. Beads of sweat dotted his skin, no longer rising just from the heat. As the trees and bushes steadily enveloped the road, so did camouflage for the many unsavory sorts who inhabited this part of the country. In the distance lights flickered on, off, then on again. Men were signaling each other.

The jeep rolled on. Miles passed with the minutes, each one seeming slower than the one before. David swept the road ahead with his eyes—Joel with his Uzi.

"How much longer?" Sparrow asked.

"Twenty miles."

Sparrow's watch told him it was nearing eleven o'clock. "That's cutting it close."

David said nothing.

The road wound between a series of hills. Lights flashed in the distance, faded, flashed once more.

"Something's wrong," said Sparrow. The two soldiers looked at him expressionlessly. "Pull over."

David did. The move saved their lives. The snipers perched somewhere up ahead fired in panic instead of by plan, their shots going astray, striking metal and canvas but not flesh. David and Joel dove from the jeep. Sparrow found the strength to follow them, although his leg made him pay for it.

"Where are they?" from Joel.

"Two hundred yards ahead."

"Left or right?"

"Both," Sparrow replied simply.

In the narrowing distance, the lights intensified.

"Three trucks two miles away," muttered Sparrow. "Reinforcements undoubtedly."

"Then we can't stay here," said Joel and he stuck his head up slowly. Automatic fire greeted it, spraying randomly over the area, ricocheting off the jeep. He hit the ground hard. "The bastards must have infrared scopes and high-powered rifles. Hell of an arsenal."

Up ahead, the lights disappeared as the trucks climbed a hill, not more than a mile and a half away now. Sparrow's eyes swept the area. It was barren and desolate. Nothing in sight. Nowhere to flee, no fortified position to make a stand. They had plenty of ammunition but no place to fire it from.

Wait . . . a few hundred yards to the right into the darkness, the land sloped then rose. Dim lights fluttered on the rise. At first Sparrow had thought they were reflections or shadows. He reached stealthily for the binoculars inside the jeep, raised them to his eyes. A small house appeared and sharpened in focus, one room by the look of it. There was movement inside and then the last of the light was gone. Candles more than likely, extinguished at the sound of gunfire.

"Grab as much ammunition as you can," Sparrow instructed.

"We going somewhere?"

"A small house on a hill one hundred yards to our right."

"The jeep?" from David.

"Too big a target. We'll have to go on foot."

"But—"

"No buts. I'll make it. The leg's still got a little life left in it."

"I could drive the jeep while you and Joel stay down in the back," David insisted bravely.

"And if you get hit, where does that leave us? Joel drives and he's picked off. I take the wheel and—"

"On foot, then." David moved his hands to join Joel's in the jeep's rear probing for the grenade bag, two extra machine guns of different caliber and additional ammunition.

"How far can you throw a grenade?" Sparrow asked Joel.

"Not far enough to get the snipers," he responded.

"But far enough to distract them, maybe make them rush their shots?"

"I can try."

The trucks weren't more than a mile away now.

"Then let's go," Sparrow said. "The grenades will provide our cover. Once we reach the hills we'll be safe." Sparrow ran his tongue along the inside of his parched mouth. There would still be just over a hundred yards to cover in the open. "Get ready." David hefted the two extra rifles onto his shoulders. Joel strapped the ammo bag to his back and held the grenade bag in his right hand. "Go!"

The three men leaped to their feet simultaneously, greeted by a barrage of automatic fire that struck the jeep and the trees behind them. Then they were running across the open field, Sparrow hustling his limp leg along till his insides felt ready to explode. Bullets stitched a mad path around them, coughing dirt into their faces and occasionally whistling by their ears. On the dead run, Joel lobbed grenades to the left and right as far forward as possible, sending up torrents of fire that led to momentary easing of the opposition's bullets.

Just twenty more yards to the hills. But the trucks were almost upon them with untold reinforcements.

Sparrow increased his pace still more, swallowed the pain that swelled throughout his broken body. A bullet sped by close enough to singe his hair. Another stung his leg. A third thudded somewhere and David went down clutching his thigh. Without losing a single step,

Sparrow pulled him to his feet and dragged him the final stretch—the two men between them having only two good legs. They spun, dove, rolled, took the hill in a half-dozen bounds. The house was just up ahead.

They had made it.

Joel crashed his full weight into the wooden door. It slammed inwards. Sparrow pulled David inside. In the corner of the room, a young boy sprang from his bed with a scream, met his mother in the middle and pressed against her.

"What do you want?" she asked in her Arabic tongue, her strong face captured by the dim light cast by a single candle. "We have nothing of value."

"We are not bandits," Sparrow comforted. "Do you speak English?"

"Yes." The woman's grip loosened around her son. "My husband taught both of us before the soldiers came and killed him." Her eyes darted toward the window and then back to Sparrow. "You are from Israel?"

"Yes."

"So was my husband. We will help you." She pushed her son off her and moved to a table where she lit two kerosene lamps. Then she approached David who was kneeling on the floor and examined his wound. "This is very bad. We must get him to a doctor."

"The men who shot him are outside in far greater numbers."

"You will fight?"

"There's no choice." Sparrow looked toward the young boy huddled against the far wall. "But you and your son might still be able to get out safely through the back."

The woman held her ground. "My name is Rivkah. If you have another gun, I know how to shoot."

Sparrow nodded at Joel who slid an American M-16 across the floor. Rivkah picked it up, jammed back the bolt.

"My son will help with the reloading," she said. "He knows guns."

The boy shook the hair from his eyebrows and crawled across the floor to join his mother.

The hut's side windows exploded inward, fragmented by bullets. Joel was already returning the fire with his Uzi. Then he hurled a grenade twenty yards to the right of the house. Screaming followed, signaling a strike. More bullets pounded the walls from all angles simultaneously. David dragged himself to the window on the other side. Rivkah followed him, tightened his tourniquet in one hand and balanced the M-16 in the other.

More bullets thundered at them. Sparrow jammed back against the wall to avoid flying glass. He glided from the house's right front window to its left front one, firing regular spurts at dark shapes silhouetted in the near blackness. The fire was returned tenfold. The cabin seemed to be baking in the heat, scorched by the bullets pounding into its frame. Sparrow sent another volley spraying the field, careful to make each shot count. He stole a glance at his watch. Past eleven. There was no chance to make the meeting with Felix. Funny how that still concerned him.

By the window, Rivkah was retying David's tourniquet. Then she abandoned her M-16 to snap fresh clips into Sparrow's and Joel's rifles. Her son cowered in the corner, not up to the task, sobbing softly.

Outside the enemy fire suddenly ceased.

"Retreating?" wondered Joel.

"Regrouping more likely. I don't like this," Sparrow muttered.

"I can't see them," said David anxiously.

"They've pulled back," from Joel.

"Or circled around," Sparrow corrected. Then to Rivkah, "What time does the sun come up?"

"A little past four."

"Too long to hold them off." Especially, Sparrow thought to himself, when the enemy would know their only hope of survival was to last until morning and would plan for that accordingly.

The silence outside was joined by silence within. Sparrow's eyes followed the field to the sloping, moonlit horizon. David and Joel kept their rifles poised on the window ledges, heads low and eyes scanning.

Nothing.

Still nothing.

Then dark shapes flashed, huddled, sprang.

"Get ready!" Sparrow screamed.

His command was drowned out by a blast near the front door. The whole cabin shook. The timbers crackled, threatening to give way and collapse atop them. Another blast, on the roof this time, showered them with splinters, sawdust, and boards. Sparrow found the grenade hurler in his sight, his head protruding just enough to make a decent target. He squeezed off two shots, one for the head and one for the belt; the first for the kill, the second to ignite the rest of his arsenal. His corpse blazed angry orange and took four of his fellows with him.

The small house popped with automatic fire. Joel's

Uzi jammed and he reached for another. A bullet tore into his neck, stood him up. A parade of fire ripped into his body and shook him to the floor with blood spurting from a dozen holes. Rivkah snaked to his window, pushing his corpse aside, and rotated her M-16 in a wide arc of fury.

On the other side of the room, a shot ricocheted off the window and stung David's eyes. His hands went instinctively up and when they came down there was a shape lunging forward from the outside. He got off three rounds but his vision was still blurry and two of them went wide. He lost the trigger, felt for it again, and then felt nothing. Sparrow watched him collapse in a flood of scarlet.

The shape that had killed him appeared in the window. Sparrow fired. Another, then still another tried to climb in. Sparrow emptied his clip. Still they kept coming. The gun was spent. He pulled the .45 from his belt and took them one at a time. He switched positions to angle himself for a better shot at the side window. Rivkah pushed the dead Joel's good Uzi toward him. Sparrow felt for it blindly.

A stunning blast punctured the front door, sent it swinging free and inward. Rivkah dove and planted herself before the shattered hinges. A sea of figures charged for the doorway. Rivkah pulled the trigger, rolled, pulled it again. Bodies piled up in the entrance. Her son sobbed fearfully in the corner, his arms wrapped tightly around his frail frame. Sparrow located the Uzi.

There was another dizzying rush at the front and he turned to help the woman fend it off. A body crashed through one of the windows and raised its gun. Sparrow blew its face into tiny fragments with the .45.

Instinctively, he turned the Uzi toward the other side window and held the trigger against a charge from without. His position was an absurd sort of spread-eagle, guns blasting toward opposite directions from both hands.

Still poised on the floor, Rivkah exhausted her clip. The refills were too far away to reach. She grabbed her husband's shotgun. A shape charged through the door and was blown backwards. A second attacker leaped headlong into the house, landing hard in front of the shotgun's barrel. Rivkah pulled the trigger again. His insides ruptured against the walls. She snapped the shotgun's trigger a third time but found only a click, had raised it over her head to strike when her stomach was ripped in two and she went down with her eyes already glazing. Sparrow turned the Uzi on her killer, exhausted it into him, and realized for the first time he was finished, or at the very least powerless to stop the boy from speeding across the floor to hug his mother's body.

"Mama! . . . Mama! . . . Ma—"

There was a blaze of fire in the doorway and he collapsed over her with his back a mass of reddening chasms, eyes held open and sightless. Sparrow spun away from the four killers rushing at him with two more at the doorway, and succeeded in firing his last round into one of their heads. But then his bad leg gave out and he struck the floor with his eyes shut and his body tied in a million taut knots to be unraveled only by death.

Sparrow expected to hear only the gunfire tearing into him. Instead, though, his ears were pierced by an inhuman, drawn-out wail followed by a whistling noise that sliced the air. His eyes opened to a massive blurred shape whirling about the room with a long, shiny blade in one hand and an automatic rifle in the other.

The shape turned his rifle on two of the killers at the same instant his sword decapitated a third. Then the rifle was dangling at his shoulder as his left hand joined his right on the sword's hilt. A fourth assailant went for his trigger, didn't find it, and looked down to see his forearm plunging to the floor. His scream was choked off by the naked steel skewing his midsection and draining his abdomen onto the floor. The last attacker turned to flee. The sword whisked down the line of his vertebrae and split his spine in two.

Sparrow's fading eyes found the biggest man he had ever seen approach him with sword still in hand. His beard was thickly tangled and he wore a sheepskin vest open at the front revealing two pistols tucked into his belt. The giant cleaned his blade of blood with a circular sweep through the air and returned it to its scabbard.

"I understand you wanted to see me, Israeli," said Felix.

NINE

Sparrow spent the ride to Al-Jauf along the last stretch of Damnation Alley in the front of the truck with Felix and the driver. In the back were some of Felix's best men, ten in all—enough to have subdued the remainder of the forty-man Arab force.

Sparrow fought for rest but his mind filled with thoughts of his daughter and grandson. It had been necessary for them to leave Israel eight years before and equally necessary for him never to see them again. Association with him might place the only family he had left in grave danger. So he had made himself stay away even though he had no one else. They were safe in America, he had told himself, safe from those who would punish him through those he loved.

It was the practical thing to do, the step that minimized the possibility of danger for them. Sparrow lived by precautions. He had been saved by them often enough to be convinced of their efficacy. Precautions were everything. Chance simply didn't exist and risk was something to be avoided at all costs.

So he had shipped his family away and moved memories into their place. Memories of his grandson growing, laughing, learning. Memories of the time they had spent together, which meant so much to a man who had forgotten what love was, no less how to feel it.

The truck pulled to a halt after twenty silent minutes in front of a nameless building on the otherwise desolate road. Felix helped Sparrow down from the truck and led him inside. His sword scabbard grazed the door frame. His two pistols were still stuck in his belt and now Sparrow noticed an assortment of knives and various unfamiliar weapons inside his vest, in addition to the automatic rifle slung over his shoulder.

"Welcome to Paradise Hole," laughed Felix.

They were inside a dimly lit bar that relied on dust for atmosphere. There were five tables spread comfortably apart, each presently unoccupied. Felix led the way toward one.

"This marks the official end of Damnation Alley, Israeli. Let's have a drink to it. The whiskey's not bad. Imported all the way from Cairo. Personally, I prefer American Jack Daniels, but you can't have everything." The giant shrugged his massive shoulders.

"In that case, make it two whiskeys."

Felix snapped his fingers and gave the order to the bartender.

"I owe you quite a debt," said Sparrow.

"Think nothing of it, Israeli," Felix passed off in his deep, thick voice. "When I heard you were looking for me, I made myself available. You have quite a reputation. I'm surprised our paths haven't crossed before."

"I still don't understand how they met tonight."

Felix leaned back and stretched. His legs reached all the way under the table. His chair, barely wide enough to support his massive bulk, creaked from the strain. "I arrived for our meeting here early, Israeli, and heard mention of four trucks with many armed men on the way and watched them pass. They weren't ordinary Libyan soldiers, though that's what they were supposed to appear as. I did some quick checking and came to the conclusion that they were dispatched to find you on the road and cancel our meeting. I rounded up my men and set out to make sure you would remain a man of your word."

The bartender returned with two grimy glasses and a bottle of Egyptian whiskey. Felix filled his to the top and Sparrow's halfway, then drained his portion in two gulps, letting out a contented moan. "If only this was Jack Daniels. . . ."

Sparrow noted the richly lacquered brown scabbard and sword handle covered with tight beige wrap protruding from Felix's belt.

"You killed the last two men with a samurai sword," he said. "Or did my eyes deceive me?"

"You saw well, Israeli." Felix refilled his glass, gulped half the contents down. "I do not like guns. Too clumsy and random. In close quarters the triggers can be deceptive things. And bullets, well, sometimes they don't work like they should." He pulled the scabbard from his belt and halfway unsheathed the blade. "But the sword does not fail. It does not jam, misfire, spend its ammo. It kills so long as the man wielding it keeps swinging." Felix rotated the blade, catching the room's murky light and sending it bouncing everywhere. "An elegant weapon that allows for a noble kill."

"You handle it quite well."

"I've had training from top Japanese masters who teach a dying Way. The Way is still vital to me."

"I've heard you're equally good with guns and explosives, as well."

Felix moved the sword to the chair beside him. "A man must understand all the weapons of his time and try to master them if he is to become a great warrior. The moment he becomes satisfied with what he knows, his progress stops, and when his progress stops, he has lost himself. I strive always to be better, Israeli. I seek to be the ultimate warrior."

"People tell me you're coming damn close."

The giant laughed heartily. "Ah, the legend of Felix. Mostly lies and rumors. Strangely, I have heard similar things about you, Israeli. 'The Lion of the Night,' they call you."

Sparrow looked down briefly. "A long time ago, perhaps. Now making it through the day is a major accomplishment."

"And that wouldn't have been achieved on this day if you too were not a great warrior." Felix tugged at his beard and nodded. "I sense great strength in you, Israeli. It is good you are humble because strength lives much better in a humble body. And yet within your soul, I feel great torment. You are on a journey, Israeli, a journey of the spirit as well as the body and mind."

"Most perceptive of you."

"In Zen they say that the wise man learns what the fool has forgotten."

"Which means?"

"That I need more whiskey." Felix laughed again and filled his glass back to the rim, sipping it this time. "There is no honor left in the world, Israeli, no nobility anywhere to be found. Men kill each other from thousands of miles away. Buttons are pressed, orders given. Innocent people fall prey to the mad dreams of fanatics. In days past there was reason, now there is only excuse. In Japan it fell upon the samurai to restore and maintain a noble tradition. A man who carried a sword did so as an admonition of his belief in truth. I am nothing more than an anachronism. A seeker of the Way. A searcher. And, when necessary, a killer. That should answer your question, Israeli."

"I don't remember asking one."

"Your eyes did and so did your thoughts. And now I have one for you. Why have you traveled a thousand miles and entered a hostile land to seek me out?"

"You're the only man who can help me."

"Help you what?"

"For starters, get to America safely."

"A man of your abilities and contacts should not find that so difficult."

"Circumstances have made it difficult. You noted yourself that the men who ambushed me only *looked* like Libyan soldiers. In reality they belonged to a different army that holds no allegiance to any flag."

"Terrorists?"

Sparrow nodded. "They want me dead. They've tried twice now. They'll try again. I can't trust anyone with position or allegiance. I need an outsider, someone with the same concerns as me but . . ." Sparrow's eyes wandered to his leg. ". . . better physical abilities."

"And you think you can trust me, Israeli?"

"If I couldn't, I'd be dead already."

"Good point. You say I have the same concerns as you. How can you be sure?"

"Because we have the same enemies."

"Most of my enemies are dead."

"Not the ones who murdered forty children in America five days ago." Sparrow watched Felix's features tighten. "They work for the same people who arranged the ambush on Damnation Alley and who are now planning an ambush on the whole of civilization."

"A strange conclusion."

"You aren't the only man who senses things."

Felix leaned back and relaxed with a smile. "My high estimations of you were justified, Israeli. I like you. I like you much. Tell me who these people are."

"That's what I'm trying to find out."

"I think you already know."

Sparrow looked away from the giant's eyes but couldn't escape the fact that Felix seemed able to read his thoughts and beyond.

"I suspect," he managed.

"That is good enough for me, Israeli. And your suspicions must take you to America?"

Sparrow nodded.

Felix finished his whiskey and tugged at his beard. "I have never been to America. This seems as good a time as any. My sword and I are at your disposal for the price of a single case of Jack Daniels when we arrive." He smiled again briefly. "We will seek the Way on the same path and perhaps someday you will tell me the truth."

"I have."

"About what drives you, I mean. I believe you when you say you are chasing especially murderous terrorists who have some horrible plot in mind. But there's more," Felix said softly, his eyes boring into Sparrow's. "It's there, deep in your soul, stretching past emotion. I can feel it. It lies under your every word, pulsates with your every breath. You are a man with a burden greater than you admit. Yet in Zen they say a man obsessed is a man lost. Tell me your burden and I can help you find your way again, Israeli."

Sparrow avoided the giant's stare. "I've told you everything."

"Only for now, Israeli, only for now."

TEN

"The news is bad, Mr. President." General Robert MaCammon closed the door to the Oval Office. Three sets of eyes followed him to his chair.

"We haven't found the transport yet?" the President raised.

"No . . . because it's not there."

"Not where?"

"Within a fifty-mile radius of the point where we lost radar contact. It didn't go down," MaCammon added for elaboration. "We can't find it because it didn't go down."

"I don't think I follow you, General."

MaCammon hesitated. To the President's right, the heads of the FBI and CIA exchanged worried glances.

"Our people in Germany believe the C-170 and its cargo have been . . . hijacked."

"General, its cargo included three F-16 fighter-bombers."

"I'm well aware of that, sir."

"Then perhaps you could summarize for the rest of us the capabilities of what we've misplaced."

MaCammon had to think only briefly. "The F-16 Fighting Falcon can reach speeds exceeding twice the

speed of sound flying at fifty thousand feet with a range
of two thousand four hundred and fifteen miles. In
short, it's the most versatile plane in our arsenal and
quite probably the most potent. It carries air-to-air
missiles and laser-guided Capricorn air-to-surface
missiles. In the wrong hands, three of the jets could
. . ." MaCammon let a shrug complete his thought.

"Whose hands, gentlemen?" the President said.
"Whose hands?"

None of them ventured an answer.

The four men in the room were a study in contrasts.
Bart Triesdale, erudite director of the CIA with a
Harvard education, had been lured out of academia to
take over the beleaguered agency's reins. Triesdale
possessed a quick, fertile mind and the capacity for
dealing with people compassionately. Individually,
these traits were as common in Washington as limousines. But together they were a rare find in capital
positions of authority, a contradiction, apparently.

Thames Farminson, chief of the FBI, was undoubtedly its most effective director since Hoover. A
midwesterner who had worked his way through college
and law school, he was a simple man who had taken
over a complex job on a temporary basis but who had
made it permanent by reducing the task to his own
level. To the computerized age of law enforcement,
Farminson added common sense and the ethic that the
good guys always win so long as they work hard
enough.

General Robert MaCammon was a military man all
the way and the devil's advocate of the group. A
decorated hero in the Korean War, he had argued
against Vietnam from the beginning, but had carried
out the orders of a soldier, nonetheless. He was a man

who possessed the ability to consider consequences as well as answers but who likewise advocated a belligerent approach to problems more often than not. MaCammon enjoyed neither the wit of Triesdale nor the country sense of Farminson. He was, though, the Defense Department's top expert on arms and a master strategist, his technical contributions to the inner circle thus being invaluable.

These three men had by attrition become the most trusted advisors to a President who had risen to the office only when his predecessor died. Then his wife had succumbed to cancer soon after he moved his chair to the Oval Office. Because he blamed the strain of the last campaign trail for taking her life, the President vowed never to preach for votes again. Without the pressure of second-term aspirations, he set himself to doing the best job possible irrespective of party or politics. He held no illusions that one man could make any great difference—but a small one was conceivable. Progress, after all, was progress. Moving forward a little, if nothing else, assured against falling backward more.

"We're doing everything we can to recover the jets," General MaCammon was saying. "We're checking every possible landing point for the C-170 within its flying range. Since it never reappeared on anyone's radar, and because its range at so low an altitude would be severely limited, we're concentrating our search no more than seven hundred fifty miles in every direction, and that's a liberal figure: France to the west, Austria and Italy in the south, and—"

"—the Warsaw Pact nations in the east," completed Thames Farminson conclusively.

"It wasn't the Russians," said MaCammon. "They've

got no use for our F-16s."

"I'm inclined to agree," echoed Bart Triesdale. "They've already got the jet's plans and designs, just as we've got the layouts for their MIG-21s. They already know what makes the F-16 tick as well as we do."

"Besides," added MaCammon, "in a military sense, the plane is already obsolete."

"So where does that leave us?" asked the President.

MaCammon and Triesdale looked at each other. The general spoke. "Unfortunately, with the very real possibility that a . . . lesser power is now in possession of them."

"I assume you've backtracked from the start of this project."

"Of course, sir. We've traced down and run checks on every person who had anything to do with the transport from the time it took off from Andrews to the time it touched down in Germany for refueling en route to Saudi Arabia."

"They're all clean, Mr. President," picked up Bart Triesdale. "Every one of them has passed every test in the book and some that aren't."

The President eyed Triesdale quizzically. "How'd your people become involved in this so fast?"

"When the transport went down, we originally suspected sabotage and reacted accordingly. The fact that we're now likely facing some form of espionage instead will make some cross-checking necessary, but nothing likely to bring anything new to the surface."

"So what you're both telling me is that we've hit a dead-end."

"Not really," noted MaCammon. "We just haven't picked up the trail yet. That transport had to come down somewhere."

"Agreed," sighed the President. "Thirty-six hours ago. That might go a long way toward obliterating your trail."

"What are the chances that the jets are being held for ransom?" suggested Thames Farminson.

"Not good," responded Bart Triesdale. "I think we'd have heard something by now or at least within the next twenty-four hours. After that we can assume that whoever has the planes is planning something far less mundane than selling them back to us."

The President shook his head. "Let's change the subject to an equally unpleasant one. What's the latest on that bombing at the old age home in New York?"

Here, Thames Farminson leaned forward. "Six dead, twenty-two wounded. Could have been much worse, though. The bomb was planted in an attaché case that was left in the dining room at the peak of the lunch hour by a couple who had come to the home on the pretext of looking for lodging for a sickly parent. An alert orderly noticed it sitting there and decided to take it up to the manager's office. It blew up when he was halfway there. Had it exploded in the cafeteria, more than a hundred lives potentially would have been lost."

"Then we were lucky this time," the President said grimly, "unlike the incident over the border in Virginia—'Bloody Saturday,' according to the papers. Whoever's behind this is picking the most vulnerable targets possible; children first, then old people. I hesitate to think who'll be next."

"That's assuming one party is behind both strikes," reminded MaCammon.

"A fair assumption I'd say," the President went on. "What's Lucifer's feeling on that subject, Thames?"

"All supposition at this point, but their latest report

states that three of the terrorists involved in Bloody Saturday have been sanctioned, leaving two at large: a big man and a dark-haired woman. According to the nursing home manager, the man with the briefcase was tall, blond and extremely broad. The woman was dark and youthful, say mid-twenties." Farminson stopped to let his point sink in.

"Not much of a connection to go on," argued Triesdale. "Could be coincidence."

"Or random choices by plainly desperate people," followed MaCammon.

"Since the man with the briefcase made his appointment at the old age home ten days ago, I think we can safely rule that out," countered Farminson.

"As well as something else, I'm afraid," interrupted Triesdale. "Routine terrorism."

"Terrorism is never routine, Bart," the President snapped.

"I'm speaking in a relative sense, of course."

"Then go on."

"These two strikes violate every rule terrorists have set for themselves. To begin with, a strike is supposed to have a purpose, a goal, something to be gained. Take the young guests at the Bar Mitzvah party hostage. Kill one of them for effect maybe to insure we'll know they mean business and will accordingly act upon their demands. Only they never gave us any demands. It was a quick strike operation all the way with nothing to be gained other than completion of the act itself. They were out for blood, not politics or money. A new high for terrorism."

"Or a new low. . . ."

"Opposite extremes with equal effects. Consider also that no group has come forward to claim responsibility for either action. None of them want any part of this. Individual terrorist groups are uncharacteristically busy denying participation and chastising the perpetrators. They've even offered to help us because they're as confused as we are and possibly just as scared. And the upshot there is that we may be facing an entirely new terrorist group with an entirely new set of rules. They didn't give us a chance to prevent a tragedy by acceding to their demands, because they don't have any. But that doesn't mean they don't have some purpose in mind."

"Specifically?"

There was no hesitation in the CIA man's voice. "These are just the preliminaries, Mr. President. We're being set up. These terrorists don't give a damn about ransoms or political prisoners, but they must give a damn about something, and whatever it is, Alexandria and Long Island were parts of it. Small parts, I might add. Insignificant in the eyes of our terrorists, or they would have contacted us by now to ask for something. That will come later . . . unless we find them."

"A task which we've placed in Lucifer's hands."

Bart Triesdale stiffened.

"What is it, Bart?" the President probed. "What's wrong?"

"It may be nothing, sir, but our liaison Bathgate is twenty-four hours overdue with his latest report."

"Any speculation as to why?"

"Could be a simple communications breakdown."

"And if it isn't?"

"Then either something has forced him into deep cover or . . ."

"Or what?"

"He's been buried for good."

101

ELEVEN

It was seven-thirty when Major Bathgate's limousine pulled up to Beta gate, the back entrance to the Quad. Dan couldn't help hoping somebody he knew would see him climb into the backseat. Didn't this beat all?

"It's over for you, Dan," Bathgate said rigidly as soon as Keiko had swung the car from the curb. "I'm pulling you out."

Confusion claimed Dan's face. "Why?"

"Because it's out of control. This thing's much bigger than I thought originally. It's not just a terrorist assault or even a whole series of them. Much more is going on."

"I thought you needed me as bait to find out what."

"They haven't made a move on you in three days and they aren't planning to while I'm around. The Doctor caught wind of something big and I think I'm on to what it was. I'll know for sure tonight."

"You're leaving me up in the air. You owe me more than that, Major." Dan looked into Bathgate's eyes. Was it fear that looked back at him?

"You're right, Dan, I owe you a helluva lot more than that. I got you into this thing and I intend to get you out before somebody starts covering the tracks."

"This have anything to do with that bombing in Long Island?"

"Indirectly. This time we got a description of the two terrorists involved. We should have a make anytime now, for all the good it will do."

"You already know who they are, don't you?" It sounded more like an accusation than a question.

"I have my suspicions and I pray they're wrong. I'm expecting an envelope to arrive within three hours. Then I'll know for sure."

"Know what?"

"That doesn't concern you."

"It did four days ago."

"Not really," said Bathgate. *I should have seen it before,* he thought. *It was right in front of me and I didn't see it.*

He looked over at Dan compassionately. Rotten business. But it didn't matter because he was finished. He'd send in his letter of resignation tomorrow, which would leave him just enough time to get the boy safely out and contact the right people.

"Dan, you've got to trust me. I'm going to have Keiko swing the car in front of the Rockefeller Library and you're going to stay in there until ten tonight. At that hour, we'll be waiting for you across the street in this car. . . . I promise to get you out," Bathgate added as an afterthought.

"Out of what?"

"Leave it alone, Dan. Don't touch it."

Keiko brought the limousine to a halt in front of the library. Bathgate ran the right sleeve of his trench coat across his brow.

Dan sat rigidly on his side of the car. "What

happened to our deal, Major? I sorta like the idea of serving my country, especially when it helps me fill a hole in my life so big that a little piece of my future slips out every day."

"Bullets make bigger holes, Dan," Bathgate said. He reached across the seat and opened the door.

Dan climbed halfway out, then swung back. "Tell me about the Isosceles Project."

For a brief instant, he thought he saw Bathgate quiver.

"Do yourself a favor," the major advised. "When I get you out of this, forget you ever heard that phrase."

"I see, like it doesn't exist."

"Hopefully."

Dan used the quiet confines of the Rockefeller Library to sort out his thoughts. Bathgate had spoken to him in shadowy statements and riddles that left him hurt and frustrated. He felt let down and, worse, unsure. What had he seen in the major's eyes? What secret had Bathgate uncovered that he was unwilling to share?

The question nagged and tore at him because he feared he might never learn the answer. The son of a bitch Bathgate wanted to pull him out. Out of what? Since Monday afternoon he had done nothing out of the ordinary; he just did it with one of the major's men always within visual contact waiting for something to happen that hadn't yet. Nonetheless, the feeling of accomplishment was there, the feeling that he was doing something to get back at the people who had driven a chasm into his life.

Still unsettled, Dan went to work on a collection of

*Newsweek*s that contained a series on terrorism. Most interesting to him tonight was the centerpiece in the international terrorist network, the Soviet Union. The Soviets hated peace. They had set up Kaddafi and Castro as their puppets in especially volatile areas of the world for the express purpose of creating chaos where none might otherwise have existed. In fact, a special branch of the KGB known as Department V was sanctioned solely to immobilize Western nations by whatever means were available (and some that weren't) to create strife and chaos during times of international crisis. The Soviets, through their puppet leaders and Department V, made it their business to recruit terrorists, train them, set them up, finance their projects—do everything but pull the trigger, though they had clearly taught the finger that would how to do it.

The same *Newsweek* contained a piece of information Dan found startling. On Tuesday April 22, just ten days away, a terrorist conference had been scheduled in Paris, right out in the open for the whole world to see, with representatives from the PLO, PLF, Red Brigades, ETA-Militar, the IRA, Baader-Meinhof, and a dozen others meeting for a convention of murderers.

The purpose of the meeting was clear: The various terrorist groups in attendance sought a means of unification in order to better and further advance their common objective of world chaos. The fact that they were holding a publicized conference in a free world city indicated the bold confidence they had in their own efficacy. Worse, the very possibility of an internationally unified terrorist front stretched beyond comprehension. Cohesion had been the only thing lacking in the underground movement for over a decade. Twenty groups working individually would more often set back each other's goals than advance them. But twenty groups working as one would form a terrorist super-structure with an inexhaustible supply of manpower and resources that even Lucifer would be hard-pressed to equal, especially if the Soviets were calling the shots. Why—

Dan sat up suddenly. The hair on the back of his neck became prickly, standing on end. He glanced around the perimeter of his carrel. A few students were sorting through books shelved near and behind him. Others turned pages and jotted notes in carrels neighboring his. He strained his eyes. Fifteen yards away a student was asleep with his feet up on the enclosed desk, snoring quietly. Another was doing a crossword puzzle.

There was nothing to be scared of.

But Dan was scared. A snakelike fear, unfamiliar and unwelcome, coiled up his spine. He couldn't define or grasp it, which made the fear worse.

He turned one way. Then the other. Still nothing. His carrel rested against a three-foot base that gave way to a window. He squinted his eyes to see outside. Reflection from the library's lights proved too much. He couldn't see outside, but someone outside would be able to see in.

The fear gnawed at him, cold and clammy, like running in an open field and catching a pursuer's steps hot on your heels. The problem of impact is fundamental. The only question is when.

Each floor of Brown's Rockefeller Library is generally the same. Rows and rows of book-filled shelving stretched for the ceiling surrounded on three sides by individual working carrels set against the windows.

The carrels were three-quarters occupied tonight. The presence of so many other students should have made Dan feel comfortable.

It didn't.

He turned quickly toward the main aisle that led students past the front of the twenty or so rows of shelved books. Two girls approached lugging huge piles of books. A security guard followed them, checking fire extinguisher gauges. The sound of light timers ticking away the seconds above rows where students had neglected to turn them off gnawed at Dan's ears.

Behind him, soles scraped quietly against the polished floor. Dan forced his shoulders to turn, lost a breath and a heartbeat. There, moving toward him, was a giant black man. He stretched two-thirds of the way up the steel shelves he passed, which made him nearly seven feet tall.

Dan stood up, moved away. The giant increased his pace. His clean-shaven head caught the light and bounced it dully back.

Dan's foot struck the base of an empty carrel. He stumbled, nearly lost his balance, found it in time to bolt down the main aisle toward the elevator.

Behind him soles pounded harder against the floor.

Dan looked for the staircase, couldn't find it, pressed the down arrow of the elevator.

Come on! Come on . . . !

The black giant swung around the corner and moved toward him. He was wearing gloves, no—just one glove on his right hand. The arm it was attached to hung motionless as he walked.

The red down arrow flashed atop the elevator doors. The black giant quickened his pace, closing the gap.

Dan was about to run when the security guard who'd been checking fire extinguishers emerged to his side. The black giant stopped, no more than twelve feet away. His stare locked with Dan's. Lennagin looked away just as the elevator doors slid open. He followed the security guard in, watched him making notes on a pad.

Dan's eyes found the giant again. The black man flashed a smile and stretched his gloved hand to one of the steel pillars that fastened the shelves into the ceiling. A creaking sound followed as the still grinning bald giant closed his fist. Dan saw the metal give, bend, twist, snap.

The doors slid closed. The elevator moved for the lobby.

It was nine-forty-five when Dan stepped out of the Rock. He was fifteen minutes early but could only hope Bathgate's car would nonetheless be in sight. Sweat dropped from his brow and underarms in steady streams. He was shaking all over and couldn't get the sight of the black giant crushing steel out of his mind.

He'd tell the major. Bathgate would know what to do. The possibility of physical harm, once so distant and unassuming, was suddenly moving in his shadow. Danger had looked at him for the first time really and he couldn't bear to look back.

Bullets make bigger holes. . . .

Dan scanned the road. His eyes halted at a black limousine parked diagonally across from the library.

Thank God!

Dan lit out for it, leaping down the two sets of four-step granite staircases leading to the Rock. He pushed past other students leaving, nearly crashed into a few

108

who were just getting there. His heart thundered in his chest. Breaths came hard. The black giant was still somewhere close by.

Dan flew across the street, feeling like he was watching himself do all this on a projector in his head. Exhaust fumes met his nose. The limousine's engine was still running. Major Bathgate was a man who left nothing to chance. Breathing easier, Dan reached for the back door—pressed and pulled.

The door was locked.

Dan rapped on the window, then pounded it. His eyes glanced furtively behind him. The black giant would by now have had plenty of time to leave the library and continue his pursuit.

"Major Bathgate, open up! Major Bathgate, it's me!"

Dan's eyes peered into the darkness. The backseat was empty. He moved to the front door. Keiko's shape filled the area before the wheel.

"Keiko, open up! It's me—Dan Lennagin. You know." Again a furtive glance behind him. "Hurry up, *please!*"

Dan's fingers dropped to the latch and pulled. The door opened. The Japanese woman didn't move. Her eyes remained focused before her.

"Keiko?"

He shook her weakly. She tumbled toward him. Something thick and warm soaked his hand.

It was blood.

Keiko's throat had been cut from ear to ear.

Dan sprang backwards, felt a scream form behind his lips but lost it. He heard nothing, felt nothing because there were no sounds or feelings able to reach him. There was only the sight of the Japanese woman with martially able hands slipping toward the passenger side of the car leaving a path of still warm blood across the upholstery. Dan might have stood there in that very spot in the street for an hour or a day had not a soft, raspy voice found his ears.

"Dan . . . Dan . . ."

The voice was throaty, nasal. Lennagin shook himself weakly from his trance and moved toward it, struck by a distant chord of familiarity.

"Dan, here. Over . . . here," it rasped again.

Lennagin moved toward a gardener's delight of round, thick bushes arranged in a neat grove.

"Here, Dan, here."

Lennagin parted two of the bushes and looked down. Major Bathgate lay sprawled beneath him, his head and shoulders propped up on the base of a tree. His trembling fingers held his trench coat over his abdomen. Blood seeped beneath them and drenched the fabric in an ever widening blotch. The coat and his fingers, Dan realized, were the only things holding his stomach where it was.

"Must . . . talk . . . to . . . you."

Dan knelt on the grass and leaned his ear close to Bathgate's mouth. Blood dripped from both corners.

"I've got to call an ambulance," Dan said because it was the only thing he could offer.

"No," muttered Bathgate. "No . . . time. Just listen." He coughed blood onto the front of his coat. His eyes closed, fluttered, opened. They were glassy, agonized. "Report came in." Bathgate fought to swallow. "The Doctor . . . was . . . right. Lucifer *is* black. Black is Lucifer. All makes sense. Should have . . . seen . . . it . . . before."

"What?" Dan was too frightened to be anything

but calm.

Bathgate was overcome by a coughing spasm that drained most of his remaining strength. "My pocket." The major looked to his right.

Dan reached down in that direction and came away with a manila envelope bloodied by Bathgate's fingerprints.

"Take it," the major instructed him. "Take it. Get out of here. Go . . . far . . . away. Isosceles active . . . again. No one to tell. Find Sparrow. Only one you can trust. Tell him to destroy Isosceles. Find him, find the Lion of the Night."

Dan gripped the envelope tightly. "I've got to get you to a doctor."

Bathgate lifted a shaking hand from his exposed stomach and grasped Dan's forearm. "No, too late. Just save your—"

The major's head collapsed forward. His hand slipped from Lennagin's forearm. His body shook, spasmed, stilled. He was dead.

Dan rose slowly, fought to keep himself in touch with what had happened. Reality flickered and tried to fade. This was a dream, had to be—why else would everything be moving in slow motion? He looked down. No dream. Bathgate was dead. *The man assigned to keep him alive was dead!*

There was a rustling in the bushes behind him. The noise shocked Lennagin back into a fully conscious state. A picture of the bald black giant who had crushed steel flashed through his mind. Then he was running, running with Bathgate's envelope held tightly in his hand. The cool spring air stung his face and dried the blood on his windbreaker. A car screeched its brakes as Dan lurched awkwardly in front of it. He passed the familiar Horace Mann English department building and swung onto a small side street, afraid to look back for fear the black giant might still be stalking him. A car took the corner too quickly, swerved toward him tires whining. Dan leaped to the curb and slammed his knee against the sidewalk. His eyes caught the driver. A drunk student, nothing more. Dan edged on, pace slowed.

Death was everywhere around him, closing fast. Violent death. The reality of it shook him alive and alert. He could be lying there with Bathgate right now. The possibility set him trembling as he moved, his sense of direction flawed but not his sense of purpose.

Up ahead, lights flickered in the West Quad, a collection of interconnected dormitories reserved almost exclusively for freshmen. A door was swinging slowly closed. Dan pushed himself for it, jammed his foot in the opening just before it locked shut. He couldn't go on. He had to catch his breath, his thoughts, his reason. His senses were dimmed to the degree that the familiar grounds seemed strange to him. He closed the door to Mead House behind him and placed his back against it.

Dan looked down. Bathgate's envelope was still gripped between his fingers. Wrinkled and caked with blood but intact nevertheless. Dan moved to the wall and slid slowly down it. He unclasped the envelope, withdrew its contents.

The first thing he saw was an eight-by-ten black and white picture of a standing figure, a powerfully built, expressionless man with light hair and eyes that seemed more like round slivers of glass tucked into his head. He was big, tall, and broad. Dan shuddered. A big man, he recalled, had been the leader of the Bloody

Saturday massacre and Bathgate had been waiting for a report on the terrorists responsible for the more recent bombing. The connection was unavoidable. The big man was behind both.

Dan felt the fear building in him layer by layer, chill by chill. He lowered his eyes to a card clipped to the bottom of the picture. Its message stunned him, brought him beyond panic, beyond fear. His heart thundered, threatening to cave in his ribs.

Lucifer is black. Black is Lucifer. . . .

The Doctor's words, repeated by Bathgate just minutes earlier.

Should have seen it before. . . .

Now Dan saw it but closed his eyes, trying to obliterate what was written on the card.

The blond man's name was Black.

Renaldo Black.

TWELVE

Dan didn't return to the fraternity right away. The possibility that the black giant was still out there in the darkness kept him perched on a flight of steps inside Mead House in plain view of the entrance. Every time the door opened, his heart raced. So far, though, only students had passed through.

Dan continued his vigil. He couldn't stay here forever but he sensed there was a reason to wait just a little longer. It took five more minutes before the reason finally revealed itself, beginning with the sound of many shoes descending the stairwell. Dan stood up and was swiftly passed by a throng of male freshmen on their way for a nighttime snack at one of the university's many snack bars.

If nothing else, hide yourself in a crowd.

In a fraternity game called kidnapping in which brothers and pledges sought equally to pursue and capture each other, that was one of the many pieces of advice handed down through the years. Before the final Mead House freshman closed the door, Dan had caught up with the group, hanging back enough not to be noticed by them and at the same time seeming a part of their motions. They would provide his camouflage,

114

just as a similar group had during D-Phi kidnapping in the fall when a group of eager pledges descended upon the area, oblivious to his presence.

Only this wasn't a game.

Dan kept pace with the group, close enough to hear their words and occasionally join their laughter. They babbled on about coming midterms, baseball practice, and plans for the summer. The throng swung into Wriston Quad on its way surely to the East Campus eatery where unused contract meals could be gobbled up at will. The destination was perfect for Dan because it would take the group right past an entrance to D-Phi.

He peeled off at the last possible second, sped by the Zeta Psi fraternity and took the circular walk to the side entrance of D-Phi. Brown fraternities are housed within regular dorms in specially provisioned space bordered by rooms occupied by nonmembers. D-Phi shared this particular complex with another fraternity, Alpha Delta Phi, as well as an upperclass dorm. Dan stuck his key into a door marked Goddard House and let his eyes lead his way in.

The stairwell was empty. The sound of his soles grazing the hard surface seemed loud enough for everyone in the building to hear. Since a silent approach upstairs was impossible, Dan took the steps quickly, hesitating only when he reached his third-floor room. What if the black giant was inside waiting for him? Dan pressed his ear against the wood and heard nothing. Acting on impulse, he jammed his key in and burst inside. If there was anyone waiting, a few screams and they'd have a whole fraternity to deal with.

The room, though, was empty, everything just as he had left it. Dan collapsed on the bed but sprang up, reversing his motion almost exactly. The fact that they weren't waiting for him didn't mean they wouldn't be coming. If anything, the opposite would be the case. This would be the first place they'd look for him. He couldn't sleep here tonight.

Considering the matter no further, Dan made for the door with Bathgate's envelope still tucked in his jacket, picking up a roll of tape from his desk on the way. In the corridor again, he relocked the door and fastened three strips of the scotch tape across its frame. He had learned the trick from an old James Bond movie. This way, come the morning he'd know if anyone had meant to pay him a visit during the night. Pleased with himself, Dan started back for the stairwell.

Finding a place to spend the night was no problem. On the fourth floor, three brothers shared a double room known as "the Box," an appropriate enough title considering that the center of the room was dominated by a piece of plywood construction the size of a double bed with sleeping quarters beneath and partying quarters above. A crowd of brothers inevitably gathered in the Box till all hours of the morning, often passed out and slept as they were.

Dan exchanged greetings with tonight's crowd but shrugged off their determined efforts to pass him a pot-filled pipe. He found a desk chair in the far right corner across from a set of empty, unmade bunk beds. He welcomed the brothers' company. Just having them in the same room heightened his sense of security, made him feel safe. He got himself as comfortable as possible and set about reading the complete contents of Bathgate's manila envelope. Somewhere within him was an urge to blurt out the story of what had happened to him that night to the happy cluster not ten feet away. But it was buried deep beneath his own sense of certainty that he had to go this alone, that telling others would only complicate an already impossible situation. He started reading.

The file on the blond man known as Renaldo Black read like a rap sheet. He was one of the top terrorists in the world, a free-lancer of German descent with links to Baader-Meinhof, the PLO, and the IRA. He had been credited with a number of hijackings and bombings and seemed particularly adept at taking the lives of innocent people for no good reason at all. He had last been seen in London nearly a year before where he had been traveling under one of sixteen known aliases. The report went on to conclude that a man matching Black's description was responsible for the bombing at the Hillside Nursing Home in Long Island and by connection was the leader of the Bloody Saturday massacre.

Dan skimmed the rest of the ten-page, single-spaced file on Black. It was dry stuff mostly; where he hung out, his pickup points, his contacts. He still couldn't bear looking at the cold face very long. Even through the picture the eyes seemed to glare back at him, threatening and omniscient.

Dan adjusted the fluorescent light above him. The stereo played the newest by the Grateful Dead and atop the Box a water-filled plastic contraption known as a bong was being passed around. Dan caught the sound of bubbles churning as marijuana found another of the brother's lungs. The bong moved on to the next in line. Dan was already reading again.

The next eight-by-ten glossy pictured a ravishingly attractive dark-haired woman with black, sultry eyes. She was shown wearing army fatigues with some sort of automatic rifle grasped in her hands. Her name according to the attached card was Gabriele Lafontaine. Last known residence, Algeria. Birthplace, unknown. Age believed to be somewhere around twenty-six. Dan looked into her eyes. Much darker than Black's but equally cold and empty. The file said she was a known associate of his. They traveled around the world together, basing their convenient alliance upon the fact that a couple enjoyed far more freedom of movement without suspicion than did a single. Here, a footnote referred Dan to a passage in the official report on Bloody Saturday stating that analysis of footprints present at the scene revealed that one of the terrorists had been a woman.

Dan had trouble believing it could be Gabriele Lafontaine. The paradox of someone so beautiful being a cold-blooded killer haunted him, because more than anything else it typified the dark, violent world he had entered. He clung to the hope that a mistake had been made somewhere with Gabriele, that they were wrong about her. As he continued with her file, though, his hope waned and then vanished altogether. She was the female counterpart of Renaldo Black in the terrorist world, known infamously for her execution of three hostages aboard an El Al jet when Italian authorities missed a demands deadline by just under two minutes.

Dan shuddered. That passage of the report brought the scene of his father's murder back to him, only this time the beautiful girl in the picture was holding the gun.

None of it made any sense. Not the death of his father or the death of Bathgate. Not a beautiful girl holding an executioner's gun. What kind of world had he entered? Thoughts of revenge left him, replaced by thoughts of survival. Everything else was superfluous.

A phone stared at him from the floor. He saw himself dialing the Providence police and telling them his story. But there would be questions he couldn't answer and answers they wouldn't understand. This stretched far beyond their capabilities. And what if they didn't believe him in the first place? Valuable time would be lost. He would be exposed, alone. No, there were other parties he had to tell his story to. And not here, not where the tentacles that had gotten to Bathgate were still reaching, probing. A plan was forming in his mind.

He had to get out of Providence, out of Rhode Island.

Go far away . . . some of Bathgate's last words.

He couldn't be safe here. Where, then?

The center of government. Eliminate the middle and go right to the people who had the information required to believe his story and the resources to deal with it. Go to the source.

In Washington. Far away enough.

Dan went back to the file. Between them, Black and Lafontaine had formed a convenient partnership fostered by a common desire to kill, nothing more. The final paragraph of her updated file indicated that the woman who accompanied the man believed to be Renaldo Black to the nursing home fit her description perfectly.

Dan flipped to another page, which contained the autopsy report on The Doctor.

The subject died of asphyxiation brought on by a crushed larynx and ruptured Adam's apple. The nasal and sinus passages showed considerable signs of hemorrhage with substantial blood loss through mouth, ears, and nasal passages. The skin around the

*throat was broken and all cartilage contracted beyond
a reasonable point. It is believed this could only have
been accomplished by some sort of steel vise capable of
exerting tremendous pressure on the order of . . .*

Dan felt a chill grip him. The picture of the black
giant crushing the steel pillar in the library froze in his
head. The coincidence was too obvious to let pass. The
giant had killed The Doctor in Los Angeles, then
eliminated Bathgate in Providence. And no doubt
existed in Dan's mind that he had come to the Rock for
the purpose of killing him as well.

Dan yawned and stretched, projecting the autopsy
report against the fluorescent light.

There was writing on the back of it in light pencil.
Dan flipped it over.

Scrawled before him was the phrase "Code Oscar is a
trigger for" followed by the drawing of a triangle.

An Isosceles triangle.

Code Oscar is a trigger for the Isosceles Project.

Bathgate had taken The Doctor's message and given
it a measure of sense, of order. Cryptic phrases strung
together into an equally cryptic sentence, but a sentence all the same.

Beneath the triangle was a column of dates beginning with April 5, the day The Doctor was killed, and
ending with May 15. One date was circled—April 21,
ten days away, a Monday. Something about the date
fluttered briefly through Dan's head.

*Code Oscar is a trigger for the Isosceles Project on
April 21.*

If it was a code, it was a damn poor one. Anyone
could have put the message together. After all, though,
Bathgate had intended it only for his own eyes.

Or had he?

Why was the penciled note so light that only holding it up to the lamp had revealed its presence? It had the look of simple doodling but somehow it was too even, too processed. What if it was a message meant specifically for him, Dan thought, once Bathgate had realized they were coming for him?

Code Oscar is a trigger for the Isosceles Project on April 21.

Written in desperation by a man who knew he was about to die, that possibility as chilling as it was real.

It wasn't hard to figure that Major Bathgate had stumbled upon something that had cost him his life, murdered quite possibly by the very people he worked for: Lucifer. Why else would his final, dying message have indicated that the international terrorist responsible for fifty deaths over the past week was working for the organization charged with finding him? Somewhere along the line the Lucifer Directive had been altered. Those charged with fighting terrorism were suddenly supporting it, backing it.

Dan leaned back and held his eyes closed. Confusion passed icily through his veins with his blood. The unanswered questions battered his mind. He was in a world foreign to him, foreign to all but a select group of professionals for whom life and death were merely relative states of being. So he would get out, get to someone for whom his story would hold credence; someone in Washington.

Tomorrow morning, first thing, he'd go to the bank and withdraw his entire account, roughly four hundred dollars. Strange seeing the net worth of his life reduced to such a petty figure, but it was enough to get him to Washington.

Find Sparrow. Only one you can trust. . . .

But how? And who was Sparrow in the first place? No, Bathgate would have to settle for the FBI in Washington. Let them find Sparrow.

Dan flipped a few more pages from the envelope and came across a report detailing the weapons used in Bloody Saturday. They were Russian Kalishnikov AK-47s and had been traced to a transplanted American arms broker in Switzerland named Lutz. The vast terrorist underground was at work, Lutz being the first link in a long chain that would lead somehow to the Isosceles Project and Code Oscar. The FBI would follow it and give Dan the protection he needed, the protection Bathgate would have provided. He'd leave Brown, leave Providence, and pick up the pieces of his undergraduate life when it was safe—though Dan couldn't help but wonder if it ever would be safe again.

III

THE TRIGGER

THIRTEEN

Gabriele Lafontaine watched the light flash its regular pattern a third time, a huge eye winking in the misty night.

"Return the signal," Renaldo Black told her and she did.

On the docks of Le Croisic jutting out into France's Bay of Biscay, a lantern was covered for a count of three, and Black steered the speedboat in for its final approach. He pulled a black ski mask over his face, as Gabriele reached for hers.

A sharp light suddenly pierced the night, illuminating the speedboat's deck.

"Turn that fucking thing off!" Black snapped.

"I am sorry, monsieur." The apology came from a short, squat man standing on the dock next to a tall muscular figure. Black regarded them both as their shapes sharpened in focus.

"Stay with the plan," he whispered to Gabriele, cutting the engine and steering the speedboat with the currents.

Three feet from the dock, Gabriele leaped out and eased the sleek black craft into position, then tied it up loosely. Black stepped gracefully onto the damp dock surface.

"You have the merchandise?" he demanded, standing next to her. "I have little time to waste, Tropez."

Tropez said nothing. The muscular man next to him, exposed biceps bulging with each breath, stiffened.

"You have the merchandise?" Black repeated.

"Monsieur, the code. Precautions must be taken," Tropez forced out defensively. A few thin strands of hair on his head were tucked neatly behind his ears. His exposed dome dripped shiny rivulets.

"I have no time for codes. The money for the merchandise. Let's get going."

Tropez gulped some air. "Do you wish to check it, monsieur?"

Gabriele watched Black shake his head. "You know the penalty for delivering faulty supplies."

"As you wish," Tropez conceded. "And the money?"

"The usual denominations. My associate will go over it with you while your man and I load the boat. Acceptable?"

"Certainly, monsieur. Most acceptable." Tropez started to dab his brow but then pulled back, as if afraid the motion might disturb the masked figure. He nodded, and his muscular assistant stepped back, revealing five three-foot-square shipping crates.

"Have they been waterproofed?" Black asked.

"Of course," Tropez assured him. "But Prometheus is a surprisingly stable explosive. In spite of its—"

"I am not interested in lectures."

"Cer-Cer-Certainly, monsieur. My apologies."

"My associate will pay you. Find an area of light so you can check the bills."

"This way," Tropez told Gabriele. She followed him toward the back of a boat house where a spotlight would allow him to count the money in rapid fashion.

Back on the dock, Tropez's muscular assistant hoisted one of the crates gently onto the foredeck. The launch billowed with the weight, accepting it reluctantly. The man was stepping back onto the dock when he caught the flash of steel before him. He thought at first it was a knife, which was good because its wielder couldn't possibly use it before his gun made its mark. He reached toward his belt and lunged in the same quick motion.

Renaldo Black flicked his wrist and the dart shot out, lodging in the target's throat. He wore the mechanism the way another might wear a wristwatch and the sling was equally inconspicuous, there nonetheless when he needed it.

The muscular man's fingers never quite found his pistol. He was caught between actions, between breaths, losing the capacity to complete either. He lived for seven seconds in all, long enough for him to feel his body strike the cold dock and plunge into the even colder waters. The waves swirled about his dying eyes, then swallowed him.

Black whipped the ski mask off, freed his blond hair, and set out to finish the loading.

Tropez looked down from the still silent Gabriele at the manila envelope.

"I see no reason to count it," he said, his eyes leafing through the green currency. "We must observe a measure of trust even in our—"

He looked back up to see the silenced pistol grasped in Gabriele's hand.

"Oh God, please no. Please!"

She should have fired right away but didn't. This marked the first time she'd touched a gun since Saturday night, and the taste of that was still heavy and dirty on her mind.

"I have a wife and children. *Five* children! Please, I beg you. For their sakes. *Please!*"

Tropez shrank to his knees, a pathetic figure really, and one that should have been easy to kill.

"It won't hurt," Gabriele promised him, but the reassurance made her task no easier. Perhaps it was the mention of children. That brought her back to Alexandria. More killing in the massacre's wake seemed impossible. She wondered if she'd ever be able to pull a trigger again. "It won't hurt."

Tropez's eyes flashed dimly at the sound of a woman's voice. His trembling eased a bit, as though a female holding a gun was less menacing. Only a weapon knew no gender.

Gabriele pulled the hammer back.

Tropez closed his eyes.

"Pleassssssssssss . . ."

Gabriele couldn't pull the trigger. She was weakening more with each second, searching for a reason to hate this pathetic man but finding none worthy of a bullet. Her finger quivered.

"Think of my family. For God's sake, mademoiselle, think of my family!" Tropez pleaded, seizing her moment of hesitation.

It wasn't his words that determined her course of action; in fact, she barely registered them. Her decision based itself purely on the practicalities of the situation. Self-defense was one thing, political executions something else still. This proved quite another. Not that she wasn't used to the killing. It just seemed suddenly harder and more futile. She held the pistol in the air and fired twice. Two soft spits echoed briefly, then faded into the wind.

Tropez looked up at her, confused and unsure, though hopeful, tears swelling down his cheeks.

"Disappear," she told him. "Disappear for a week, at least. Stay clear of your family or I'll come back and kill you. Understand?"

"Yes! Yes! . . . Thank you, thank you. . . ."

Tropez was on his feet. He backed up pitifully, turned and scampered away.

She raised the gun for his back. How easy it would be to take him now, a faceless figure fleeing through the night. But in front of the figure was a man with a family and to kill one she had to kill the other.

Gabriele Lafontaine lowered her gun and started back toward the dock. It mattered little that she'd let Tropez live, at least in the pragmatic sense, because he didn't know enough to do them or the plan any harm. But in another, far more important sense the ramifications of her action were profoundly hazardous. She had felt pity. Worse, she had *felt*.

One of the cardinal rules she lived by had been broken and she found herself vulnerable. Strange thing about rules; once one falls, others have a tendency to tumble after it.

Gabriele blocked out the thought and quickened her pace to rejoin Renaldo Black.

FOURTEEN

Sparrow was exhausted. He had slept only four hours of the past forty-eight and the strain was telling on him. His years on the kibbutz had been filled with lazy days and sleepy nights. The sudden switch back to his life style of a decade earlier came as a shock to both his system and his sensibility.

He had put his life totally in the powerful hands of the mysterious Felix and thus far those hands had ably done the job of getting him safely on his way to America. From Al-Jauf they had traveled north by truck to the oil refinery at Mersa Brega. Then came a long and dangerous drive across five hundred miles of coastal road to Tripoli. A brief layover followed, after which Felix arranged passage for himself and Sparrow aboard a cargo plane en route to the Algerian city of Sfax. Now they were on their way by train to Algiers, just the two of them. Felix had left all of his men behind in Tripoli, a move which reduced their measure of comfort by the amount of fifteen superb soldiers.

"Why Paris, Israeli?" Felix asked in their private compartment, referring to the destination for which Algiers was a stopover point. The giant carried both his sword and rifle in a gun bag always within arm's reach.

His two pistols remained tucked in his belt. His many knives and other assorted weapons stayed hidden in his sheepskin vest.

"I know a man there who can give me certain information I need."

"The one you called from Tripoli?"

Sparrow nodded. "An old associate who owes me a few favors."

"Perhaps I know him."

"Constantine Depopolis."

"Ah, the one-eyed pirate of the seas."

"Not anymore."

"But for years terrorist gunrunners sailed in fear of his ghost ship, which appeared out of nowhere to arbitrarily dump their cargoes overboard."

"He's moved into a different line of work."

"One that will give him access to information about the butchers who killed those children?"

"One at least."

Felix leaned forward. "It seems, Israeli, that you are chasing after that which you already possess."

"I must be sure."

"That is a luxury men of our kind can seldom afford." Felix watched Sparrow's eyebrows flicker at his use of "our." "You are a man too much like myself."

Sparrow stretched his weary muscles, conspicuously leaving his limp leg in place. "Not really."

Felix chuckled. "The body, Israeli, it matters little. It makes up but one-third of the essential triangle, and the other two legs—the mind and the spirit—are far more important for a roguish samurai *or* the famous Lion of the Night in seeking the truest Way. And in mind and spirit we are the same."

"But what of our motivations?"

"I have none. Politics, Israeli, motivations are all politics. All over the world men kill each other over whose god is stronger and whose way of life is better. Men try to force their ideas on others and if those others resist, the men abandon the preaching and reach for the rifles. The only absolute truth of the Way is that there is no absolute truth."

"Zen?"

"Common sense. Something this world of yours seems very short on."

"It's your world, too."

"Only by default." Felix struck his massive chest. "My way of life is the way of the sword. I seek inner peace, but all around me there is turmoil. Living alone on a mountain is not the answer either, because sooner or later some man with a gun will climb the mountain and claim it for his people because his way of life is best. Guns make marvelous persuaders, don't you think, Israeli?"

Sparrow nodded. "And right now, my friend, the whole world is playing Russian roulette."

Outside the train squealed to a halt in the station at Algiers.

They took a cab into the city's port section.

"You will not find a better gathering point for the scum of the earth," said Felix. "A den of the lawless, all with nothing to lose. Police stay clear of this section. Murders are routine. Criminals and killers walk around free with guns strapped to their waists or slung over their shoulders. Victims are claimed every night, their corpses dumped into the water. Nobody misses them."

"You expect to find us a boat here?"

"In Algiers, Israeli, one can obtain anything for a price, including a seaworthy captain."

"We could also retain one in a more . . . respectable port."

"Which is exactly what the people chasing you—now us—would expect our strategy to be."

Sparrow shrugged, accepting the point. Together they walked across the dirt-layered street, Sparrow struggling to keep Felix's pace. His limp leg grew worse when he went long periods without sufficient rest. They stopped before an English-speaking bar named The Port of Call. Music and shouting blared from the inside. Felix hesitated before leading the way through the door.

"The toughest bar in all Algiers, Israeli," he explained. "A gathering point for the scum of the earth like no other I have ever seen." Felix fingered the sword wedged through his belt. His rifle had been left in a safe place with a contact. "There will be men inside with boats. Perhaps, my friend, you should wait for me out here."

"I appreciate the concern, but I'm going in."

Felix smiled. "I thought as much. Stay on your guard. Throat-slitting is a misdemeanor in this section of town."

The big man opened the door and Sparrow followed him in. The room was dimly lit and smoke infested. The music sprang from a juke box in the corner. At a table in the center, a small crowd had gathered around an arm-wrestling contest between two gargantuans with arms the size of tree trunks. A thick-haired man with a tattoo of a dragon on his monstrous bicep seemed to hold the advantage. Sparrow scanned the rest of The

Port of Call. Large men with cold eyes abounded. All
seemed to wear pistols at their sides. Women bathed in
cheap perfume and tight clothes paraded this way and
that, displaying their wares while searching for the
highest bidder. Those who'd found one were comfortably perched on his lap. The unfortunate single males
guzzled beer, seldom smiling.

A cheer went up from the center table. The thick-
haired monster with the dragon tattoo had won. The
loser walked away holding his elbow. Sparrow noted it
looked broken. Someone slammed a coin into the juke
box, kicked the machine, and the song changed. He
kicked it twice more and laughed.

"The sailors hang out in the back, Israeli," Felix said.
"We should make our way over there."

Sparrow held his ground. "You go. I'd only get in the
way and force more questions to be raised than you
could answer. It's a lot easier for one man to book
passage than two."

"A good point. Be on your guard, though. I'll be just
around the first partition."

"I can still take care of myself."

"Of that I am sure, Israeli."

Felix made his way through the crowd, drawing long
stares from the clientele. Even in a place like this, his
massive frame and diverse arsenal stood out. Sparrow
found an empty table in sight of the door and pushed a
single chair around so that it was against the wall.
Reassuringly, he patted the .45 concealed beneath his
baggy shirt. A boy came over wearing an apron.

"You wish a drink?"

"Whiskey."

"No whiskey."

"Scotch then."

"No scotch."

"How about bourbon?"

The boy pinched his nostrils. "Very bad."

"Beer okay?"

The boy nodded. "Three kinds. Which one you want?"

"The best." Then, after a quick glance around him, "Something imported."

The boy took his leave.

Sparrow continued to monitor the bar with his eyes and ears. Three poorly matched couples were dancing in the middle of the floor. A small man stood up on a table and challenged three hulking friends with a knife. One of the three pulled the table from under his feet and the small man went flying. Laughter filtered through the room. Sparrow felt distinctly uncomfortable. It wasn't just the surroundings, though they certainly weren't cordial. He had ventured out in public as little as possible for the last eight years. The older he got, the more he wanted to be with himself and those he knew well. A roomful of strangers with knives in their pockets and guns on their hips didn't fill either criterion.

"Is this the cripple?"

Sparrow turned swiftly in the direction of the door. Three men had entered wearing blue navy pea jackets and navy watch caps, all large, the speaker toothless. His question was aimed at the curly-haired hulk with the dragon tattooed on his arm, the winner of the arm-wrestling contest.

"That's the one," the hulk confirmed.

The three sailors edged forward, the speaker at their

lead. "We don't like cripples here."

Sparrow said nothing, reached for his .45.

"And we don't like old men, either. Gives the joint a bad name." The speaker whipped a knife from his belt. "You know who I am, old man?"

Sparrow had the .45 out of its perch.

"Name's Billy Bags. They call me Cutter around these parts. I make it a point to slice someone up every time I get into port." The arm wrestler moved to his side. Billy Bags held the knife menacingly before him. "I enjoy cuttin' old men up best of all."

He charged forward, the glinting blade in line with Sparrow's throat. Sparrow let the outstretched arm pass halfway across the table before shifting his weight forward and hoisting upward in the same motion. The wood splintered against Cutter's face, sending him reeling to the floor. At impact, the .45 slipped from Sparrow's fingers. He didn't dare risk a moment to retrieve it, because the moment plainly didn't exist. The sudden turn of events stunned Cutter's fellows long enough for the Israeli to lurch one way and twist the other, moving as fast as his body allowed. He caught one with an elbow to the ribs and the other with a solid knee to the groin.

Cutter charged at him again but Sparrow side-stepped and kept him going off balance to the floor. He landed near his knife and reached out to retrieve it. Sparrow saw this motion unfold and spun to beat him there, might have succeeded had not he used his limp leg as the pivot point. It buckled, betraying him at the same instant a fire-breathing dragon flashed before his eyes as the arm wrestler grabbed him from behind, interlocking his fingers. Sparrow felt the pressure on his neck, twisted in a classic escape maneuver with no results, then tried another also to no avail. The arm wrestler tightened his grip and dragged Sparrow backwards. The dragon grew with each flex of his massive bicep.

Cutter rose back to his feet and moved slowly across the room, his knife jabbing at the air.

"Fights pretty good for a cripple, don't he? Well, after tonight he won't be fightin' no more, I say. I'm gonna cut you up and use your Jew hide for fishin' tomorrow, old man." The knife flashed before Sparrow's eyes, headed for his throat. "Anyone who don't want to get hit by crippled blood move back so you can avoid the flood."

The arm wrestler laughed again. Cutter's blade whipped forward, then suddenly vanished in a blur from his hand. He uttered a cry of anguish and held his shattered fingers in his good ones.

"What have we here?" Felix reeled in his ball-and-chain and stuck it back in his sheepskin vest. "What might this be?"

"Ain't none of your affair, mister," Cutter said from a squatting position, passing a second blade from his ruined fingers to his useable ones.

"The old man means nothing to you. Leave him alone and let me buy you a drink."

"Fuck off!"

Before the curse was even completed, Cutter had hurled his second blade for Felix's heart. Moving with the air, Felix glided from its path and unsheathed his sword at the very instant Cutter went for the gun in his belt. The sailor had a draw like lightning, quite unfortunate in this case, because as he snapped the pistol out, his forearm tore into the razor-sharp edge of Felix's blade. In his own mind he had pulled the trigger, which was impossible since his elbow and all beneath it were lying in a bloody heap on the floor.

Sparrow jerked from the arm wrestler's grasp and dove quickly to the floor, watching Felix make a diagonal cut from another sailor's right shoulder through his left hip. Then he was drawing one of his pistols and firing it point blank into the onrushing midsection of Cutter's other henchman, blowing him backwards.

The arm wrestler bolted forward with a furious scream that ended when the point of Felix's sword sliced through his muscular neck and emerged from the other side. Felix withdrew the blade and the body crumpled to the floor. He stuck his pistol back in his belt, spun the blade with a flick of his wrist to clean it of blood, and returned it to his scabbard.

"Let's get out of here, Israeli," he told Sparrow, helping him to his feet and stealing a final glance at the man called Cutter, now wailing in the agony of his severed arm. "Before anyone becomes too interested in our handiwork."

Keeping his eyes ready for other potential assailants, Felix backed toward the door, picking up Sparrow's pistol on the way.

"I found us a boat, Israeli," he reported when they were outside. "A trawler. The captain would be more than happy to help us on our way to Paris."

"Is he reliable?"

"In Algiers, no one is reliable."

"Time is more important anyway," Sparrow said. "It was no accident they attacked me in the bar."

"How can you be sure?"

"How else could that man Cutter have known I was a Jew?" Sparrow paused. "They've found us."

"And failed again."

"I'd prefer not to wait until the next attempt. Will the captain you found leave tonight?"

"He will now."

FIFTEEN

Sparrow met Constantine Depopolis for a late lunch at a cafe in the center of Paris the next afternoon.

The trawler Felix had retained for them in Algiers had taken the Strait of Gibraltar to Lisbon where it docked after an uneventful fourteen-hour journey. Sparrow had slept almost the entire time, waking up on a few occasions always to find Felix wide-eyed and watchful. In Lisbon they had chartered a jet, arriving in Paris just in time for the meeting with Depopolis.

Sparrow had spent most of his waking hours during the journey reflecting on his past. His wife had died fifteen years ago, two years before their grandson was born. The story in Jerusalem was that terrorists had killed her for revenge, but in reality it had been a stroke. Then he recalled the day, eight years ago, when he had informed his daughter, son-in-law, and grandson of their impending move to America for security reasons. His daughter knew him well enough to understand his reasons and not argue with them. What he did he did because it was best and safest. The logic was simple. Explaining the situation to his five-year-old grandson was a bit more painful.

"I don't want to go, Papa," the boy said stubbornly,

his face upturned into a familiar mask of determination.

Sparrow took the child into his lap. "It is for the best."

"What about my friends? What about my house? What about . . ." The boy searched desperately for more examples.

Sparrow saved him the trouble. "When you play games with your friends, you are the leader, are you not?" The boy nodded. "And you dream someday of being a great general of our nation and leading far more than just games. Am I right?"

The boy looked at his grandfather with astonishment. "How did you know?"

"Because I look into your eyes and see myself. We are much the same, you and me. But before you can grow up and give orders you must learn to take them. You must learn to do what is best for your nation and your family. It is never easy and it often hurts, but still you do it. Do you understand?"

The boy nodded courageously. "I will go to America."

"And someday you will return here a general."

The boy tightened his hold on Sparrow's shoulders. "Will you visit us in America, Papa? Will you visit us often?"

Sparrow tousled his hair. "Would you expect me not to?"

The boy hugged him tightly. "I love you, Papa."

Sparrow was glad for the hug because it saved the boy from seeing the tears welling in his eyes. He had lied to his grandson—there would be no visits. Trips to America would forfeit the very security he was establishing by sending his family there. He could not allow himself to be associated with them. The risk was too great. Their safety had to be insured at all costs. So the lies began. Sparrow hated the lies that had forever dominated his professional life and always seemed to squeeze their way into his personal one as well. The lies were everywhere, becoming easier to tell but no less easier to bear. Each lie brought him further from the great truth he had seen once as a bright beacon in the future rising above the darkness of the past. But as the days went by, and the future grew into the past, the darkness had swallowed it. A dim glow on the horizon, that was all that remained. The rest had vanished with his dreams, his ideals.

And he was on his way to America. Even the lies weren't sure anymore.

"I'll wait outside, Israeli," Felix had said when they reached the cafe.

"Aren't you hungry?"

Felix shrugged. "Restaurant food is difficult for me. Besides, if problems arise it will be from out here. I prefer to remain by the door just in case, to solve them."

"Thank you."

"Think nothing of it, Israeli. Just say hello to the one-eyed pirate for me."

Constantine Depopolis was one-eyed but he looked nothing like a pirate. His white, double-breasted suit covered a black polo shirt tight over still wide shoulders. His raven eye patch lent him a look that was dignified, even fashionable, and hardly menacing. His hair was black too, neatly styled and combed straight back off his forehead and over his ears. His skin was fresh and deeply tanned, his face showing its few wrinkles proudly. The years had treated Depopolis well and he had returned the favor.

"Ah, my old friend," he said, rising to his feet with a smile as soon as Sparrow crossed the floor. "It has been too long."

Sparrow extended his hand only to have Depopolis bypass it, hugging him tight and hard, slapping him at the shoulders.

"How is life treating you?" the Greek asked, pulling back a bit.

"Well, until a few days ago."

"Ah, the subject of your visit . . ."

"You have the information I requested?"

Depopolis offered him a chair and returned to his own. "Have I ever failed you, Sparrow?"

"I'm too old to remember."

The Greek laughed, reaching across the table to slap Sparrow on the arm.

"We go back a long way, don't we?" Depopolis reflected, and in one long instant he remembered it all.

For many years he had sailed the high seas as a smuggler, a modern-day pirate who pilfered whatever riches ships unlucky enough to pass his way had to offer. He was a legend in every port of Europe and an enigma to the many coastal patrols he eluded. He had been caught only once, by the irate owners of a pirated drug shipment, and for punishment lost his right eye to a branding iron. But only one eye is needed to steer a ship, and Depopolis had returned to the seas with fresh vigor and resolve and had prospered, even as a massive fleet coordinated by European drug runners was preparing to launch against him.

Sparrow had sent ships to head it off within hours of

the battle that would have certainly cost the Greek his ship and probably his life. The Israeli knew that almost all terrorist arms shipments traveled by water. A terrorist is nothing without his guns, so Sparrow concocted a plan to give Depopolis sanction on the high seas to raid the gunrunners' ships, confiscate their cargo, and be paid exceptionally well for it. Accordingly, the Greek played havoc with hundreds of terrorist cargoes, indirectly saving thousands of lives and throwing the entire network into disarray.

Sparrow, meanwhile, found that not only had his strategy gained him a new advantage over terrorist gunrunners, but also a loyal, lifetime friend. And when he moved on to other ventures, he took Depopolis with him, placing him at the head of an intelligence unit dedicated to stopping all terrorist arms shipments at the source and clearing the seas of gunrunning altogether. The years had passed, and eventually the two men went their separate ways. But Depopolis maintained his own private intelligence operation and strike force, utilizing computers as often as twin-engine hydrofoils to find and intercept illegal arms . . . and resell them to legitimate countries. Once a pirate always a pirate.

Depopolis pushed a manila envelope across the table at Sparrow. "Inside you will find a picture of the man responsible for Bloody Saturday. A most unsavory sort, I must admit, the kind I'd hang from the mainsail as quickly as I'd piss in the ocean."

Sparrow slid the photograph out and studied the hard face framed by blond hair. "Renaldo Black . . ."

"Know him?"

"Only by reputation."

"And quite a reputation it is. . . ."

"How'd you come by the information so fast?"

"The American intelligence computer has no secrets from me, old friend." Depopolis rested his hands on the table and leaned forward, lowering his voice. "You didn't come here just to pick up a photograph, though."

"No," Sparrow conceded. "I need more information."

"Certainly, there's no information I can pass on to you that you don't have access to yourself."

"It concerns Lucifer."

"Ah, our former associates. . . ."

"Not really former."

Depopolis looked puzzled. "But we both left their employ eight years ago."

"And I've kept my eyes on them the whole time since."

"Ah, watching for something specific I presume, old friend."

"And I saw it six days ago in America."

"Bloody Saturday. . . ."

"Exactly."

"Ah, and you think Lucifer was responsible for such a horror through Renaldo Black?"

Sparrow nodded.

"But why?"

Sparrow looked Depopolis square in the eye. "Isosceles," was all he said.

The Greek's rich features paled. His lips quivered, words struggling to form behind them. "But that's . . . impossible."

"I don't think so."

"But Isosceles was defensive in nature, *totally* defensive."

"Only in theory, a theory easily changed."

"You've been anticipating this, old friend."

"Preparing for it, at least." Then, distantly, "For eight years now."

"Since you left Lucifer."

"Since the emerging leadership decided it was in the organization's best interests to *have* me leave," Sparrow snapped bitterly.

"Then you're sure about Isosceles?"

Sparrow nodded slowly. "The massacre marks a commitment to it on Lucifer's part."

"Then they must be stopped." Depopolis's face grew grim and taut with determination. The point of his tanned chin stuck forward as he spoke. "I am at your service, old friend. Whatever you need is yours for the asking. Ships, troops, I could assemble an army in three days. I could—"

"For now, just answer one question. Have any high-yield explosives changed hands lately?"

A trace of a smile crawled over the Greek's lips. "Ah, old friend, it's like the old days." The smile vanished. Depopolis began tapping his fingers stiffly against the table top. "Your search for black market high-yield explosives, is it limited to those of the missile variety?"

"Not really, I suppose."

"Ah, then perhaps I can help you. I received a report this morning that a large quantity of Prometheus plastic explosives exchanged hands recently right here in France."

"How much?" Sparrow asked eagerly.

"A hundred and fifty pounds."

"Good God! In one shipment?"

"Unfortunately."

"And the parties involved?"

"That's what the report to my office was about. The dealer who delivered the *plastique* and his guard have disappeared."

Sparrow's face turned to glass. The slightest expression might have cracked it. "Can you help me get to America?"

"I'd sail a boat myself if need be, old friend."

"I'm afraid we won't have time for that. We may not have any time at all."

Depopolis regarded Sparrow tentatively. "The missing Prometheus shipment, old friend. What does it mean?"

Sparrow held his stare. "The trigger. You've shown me what they're going to use for the trigger."

SIXTEEN

For Dan Lennagin, sleep did little to sort out the problems that plagued him. He woke up cramped and uncomfortable in one of the Box's extra beds. If anything, he felt more confused and frightened than he'd been when he'd finally been able to shut his eyes.

The first order of business was to return to his room. It was still his home here, something that represented security, and he missed it. Before entering, he carefully inspected the transparent tape he'd affixed to the frame. All three strips were unbroken, a sign the room hadn't been entered during the night. He turned the key and stepped inside.

The room was a shambles. His books were scattered everywhere, his desk drawers pulled out and emptied randomly. The clothes once in his dresser littered the rug. Feathers from his down jacket fluttered in the air. The refrigerator sat open, its contents spilled atop his desk.

The room had been searched, that much was clear. Equally clear, however, was the fact that the intruders hadn't left with what they had come for, because Dan held Bathgate's manila envelope under his arm right now. They had torn the place apart in their search for it.

But there was more. Why had they bothered to return the tape to the outside of the door and in the exact places he'd left it? Why bother if they had made a mess of the room to begin with? Surely, anyone skilled enough to notice tape and return it to its precise pattern could search a room and leave no trace of his presence.

Unless they *wanted* him to know they'd been there. Dan sat down on the bed shivering slightly. Their search had turned up nothing so they'd disrupted the order of his room to similarly disrupt the order of his mind. They wanted him to know they had been there, were *still* close by. He had what they wanted, and more than Bathgate's envelope, they wanted him.

Dan pulled a Providence *Journal* from the corridor and began pouring through it. He'd leave for Washington as soon as possible, and he wanted to bring evidence of what had happened to Bathgate last night with him. Certainly there would be mention of the killings in the paper.

But there wasn't. The *Journal* carried not a single word on the murders of Bathgate and Keiko. How could that be? Someone would have stumbled upon the bodies not long after he fled the scene. The police would've been alerted, the reporters not far behind. None of this had happened.

"I heard you slept in the Box last night. . . . Now I can see why."

Dan turned with a start to find Peter Brent in the doorway. "Somebody's idea of a bad joke."

"Really?" from Brent skeptically, stepping inside. "Somehow I don't buy that."

"All right. So maybe one of my many enemies decided to get a little revenge."

Peter smiled. "The place looks too good for that." The smile disappeared. "What's going on, Dan?"

"Why does something have to be going on?"

"Well, besides the fact that your room looks like we just held Hell Night in it, you bagged the Fraternity Presidents' meeting last night. Remember? Come on, try real hard. You're the president of the presidents, Danny boy. Under your brilliant leadership they've made a stand to force the university to strengthen fraternity charters. Last night's meeting was the big showdown. Except you forgot to show up. And the rest of the guys were too confused to take up the slack, so the deans ate them up and the charter strengthening got screwed. I know how much it meant to you, which means I know you must've had a goddamn good reason for missing the meeting. Now tell me what the fuck is going on with you!" Brent demanded, revealing a side of himself Dan had never glimpsed before.

"I can't tell you."

"I'm your friend, Dan. You can."

"You're my friend, which is exactly why I *can't*."

"When something's eating me, I always feel I can come to you. I'd like to think you felt the same way toward me."

"I do. It's just that this is . . . different."

Brent's expression softened. "It must be, Dan, because I've never known you to forget your responsibilities or your friends, and the last couple days you've been doing a good job forgetting both. I didn't mean to blow up at you before. It's just that if you're in trouble I want you to know that I'm—"

"I have to leave for a while, Pete. I don't know how long I'll be gone, but I'd appreciate it if you'd square everything with the guys for me."

Brent's eyes flashed distantly. "Sure thing." A pause. "Except I think you'd be a whole lot better off if you got whatever's eating you off your chest."

Dan shook his head. "I can't now. Trust me."

"Anything else I can do?"

Dan regarded his friend warmly and shook his head again.

Peter was about to push a smile forward, then decided just to speak. "On your way wherever you're going, you think you could drop this at the bank?" He produced a blue check from his pocket. "It's the refund the university owed us for the furniture. Thirty-two hundred. I picked it up last night after you forgot to."

Dan took it from Brent's outstretched hand and pocketed it absently. "What would I do without you?"

"Flunk Engine Nine, because I haven't returned your notebook yet. I'll drop it off before lunch. Just leave the door open."

"No sweat."

"And, Dan, whatever's going on, be careful, okay?"

"For sure."

He closed the door behind Brent and locked it, an agenda firm in his mind. First he changed his clothes. Then he moved to the desk and withdrew the contents of Bathgate's envelope and placed them in a fresh one of his own, a little smaller, to make carrying the material easier. The envelope would never leave his person. He tucked it into the inside pocket of his windbreaker, then carefully checked the room and catalogued it, searching for anything else he might need for the trip. Additional clothes were out of the question, being too much of a tip-off of his intentions to anyone who might be watching. He would go to the airport right from the bank, the plan being to catch them off guard. The bank . . . he was almost to the door when he remembered his statement savings book was still in his drawer.

His heart picked up speed as soon as he hit the pavement outside D-Phi. They could easily be watching him now, probably were. So he'd walk among crowds, avoid being alone at all costs especially in confined spaces. The calm he felt in determining his strategy surprised him. He was changing, evolving, not the same person he had been last week or even yesterday at this time. His brother had once told him that was the way it was in Vietnam. You changed fast because you had to if you wanted to stay alive. There was no middle ground at all, no compromise. Everyone was a professional, at least those who lived. Everything added up to survival.

A chorus of bells chimed in the near distance. One series of classes was ending, another just about to start. Dan had timed his exit from the fraternity perfectly. The sidewalks for the next ten minutes would be flooded with people. He found the flow of traffic leaving Wriston Quad and became part of it. He reached the Green—a large grassy area crisscrossed in several directions by sidewalks—with a springy stride and watchful bright eyes that belied his predicament. He felt confident enough to stop at Brown security headquarters en route to the bank. The newspaper had totally ignored the previous night's murders. He wanted to know why.

"Anything funny happen last night?" he asked the blue-uniformed guard behind the main desk.

"Nothing special. Why?"

"I was coming out of the Rock around nine-thirty last night when I thought I heard someone scream."

"You call us then?"

"No. I had a big exam this morning. I guess I wasn't thinking straight."

"Doesn't matter anyway," the guard behind the desk said. Dan realized he'd never seen him here before, and as a fraternity president he had come into contact with just about all the guards at one time or another. A scar ran across the man's right eyebrow. Not an easy face to forget. "Nothing went down last night in that area other than a bicycle snatching. Maybe that's what you heard."

"Maybe," Dan echoed, unsatisfied.

He started for the door. The guard eyed him strangely.

"Have a nice day," the scarred man said.

"You too."

Dan reached the corner of Thayer and Waterman, just two blocks from his bank, and waited for a bus to pass by before crossing the street. A new dimension entered his strategy. Thayer Street was a popular route and the buses were inevitably crowded. He'd hop on the first one he saw after leaving the bank with his money and switch a few times through Providence to throw them off the trail if they were still on it. His mind worked fast, storing his options for further reference. Nervous energy countered his fear and made its effects negligible. He reached the bank angry at himself for having been lost in his thoughts the final stretch of the way.

Dan filled out a withdrawal slip for all but a token of his savings and joined the inevitable line. He had no passbook, just a bank-provided accounting folder in which he kept track of his own transactions. Statement savings, they called it. The interest was better by almost a point, a dollar a year maybe. His turn came up.

Dan moved to a teller's station, exchanged perfunctory smiles with her, and handed over his withdrawal slip. Her fingers glided across a computer-controlled keyboard, feeding information in from the slip. The machine coughed up a bit more of the white paper from the roller that confirmed the transaction. The teller repeated the process. The machine coughed succinctly again.

"Are you sure you wrote down the right account number here?" He took the withdrawal slip from her extended hand. "It didn't go through." The teller's smile was gone.

Dan checked the number and found it correct. "What do you mean?"

"The computer says your account's been closed."

Dan shrank back stunned, his eyes glassy. He wasn't sure he said anything else to the teller and doubted she could have heard him anyway. He wanted to say a mistake had been made but knew one hadn't. Everything was suddenly clear to him: Lucifer was doing its utmost to isolate him. They had drained his account because they knew without money he was helpless, trapped, a prisoner.

Their prisoner.

He exited the bank dimly, his resolve and enthusiasm wiped out with his savings. He had underestimated the opposition's reach and power. Access to and control over computer tapes were obviously within Lucifer's domain. The potential of their reach was limitless, and they were reaching for him. A bus crept past him and squealed to a halt. Dan caught up and boarded it on impulse. He needed time to collect himself, to think. The bus ride served only to further scatter his thoughts.

Every passenger who boarded or met his eyes belonged to the vast forces of his enemy. There were no walls on the bus, no place to hide. He had never felt so alone before or so weak. He was at the mercy of a faceless entity who could manipulate computers as easily as eliminate people who stood clumsily in its way. How could he expect to beat them?

He had to figure it out somewhere where he felt safe.

He had to get back to D-Phi. The house. His home. . . .

Dan returned to Thayer Street via a different bus some twenty-five minutes later and exercised the same degree of caution in returning to Wriston Quad as he had in departing from it. The closer he got to the house, the higher his spirits rose.

Until he heard the first sirens. They found his ears when he passed under Wayland Arch at the entrance to the Quad. His stomach knotted. He broke into a run, swung right quickly toward the clouds of smoke gathering in the sky. The horribly corrosive smell of a chemistry experiment gone wrong invaded his nostrils. A fire engine crawled carefully down a section of narrow walk. A rescue squad followed in its wake.

Dan turned a corner and stopped dead. D-Phi was engulfed by smoke. The crew of one fire engine struggled for better position to hose it down. Orders were shouted. People rushed everywhere. They blew up the house, Dan thought, they blew it up and it's my fault. Guilt swam through his stomach, swallowing the fear. His mouth was parched and bitter. Then the mist before his eyes cleared and so did the smoke. It was all coming from one window on the third floor.

His window.

It had been blown out frame and all, and had taken a

portion of the surrounding bricks with it. As far as he could see, though, there was no other damage to the building. The explosion had been contained in his room.

Dan allowed himself to hope. Maybe no one had been hurt. Maybe they had blown up his room not knowing he wasn't there. But there were too many rescue squads, and an organization capable of wiping out even a meager bank account was unlikely to make such an error.

It was a different error they had made and Dan recognized it with horror and pain being carried out on a stretcher. A white sheet covered a supine figure past the face. Only the figure's hair was exposed. Curly hair—his hair. . . .

Peter Brent's hair. . . .

The truth struck him like a strong wind and nearly buckled his knees. Somehow reason slithered through his shock and he saw what had happened, saw it in living color projected on a movie screen in his head. They had wired his room with explosives and waited for his expected return from the bank. When Peter Brent, his look-alike from a distance, entered through the unlocked door they had set the explosives off. So Peter was dead, blown to bits because he stopped by to drop off Dan's Engine 9 notebook.

It wasn't fair! It wasn't goddamn fair!

The shock cushioned him, kept him away from shedding tears but not from pondering them. Amidst the haze he saw the truth: Peter was dead and it was his fault. He had caused his best friend's death. There would be no more California smiles, no more problems to help him solve. . . .

Dan felt himself grow faint from the hurt. Then

someone he knew seemed to catch a glimpse of him. Instinctively, he ducked around a corner. His mind was working again; reasoning, planning. It made him feel dirty and cruel. But he saw his way out. The stretcher carting a curly-haired corpse from the scene would be a signal of success to the killers. It wouldn't be till later that the truth became known. He was free until then. He had time to act, to plan.

From deep within him, the strength came to run, run as fast as he could around the corner, skirting the grass border of the cement walk and challenging the rush of people hurrying to the scene of the explosion. He seemed to be the only person moving away from it but that didn't matter.

He thought of his father.

He thought of Peter Brent. . . .

And his hand dropped into his jacket pocket and touched the check for $3,200 Brent had given him to deposit. He'd had the money he needed all the time. The world suddenly sharpened in focus. He saw everything in crystal clarity, including his means of escape.

"Say what, man?" Tommy Lee Hudson squinted his features into a disbelieving stare.

"Did you mean what you said the other day, about owing me something you could never repay?" Dan repeated. He had come to Tommy Lee's room direct from D-Phi.

"If I said it, I meant it. But you didn't sprint over here out of breath to have me repeat my debts."

"No, I came here to erase them. I'm in trouble, Tommy. I need your help."

Tommy Lee's expression tightened. "Just name it."

"Still got that rejuvenated Mustang of yours?"

"Hottest set of wheels on campus."

"I'm in trouble."

"You in trouble? Come on. . . ." Hudson studied Dan's eyes. "Jesus shit, you're fuckin' serious! Where you need to go, man? Just name the destination."

"The Bonanza bus terminal downtown. But I don't want you to drive me, I want to borrow your car."

Tommy Lee's mouth dropped. Dan knew he never lent his car to anyone, no matter what. But he couldn't let his friend play chauffeur because that might place Tommy's life in jeopardy. One death on his conscience was enough. He'd stop at the bank to cash the D-Phi check and then take the hourly express from the terminal to Boston's Logan Airport where he'd catch the next plane to Washington.

Tommy Lee's face fell into a smile. He dug into his pants pocket and came out with a set of keys.

"Take good care of her," he said, handing them over.

"With kid gloves. I'll leave her in the terminal parking lot, keys under the seat." Dan paused. "This makes us even, Tommy."

Hudson shook his head, still smiling. "No way, man. Shit, for what I owe you, I'd drive ya to a fuckin' KKK barbecue."

"Logan Express now boarding on platform seven."

The stocky man with the scar running through his eyebrow studied the curly-haired youth superimposed between the cross hairs of his rifle sight. The target rose from his seat in the bus station terminal and stretched uneasily, scanning the area around him. No matter, the stocky man reflected, his eyes would do him no good. He stood out of sight fifty yards away in the corner of a darkened repair bay.

While witnessing the aftermath of the explosion he had caused, the stocky man had noticed with no small degree of shock Lennagin lurking among the crowd. A chill had gripped his spine. Somehow he had made a crucial mistake that would cost him more than his job if it was not corrected immediately. There hadn't been time to issue a report and call for reinforcements. There had been time only to follow Lennagin from the fraternity and wait for the opportune time to make his amends.

He moved the barrel a fraction to the left, keeping his target locked in the grid. He pawed the trigger. Once pulled, the rifle would release nothing so mundane as a bullet, but a miniature dart loaded with fast-acting poison. Lennagin would be dead before he hit the ground, a victim of an apparent heart attack. The target reached the front of the boarding line, extending his ticket to the driver.

It was time.

The stocky man with the scarred eyebrow steadied his rifle and curled his index finger inward. The trigger gave at the precise moment a heavy arm jerked him backwards. The poisoned dart struck the side of the bus harmlessly as the arm raised to his throat and tightened. The stocky man's fingers groped for the face behind him but had locked only on air when the stiletto plunged through his third and fourth ribs, puncturing his heart.

He was dead before he hit the ground.

A tall, muscular man emerged into the light, his stiletto conveniently back in its sheath. His face was harshly angular but plain, neither warm nor cold. His features were generally nondescript, save for the conspicuous contrast between his ash-gray hair and heavy, jet black mustache.

He approached the bus slowly, not wanting to attract any undue attention to himself. Still, he was the last passenger to board and the driver had to reopen the door to collect his ticket.

He took a seat in the front so he could watch the curly-haired young man, whose life he had just saved, in the mirror.

It was going to be a long trip.

SEVENTEEN

The bus got Dan Lennagin to Logan Airport just in time to catch the four o'clock plane from Boston to Washington. He paid for his ticket with some of the cash he'd acquired from the bank in return for the D-Phi check, and then boarded immediately, his only luggage being the manila envelope tucked carefully in his inside jacket pocket. It was his life insurance and not to be taken lightly. Once in Washington, it would add credence—a measure of proof—to his story.

He was issued an aisle seat and reclined comfortably in the moments before takeoff, feeling reasonably safe. His mind couldn't keep up with all that had happened. He replayed the day's events and found himself chilled by fear and hurt again. Hidden reserves of strength had kept him going this far. He hadn't had time to think. Now he did. There were problems to consider.

He had already decided to make the FBI the recipient of his story and envelope. He had read enough times that the Bureau was the best of the three letter agencies at purging itself and would thus be the most likely to be free of Lucifer infiltration. What was more, he had the best chance of finding someone with an open ear at the J. Edgar Hoover Building. Somehow he couldn't see himself talking to the CIA, Secret Service, or NSA—and as for the latter two, he didn't even know how to contact them.

So it would be the FBI . . . but not without hassles. By the time he reached Washington and got settled somewhere it would be in the vicinity of seven o'clock. Seeing an agent tonight would be a difficult task and tomorrow was Saturday, which could prove no easier. He'd have to have a story ready, something that would make them see him on such short notice without passing him off as a crackpot—which is what he'd undoubtedly sound like. He'd make them give him an appointment.

Then he'd show them the envelope, Bathgate's last remains.

The jet jockeyed into the air. The head stewardess completed her perfunctory instructions before Dan even realized she had started.

He felt lousy. His stomach was doing cartwheels and his head wouldn't stop spinning. He held his eyes closed but Peter Brent kept smiling at him, and when he blocked him out, Major Bathgate appeared with a desperate plea and his guts falling out. His brother had told him what it was like in Nam at first before you became conditioned. About how your buddies got blown apart by land mines or had their heads emptied by snipers. And the only thing that stopped you from weeping for them was the realization that it could have just as easily been you, and that you might be next. That was the kind of world he had entered. Still he wanted to weep.

A few minutes after the jet seemed to level off, a stewardess came round with a pushcart and asked him if he wanted something to drink. He asked for ginger ale, then added whiskey to the order for an additional two dollars. It was just one drink, he reasoned. Maybe it would help relax him.

While the stewardess was mixing it, a nondescript male passenger who'd been sitting three seats behind Dan brushed by her on his way to the men's room. Her trained "excuse me" smile prevented her from seeing the man drop a small pill into the plastic glass. It had dissolved by the time she looked down, as though it had never existed in the first place. She started to hand it to Dan.

Before he could take it, though, another man tripped on a bulge in the carpet and crashed into him. The glass went flying, splattering its contents across the aisle and drenching Dan. The man muttered an apology and patted the wet spot on Lennagin's jacket, apologizing uneasily again. There was something vaguely familiar about the man, as though they had met recently before. No spark of recognition, however, filled his eyes when they met Dan's. It was probably just his looks, Lennagin concluded thoughtlessly. The black mustache and gray hair made an incongruous match.

The man poured out one more apology before leaving. He smiled, and the embarrassed gesture distracted Dan from the action of the stranger's right hand sneaking something into his right suit pocket. He sauntered away.

The man with the black mustache had watched the action unfold near the boy's seat with a hint of amusement. It looked clumsy to him in its slowness. His latest assignment should've proved arduous, but his inept opponents seemed determined to make it easy. Actually they weren't inept at all, just no match for him. But the man was no one to brag, even to himself. Brief physical contact with the boy had been deemed necessary hours ago to obtain what now rested in his pocket. His opponents' actions had made him act faster than he would have preferred. Now the boy had seen his face, which could cause a problem later. The man returned to his seat, noting the position of the passenger with the pill on the way. There would be time to deal with him later.

Dan quickly drained his refilled glass and fell off into an uneasy slumber. He awoke with a start more than a half-hour later. The man with the gray hair and the black mustache! He'd ridden the Logan Express from Providence as well! Dan remembered seeing him climb on. He recalled the feeling of his hand wiping the soaked area of his jacket earlier. A powerful hand attached to an arm like iron forced into gentleness.

Dan's stomach sank. He lost a breath. His right hand dropped hastily into his windbreaker for the inside pocket.

Empty.

The envelope was gone!

He wanted to scream out that he'd been robbed, but to whom? And what to offer as an explanation? Any outburst would lead to uncomfortable questions he couldn't answer. Problems would result, delays perhaps. He'd be noticed. A nagging feeling tore at him, frustration mixing with helplessness. He was alone and his life insurance was forfeit. There was no choice other than to find the man with the black mustache. He rose from his seat and started slowly down the aisle.

The jet was a DC-10. Plenty of places to hide, to maneuver. His plight was all but impossible even before the captain announced he was beginning descent into the Washington area and the seatbelt sign had been turned on again. Reluctantly, Dan went back to his seat. Otherwise, he'd have stood out too much, another element of his strategy lost.

What strategy did he have now, though? Everything had been based around the envelope, his sole proof that the events of the last week had really happened. He had committed most of its contents to memory.

Code Oscar is the trigger for the Isosceles Project on April 21. . . .

But would the FBI believe him without proof? He had nothing but a story now and a crazy one at that.

The plane landed, taxied toward the terminal. Passengers rose from their seats, clutching for overcoats or briefcases or handbags. Dan searched their faces for a black mustache surrounded by gray hair. There was none. He was confused. Would it be better to remain on the plane until the very last to check for the man, or would a better strategy be to dart off at the front of the line and wait for him at the gate?

Dan chose the latter. He pushed his way past as many bodies in the aisle as he could, emerging into the terminal among the first fifty off the plane which meant the man he sought must have been among the first forty-nine, because he was nowhere to be found.

Meanwhile, back on the jet a stewardess shook the shoulder of a sleeping man dozing three rows behind where Dan's seat had been. His eyes remained closed so she shook him harder. The man slumped over, supported only by his seatbelt. The stewardess screamed.

The man was dead.

Dan found an available hotel room at the Hilton through the courtesy phones located in Washington

National's lobby. As he made the trip into town in the hotel limousine, a contradiction nagged at him: If they could get close enough to him to steal the envelope, why not kill him as well? The maneuver made no sense.

Unless Lucifer hadn't been behind it.

But then who had? Was there some factor here that he hadn't considered yet?

He'd let the FBI find the answers. Once in his room, the Bureau was the first number he dialed. He was surprised when someone answered at seven-thirty on a Friday night.

"Federal Bureau of Investigation." A female voice.

"I'd like to speak to an agent please," Dan stammered. No matter how long you rehearsed a line like that, it never came out right. *I'm botching it,* Dan thought.

"I'm sorry, all offices are closed right now. If you'll call back Monday morning during regular business hours, which begin at—"

"This is an emergency."

"What is the nature?" the voice asked plainly.

Dan began his equally well-rehearsed story. "I've come down here from Brown University where I serve on the Student Affairs Committee. A radical group is planning something big, so I need to talk with someone big."

"Are you sure this can't wait till Monday?" the voice asked routinely.

"I wouldn't be calling now if it could."

"What is the nature of your suspicions?"

"Guns have been smuggled onto campus by a black militant."

"Have you spoken with the local or university authorities?"

"They don't believe me. Think I'm overreacting or just plain making the whole thing up. I'm not, so I spent my own money to come down here and talk to somebody who'd listen."

"All the same, a Saturday meeting is quite irregular."

"So are the circumstances."

A pause. Dan heard a typewriter rattle briefly on the other end of the line.

"Tomorrow morning at nine o'clock. An agent will meet you in the lobby. Your name please."

Dan almost gave her the false one he had registered in the hotel under. "Dan Lennagin." He hesitated. "What will his name be? The agent's, I mean."

"Sorry, sir, I'm afraid I don't have that information available. It will be whoever's on call. . . . Are you quite sure this is an emergency?"

"Absolutely."

At precisely eight-fifty-five the next morning, Dan climbed the steps of the J. Edgar Hoover Building, which turned out to be right across the street from the Justice Department and the Federal Energy Administration. A powerfully built man with wide, droopy eyes underlined by bags held the door open for him, then shut it tight.

"You Lennagin?" he snapped.

Dan nodded.

"Name's Quinn, kid, Paul Quinn. I'm on call today so you drew me. Sort of like when they take you to the emergency room and get some doctor to trade his golf club for a scalpel. That's who your life depends on."

"The analogy's not far off," Dan said, taking Quinn's outstretched hand. His grip was firm.

"Let's go up to my office. I don't play golf so I'm not too pissed about you ruining my Saturday."

Quinn had a deceptive, lumbering look to him, cold yet compassionate—his expression constantly held like a crocodile ready to snap. His receding hair had once been curly. Now it waved irregularly over his scalp exposing skin in several patches. He carried his mouth a bit to the side, a kind of perpetual snicker that once might have been a grin. But the rest of his face was sharp and sensitive.

He offered Dan a chair in an office that was small but functional, littered with papers, reports and technical manuals.

"You told the night operator your being here represents an emergency," he opened, taking the seat behind his desk.

"It is."

"Well, if it's the old thing about student radicals hatching plots to take over the administration building, I've got to disagree."

"It's not," Dan assured him.

"Good. I don't like investigating kids. There's something dirty about it and I have to keep my hands clean to be able to look myself in the mirror." Quinn paused and smiled faintly. "I've got a daughter starting at Vassar in the fall. She thinks my job sucks. Sometimes she's right," the agent said with a twinge of bitterness. "I don't like being here on Saturday."

"Either do I."

"So stop wasting both our weekends and come to the point. Don't want to disappoint the Student Affairs Committee at Brown, do you?"

"Brown doesn't have a Student Affairs Committee."

Quinn looked across the desk at Dan quizzically. "Huh?"

"I sort of made it up so you'd see me today. I couldn't wait till Monday. My life is . . . in danger."

Quinn leaned back, started to smile then stopped. "I hate to believe you because it'll beat the hell out of my weekend, but somehow I get the feeling you're telling the truth. What happened, you get mixed up with the wrong sort of people or something?"

"Exactly."

"Drugs?"

"No."

"Underground protest movement?"

Dan shook his head.

"That doesn't leave a whole helluva lot considering you're still in college."

"It didn't until last week. . . ."

And Dan went on to tell him everything, starting with the phone call from The Doctor, the appearance of Bathgate, his being set up as bait, the existence of Lucifer, Bathgate's murder, the events of the past few days, his flight from Rhode Island, and the disappearance of the envelope. In all the story took more than a half-hour to tell, with Quinn stopping him regularly to ask questions—a good sign, Dan reckoned. At least the FBI man was listening. On the other hand, he had to admit that putting the facts of the story together in a neat little package made it seem even more incredible and confusing. He bit his lip when Quinn sighed loudly at the end.

The agent's face was slightly pale. "Frankly, Lennagin, I don't know what to make of all this."

"You believe me?" Dan asked hopefully.

"Look, Lennagin, this is real life, not some drummed-up movie where men with government pensions turn deaf ears to innocent people who fall in off the street with some incredible story to tell. We *do* listen, but that doesn't necessarily mean we believe. That part requires proof. What'd you say happened to that envelope?"

"It was stolen from me on the plane."

"From inside your jacket?"

"That's right."

Quinn raised his eyebrows. "As I said, I can't let myself believe you yet, but neither can I discount the fact that you've got access to names and information you couldn't get out of any library. You did mix them up a bit, though. Bill Bathgate's an old friend of mine. We belong to the same country club and all that. One of his sons goes to school with my youngest daughter. But he works for the State Department, has for twenty years."

"That's the way he wanted it to seem."

"Hell of a cover."

"That's the point."

"And you're telling me he was somehow associated with a secret organization I've never even heard of."

"Yes, I am."

"And that this secret organization, named Lucifer, murdered him two days ago."

"I can't be sure of that. It just seems to add up. They killed Bathgate because he was on to something."

"Project Isosceles. . . ."

Dan nodded. "Like the triangle."

"Thanks for the geometry lesson. And, ah, Code Oscar is the trigger that's going to set it off on April—what was it?"

"The twenty-first."

170

"I see," Quinn acknowledged, nodding deliberately. "Then there's Renaldo Black and Gabriele Lafontaine."

"They killed all those kids in Virginia. Bloody Saturday."

"It seems you know more than every law enforcement agency in this country."

"Bathgate knew more. He just passed the information on to me."

"In an envelope that disappeared."

"Right."

"Which he gave to you after some monster with a steel arm chopped up his guts."

"Two in a row."

Quinn leaned forward, angered. "Don't be snide with me, Lennagin. I'm not a street cop from Providence, I'm a Washington desk jockey. I've got an undergraduate degree from Princeton and a law sheepskin from Harvard and every night before I fall asleep I wonder why the hell I'm not in private practice. I've been on this job for fifteen years and have been passed over for promotions so many times that my head's got tread marks all over it. I make forty thousand a year and I've got a mortgage six times the size of your student loan Bill Bathgate so amiably offered to pay up. My kids don't think a great deal of me and my wife wonders even more than I do why I'm not in private practice. So the last thing I need is some snot-nosed asshole coming into my office on a Saturday with a story that's more jumbled than a Rubik's Cube."

Dan felt his face flush. "Look, *Mister Quinn,* I don't need someone to blow my nose for me. What I need is somebody to keep me alive. You see, somebody tried to blow my head off yesterday. I like my head, Mr. Quinn.

Even though there are a dozen professors at Brown who'd tell you I don't use it often or well enough, my body would look pretty strange without it. And the people with the bomb who killed my friend aren't finished yet, not by a longshot. If they find me, my *body* will be the thing that's more jumbled than a Rubik's Cube and all the pieces are gonna fall right on your desk, which just might make *you* feel like a pretty big asshole." Dan thrust a trembling finger at the phone on the desk before him. "Call up the Providence police, Mr. Quinn. They'll be more than happy to tell a person of your stature about the explosion at Brown yesterday, one death resulting."

Quinn eyed Lennagin closely. "You finished?"

"Without your help, I just might be."

"You might just get it."

"You . . . believe me?"

"I don't want to," Quinn said softly, "at least not everything you say. The implications are a bit too much for a desk jockey like me. I say Bill Bathgate worked— er—works for State. You say otherwise. If you're right, he must've had the best damn cover of any man in Washington. And when those kinds of covers get pulled off it's time to pack it in and head for the hills." Quinn frowned. "He was also a damn good friend with a family that thinks highly of him."

"Thought," Dan corrected.

"So you say."

"Because it *happened*. It's the *goddamn truth!* You've got to do something fast!"

Quinn's face soured. "Look, Lennagin, I don't like being told what I have to do or at what pace I have to do it. You race in here with your tongue hanging out your ass expecting me to buy a story that's got shit stains all over it. I'm going to try very hard to forget this conversation but I sincerely doubt I'll be able to and will probably end up checking out these claims of yours, wishing the whole time I was writing my own legal briefs instead."

"I just hope you finish before somebody writes my obituary."

"You're getting snide again, kid. That's not the way to gain friends and influence people," Quinn said smugly.

"It's a funny habit I pick up when somebody's trying to kill me and nobody wants to listen."

"I've listened, Lennagin. What else do you want me to do?"

"Some protection would be nice. You know, big guys with big guns."

"This is Washington, Lennagin, the *real* FBI. I'm not Mike Connors or Efrem Zimbalist Jr. and we're not in the business of handing out protection to every nut who runs in off the streets screaming conspiracy, especially on Saturdays. The government shuts down on weekends. If a war breaks out, pray it waits for Monday."

"Except *I* might not be able to wait for Monday."

"You're breaking my heart. But don't worry. It won't take until then anyway. The morning's shot so I might as well forget the afternoon too. Curl up with the computer for a couple hours and check out your story. You get back to your hotel and don't move until you get my call. You'll get one either way. Who do I ask for?"

"What?"

"Come on, kid, I assume you had the smarts not to register under your own name."

"Right. Ask for Peter Trench."

"Original."

"I'm full of surprises."

"Anyway, I'll give you a number where you can reach me in case anything comes up before I get back to you."

Dan hesitated. "Thanks, Mr. Quinn. I really mean that."

"Don't thank me yet, kid, because if I don't find anything, God help you. . . . And if I do find something, God help us all."

EIGHTEEN

Dan reclined uneasily on his bed at the Hilton, waiting for the phone to ring with a call from Paul Quinn. On the way back from the FBI he had stopped at a department store and purchased three pairs of pants, six shirts, socks, underwear, and a tote bag to carry them all in. Wherever he went next he'd certainly need more clothes and he had more than enough cash left to buy them.

The final thought brought an ironic smile to his lips. He had stolen $3,200 from his fraternity. The house would be in desperate trouble by the beginning of the week unless he was somehow able to return it. But at this point the money was missing and so was he. Peter Brent had been murdered in his room. Would the brothers have called the deans, the police, his family? And what steps would those people be taking now? He'd have to call his mother at least, set her mind at ease that he was safe.

Come on, Quinn, call!

The phone rang. Dan snatched it.

"Hello. . . . Hello?"

No sounds. Not even a click. There was no one on the other end.

The dial tone returned. Dan slammed the receiver down.

Please, Quinn, please. . . .

There was a knock on the door. Dan crept slowly toward it.

"Who is it?" he asked, braced against the wall.

"Maid," a soft female voice came back.

"Hold on." He moved his eye to the peephole. A white uniform stared back at him. He could see half a cart loaded with towels and cleaning tools. "Okay." He slid off the chain and undid the bolt. The door swung free.

The maid smiled.

And maybe if his thoughts weren't still behind him on the phone, Dan would've realized the bed was already done—which meant she had already been there.

As it was, the realization struck him only when a white shoulder crashed into his chest, rocketing him backwards. The maid clung to him, dug her hands into his throat. His fingers grasped her hair and came off with a wig. A man was revealed, a big man, big enough to fill out the baggy outlines of a maid's white uniform. He was stubble-haired, with a marine crew cut. A square head sat atop his sinewy, square frame layered with muscle.

Dan clenched his hands together and pounded the man's nose. His grip weakened and Lennagin pulled free, scrambled to his feet, and rushed for the closed door. But the assailant's steellike fingers found his ankles and brought him back down. His chin struck the luggage rack, sending shock waves through his neck. His teeth smashed together. The room's light faded.

Out of pure instinct one of his legs snapped back from his prone position and caught the big man on the side of his face. He gasped, let go again. Dan rolled away, stood up, and faced him. The man wasn't much taller than he but was all muscle from the neck down. His arms swayed circularly before him as his feet assumed a karate stance. The man charged, lashing out with a vicious strike. Dan sidestepped and got his arm up in time to deflect part of the blow. It grazed off his side with still enough force to split his breath in two.

Before it had come back together, Dan barreled at the man, going for the knees with a sure football tackle. But his target avoided him easily and landed a sizzling kick square in his jaw, slamming him against the wall. Dan tried to move but his body betrayed him and another kick caught him in the stomach. He started to slump for the floor, blood seeping from his mouth.

The muscular shape grasped his shoulders, stopping his descent. Then he was being blasted against the plaster. Once, twice, three times till the room shook, along with everything inside him. His brains felt like they were sliding down his skull into his throat.

Strangely, scattered thoughts managed to float through his mind. The idea of physical violence had never bothered him before because he'd never been on the receiving end of so much. The possibility that someone of his size and strength could be the recipient of such a pounding had never occurred to him seriously. . . .

177

With the force of every weight he had ever lifted, Dan hurled his wrists under the big man's arms and sent them weakly into the air. A quick dodge to the side and his fist was connecting with the bony face before him. The man lurched backwards, stunned not injured, his black stubble seeming to sharpen at the edges.

Dan lunged awkwardly at him, another fist floating through the air. The stubble-haired man caught it and twisted. Dan gasped, was about to scream in agony when a callused palm struck him hard under the chin, spilling him backwards.

The big man flashed his knife.

Dan saw it and backpedaled. But his assailant covered five steps to his crawling one. The knife was swinging down. Dan hit the carpet, heard the blade swish into something soft, and wondered for a moment if it was his flesh.

The big man tore the knife free of the chair upholstery, shifted it agilely to his other hand. The blade loomed overhead again. Dan pushed himself backwards and considered rising, deciding against it for lack of time. His back struck the glass door leading to the balcony. His feet got tangled in the stubble-haired man's legs, halting his movement. The man smiled and readied the knife slowly, prolonging the motion.

The blade began its descent.

Dan grabbed the big man's arm before the knife pierced his flesh and pulled with all his might. Fortune smiled. He caught his assailant weightless and off balance, at the weakest point of his cut. The big man stumbled for a second, then tried to regain the footing he'd lost. Too late. His arms hit the glass an instant before his face did. The pane shattered. Fragments splintered and leaped through the air. The man's face and forearms filled with blood. Slivers of glass stuck out from his skin.

Dan jumped on his back as he dazedly sought to rise, curled an arm under his throat and started to jerk the massive head back. He'd pull until he heard a snap, until the prickly head hung limp in his hands. But the big man was too strong. He tensed his massive neck muscles against Dan's leverage and resolve. His bloodied arms flailed wildly, located Dan's head, and then sharpened their accuracy. Impervious to the blows, Dan kept wrenching the huge head toward him gaining precious inches. Then ten thick fingers found his curly hair and pulled with fantastic strength forward until his own head struck the concrete of the patio. Huge, blood-soaked hands caught him, lifted him, spun him, drove his back against the railing.

Nine stories below traffic filtered down the main streets of Washington.

Trembling fingers found his throat and he struggled to pry them off, succeeding only in a stalemate that cost him his breath. His eyes found the big man's. They were bulging, mad, surrounded by a face lined with scars and imperfections. His nose was flattened and his ears maimed like a boxer's or wrestler's. The man tightened his grip. Dan increased his resistance. His toes stretched to reach the cement. He was being lifted up. The man was trying to throw him over the balcony!

In fact, he nearly succeeded, letting go only when Dan's belt jammed beneath the steel grating. His body dangled in limbo suspended between the patio and the

busy intersection nine stories below. The man jerked
the belt free. Dan's head struck the railing and fell
toward the prismatic tiles of the patio. One of his hands
got there first. The other attached itself to the railing
against the stubble-haired man's concerted efforts to
toss him over the side. One of his legs fell from its
perch, flapping in the air. The big man stepped back
and lunged forward with a kick to his stomach.
Another. And another.

I'm going to die, Dan thought, I'm going to die....

Then he saw the knife gleaming a few inches away.
His fingers scraped across the tile, felt for its hilt. His
other leg slipped from its twist around the railing and
joined the first in midair. His stomach and side felt
crushed. Blood crawled up the sides of his throat. The
big man had stopped kicking, was going for his
shoulders now to heave the rest of him over.

His hand grasped the knife at the very instant the big
man jerked him upward. He jammed it forward and up.
The blade tore into something, hard at first but
growing strangely spongy and soft. Then there was a
swishing sound, followed by a light thud as the hilt
reached flesh.

The big man stumbled backwards gasping, hands
reaching for the hole in his abdomen that stretched
through his thorax. His sudden motion pulled Dan
from his precarious perch and he landed hard on the
tile of the balcony. He looked up to see his glassy-eyed
assailant crash backwards through what was left of the
door pane. He hit the rug with one thump, and then
another, his fingers still cradling his stomach in a lock
around the knife's hilt. His breathing was hard,
irregular. Finally it stopped.

Dan crawled through the shattered glass door and looked down at the motionless frame. The rest of his room was a cascade of meaningless shapes and shadows, none of which held any essence. His purpose, his identity, his reason for being there fled him. His eyes blinked and breaths came with astonishing deliberateness. He leaned over the corpse's still chest and listened for a heartbeat.

Hot, acrid breath found Dan's face at the instant thick, scarlet fingers dug into his throat. He screamed, tried to pull away, couldn't. The grip had only a fraction of its previous force but it was enough to choke his air away, though not enough to prevent Dan from wrenching the knife free of the midsection it had been lodged in and plunging it back through flesh and bone.

Dan pulled free.

The big man reached out for him, flailing the air. His fingers had almost reached their target when a violent spasm overtook them. The massive body shook volcanically, then finally lay motionless. Dan stared at it with unseeing eyes, not believing the big man was dead. He couldn't be sure how much longer it was before he pushed himself to a standing position and let the knife slip away.

He didn't feel his own pain yet; that would come later. Instead he felt only death, the cold reality of violent death upon him again.

A rush streamed up his throat. He made it to the bathroom just in time to vomit into the toilet. When there was nothing left inside him and the dry heaves started, he moved to the shower and turned the cold water on over his head from outside the tub.

A man lay dead not thirty feet away, a man *he* had

killed. His fingers started trembling, then his whole body. He wanted to cry but lacked the energy as well as the capacity.

The cold water kept streaming down.

Dan dropped to the floor and moved his head further into the tub, as though to lose himself in the icy jets.

NINETEEN

How much time passed, Dan didn't know. The cold water felt good, helped clear his mind.

His body was another matter. Not one part of it was spared the pain, his head least of all. The constant throb threatened to shatter his eardrums and split his temples. Each breath brought a deep shot of pain to his right side, the side the dead man had kicked repeatedly. Ribs might very well be broken, or at the very least badly bruised. His palms were cut, though only superficially. His stomach felt like it was knotted on the inside.

He switched off the water and eased himself away from the tub. The motions hurt, came slowly. He reached for a towel and draped it over his soaked head. Then he sat on the floor and fought with his mind to think.

They had found him; that much was obvious. And also obvious was how wrong he had been about believing himself capable of functioning in their world. Seeing others die is one thing; almost dying yourself is something else totally.

Dan forced himself to rise to a standing position. The mirror looked back at him, a stranger in the glass.

His face was a mess, all puffy and bruised. He paced the bathroom gingerly, found he could move so long as no sudden motions were required, that possibility seeming remote.

He threw his soaked and bloodied clothes off into a clumsy pile and chose a new outfit from the modest wardrobe he had purchased that morning. Then he pocketed the $2,800 he had left and gathered up his tote bag. He was finished in the hotel, finished altogether unless Paul Quinn found some reason to believe his story.

Paul Quinn . . . why hadn't he called? No matter. Dan would call the number Quinn had given him . . . in case something came up. Well, it had. The agent would understand. The dead man in his hotel room offered new proof that his story was true.

"FBI emergency exchange," announced a man's voice.

Dan couldn't remember dialing. "I need to speak to special agent Paul Quinn. Quick, please!"

"Could you repeat that please?"

"Paul Quinn! I need to speak to him. You've got to get him. He gave me this number in case—"

"I'm sorry, sir, we have no agent by that name."

The receiver slipped from Dan's fingers.

Paul Quinn didn't exist, at least not as an FBI agent. Lucifer had set him there this morning to learn what Dan knew before dispatching the stubble-haired man to kill him. The first half of their plan had succeeded brilliantly, though not the second.

Suddenly something else was very clear to Dan. The stubble-haired man certainly hadn't acted alone. There would be more of them in the building, backups they were called. They might be on their way up to the room right now!

Dan grabbed his tote bag and bolted into the corridor. Once in the elevator, he pressed L, no destination beyond that yet determined. The compartment was deserted and thankfully made no stops during a rapid descent to the lobby. The doors slid open, beckoning him out.

Dan froze.

Two men were standing before him, a spark of recognition in their eyes.

Dan's forward motion stopped. He edged back, hit the button marked "close door." The door closed but not before the two men, both clad in three-piece suits, had entered. They looked at him, eyes betraying their intentions. One moved his hand toward his jacket. The other tautly stood his ground.

"Hold that door!"

The shout came at the instant the rubber on either door smacked together. Dan's right hand shot out before the two men could react and pressed the button marked "open door." The machine responded. The doors opened to the lobby again. An elderly couple entered followed by a bellhop lugging a pushcart jammed with suitcases and packer-bags.

The bellhop pushed 10. "What floor, buddy?" he asked Dan, looking at his bruised face with suspicion.

"Eleven," Lennagin answered without missing a beat.

The bellhop pressed it. "You guys?"

The well-dressed men looked at each other. The shorter one spoke. "Same."

The elevator started to move.

Dan felt cold sweat dripping from his underarms. He had to act fast, but not too fast. He couldn't hope to take the two men on, not without a weapon. What, though, could he use?

The men exchanged nervous glances. Their eyes turned furtively toward Dan. He looked away.

There had to be something. . . .

4 . . . 5 . . . 6 . . .

A fire extinguisher was perched on the wall above him to his right. He could reach it if he was quick enough, spray the man with foam, and make his escape while they were blinded. But how did he know foam was contained inside? Why not water? Where would that leave him? He'd dampen their suits while they used their guns. The extinguisher was small, not much pressure, certainly not enough.

7 . . . 8 . . . 9 . . .

The tenth floor was coming up fast. The doors would open and his cover would depart.

Cover! That was it!

The timing would have to be perfect to buy him the seconds he needed. Minutes were a luxury, hours at this point plainly unthinkable.

The doors slid open. The bellhop started his cart forward.

Dan swung his tote bag up and around, smacking the two well-dressed men across their heads, knocking them off balance. Then he leaped over the cart, crashed into a matched set of luggage and sent it lurching behind him before the two men had a chance to recover. Another double swipe with his arms and the cart had been emptied. The two men regained their footing and shoved the sprayed suitcases and tote bags aside only to have the old couple stumble in their path and block it. Finally they pushed their way out of the elevator and surged into the corridor. The emergency exit was just up ahead to the left.

The door had already closed behind Dan.

They had lost only a few seconds, ten at the most. But it takes only two and a half to plow down stair flights at the breakneck clip Dan was moving. He reached the lobby before they were even halfway down, raced out of the hotel, and jumped into the first cab he saw, telling the driver to drive somewhere fast.

Anywhere. . . .

In the Hilton's switchboard operations room, a man with gray hair and a black mustache made sure the unconscious operator looked comfortable inside her receptacle. She would awaken shortly with a slight headache, feeling as though she had simply faded off. The drug he'd given her was that effective.

The man smiled. He had to isolate the boy, keep him from the protective clutches of the FBI. Otherwise, everything would be ruined, all his planning. And he had succeeded. What's more, he knew where Lennagin would go next. He knew how the boy thought.

His plan was working perfectly.

Quinn had wasted no time going to work. Dan Lennagin's story intrigued him. Though he didn't yet believe it, neither could he pass it off. Everyone in the Bureau had his own way of reading people. For Quinn, it was the eyes. They never lied. Lennagin's had been nervous, distant, unsure.

The boy was scared. Quinn wanted to find out what was scaring him.

He started the moment Lennagin had closed his office door with a call to the twenty-four-hour number of the Department of State.

"Yes?" a female voice answered.

"I'd like to speak with Major William Bathgate."

"Major Bathgate is in the field. Can I take a message?"

"Not unless you've got an hour to spare."

"Excuse me? Is this an official call?"

"Look, miss, I'm calling the emergency number on a Saturday afternoon when I'd much rather be watching cherry blossoms sprout. Let's say it's not social."

"Can I have Major Bathgate call you?"

"I'd rather call him."

"I'm afraid I don't have a forwarding, Mr. ah—"

Quinn was not about to give his name. Let them spend some time tracing it down.

"When was the last time he checked in?" Quinn asked.

A pause. "I'm afraid I don't have that information."

"Has he checked in in the last three days?"

"I'm afraid I don't—"

"—have that information. Yeah, tell me about it."

Quinn hung up, edgy. He left his office and took the elevator to the fourth floor and the computer room. It was Saturday; a booth would surely be open, all of them probably.

Minutes later he stood before a set of sliding steel doors. He placed his plastic building card into a slot that swallowed it up and then quickly spit it back out. A green light flashed, the doors opened, and Paul Quinn stepped into the nerve center of the greatest crime-fighting organization in the world. He shoved his card into a second slot that coughed it back at him even quicker than the first. The door to one of the closet-sized terminal rooms swung open. He entered, closed the door, and locked it behind him. Awkwardly, he felt for the snub-nosed he carried everywhere these days and was reassured to find it secure in its holster.

A keyboard sat on a desk before him. The ceiling light had been activated automatically once the machine had accepted his card. He sat down and flipped a switch on the underside of the terminal. The keys sprang to life, bringing Quinn in touch with a boundless volume of information concerning criminal activity, the American intelligence system, and related subjects. The computer complex was known as DORIS, an acronym for Data Operations and Resources Intelligence Systems. Technically this cubicle and the room that contained it didn't exist. Technically he was fifteen years, four never-to-be-seen promotions, and a dozen security levels away from being cleared to use it. He was placing everything on the line, up to and including his career. Some career. They had stifled him in the Bureau because he was too smart. He had stuck with the job first on principle, then by habit, and finally out of just plain fear of anything new. He'd hit forty last week, that magical age. Nothing seemed possible anymore. The future was drying up around him.

Quinn started typing.

"Good morning, DORIS." He watched his words light up on the screen, centering themselves.

Then the computer. "GOOD MORNING. REQUEST IDENT."

Quinn started typing again. "Special agent Paul Quinn. Clearance one, double zero, A-X."

There was a short pause. "GOOD MORNING, PAUL. NICE TO SEE YOU HERE ON A SATURDAY. SORRY BUT YOU DON'T CLEAR."

"Emergency override Julius-squared," Quinn typed.

"AUTHORITY?" the machine asked him.

"Director Able."

Another short pause. "CLEARANCE CON-FIRMED. WHAT CAN I DO FOR YOU ON THIS FINE SPRING DAY?"

"Request IDENT on several names and terms."

"READY."

"Term—Lucifer."

"NO DATA."

"See subdivision under organizations."

"I ALREADY HAVE, PAUL. SORRY, STILL NO DATA."

That's okay, sweetheart, Quinn said to himself, *figured that much.* He went back to the keyboard.

"Term—Project Isosceles."

"NO DATA." The reply came almost as soon as he had finished typing. It was like dialing a local phone number.

"Check under Confidential Projects Division."

"STILL NO DATA. SORRY AGAIN, PAUL. I HATE TO DISAPPOINT YOU LIKE THIS."

Hardly a disappointment or a surprise, Quinn thought. Now for the good stuff.

"Request IDENT on man, anonym—The Doctor."

This time it took a bit longer. The results surprised Quinn, because until they flashed on the screen he had clung to the hope he'd find nothing to confirm Lennagin's story.

"REAL NAME: TREVOR HASTINGS. AGE: 48. OPERATIVE IN CIA FOREIGN SERVICE DIVI-SION SPECIALIZING IN COVERT OPERA-TIONS. AFFAIRS INCLUDE CHILE, ANGOLA, UGANDA, IRAN. DETAILS REQUIRE ADDED

CLEARANCE. LEFT CIA IN 1982 TO WORK FOR DEPARTMENT OF STATE SPECIAL SECTION UNDER MAJOR WILLIAM BATHGATE. . . ."

The machine spit out more information, enough to fill five typewritten pages. Quinn only skimmed it. His mind was elsewhere. Not only did The Doctor exist but he *was* connected to Bill Bathgate, just as Lennagin had said. The kid might have heard of The Doctor and Bathgate individually but linking them together was downright impossible. And knowing Hastings's field name? That was even more so. Unless . . .

Quinn's fingers found their way back to the keys. "Request Doctor's present status."

"STATUS TERMINATED."

"Elaborate."

"EXPLAIN."

"Was The Doctor executed?"

"STATUS TERMINATED. NO FURTHER DATA."

Quinn's fingers were sweating now. "Request IDENT on man Renaldo Black. Alias probable."

The machine took longer than it had with The Doctor, all of ten seconds total.

"RENALDO BLACK: INTERNATIONAL, FREE-LANCE TERRORIST. LINKS TO FOLLOWING GROUPS ESTABLISHED—PLO, PLF, BAADER-MEINHOF, RED BRIGADES, IRA, OTHERS. TRAINED IN LIBYA 1972-3. BELIEVED TO HAVE ASSISTED IN OPEC RAID UNDER CARLOS IN VIENNA 1976. ALIASES AS FOLLOW—"

Quinn nervously pressed the INTERRUPT key. "Request present status."

"PRESENT STATUS UNKNOWN."

"Request present position."

"PRESENT POSITION UNKNOWN."

"Request hypothesis on possibility Renaldo Black was involved in and/or masterminded Virginia massacre April 4."

"INSUFFICIENT DATA."

"Speculate, DORIS."

"YES, PAUL. SUBJECT TRAINED IN LIBYA EXTENSIVELY WITH RUSSIAN KALISHNIKOV AK-47 IN YEARS PREVIOUSLY STATED. PSYCHOLOGICAL PROFILE RED LINES PSYCHOPATHIC TENDENCIES AND STRONG INCLINATION FOR MASS MURDER. SEXUAL BASIS SUSPECTED. NO FURTHER SPECULATION POSSIBLE. ANYTHING ELSE, PAUL?"

Quinn's eyes looked at the screen but saw nothing. Dan Lennagin knew more about Renaldo Black than the computer.

"PAUL?"

His name flashing on the console lifted him from his daze.

"Request IDENT on woman, Gabriele Lafontaine. Alias probable."

The computer's answer came almost immediately.

"GABRIELE LAFONTAINE: INTERNATIONAL, FREE-LANCE TERRORIST. FIRM LINKS ESTABLISHED TO BAADER-MEINHOF GANG. OTHERS STRONGLY SUSPECTED BUT NO CONCRETE INFORMATION ON BANKS CLEARED FOR YOUR EYES. SPECIALIST IN—"

Quinn hit the INTERRUPT button again. "Request status as it pertains to Renaldo Black."

"CONNECTIONS ESTABLISHED. TWO ARE BELIEVED TO HAVE BEEN INVOLVED IN IDEN-

TICAL TERRORIST ATTACKS NUMBERING
FIVE OVER THE LAST TWO YEARS. SPLINTER
GROUP UNDER INVESTIGATION. . . ."

There was more but Quinn didn't read it. Lennagin
might have stumbled upon the names of Renaldo Black
and Gabriele Lafontaine. Information linking them
together, though, was classified, not something you
read casually in *Time* or *Newsweek*. Yet the boy knew.
The small room suddenly felt extremely cramped.
Quinn was hot and his shirt was sticking to his skin in
more places than it wasn't. His underarms were soaked
and he cursed his deodorant. He glanced around him,
not feeling very safe. If part of Lennagin's story was
true, then all of it was. If they got Bill Bathgate, they
could get him.

"PAUL?" The computer was flashing his name
again. "PAUL?"

Quinn thought for a few moments. "Request reverse
IDENT."

"WORKING."

"Tall, black man. Bald head. Very large." Quinn
paused. "Tremendous strength. Potential prosthetic
attachment."

The screen stayed blank. He hoped it would remain
that way. It didn't.

"POSITIVE IDENTIFICATION OBTAINED,
PAUL. SUBJECT KNOWN ONLY AS TUNG-
STEN. INTERNATIONAL CONTRACT ASSAS-
SIN USUALLY IN EUROPEAN ARENA. THIRTY-
SIX REGISTERED HITS. PROSTHETIC DEVICE
CONFIRMED AS STEEL ARM ATTACHED FOL-
LOWING EXPLOSION SEVEN YEARS AGO AT
REQUEST AND EXPENSE OF THEN PRESENT
EMPLOYER. . . ."

"Oh shit," Quinn muttered.

Meanwhile, Dan Lennagin had determined his destination.

"Washington National," he told the cab driver.

He was totally alone now. There was no one he could trust. His life rested squarely in his own hands. They had tried to kill him in the hotel. They would try again. But the morning's failure had shown him something; he too could kill. The enemy had become his unwitting teacher. A drive filled him, an anger. People would have to pay for Peter Brent . . . and his father. For now, he was the only person who knew enough to make them.

Somewhere in him fear pushed itself forward and he pushed it back. Was it vengeance he wanted or safety? He didn't know anymore. Perhaps the latter could be accomplished through the former. He would hunt those who hunted him and find the secrets of the Lucifer Directive. Bathgate's envelope had contained the name and address of the arms dealer who had sold Black his rifles: Stettner Lutz in Switzerland.

A place to start.

The man with the gray hair and black mustache stepped into a phone booth at Washington National Airport.

"You took quite a chance," the man on the other end charged in their native language when he'd finished his report.

"It was called for."

"I hope so."

"Besides, precautions were taken. The old couple in the elevator were our agents. They would have taken steps to keep the boy safe had it become necessary."

"And the dead man in his room?"

"I let him sneak by me."

"You knew Lennagin would kill him?"

"No, but I had to keep the boy on his own. The man's appearance conveniently became part of my plan. A link by Lennagin with the FBI would have destroyed everything."

"You will follow the boy to his present destination?"

"I will meet him there."

"You can predict his moves that well?"

"I've come to know him. He's learning fast. By all rights he should be dead already."

"If your mission fails, Colonel, in two weeks we might all be."

TWENTY

The phone ringing on the desk jarred Renaldo Black from his chair in a luxury apartment high within the Watergate complex conspicuously lacking adequate furnishings. Black placed the receiver on the blotter and switched the call to an amplifier.

"So your efforts to kill Lennagin failed," a voice from Houston, scrambled by distance and device, charged. "You assured me there would be no problems."

"I failed only today," Black said evenly. "Your people failed twice. If they had done their job, Lennagin never would have reached Washington to begin with." Black glanced into the darkened right corner of the room where a huge shape stood silhouetted against the drawn blinds. "We should have used my man to dispose of him when we had the chance."

"The same way he disposed of Bathgate? I think not. We were lucky to get the disposal unit in before anyone besides Lennagin stumbled upon the bodies. A more subtle means was called for."

"Subtlety got two of your men killed."

"Subtlety had nothing to do with it. One body was

found in the repair garage of the bus depot, the other in his seat on the plane in Washington. Both executions were very professional, certainly not Lennagin's work."

"That raises an interesting problem. Perhaps the boy has discovered a guardian angel."

"Which he had no need of in the hotel this morning," the man from Houston snapped. "You told me you would pick a good man."

"I did."

"Then you're telling me this college boy was better."

"Luckier and more desperate. Together they often amount to being better, yes."

"And where will this desperation take him now?"

"Out of the country for sure on what he thinks is our trail."

"Isn't it?"

"Only if we let it be. We can use this to our advantage."

"Our advantage would be to kill the boy before he leaves the country."

"Even if we could find him, I disagree," Black countered smoothly. The voice of reason was not one he was accustomed to using. "We need him alive for a while longer."

"For what reason?"

"To find out who guides the wings of his guardian angel. Someone seems to want him alive very badly, which makes that person our enemy."

"One of Bathgate's holdovers, perhaps."

"The Doctor was the last one. Tungsten most ably took care of him."

The huge, black shape stepped out of the room's shadows, flexing his ungloved steel fingers. They crackled slightly. He smiled.

"Then how do you propose we go about discovering this angel's identity?" the man from Houston asked.

"I'll leave that to Gabriele. She's already on her way to Europe and might even beat Lennagin to his destination. Don't worry, the boy is harmless. He can't do us any further damage."

The man from Houston thought briefly. "I can't understand why he didn't return to the FBI."

"I'd wager our mysterious guardian angel is behind that somehow. No matter. I'll handle the boy."

"We're working on a very tight timetable. No room for slipups, Black, no room at all. Speaking of which, how are you coming with the explosives?"

"Almost all one hundred fifty pounds have been molded into the proper shape. We'll have the *plastique* in place twenty-four to forty-eight hours prior to the moment in question."

"Isosceles depends on it," the voice from Houston said. "The trigger must be effective for the project to work as we want it to."

"Which leaves Sparrow as our only obstacle. How many times now have your people failed to eliminate him?"

"We were unaware of his link-up with Felix until Algiers," the man from Houston said with uncharacteristic defensiveness. "Our . . . failures are no longer the issue. We traced Sparrow to Paris and from there we suspect he's found means to reach America." A pause. "He'll be coming into Washington National Monday afternoon."

"How do you know that?"

"Lucifer is not without resources. He's yours, Black. I want him taken out in the airport before he speaks to anyone."

"I'll handle it personally." Black's eyes darted to the dark corner. "And I'll bring Tungsten along to finish off his apelike friend."

The black giant smiled again and closed his fist around a brass figurine, compressing it into a tight little ball.

"Don't let him slip by," the man from Houston warned. "Any association on his part with our friends in Washington might prove costly to our plans."

"Leave it to me," Black assured him. "Leave it to me."

One hour after Paul Quinn had finished his dialogue with the computer, a black limousine with government plates drew to a halt in front of the J. Edgar Hoover Building. Quinn approached it slowly.

"Get in, Paul," a voice instructed from the backseat through an open window already sliding closed again.

Quinn opened the door and settled himself into the spacious seat. Next to him sat FBI director Thames Farminson. Farminson tapped his knuckles on the soundproof glass that sealed them from the front seat. The driver nodded and pulled the car back into traffic.

"Where we going?" Quinn asked.

"White House. The scenic route. I'd like to be sure I know what I'm taking in with me. Any luck locating Lennagin?"

"No, and I just got a report from the emergency team I sent over to the Hilton. They found a body in his room that belongs to some brute I'm sure will turn up on our software."

"You think Lennagin killed him?"

"Only because the guy was trying to do likewise to him. Must have been a helluva fight judging by the mess the room and the corpse are in. Anyway, the kid left the hotel in quite a hurry. Didn't take all his clothes and left his bill outstanding."

"Maybe he's coming back."

"Would you?"

"Now that you mention it, no. But why didn't he come back to you?"

"I don't know. Something must've spooked him. It wouldn't have taken much under the circumstances."

"They might have caught up with him after he left the hotel."

"Sure. But I'd rather proceed on the notion that he made it out. The kid's no pro but he's got damn good instincts and takes precautions. I think he's still alive."

"And headed where?"

"My guess is Europe. He must figure he's alone and somebody damn near killed him this morning. So I think he's going after them. I think he's going to try and track them down."

"How?"

"The kid's not a total amateur. His old man was the guy who got knocked off in South Africa about a dozen years ago. So Lennagin is obsessed with terrorism. Even before Bill Bathgate walked into his life, he had names and places stored in his head, certainly enough to help him get started."

"Help him get killed, you mean."

"Maybe. Maybe not."

"You seem to have a lot of faith in this boy, Quinn."

"I like him, that's probably all. But you should hear him talk. Scared but cool. Trouble is I didn't listen. I feel like shit, if you'll excuse the expression, sir. I should have kept him in the office while I ran the check. But when some curly-haired kid with dimples walks into my office looking like something out of the Hardy Boys, my major question seems to be why did he ruin my Saturday. Beats the hell out of first impressions." Quinn hesitated. "So how much of what the kid said is true?"

"About Lucifer, you mean?" Farminson said frankly. "I'm not about to insult your intelligence by being coy or claiming it doesn't exist, Paul. Before this is over, you'll wish I had. The fact is, though, that I just don't know. I haven't had time to check all the channels. The issue at hand is whether Lucifer's changed sides. Whether they have or not, it's hard for me to believe that their people were responsible for Bloody Saturday and the bombing on Long Island."

"According to Lennagin, Renaldo Black was the main trigger man."

"Then by implication Lucifer loaded his gun. But it doesn't make any sense."

Quinn fingered his chin. "Maybe it does, sir. I never even heard of Lucifer until four hours ago and if I had stayed home today it's likely I never would have. But it stands to reason that over the years their people have crossed paths with just about every terrorist around the world at one time or another. So let's say, just for the sake of argument, they want to turn the tables for a while but they don't want anyone to know about the shift. They'd have a whole phone book of people to do their dirty work for them. Why, then, settle for a guy playing second fiddle at the church picnic when you can have the Sunday organ player himself?"

"Renaldo Black. . . ."

"His file indicates nobody plays the terrorist tune

better. The man's a psychopath. He'd shoot kids as quickly as he'd pick his nails." Quinn and Farminson shared a deep breath. "What about the rest of what Lennagin said, sir? About Code Oscar and this Isosceles Project?"

"I haven't the slightest notion, Paul. Lucifer exists outside the traditional intelligence system. All things considered, they could have hatched any plan they wanted, free of the reins that restrict the rest of us. That was their whole basis to begin with—the Lucifer Directive it's called. They needed freedom, autonomy. We cut the red tape for them."

"And now they've wrapped it around our throats," Quinn reflected.

Farminson made no comment. They were almost to the White House. He spoke finally with his gaze fixed faraway out the window.

"Ever meet the President before, Paul?"

"Didn't even vote for him."

Does anyone have anything they'd like to add?" the President asked when Quinn had finished his story. He had spoken articulately for twenty minutes, glancing down at his notes only occasionally. He found his mouth was very dry and wished he had taken a drink before entering the Oval Office. Water, though, would have done nothing for the bad taste he had as well. He felt he'd let Lennagin down and wanted desperately to make it up to him somehow. He had taken a chair directly before the President and had struggled the whole time to look him in the eye, shifting his gaze rarely toward Farminson, his superior, or Bart Triesdale and General Robert MaCammon, men he knew only by reputation. He'd be a fool not to admit that the whole scene awed him a bit.

"I don't like to add this, but I must," sighed MaCammon. "After Thames reached me on the red line, I pulled out all the stops to contact Major Bathgate. No luck. He just doesn't exist anymore."

"Then you agree with the story this Dan Lennagin told Mr. Quinn here."

"That part of it, yes."

"And I can confirm another part," added Triesdale. "Something funny's definitely afoot at Lucifer. I went through all the usual channels and drew a blank. Then I tried a few unusual ones and got the runaround. When I tossed the name Renaldo Black at them, they professed ignorance, and the trouble is I believe them."

"Trouble?"

"Yes, sir. I think whatever's happening originates at the top, the *very* top: the head of Lucifer and its operating board, none of whose identities we know."

"Wait a minute," interrupted the President, "are you telling me none of us has any idea who controls Lucifer?"

"That's right."

"Then how do we make contact, keep a monitor on them?"

Triesdale hesitated. "Through Bathgate. But I'm continuing some discreet inquiries."

"Why keep them discreet?"

"Because we're still not sure how deep the penetration is and we don't want to give away that we're onto them. Right now, that's the best thing we've got going for us."

"Which isn't saying a whole helluva lot."

"No, it isn't."

The President nodded deliberately. "Let's proceed on the supposition that everything Paul has just related is true and that Bart is correct in his assumption that penetration has occurred only at the top, what exactly are we facing?"

"An organization," began General MaCammon, "with unlimited manpower, resources, and money with access to every file and computer tape in the country and a network of agents who can kill without spending a single hour at the typewriter to justify their actions."

"Is there any way we can shut them out?"

"We'd have to change every computer key and cipher from Defense all the way to NSA. It might take months."

"What about recalling their agents?"

"Their mandate is international. We wouldn't get far enough for it to matter. In any case, if Bart is correct about this operation's springing from the top, it wouldn't help us."

"And yet," picked up the President, "with this vast network of agents we can't even hope to locate, they still recruited an international terrorist. Seems superfluous and dangerous. Any ideas why they'd take the risk?"

"Because their plan was to have only the inner circle know the truth," replied Thames Farminson, "the barest minimum possible. It's my guess this didn't include any of Lucifer's rank-and-file or group station leaders. But then Major Bathgate stumbled onto the truth and Dan Lennagin stumbled with him. The truth leaked out, spoiled the shadow of their plan but not the substance of it. Lucifer wanted to come out of all of this with their faces washed and hands cleaned so they'd still be the good guys and a hundred times more important to us to boot. That, of course, has changed."

"Which takes us up to the Isosceles Project," said the President. "If I remember my geometry correctly, Isosceles refers to a type of triangle—'tri' meaning three. General MaCammon, how many F-16s did we misplace?"

"But with those planes, they could . . ."

"Precisely," interrupted the President. "And at this point it seems logical to assume that the Isosceles Project will make use of the jets somehow in what will appear to the world to be another terrorist attack. But that's getting ahead of ourselves. Let's turn our attention to another element of Lennagin's story. Bathgate told him that Sparrow was the only man he could trust. Who is Sparrow?"

"A man greatly responsible for the founding of the state of Israel and its early sustenance," Bart Triesdale responded, opening a file on his lap. "Sparrow's something of a legend in intelligence circles. He was one of the early leaders of the Haganah, later transferring his efforts to the Mossad and Israel's counterterrorist strike forces. He worked within these groups as an advisor and participant until 1972 when he left to expand his ideas into an international arena."

"How?"

"Lucifer. The whole concept was his idea."

The President's mouth dropped to better swallow the bombshell. "So we have him to thank for all this. . . ."

"Not exactly. Sparrow officially retired, some say under forced conditions, from Lucifer eight years ago, retired to a kibbutz that was raided by enemy forces last Monday."

The President noticed the folder on Triesdale's lap.

"You seem to have quite a bit of information on him at your fingertips."

"I pulled his file this morning, one hour after a coded message arrived via an ancient channel in an ancient cipher informing us that he had vital information about Bloody Saturday. A teaser obviously for something else, suggested perhaps by the fact that the code he used has been deactivated for eight years, dating back to his final days with Lucifer. Significant, I think. The end of the message stated that he will be arriving at Washington National at two P.M. Monday and would like to be brought in."

"Does his file give us a clue as to what sort of man we're dealing with here?" the President asked.

"Considerably more than a clue, sir. The file begins in the early 1940s when Sparrow—then Joshua Cohen—was still a teenager. He had broken free of a death train after his parents were murdered and made his way somehow to France. Walked almost the whole route, from what I understand, with a mangled thigh, courtesy of the Nazis. Never healed right because of the journey and he sentenced himself to a limp for the rest of his life."

"But he reached France."

"In time to become a soldier in the Resistance. No, more than a soldier, a personal war machine. They called him the Lion of the Night and he did more damage to the Nazis than any other single man in Europe. Ever hear of the Children's Resistance, or *La Résistance des Enfants?*"

"No."

"Funny thing about kids. Even animals like the Nazis trust them at first glance and allow them considerably more freedom of movement than adults.

206

Sparrow, the Lion of the Night, recruited boys and girls who, like him, had lost their parents to the Nazis and turned them into a covert fighting unit with a hundred advantages over the best adult underground force. They could get into places adults couldn't and were never suspected of the acts they were responsible for, bombings mostly. A little boy walks into a restaurant holding a book satchel, leaves without it, and seconds later the Nazi-filled restaurant blows up. Schemes like that were carried out countless times. A few were kamikaze in nature."

"My God," uttered the President, and repeated, "What kind of man are we dealing with here?"

"A man who will do anything he has to in order to survive. A man whose values were formed during the months he lived in the woods to avoid being butchered by the Nazis."

"And the Nazis never caught on to *La Résistance des Enfants?*"

"It was too late by the time they did. For all intents and purposes the war was over. But it never ended for Sparrow, not really. He headed for Palestine on Liberation Day before De Gaulle reached Paris and joined up with the Haganah. Using his French contacts, he was able to smuggle in more arms than the rest of the Jewish network combined. The consensus is that the Israeli War of Independence never would've stood a chance if not for his bullets. Sparrow was a hero in every sense of the word, but a hero who was never satisfied. He became a leading figure in the Mossad when that organization was formed in 1951 and constantly refused promotions to administrative levels so he could stay active in the field. He had been a soldier too long to do anything else, and he seemed none the worse for wear."

Triesdale paused and glanced down at the file on his lap.

"The '67 Six-Day War came along and Sparrow's intelligence reports were responsible for Israel's strategic coup of taking out all of Egypt's air force before it got off the ground. Then a rift developed. Those same intelligence reports indicated Israel's only hope to avoid another war or two within the next decade would be to occupy Cairo and demand unequivocal surrender. Make no mistake about it either, the Israelis could have done precisely that if they'd wanted to. But more moderate heads prevailed with the help of some outside pressures and their forces stopped after the Sinai. Sparrow soured and was frustrated time and time again in his attempts to prove that Israel had to seize the advantage before 1970 or risk losing all the ground, physical and otherwise, she had gained. Eventually he gave up, turning his attentions to an equally pressing matter: terrorism, first solely as it connected to Israel, later on an international scale."

"Then he formed Lucifer," interjected the President.

"From the top down," continued Triesdale. "We've been through the specifics of how the organization functions before. Suffice it to say now that Sparrow served as its director up until eight years ago when he elected to retire to a kibbutz."

"Or was forced to," from General MaCammon.

"We can't be sure. Lucifer doesn't advertise such facts."

"Either way," began Thames Farminson, "he's back in the field."

"Running just like he did from the Nazis in the 1940s when he escaped from that train, and his predicament seems just as desperate," added the CIA man. "He's become the Lion of the Night again, which is all the more reason why we need him. He understands the terrorist mind better than anyone, because he thinks like they do."

"Considering our present predicament," noted the President, "the timing of his transformation is extraordinary."

"And I doubt it's coincidence," theorized Triesdale. "When Sparrow left Lucifer, whatever the circumstances were, he dropped out totally. No advice, no consultation. For security reasons, he obtained a new identity for his only surviving family—a daughter, her husband, and their five-year-old son—and sent them to live in America, here in Washington specifically, where he felt they'd be safe. That gave him a total out with no strings attached, because no one could get to him through his family. Now his home is attacked and he wants back in again, all this at the very time the organization he founded has apparently turned."

"Obviously we've got to bring him in," concluded the President. "But we can't afford at this point to take anyone else into our confidence. If word leaks out about what's going on, it'll be impossible for any of us to maneuver."

Paul Quinn leaned forward. "If I might make a suggestion, sir, we could use me to lead the recovery team at the airport come Monday."

The President frowned. "With all due respect, Paul, you're no field man."

"With all due respect, sir, I became one when I stepped into this office. Necessity makes different men out of all of us. Just ask my wife."

"I can brief him on everything he needs to know to

run the operation smoothly, Mr. President," Thames Farminson offered.

But Quinn wasn't finished. "And after that briefing is finished, I'd appreciate one on the best way to bring in Lennagin."

"Out of the question!" boomed Bart Triesdale.

"I don't think so," Quinn went on. "Besides the fact that I'm partly responsible for sinking this kid further into the mess he was already in, I'm the only person he would certainly recognize and might trust."

"Why only 'might'?" from the President.

"Because I can't figure out for the life of me why he didn't come back to the Bureau after he took care of the linen lady with the crew cut. Maybe somebody wants him to stay clear of us. I just don't know."

"But you still want to go after him."

Quinn paused, just long enough. "I've *got* to go after him, sir."

The President thought briefly, unconvinced. "Let's table this for the time being and concern ourselves with the coded message Bathgate left for Lennagin. Paul, would you repeat it please."

Quinn steadied his nerves and spoke. "Code Oscar is the trigger for the Isosceles Project on April twenty-first."

"So now that we have a limited idea of what Isosceles may involve—our missing F-16s—let's turn our attention to the trigger intended to set it off. What is Oscar? The floor is open, gentlemen."

"Oscar . . ." came the voice of Paul Quinn, swift and uneasy.

The President noted that Quinn's expression had gone pale. His face seemed on the verge of slipping into the cleft in his chin.

"Paul? What's wrong?"

Quinn looked up. His eyes emptied. "I'll tell you, sir, but you may end up wishing I was in private practice more than my wife does. It's Oscar that's wrong . . . eight days from now—Monday, April twenty-first. That's the night the Academy Awards have been rescheduled for."

TWENTY-ONE

Bart Triesdale's pocket evaluation of Sparrow had not been far off the mark. His success in hunting terrorists down and predicting their movements was due more than anything else to the fact that he thought much the same way they did. To visualize their desperation, all he had to do was recall his own during the undisciplined years of embryonic Israel when a man's words were worth nothing unless they could be backed up by bullets. Similarly, a terrorist lives in a self-made world of moral and mental limitations, his path no less confined than a bullet's. Know the path and you know the terrorist.

Sparrow knew the path. He often wondered how far the similarities between himself and the people he had spent a lifetime chasing stretched. "We're the same," one terrorist had told him en route back to Israel to stand trial. "You know that, don't you?"

Sparrow hadn't answered him and had done his level best to forget the question over the years. It nagged at him because he knew the true answer and it, more than anything else, was an admission.

We're the same. . . . You know that, don't you?

Yes, he thought, yes. . . .

212

"Did you say something, Israeli?" Felix asked him.

"No," Sparrow mumbled.

Their plane was taxiing down the main runway of Washington National Airport. More than forty-eight hours had passed since Sparrow had sent his coded message to the CIA stating that he had information vital to the massacre in Alexandria in a cipher certain to arouse curiosity. He assumed the Americans knew of his past and would be eager to accept his help. He had no idea, though, whether they even suspected the truth behind what was happening. If not, he'd have a difficult job ahead of him.

The plane had come to a halt and people were jamming into the aisles. Felix eased his monstrous bulk from the seat's restrictive confines and tried to stretch. It had been a long journey, with many plane changes along the way for security reasons.

"I don't think I am going to like America, Israeli," he shrugged in an uncharacteristically soft voice.

They had obtained clothes more suitable for American wear in Paris, but Felix felt distinctly uncomfortable and uneasy in his. What's more, his wardrobe didn't include any of his weapons, all of which he'd been forced to smuggle in his baggage. All told, he felt naked and unsure. This wasn't just a foreign country for him, but a foreign world of restrictions and laws. Felix wasn't used to restrictions, even less so to laws. He had spent his life in a world where a man wore a gun as freely as a watch. Wind the watch, fire the gun. It was not hard for both to become daily rituals.

Sparrow and Felix waited for the rush to subside and then settled into the aisle.

"Some business first," Sparrow said with a wink when they approached the men's room.

In fact, his visit to the lavatory had as its sole purpose the removal of his .45 from the special compartment of the tote bag Depopolis had provided him with. It was the same kind hijackers used, the false bottom screened by special lining that blocked out standard airport X-ray devices. He emerged with the gun comfortably tucked in his belt and hidden by his jacket.

"Shall we greet America?" he offered Felix.

The giant shrugged and followed him into the terminal building. Sparrow's coded message had included nothing more than the time of his arrival, so the Americans couldn't know at which gate to meet him. They'd be waiting instead at the main airport exit. Sparrow followed the signs down the long, apparently endless corridor. His eyes swept right and left, unsatisfied in spite of his security precautions but comforted by the cold steel of the pistol pressed against his flesh. Men with cases in hand or overcoats slung over their arms inevitably drew a second look; too easy to conceal a weapon to be used once they were by you. Sparrow readied himself each time one passed.

"Easy, Israeli," Felix soothed. "It is looking as though you like this country as much as I do."

Sparrow forced a smile and shifted his gaze down the corridor. A baby carriage sat unattended outside the door to the woman's lavatory. An odd sight, he noted, but hardly a threatening one.

Renaldo Black stood near a row of pay phones, perpetually in line to use the next one that opened up. He had chosen a baby carriage because it was the only thing that, first, wouldn't seem out of place in an airport and, second, wouldn't attract people too close to it. A sleeping child was one of the few truly respected private possessions. People might pass near the carriage and try to steal a glance inside, though they'd never draw near enough to notice that this child was strangely quiet.

The doll was amazingly lifelike really and voiced no objections over sharing its carriage with a device about the size of a shoe box, loaded with some leftover Prometheus *plastique,* enough to do quite a job in a confined space. Two wires extended from the top of the device, like antennae from an insect. When the time came, Black would press his detonator and an electric charge would soar from the right wire to the left one and the bomb would be set off. He caught sight of his two target figures approaching and turned toward the wall. He couldn't chance forfeiting the plan at this point by allowing the old Israeli or his henchman to recognize him. So he counted their steps mentally, finger on the button and ready to press when the count was finished.

Ten . . . eleven . . . twelve . . .

The magic number was forty. He could see them walking in his mind, keeping perfect pace with their stride. He had thought everything out so it would be foolproof.

And it would have been were it not for the exuberant spirits of a youth with a soccer ball disembarking from the same plane. Feeling a sudden release after his long, confined flight, the boy heedlessly kicked the ball down the long corridor, then froze as he saw his third boot heading directly toward a baby carriage parked to one side.

The impact of the soccer ball forced the carriage to slam hard against the wall. As it tipped back in the other direction, the two vibrating wires grazed each other, creating a spark. The explosion that followed incinerated the plastic doll in half a second and tore out a huge chunk of the wall. Those closest to the blast felt as though the wind had been smashed out of them from both sides and fought futilely to get it back as consciousness was stripped mercifully away. Parts of the ceiling showered down on others fortunate enough to catch only the whiplash of the blast, which tumbled them from their feet and set them hugging the floor for comfort. It was difficult to separate cries of fear from those of true anguish and few bothered to try, as an emergency alarm wailed in obscene counterpoint.

Felix was the first one back on his feet, followed closely by Sparrow. That the bomb had been meant for them neither doubted, nor did they question whatever stroke of fate had saved them from it even as a punctured soccer ball dribbled by.

Sparrow inspected the damage wrought by the bomb. Destruction and suffering were things you never got used to. A full thirty seconds had passed since the explosion. Time crawled.

Then he saw the blond man. Smartly dressed, his face expressionless, he was a calm bystander amidst the panic, viewing the scene with disappointment and confusion instead of shock. Sparrow could tell this from his cold, icy, lifeless eyes. People were rushing toward the scene, official and otherwise. The motionless blond man stood out among them. Sparrow edged forward. The blond man backed away, turned.

"Black!" Sparrow screamed, giving chase now, the .45 whipped from his belt. *"Black!"*

Renaldo Black stepped calmly into the crowd forming behind him and became part of it. Sparrow held the

.45 low as he crashed through the expanding mass of people in search of the blond man. Seconds ticked away. Frustration tore at him. Somewhere his leg throbbed but he didn't feel it. Sweat slipped down his face and made a neat pile by his chin.

"Black!"

The tall, V-built blond man was strolling calmly away, free of the crowd. He didn't look back.

Sparrow caught one glimpse of him, then lost him again. A sea of people closed around him, clashing from different directions. They had come out of nowhere. It was part of Black's escape route. The terrorist had counted on the explosion to have precisely this confused effect. The Israeli tucked the .45 into his belt and pressed forward.

Black was gone. Sparrow shouldered his way through the mass and started running. His breath failed him first and his eyes went next, even before his leg. He swiped at his face with a jacket sleeve to fight off the sweat. It was over, the quarry lost.

He kept his path toward the main exit.

Up ahead, a blond head rose above the rest. Black fought down the desire to look back for Sparrow. His count had reached twenty-nine when the bomb had gone off. The angle he had chosen allowed him a view of the carriage and the blur whirling toward it, so he realized the failure an instant before the premature blast confirmed it. He had flinched more at the crash of the ball into the carriage than at the explosion itself. At that point he should have turned and fled but a chance had still existed that his count had been off and Sparrow was dead anyway. When the Israeli rose from the floor, he still couldn't leave, couldn't resist stealing a look at the man he'd have to kill another time.

Foolish really, but he hadn't expected Sparrow to recognize him. Obviously there was something here he hadn't considered. . . . But what?

Sparrow saw the blond head flicker before him and quickened his pace. But his soles struck the floor too hard, forfeited his position, so he slowed slightly, wondering what had happened to the days when he could stalk his prey silently over any surface. He was gaining on Black; slowly, but gaining all the same.

Just one shot, one clear shot. . . .

Sensing Sparrow's presence, Black dodged by some people and spun around others. He had the long, loping stride of an athlete. He could move much faster if he desired but decided against it because a faster pace would clear the way for the Israeli to reach him. He was thinking quite rationally, far from tired, and with a new strategy in mind.

Sparrow was moving on borrowed breath. His heart thundered its objections. His bad leg wasn't being fooled anymore and had fallen back to a limp. He kept Black in sight, thought of drawing his gun and using it here, even though there were innocent people to think of. One shot, he could take him with one shot. Before too much longer, he'd have to take the chance.

Sparrow ripped the .45 from his belt. Before him, people screamed, scattered, hit the ground.

"Black!"

The barrel was poised at his target's back, just forty feet away. Sparrow held his ground in combat position, pawing the trigger.

Black dropped out of the scene, disappeared. Sparrow shook sense to his eyes, scolding them for accepting this illusion. But wait . . . up ahead, was that an—yes! An escalator! He sped toward it, reached it just as the people Black had crashed by had picked themselves up again. His limp leg prevented him from taking the same path.

When he reached the main airport level, Black was gone. Undaunted, Sparrow moved for the exit doors, pistol back in his belt. The Washington sun greeted his eyes harshly. Streams of people littered the sidewalk in rows four deep. There were taxis, buses, limousines, cars, hotel transports. Black could be waiting for any one of them. Sparrow searched the crowd. From behind people looked astonishingly the same.

"Where are you?" he asked aloud. "Where are you?"

Sparrow's initial movements had confused Felix. He quickly gave chase only to collide bodily with a group of women lugging shopping bags. His stride was broken. He felt distinctly uncomfortable among so many people in so cramped a space. Still, he reached the main airport level just moments behind Sparrow, following his path almost directly. Felix searched for him first on this level, then above on the observation deck. He was nowhere in sight.

But someone else was.

Felix felt his presence before he actually saw him and even then he wasn't precisely sure what he was feeling. But he knew what he saw. On the observation deck, a black monster of a bald man glared down at him, leaning slightly over the railing. He wore a glove on his right hand but not his left. There was something strange about the way he held his hidden fingers.

Tungsten smiled.

Felix smiled back.

Tungsten backed away from the railing, turned, and

walked off. Felix didn't follow.

There were few things he was truly certain of but one of them was that he would meet the black giant again another day.

Desperation surged through Sparrow. His eyes had deserted him and his sensitivity was blurred by strain and fatigue. Black could be anywhere or nowhere and with each passing second the latter grew more likely. Sparrow spun lazily to his rear. The sleeve of a brown suit jacket peaked out from the top of a garbage can. Sometimes the best disguises are made up of less clothing, not more. He scanned the crowd again, filtering all out except for those in shirtsleeves on a brisk spring day.

A man with blond hair turned slightly. There he was!

"Black!"

The terrorist didn't so much as turn. A bus squealed to a halt before him. People jammed toward it. Black let himself be engulfed.

The Lion of the Night sprang backwards and leveled his .45 into the crowd. People screamed and dropped, clearing his bullet's path. His eyes locked on a blond head, held it amidst the chaos. The shot would have to be perfect. There wasn't an inch to spare. He edged his finger to the center of the trigger for his last chance at Black, knowing the terrorist was about to spin with gun in hand. Sparrow started to squeeze, felt something plow into him and take him down from behind.

Black *had* spun. But his gun moved back into its holster under his armpit as soon as he saw the two airport security policemen wrestling the old Israeli to the ground. He boarded the bus and watched the action until it rumbled forward and the Lion of the Night was left behind.

The security officers held him by either arm, their grips tight and sure. One of them had his gun; Sparrow didn't know which nor did he care. He'd been about to kill Renaldo Black and the bastards had stopped him. Damned Americans never could get things quite straight. . . .

He didn't know where they were taking him and didn't bother to ask. One of them had twisted his left arm into a hammerlock, a supposedly invincible hold from which Sparrow knew a half-dozen escapes. He used none, just let himself be led painfully along.

Then a man stepped into their path flashing a badge and an ID, breathing fast and irregularly, sweat streaming from his brow.

"Quinn. FBI," he announced. "This man belongs to me."

The two security officers looked at each other. One spoke. "Look buddy, we got orders. Besides—"

"Good," Paul Quinn snapped. "Put it all down in your report. But this man's an Israeli citizen and I've been sent down here to pick him up. So unless you want to swap your guns for tampon sweepers in the lady's room, hand him over nice and polite along with the gun you rudely confiscated."

The two officers released their holds, one reluctantly jamming Sparrow's .45 into Quinn's palm. They stormed away angrily, eyes following the FBI man's motions.

"Sorry the welcoming committee was late but you ran right past us," Quinn said, placing the .45 in his pocket. Up ahead Sparrow saw three more agents standing just inside the airport lobby. "Special agent Paul Quinn." He extended his hand. "And if you're not Sparrow, I'm in for a helluva bad time." Wordlessly, the Israeli gripped his outstretched palm. "Helluva reception you got."

"You might call it that."

"Who were you about to shoot at? The bomber?"

"Renaldo Black."

"Jesus Christ . . ."

"But he's gone now." Then, distantly to himself, "And with him may well have gone our chances of stopping Isosceles."

Quinn froze at mention of the word. "You know about Isosceles?"

"A little," Sparrow said softly, relieved by the American's recognition. "The project was my idea."

IV

ISOSCELES

TWENTY-TWO

When the plane finally came down in Zurich, Dan was exhausted. He had never been a good traveler, though the arduous trek just ending would have strained the patience of even the best. There had been a bumpy flight across the Atlantic, a frantic plane change in Paris, and a cold dinner en route to Switzerland.

The only good thing to come from the journey was that he could move freely now without sending waves of pain through his ribs. Virtually all the swelling on his face had gone down as well, so the bruises would no longer make him recognizable. He was thankful for that much, at least.

He had occupied himself during the long trip both with his plans, of which there were few, and his drives, of which there were many. He couldn't sit back and wait patiently for Lucifer to come for him. He had to track them down, learn something that would help expose their shadowy existence and true ends so as to find himself allies in the press or politics. His defense would be attack. All he needed was proof.

His search for it would begin tomorrow with a scrap of information recalled from Bathgate's file: 17 Bahnhofplatz in Zurich, the office of transplanted American Stettner Lutz, the arms dealer who had sold Renaldo Black the rifles he had used in the massacre of forty children. Lutz promised to be the first link in what promised to be a very long chain that would lead Dan ultimately to Lucifer.

He had a jump on them and had to make it last. Earlier lessons the organization had taught him were not lost. There was a role to play. Accordingly, from Paris Dan reserved a room in one of Zurich's most exclusive hotels, the Baur au Lac located near the end of the fashionable Bahnhofstrasse, overlooking Lake Zurich, and found a cab without delay at the airport to take him there.

He had booked the least expensive room available but the conversion table confused him. At the hotel the assistant manager helped him transfer a portion of his American money into the proper Swiss denominations and escorted him personally to the elevator. Dan appreciated the courtesy more than he could say, although he didn't fully understand it. His clothes didn't fit the prestigious Baur au Lac, and neither did his age or lack of luggage. Perhaps that was it; he was an oddity. That would make him easier to spot—in which case he might have chosen the wrong hotel.

"If there's anything else I can do for you, monsieur, please do not hesitate to call on me," the mustachioed assistant manager offered.

"There might be," Dan said and tried to pass the man a tip.

The manager begged off. "There is no need."

"But—"

"You are our guest, monsieur. Courtesy comes at no extra charge."

Dan forced a smile and stepped into the elevator.

Right hotel, after all.

But it was time to think of Stettner Lutz.

It didn't take Dan long to learn that the Bahnhof-platz was perhaps the only unfashionable section in all of Zurich, lined with decrepit buildings used as shelters for persons waiting for public transportation. The taxi driver drove past them, doubled back and parked in front of one across the street and isolated from the rest.

"You are sure this is the place you are looking for?" he asked in decent English.

"Yes," Dan said, counting out the proper number of Swiss francs to pay him.

His question was not ill-founded. Number 17 Bahn-hofplatz proved to be the most decrepit building of them all, longer than it was wide, windows either cracked or boarded up. The bricks of which it was built were more black than red. The building seemed on the verge of tumbling into the ground on which it was set.

Dan paid the driver and stepped out of the car, glancing around him. This former Bahnhofplatz trans-port depot would make a fine arms warehouse indeed, especially for a man like Lutz who was on the move constantly. Who would expect such an outfit to be set up in the center of Zurich? People of all ages milled about the mall, waiting for their bus or tram, eyes raised to the sky to check the weather. None ventured near the warehouse, respecting the signs scrawled in a language Dan couldn't read. A boy tossed a rock through a still whole window and fled around the corner. Dan had trouble believing there was anyone inside to hear the crash. Had Lutz already moved his business elsewhere? Suppressing the thought, he approached the front door.

The problem, of course, was that while Dan had good reason to see Lutz, the reverse was not true. The solution was to appear as an interested—and wealthy —party in the wares Lutz had to offer. But he also needed a sponsor, a contact high up in the terrorist world to make his story seem credible. Dan had found an unwitting one: Renaldo Black.

He walked through the brisk Zurich wind up a dirt walk and climbed a set of rickety steps to the front door. There was no knocker or bell, so Dan hammered his fist against the wood. When no response came, he hammered harder.

Footsteps approached and stopped. The door creaked open enough for a set of dark eyes to peer out.

"I'm looking for Stettner Lutz," Dan said with a calm that surprised him.

"Never heard of him," the owner of the eyes snapped, in English.

"Mr. Black told me otherwise.'

"Black?"

"Renaldo Black."

The door opened a bit more. The owner of the dark eyes was thin and gaunt, dressed in dirty work clothes. He smelled of perspiration.

"What's that got to do with anything?" the man charged.

"I'm in the market for some . . . merchandise. Renaldo Black thought I might be able to find it here."

"Depends on the specifics."

"Are you Lutz?"

"No."

"Then the specifics will have to wait."

"Mr. Lutz don't see anybody who walks in off the street."

"Mr. Black would be most disappointed if he failed to make an exception."

The thin man sized Lennagin up, couldn't quite figure him. "I'll go tell Mr. Lutz."

"Give him this." Dan whipped a hundred franc note out of his pocket and tore it neatly in half, handing a section to the man in the doorway. "Tell him the rest of this bill and a whole lot more are being kept outside."

The man smiled. He was missing all his front teeth. "I'll tell him."

The man closed the door. It was five minutes before he returned.

"Mr. Lutz thinks he'll see you."

"Thinks?"

"Yeah. See, before you go in, I'm gonna search you. If I find anything on you that might make Mr. Lutz nervous, I'm gonna slit your throat and the boss won't know the difference."

Inside the doorway, Dan submitted to a fairly thorough body search that turned up nothing.

"You got an ID?"

"I didn't bring any of them with me. Doesn't always pay in my business."

"Mr. Lutz won't like it."

"I don't need a wallet to carry money."

"Sure. Let's go."

The thin man led Dan down a narrow corridor set between two huge rows of shipping crates. They walked side by side. The warehouse was dimly lit and smelled terrible. The floor had a good layer of dust on top of it, clean only in square slots where crates had recently been lifted away. The crates he saw still lined up around him had only numbers on them for markings. Some were larger than others. Dan tried to guess their contents.

"Here we are," the thin man said when they reached a wooden door with countless chips decorating it. He knocked. "I got him with me, Mr. Lutz."

"Bring him in," a raspy, nasal voice instructed.

The thin man opened the door and followed Dan inside. The air was stained with cigar smoke that hovered in huge clouds near the ceiling. Behind a metal desk cluttered with a mess of papers sat a man who seemed at once to be all stomach. He had no neck, just a round, nearly bald head that looked like a simple extension of his blubberous torso. Dan counted three chins wavering between puffs of the monstrous cigar wedged into his mouth.

"So you're one of Black's friends?"

"Yup."

"You got a name?"

"Quite a few of them."

"Which one you using today?"

"Dan sounds good."

Lutz took the cigar from his mouth and rested it on the tip of an ashtray. The motion seemed difficult for him. "Okay, Dan, my man Bernie there delivered half a hundred franc bill from you. Around here that don't buy much."

"Your merchandise might not be worth any more."

The fat man leaned a bit forward. "Don't fuck with me, boy. I used to chew on punks like you."

Dan's heart was racing. He hoped Bernie didn't notice. "I came here to do business, not to discuss your dental work."

Lutz laughed. The laugh fell into a cough. "I like you, kid. You got pizzazz. Sit down and let's powwow. See if I got the goods you're looking for. And if I don't, nobody does."

"So I've heard."

"Yeah, I got a good rep in the business. Sell only the best merchandise dirty money can buy. Funny thing is a lot of it ends up back in the countries where the stuff was made in the first place."

"Strange world," Dan said.

"I told you to sit down."

"You asked me to. And I don't do business with third parties in the room."

"Bernie's my partner. Heightens my sense of security."

"I don't like being outnumbered when I talk business."

"We're all friends here, kid."

"My point exactly."

"Bernie don't like being on the outside of things. He might get angry."

"Tell him to visit a dentist."

Bernie clenched his hands into fists. Lutz laughed again, fought off the cough that ordinarily followed.

"Go to lunch, Bernie," the fat man told him. "But don't bite down on any hard sandwiches." This time, the cough beat him.

Bernie closed the door and was gone.

Dan sat down, tried to look hard. It wasn't easy. All his life, his appearance had never measured up to his age. He looked perpetually younger than he was, too young certainly to play the role of a hard-boiled terrorist. Unless he made his boyish looks work for him. There was a way.

"You'd be dead now if you was a cop, you know," Lutz told him.

"Oh?"

"See this phone? Whenever somebody official's planning a visit I get a call at least five hours in advance. Whole place gets moved out in that time. Once in a while hotshots show up all alone. Nobody ever sees them again."

"I'm glad we're on the same side."

Lutz leaned as far backwards as he could go. "So you're one of Renaldo Black's boys. You tight with him?"

"Depends."

Lutz winked. Even his eyelid was fatty. "You know what I mean. It's common knowledge that Black don't love straight."

Dan remembered reading about the terrorist's sexual preferences in Bathgate's file on him. "I like to fuck. So does he."

"Each other?"

"When the spirit moves us."

Lutz's three chins dropped for a smile. "I like the way you talk, kid. But you don't look like Black's type. Your face ain't got enough holes in it, your hair's too neat, and you're a little too soft around the eyes. Now, take the last crony of Black's who was in here." Lutz looked him right in the eye. "The one who picked up the shipment of Uzis. . . ."

Dan held Lutz's stare. He was being tested and he knew it. His mind worked fast, determined his response. If it was wrong, he was finished. Bernie would gladly see to that.

"First of all, Lutz, Black likes little boys—the

prettier the better. And second of all they were Kalish-nikovs and he picked them up himself." Dan stood up angrily. If the maneuver had failed, he'd now be able to make a run for it. "I don't like being tested. How about I take my business elsewhere?" He held his breath on the last word.

"Sit down, kid, can't be too careful in this business. Renaldo always picks up his merchandise himself. But only someone who knows him would know that."

Or someone who's read his file, thought Dan. "You through playing games?" He was breathing easy for the first time since he'd entered the room.

"Yeah. I got something you might be interested in. I know a guy up in Germany who can get you a boy real cheap for keeps. Friend of Black's as a matter of fact. I used to be in the business when I was younger. Take my word for it, if you got the same tastes as Black, these kids would be right up your alley."

Dan forced himself to continue the charade. "What's the price?"

"A couple thousand marks. Cheaper maybe 'cause you know me."

"I'll let you know."

"Make it fast. Demand's pretty high these days. Little boys are sellin' bigger than machine guns. Maybe I'm in the wrong business now."

"Not for my tastes today you're not."

"What you in the market for, kid?"

Dan knew quite a bit about guns from the magazines his brother had always left lying around the house. They had gone to the range together on several occasions and although Dan didn't share his brother's interest, ironically he came close to sharing his marksmanship and even his knowledge.

"German machine pistols," he replied evenly. "Mausers."

"Shit, those are hard to come by and damn expensive when I can get them. They haven't made any since World War II. They got hardly no circulation these days."

"They're still the finest handguns ever made. One squeeze fires all twenty shots in the clip. Damn pistol has the power of a rifle at one quarter the size, and it's concealable to boot."

"Okay, kid, you sold me. Trouble is, I ain't the buyer. What you plan on using them for?"

"Is telling you included in the agreement?"

"Just friendly curiosity."

Dan smiled for the first time. He was getting caught up in the game, the role. "You been straight with me, so I'll be straight with you. We're gonna make a lot of in-close hits in crowded places and we don't want to be seen or noticed. We figure Mausers will be perfect."

"Except you'll need silencers."

"Right."

"Cost you extra, a small bundle if I have to have them made up special."

"Don't worry about the money."

Lutz's chins sank into another smile. "Music to my ears, kid, music to my ears. You still in with Black?"

"Sort of. After the Virginia thing, we split off into separate groups. Made sense, we figured."

Lutz nodded. "I knew he wanted those Kalishnikovs for something big. . . ."

"In a month you'll be saying the same thing about my Mausers."

"Only you've presented me with a problem, kid. It

might take a couple weeks to even locate Mausers. How many we talkin' about?"

"Say twenty and a couple thousand rounds of ammunition for starters."

"Whooooo! That'll cost you twenty-five thousand good old American bucks without silencers and expenses."

"Doesn't sound like the price you'd charge your best customers."

"Ah hell, my friend in Germany owes me a few favors. I'll throw in one of his boys at no extra charge."

Dan made his eyes gleam. "Sounds fair to me. What the money people don't know can't hurt them."

"Speaking of money, you gotta leave a deposit."

"A thousand okay?"

"Plenty."

Lennagin started for his pocket but then pulled back. "You wouldn't happen to have a sample Mauser lying around, would you?"

"As a matter of fact, I would," Lutz smiled. "How 'bout I give it to you as a sign of good faith?"

Dan grinned sheepishly and nodded. Lutz pushed his obese frame from the chair and waddled across the room toward a locked cabinet. From behind, his body had the look of a massive block, all one piece with nothing to distinguish where one part of the bulk ended and another began. He stuck his key into the lock of the cabinet and turned to smile at Dan.

"My private collection," he announced, sticking his hand inside and coming out with a sleek-looking square pistol differentiated by its extra-long clip. "A German Mauser," he proclaimed. "The world's first and best automatic pistol." He handed it gingerly to Dan.

Lennagin took it and tried its weight. Smooth and easy. He was no expert with guns but he knew a good one when he felt it.

"Loaded?" he asked.

"Sure. I didn't want to insult your intelligence by taking the clip out."

"I appreciate that."

Lutz waddled back to his chair. He thudded back down with a heavy sigh. "Now how 'bout my deposit?"

"Coming right up."

Dan pulled a wad of bills from his pocket and started to hand it across the thin desk. Lutz rose halfway out of his chair, the motion prolonged and imbalanced. The opportunity was there. Dan grabbed for it.

In a single swift motion, he shoved the steel desk backwards so that the lip caught Lutz in his monstrous stomach and jammed him against the wall. The fat man's mouth fell open for a scream so Dan, not particularly wanting to face an angered Bernie rushing through the door, threw all his weight into the desk again. The flesh before it gave, sagged. Lutz gasped. His head fell to his chest. Then Dan was alongside him, slamming his head hard against the wall. Lutz's eyes glazed, filling with fear. Dan stuck the point of the Mauser's barrel against the fat man's temple.

"I want Black," he said, surprised his calm hadn't deserted him when he dropped the ruse. "And you're gonna help me find him."

"I can't."

Lennagin pushed the barrel forward till its steel scratched flesh. He cocked the trigger.

"Black's a customer—that's all," Lutz pleaded. "I don't know him any way else."

"You must know how to contact him."

"No. Contact was always initiated by him." A pause. "You're dead, kid. You know that, don't you?"

"You're probably right," Dan told him, "which means I've got nothing to lose by pulling the trigger and painting the walls with your brains."

"You're a fool, kid."

"A fool with a gun. I want to know how I can find Renaldo Black."

Lutz managed a smile. His lips trembled. Blood dripped down the side of his face from the spot the barrel had made its imprint. "You know something, kid? You don't scare me. Shit, ten years ago I sold punks older than you for a living. I think I'll tell you what I know. It's the least I can do to help you get killed because you're crazy enough to go where I send you and there they'll kill ya sweet and sure. Don't run no friendly over-the-counter business like old Lutz. No way, no how. Yeah, I'll tell ya and then I'll look forward to reading about your body being dragged out of the water with more holes in it than a pin cushion."

"Stop stalling!" More pressure from the Mauser. "Talk!"

"Fuck the gun, punk. I'm just puttin' my thoughts together." Lutz paused for a narrow smile. "That guy I mentioned who's in the flesh-peddling racket is also Black's German contact. If anyone can assure you of a nice, painful death, it's him. His name is Wolfgang Bauer and he works out of a bar in Hamburg, Germany."

"Give me the address!"

"Easy does it, kid, easy does it. The bar's called Der Vergnügen, and it's right on the main drag in the Reeperbahn section of the city. You can't miss it, just look for big red letters overlooking the Herbertstrasse.

Lovely neighborhood. Makes this one look classy."

Dan committed the address to memory. "How do I know you're not lying?"

"Because I want to hear about how Bauer kills you. Burn up your insides real slow with a hot poker up your tight ass—something like that. Maybe he'll just sell you to the highest bidder."

"I don't expect you'll be calling Hamburg to warn him that I'm coming."

"If I did, I'd have to admit that I gave you his address. Not too smart for a man in my position."

"That's what I figured."

"Don't matter anyway. You're dead, whether I kill ya or somebody else does."

"That remains to be seen," Dan said. He shoved Lutz's desk away from the wall and stripped the fat man's belt from his massive waist. "Put your hands behind the chair."

Lutz obliged. "What do I do if my pants fall down?"

"Chew on your prick . . . if you can find it." Dan finished tying. Then he found a filthy towel hidden on the desk and rolled it into a small ball. Holding Lutz's head back, he jammed it into his mouth. The fat man stifled a cough, tried to spit.

Dan backed away, Mauser by his side. Lutz's eyes followed him to the door. He turned away long enough to turn the knob and start the door open. He looked back at Lutz one final time, was about to speak when something cold and hard stuck itself into the back of his head.

"Drop the gun," said Bernie.

TWENTY-THREE

"Where the hell you been?" Lutz asked his toothless thug while he was undoing the belt, keeping a close eye and loaded revolver on Dan, who was presently hugging the wall.

"I thought I heard something outside."

Lutz rubbed his hands together to restore the circulation. "Don't try thinking from now on, okay?"

Bernie shrugged, glanced at Dan. "What do you want me to do with him?"

"Kill him, asshole, but don't do it here. Do it somewhere where you can get the body hid right away. I don't want nobody asking no questions. No corpse, no questions."

"Got ya."

"Then get the hell outta here. I don't want to see your face again till the kid's been burned."

Bernie flashed a toothless grin. "No sweat."

Then he had Dan by the arm in a terribly strong grip for a man who didn't look like he had a muscle to speak of and led him from the room down the narrow corridor where he could still make out his footprints from twenty minutes before. Dan looked for a means of escape, searched his mind for a plan, and then realized he was finished. His only worthwhile actions the last few days had been instinctive, like killing the man in his Washington hotel room, or answering Lutz's questions smartly, or coming to Zurich in the first place. His thoughts were his problems. Thinking slowed him down. Trouble was he didn't know enough not to think. Too few lessons had been learned. No more, it seemed, would be.

He mounted a few futile attempts to escape from Bernie's grasp and found each stifled with a painful wrench of his arm or a hammerlike hand to his head.

They were almost at the front door when Dan heard the explosion. It echoed through the warehouse's shabby walls and stung his ears.

Bernie felt it even more. He had been blown backwards, separated from his pistol with a huge red hole swelling in the center of his chest. He crashed into a row of numbered crates and toppled over them. Before Dan knew what was happening, a figure whirled past him in line with the door to Lutz's office. As if on cue, the fat man emerged with a machine gun poised in his hands. He found the trigger but never pulled it. The first bullet caught him in the neck, the second dead-on in his forehead. Lutz gazed up, as though to look at the wound, and then thudded hard to the floor.

The gun-wielding figure spun toward Dan and stood stark still. A long time ago, Lennagin might have raised his hands slowly over his head or pleaded some conciliatory words, but not today.

The figure stuck its pistol into the pocket of an army fatigue jacket worn over faded blue jeans. It swept a free hand across its head and came away with a blue cap.

Long, blond hair dangled freely, stretching past her

shoulders. Her eyes were blue and cold, her face beautiful but tight in its determination; her mouth slightly bent, smileless.

"Let's get out of here," she told him.

"Who the hell are you?"

"Name's Jill Levine. The fat bastard in the heap over there sold the guns that butchered my family."

She drove him back to the Baur au Lac, passing by nerve centers for the banking and insurance industries throughout the world, first on the Bahnhofstrasse and then on the Talstrasse as they drew closer to the hotel.

"Alexander Levine was your father?" Dan asked uncomfortably once she had pulled the car into traffic.

"And Susan Levine was my mother and Jason Levine was my brother. I didn't come home for his Bar Mitzvah. Too busy educating the natives in some worthless African country."

"You killed Lutz for revenge."

"And I'll get the others too."

"I was hoping you did it to save my life."

"A happy coincidence for you. I couldn't have cared less. I did figure, though, that since the fat man was having his goon dispose of you, we might have a few similar interests."

"More than you can imagine." Dan hesitated. "Twelve years ago, terrorists killed my father on a plane in South Africa."

Jill's eyes flashed with surprise. "Your old man was the guy whose number got drawn? Well, I'll be damned. . . ."

"We both are, but for our presents—not our pasts."

"Then I don't suppose your meeting with Lutz had

anything to do with your old man."

"No. I'm after somebody, too." Dan looked at her closely. "Does the name Renaldo Black mean anything to you?"

She screeched on the brakes, stared at him with blue eyes blazing with fury. "That's the son of a bitch who butchered my family! How do you know him?" she demanded.

"It's a long story and tends to get complicated in parts. Suffice it to say he stepped into my life along with a host of others—some good and some bad. I ran away because I couldn't tell the difference anymore. And the only way I can get back home is to find some answers. I figure Black has them."

Jill's stare softened. "Where is home?"

"Up until a few days ago, it was Brown University in Providence, Rhode Island, where I faithfully served Delta Phi as its president."

"I applied to Brown," she told him.

"Get in?"

"It didn't matter. I decided not to go to college right away. I wanted to travel, see the world, meet new people. That was three years ago. I've been traveling, seeing, and meeting since."

"It doesn't sound like the experience exactly overwhelmed you."

"It was okay for awhile. I got bored. Matter of fact, I'd just about decided to pack it in when the news reached me about what happened to my family, three days late and sketchy, but leaving no room for hope. I guess it was better that way. Made me feel guilty as shit and so God-awful lonely."

"Guilty because you weren't killed too?"

"Maybe. That was one of several options I tossed

about in my head for a couple days."

"And then?"

"Look, Lennagin, I got no room right now in my life for questions." Here she increased the speed of her Fiat.

"Which means you must figure you got all the answers."

"I had enough of them to get Lutz. I'll find more to track down Black."

They had reached the Baur au Lac. Jill Levine hit the brakes hard. "This is where you get out, college boy."

He did but rested his hands on her open window before moving for the door. "This may sound corny but since you saved my life, I figure I owe you something."

"You're right, it does sound corny."

Dan ignored the statement and its tone. "I know how tired and hungry this being alone has made me. The food's not great in the hotel but it fills you up and, besides, you're the only one I've met since the bottom dropped out of my life who seems to understand what I'm going through. I'd like to hold on to that for a while longer."

"You want to get into my pants, Lennagin?"

His hands slipped from the door. He fought for a rejoinder but came up empty.

"Don't be shy, college boy," she snapped at him. "When your family gets butchered and you take to chasing after their killers with guns in both pockets, you'd be surprised how simple sex can be."

They continued their discussion in his hotel room after each had taken a long, hot shower. Jill redressed in front of him without so much as flinching. Clearly she felt as comfortable naked as she did fully clothed, unlike other girls Dan had known. To him she resembled a *Playboy* centerfold come to life. Without clothes her physical perfection seemed drawn by an artist with every line, hair, and muscle symmetrically in place. She caught his staring eye and teased him with a wink, tucking a blue work shirt into her jeans and tousling her hair in front of the mirror.

"You're pretty good with that gun," Dan said lamely, noticing the revolver resting on the dresser.

"Comes with the territory," she told him. "I've spent over three years in two dozen African and Third World countries you probably never heard of. The governments often didn't take too kindly to American idealists spreading the new math to their people. Today, the alphabet, tomorrow a revolution—all that sort of shit. Anyway my jeep got run off the road in the middle of Ethiopia's bush country one day and I had to hide in the grass and trees for twelve hours hearing soldiers' boots slashing the ground near me the whole time. I got out of that one and figured it was time to carry some protection. So I picked up a few guns on the black market and practiced five hours a day. I couldn't afford to be anything but an expert."

"You ever have to use them on anybody before today?"

"You'd be surprised what the sight of a girl holding a gun does to man, Lennagin. Most of the time unfriendly soldiers or government hatchet men shrank back and left. A couple times they didn't. I'm still here and they're not. That answer your question?"

"For sure."

"What's the rest of your story? How'd you get in to see Lutz? He's not in the habit of accepting new clients off the street."

"I told him I was one of Black's boys . . . in more ways than one."

"And he believed you?" she asked incredulously.

"I can be very convincing when the walls are closing in around me."

"All the same, if Lutz had had any mind at all he'd have shot you long before I appeared on the scene. What led you to him?"

"Same thing as you and for the same reason. I knew he was the one who sold the Kalishnikovs that were used—er—against your family, so I figured he might provide a link to Black."

"And did he?"

"I'm not sure. He gave me an address in Hamburg, Germany."

She swung suddenly toward him, her eyes alive and burning with more emotion than he'd thought she possessed. "Where in Hamburg?"

Dan pulled the address from his mind. "In the Reeperbahn section. A bar named Der Vergnügen located on the main drag."

"Near the Herbertstrasse?"

"Overlooks it, Lutz told me. But how did you—"

"Looks like you were good for something after all, something big." He saw her smile for the first time. It vanished quickly. "What about a name? Did Lutz give you a name?"

"Bauer."

"Wolfgang Bauer?"

Dan nodded.

Her smile flashed again, longer this time. "Holy shit! You hit the goddamn jackpot!"

"I don't get it."

"How could you? You probably never been out of the friendly confines of America before, college boy. You probably know as much about terrorism as I do about English literature."

"I don't know so much about English literature. But I've been reading books about terrorism since I was twelve years old."

"All you can get out of them is footnotes full of political bullshit. But this is the real thing."

Dan looked at Jill quizzically.

"A bar called Der Vergnügen, college boy. One of the dirtiest, filthiest, scummiest places on earth. On the main floor, you can buy booze and women. And if that doesn't suit your tastes and your pockets are pretty well lined, there are plenty of boys, girls, and drugs located in the lower level. Anything you want can be obtained for a price in Reeperbahn, and Der Vergnügen is a major center for finances and supply. But the real fun goes on upstairs. That's where Bauer hangs out as a member of Germany's never-say-die terrorist group. The bar is one of its main headquarters."

"Baader-Meinhof?"

She smiled at him. "You get an 'A' for the course, college boy, but don't let it go to your head. I'm sure the books told you that the Baader-Meinhof gang is just a 'hanger-on' terrorist group. In many ways they are, little more than skeletal these days, actually. Ran out of money a few years back and never quite recovered. Then they discovered a new market: kids. They've bankrolled a new awakening literally with blood money. You'd be surprised how many bucks a little boy goes for these days. Baader-Meinhof takes the cash and invests it in supplies and the recruiting of every psychopath in West Germany into their numbers. Der

Vergnügen promises to be teaming with them. But that's not going to stop me from making the trip."

"Why?"

"Because, Lennagin, that little piece of information Lutz passed on to you has saved me two weeks' work. That's how long it would've taken me to track down one of Renaldo Black's contact points. You can't throw those kinds of gifts away. I suppose I should have known Baader-Meinhof and Der Vergnügen was the logical location, but under the circumstances my mind wasn't functioning as smoothly as it should have been."

"You seem to know quite a bit about terrorists yourself."

"And all of it from experience, Lennagin, not books. In the Third World countries I've been puking in for the last million years or so, terrorism is a way of life. Most people who know as much as I do about the inside got dumped in a river a long time ago. I guess I was a little bit lucky and a little bit good. Either way, Lennagin, you've given me reason to press my luck and my skill a while longer." She paused. "Der Vergnügen will lead me to Black."

"Then you'll kill him?"

"Just like I killed Lutz."

"Black's no fat tub of lard with a cretin for a henchman."

"My guns don't discriminate."

"You won't be able to do it alone."

She moved toward him, eyes twinkling. "For somebody who just missed leaving his brains at a warehouse, you're getting pretty uppity, college boy."

"You and I are after the same thing, though for different reasons. You saved my life and I saved you two weeks. I figure that makes us even—good point to start a working relationship from."

"I work alone, Lennagin."

"So did I until three hours ago. Amazing how a gun to your head changes your perspective. You're going to Hamburg and so am I. It makes sense we go together."

"Not to me it doesn't."

"Why?"

"Because you're an amateur."

"Not any more than you. You lost your family; I lost my father and my best friend. We've both got scores to settle and an equal right to settle them. We're both driven by rage and pain with a little bit of fear added for good measure."

"Except I want Black for revenge. You want him for . . ." she groped for a word, ". . . proof."

"So who's more the amateur?"

Jill's face upturned quizzically. When she spoke again her voice was lower, yielding. "I suppose you've got a plan to get us up to see Bauer at Der Vergnügen too."

"I won't go in blasting with both pistols, that's for sure." Dan thought briefly. "I got in to see Lutz, didn't I?"

"You said it yourself before, though. Lutz was different. Small-time compared to what we'll be facing in Hamburg."

"Except Bauer must be a businessman as well as a terrorist. Like you said, he's bankrolled a good portion of the new Baader-Meinhof by selling little boys on the Reeperbahn."

"So?"

"So there's my in. I'll be a shadowy American who's come to Hamburg in quest of the particular products he dispenses. Good old American dollars waved in front of his face might distract him long enough for us to get what we really want."

Jill smiled at him, nodding. Her perfectly formed breasts swayed as she edged forward. "I like the way you talk, Lennagin. We might not make such a bad team, after all."

"Then we'll leave for Hamburg tomorrow. . . ."

"Not so fast," she resisted. "I'm already resigned to getting myself killed, but you're a different story."

"That's my decision. What's yours?"

"Tell you what." She sat down next to him on the bed, her eyes the softest he had seen them yet. "I'll think about it while we eat and decide while we screw."

Morning came with a knock on the door before seven A.M. Dan rolled out of bed, hardly rested but feeling refreshed, careful not to disturb Jill. But an arm tugging at him as he tried to move told him she was already awake.

"Giving up so soon?" she sighed. All night long she had been in control, teacher to student. He was at her mercy and both of them knew it. Dan had lost himself totally in her and wanted to lose himself more.

The knocks came again in a series, louder this time. Dan smiled at her and pulled away. "I better get that."

Jill held a sheet against her chest, her pistol tucked under it. Dan pulled on a pair of pants and moved to the door.

"Mr. Lennagin," greeted the small, mustachioed assistant manager who'd been so helpful and friendly upon his arrival, "I'm most sorry to disturb you at this early hour but I'm afraid it's necessary. May I come in?"

"Well . . ."

Before Dan could complete his objection, the small man had pushed his way through the door and closed it behind him. He exchanged a cursory, disinterested glance with Jill and looked back at Lennagin.

"I am very sorry to have to force myself upon you, but circumstances have arisen that might interest you. I felt it was in your best interest to be informed immediately."

"Of what?"

"Zurich is a beautiful city, Mr. Lennagin, but we have our problems just as your American cities do. There was a murder yesterday afternoon on the Bahnhofplatz. A most unsavory sort named Lutz who was rumored to have been involved with criminals and terrorists. Sold them weapons, I believe."

"How does this concern me?" Dan asked. Could the manager sense his nervousness?

"Oh, I'm not saying it does. Please excuse my manner. If I may continue, though. . . ."

"Please."

The assistant manager locked the door and chained it. "The Zurich police applaud Lutz's killing. They would prefer to reward his murderer instead of tossing him in jail. It is thus doubtful a serious investigation will be mounted at all. Officially, the whole matter will be filed and forgotten. Unofficially, however, Lutz had many friends who are not at all pleased with his murder. They have asked many questions, sent people canvassing the city. It seems two young people were spotted in the vicinity of Lutz's warehouse at the approximate time of the killing. The boy, I'm told, had curly hair. He was with a blond girl." The final statement aimed at Jill.

Dan started to say something. The manager just kept speaking.

"Three of Lutz's friends appeared in the Baur au Lac's lobby not fifteen minutes ago. They were well-dressed and carried briefcases. I cannot speak for what was contained inside. They asked me if two young people meeting the approximate descriptions I just gave you were staying here. I told them I seemed to remember a boy with curly hair checking out yesterday afternoon. They seemed satisfied but they are certain to return, perhaps before noon. They will bring official papers to force me into compliance. Zurich is also not free from corruption."

"Have you called the police?" Dan asked calmly.

"Funny thing about our police," the manager told him. "They do not wish to get themselves involved in the case from either side. They will not actively search for the killers of Lutz but neither will they protect them. In their minds the problem doesn't concern them. The rats, they say, will eat each other. So wherever these two young people are, I'm sure you understand they are in very grave danger."

"Yes."

"They will, of course, try to escape. Who can blame them, these two young friends of ours? They will not get very far, though. All the airports and rail stations are being watched by the friends of those with the briefcases."

Dan swallowed hard, looked furtively at Jill's blank face.

"But fortunately," the mustachioed man continued, "there are many people in Zurich in positions like mine who are well schooled in arranging passage for people who otherwise would be stuck where they are. Many have crossed our path before in not too different predicaments from this boy and girl. We frequently support their efforts without questioning their motivations. We feel they have done a service to our city and that we owe them something in return. When they are able, they pay us. When they are not, they don't. It matters little. Most of the time we get them safely to France or Germany. Sometimes we fail. Always the effort is made." A pause. "It's splendid in Munich this time of year."

"What about Hamburg?"

"Cold, and a long trip, but worth it depending on your desires. Of course, the key to any of these escapes is timing. They must be executed—pardon my choice of words—with the utmost of precision. Every second counts. The men with the briefcases tend to catch on to a trail quite fast."

Dan thought quickly. The manager's offer could easily represent the perfect set-up. Why trust him? To begin with, Dan reasoned, he could easily have had them killed last night. But more important, he had a gut feeling the man's intentions were honorable. Not much to go on perhaps, but feelings had gotten him this far and he was learning more and more to heed them without question.

"We'll be downstairs in twenty-five minutes," Dan said.

Actually, it was only twenty minutes later when the elevator deposited them in the lobby. People looked over, taking notice. Jill's fatigue jacket and jeans weren't in fashion. Their stares didn't faze her in the least. She walked with one hand by her side, the other in her jacket pocket where it cradled the grip of her revolver. A knapsack straddled her shoulders, containing, she said, all her possessions worth a damn. Dan felt an overwhelming urge to reach down and take her free hand in his. Warmth and trust had been out of his life for five days that seemed like months. Now he had them back and wanted to reassure himself of their presence. He moved his fingers lower but the hand was gone. Their eyes met, hers scolding him.

How can I move fast if I'm locked to you? they challenged.

He moved his fingers back up and felt very cold again. The sensation of relief, of companionship, of security, was gone. The two of them were both still alone. They were just alone together.

Dan squared away his bill with the assistant manager, keeping up a front of normal proceedings. The bearded man then led them toward a side exit, babbling the whole way but saying exactly nothing.

A van was parked outside with the name of a Zurich newspaper printed on its side. It sat near the curb with its engine running.

"It will take you to Munich," the assistant manager explained. "From there, you will have to arrange your own passage elsewhere."

"I don't know how to thank you," Dan said lamely.

"It is I who should be thanking you," the assistant manager said as he opened the rear doors of the van, beckoning them to enter. "Have a safe trip." The doors closed. Blackness swallowed them.

They found seats on piles of a Swiss morning paper bound for Germany. The driver made the trip every day. The back of the van was never checked. He knew the border guards. Their pockets were fatter because of him.

Dan leaned back and closed his eyes in silence, thinking of what they might find in Hamburg and fighting to close his nostrils against the bitter stink of newsprint.

Jill Levine kept her eyes open, studying the half-sleeping figure next to her, picturing his soft curls tossing about her while they had made love the night before. She smiled, but the smile fell immediately into a sigh.

Gabriele Lafontaine had remembered what Jill Levine, who had never existed in the first place, had forgotten.

Dan Lennagin had to die.

She had to kill him. In Hamburg. It was all arranged.

The boy was innocent, just as her parents and so many others were innocent. Why did they have to die? Why did the boy have to? There were no answers because the questions were not allowed, rule number one of the life she had chosen. She was committed to it, doomed by the commitment.

Gabriele Lafontaine felt for the boy's hand and squeezed it.

In the lobby of the Hotel Baur au Lac, a tall-gray-haired man with a jet black mustache watched the newspaper van pull away from the curb. Matters had certainly taken a turn for the better.

He smiled inwardly and made his way toward the service desk to arrange passage to Munich.

TWENTY-FOUR

The President arrived late for the early morning meeting, just as his secretary finished distributing mugs of coffee to the waiting occupants of the Oval Office.

"I apologize for my absence yesterday but there would have been too many suspicious people if I had canceled out on the governors' conference." He moved toward Sparrow, who rose to greet him. "I've been briefed on the nature of Isosceles, but I'd like to hear exactly what it is in your own words."

Sparrow took his seat again. "A retaliatory contingency to be used in the event of a major terrorist attack. At least that was the way we defined it over a decade ago."

"And how did you define 'major'?"

"Something that caused severe disruption of the orderly flow of things. It could have been an assassination or even the detonation of an atomic bomb by a terrorist group. I felt Lucifer needed an equalizer, a response to dissuade such actions." Sparrow took a sip from his mug. "The Isosceles Project, as its name indicates, was a three-pronged attack plan whereby Lucifer would launch assaults on—and reasonably obliterate—three terrorist strongholds across the globe as this response."

"You said obliterate," noted MaCammon. "That sounds to me like a triad air strike."

"It most certainly would have included one," confirmed Sparrow. "The vast resources of Lucifer included access to a limited supply of on-call fighters and sufficient ammunition for them."

"But you never made use of either."

"Under my plan we weren't supposed to. Isosceles was meant to function more as a deterrent. We leaked word in the right places that extreme force on the part of terrorists would be met by even *more* extreme force. In any event, my final two years with Lucifer passed with Isosceles remaining purely a concept. But gradually the Lucifer leadership changed, became more radical. They were struck by what they thought to be the brilliant logic of Isosceles and were determined to make things happen instead of waiting for them to happen. They searched for a legitimate reason to move Isosceles into operation and when none arose, they contemplated creating one on their own."

"Toward what purpose?" asked the President.

"Destroying terrorism at its source at any cost. Blasting terrorists from their underground lairs where they'd have to make account and fight in the open. But they still needed a rationale."

"I get the feeling this is where America comes in. . . ."

"Two major factors made her a logical choice. In the first place, your country at this point had been free of direct terrorist assaults, thanks mostly to your borders. Access into America and escape out is not nearly the simple matter it is in Europe and the Mideast. It's often as easy to move from country to country across the

Atlantic as it is to move from state to state here. You have oceans on two sides of you and allies on two more. Whatever they wish to make you think, terrorists will virtually never undertake a mission where a near certainty of capture or death exists, and in America that has always been the case." Sparrow paused. "Just as important, though, is that Americans grow angry before they grow scared. It's your nature, your 'Way,' my friend Felix would call it. So anyone looking for a justification to launch Isosceles would need look no further than your shores."

"And that's what Lucifer did?" questioned the President.

"The emerging leadership tried to but was stifled by the old guard. I went yet a step further. I threatened to expose their plot to the American Administration of eight years ago and all subsequent Administrations since. They begged off, promised to deactivate Isosceles even as I . . . retired."

"You set yourself up as a target for them," surmised Farminson.

Sparrow nodded. "I had confidence in my abilities to defend myself, and more than that I knew my threat was the only way of insuring I'd know Isosceles had been activated well before the triangle of attacks was launched. How? They'd have to kill me to insure my silence. So I set a trap with myself as bait. It was sprung with an attack on my kibbutz two days after the massacre in Virginia."

"Obviously, though, Isosceles wasn't launched in the massacre's wake," noted the President.

"Because alone it wasn't enough to justify activating the project. More was needed. The bombing in that home for the aged. The airport explosion yesterday.

Small fuses leading to a major trigger."

"The Academy Awards six days from now," muttered Paul Quinn.

"The timing would be perfect," added Sparrow.

"Why?" from the President.

"Because an open terrorist conference has been scheduled in Paris for April twenty-second. I'd guess, gentlemen, that an attack on that conference is one of the three legs of Isosceles."

"Then our strategy is obvious," the President said, with conviction. "We'll cancel the damn awards. Make up an excuse. Maybe we can arrange to have somebody else go on strike for a while."

"I don't think that's the answer," argued Sparrow. "Not at all, because we have to face the fact that if we take the Oscars away from them, Lucifer will find another rationale for launching Isosceles—another trigger. We might buy ourselves time but we'd lose everything else, considering we might never discover what their new trigger is. We're not dealing with ordinary terrorists here. We're dealing with an enormous international organization."

"Who have put a murdering psychopath atop their operation," added Thames Farminson. "Renaldo Black."

"Don't underestimate him," Sparrow advised. "He's the best in the world at what he does. God knows that must have been the reason Lucifer recruited him."

"Why not just use their own people from the start?"

"Because the cover had to be perfect, and it would have been if that Major Bathgate of yours hadn't caught wind of what was going on. The plan was to have no Lucifer operative contribute anything to this phase of the operation. The director and the board of controllers would be the only ones needed to coordinate matters, and the rest would be left to Black. That way, the organization's credibility would be maintained. Lucifer would come out of this whole thing smelling like a rose with their nose high, ready to avenge the horrible tragedy."

"But Lucifer did sanction three members of the hit team used in Bloody Saturday," Farminson pointed out.

"Who had absolutely no idea they were actually working for the people that ended up killing them. Black made all the arrangements. Then, it's my guess the Lucifer hierarchy provided him with enough information to stay clear of the dragnet that covered three of the men he had retained. A perfect formula, really. With them out of the way, Black and Lafontaine remained the only link with what was truly going on."

"What if Lucifer knows we're onto them?" asked the President. "What if they know we're aware of their plan to use the Academy Awards as a trigger?"

"One does not necessarily imply the other. Undoubtedly they know we're onto them, because there's no escaping the fact that they're aware Lennagin reached the FBI. But they have no way of knowing how much information the boy possessed and passed on. He slipped from their grasp in Providence, and the contents of that disappearing envelope Bathgate gave him remained a mystery. So they can't be sure we know about the Oscar ceremony, and even if they did, it might not change things. We won't be facing machine guns or grenades in Los Angeles." Sparrow swung to his right. "Mr. Farminson, what did your analysis show of the bomb at Washington National?"

"An extremely volatile plastic explosive."

"Prometheus, to be exact, and nearly one hundred fifty pounds of it are still unaccounted for."

"My God," muttered General MaCammon, the only other man in the room familiar with Prometheus. "How can you be sure?"

"I'm not. But one hundred fifty pounds was smuggled out of France last week and the supplier has disappeared. It adds up."

"What exactly are Prometheus plastic explosives?" asked the President.

"Why don't we let General MaCammon answer that?"

"Per ounce, the most potent explosives of their kind known to man," MaCammon responded after a barely perceptible pause. "It was developed by the Cambodians, interestingly, during their latest escapade in Vietnam. Not nearly as dangerous as other *plastique* to work with. It can be molded into any shape, tempered to any consistency, and coated with any paint or finish without losing any of its potency. It can be set off by time trigger, heat trigger, any trigger imaginable. And a hundred fifty pounds properly placed, well . . ."

"Go on, General."

"A hundred fifty pounds properly placed could level a city block."

"The Los Angeles Music Center where the Oscars are going to be held is less than the size of an average city block," noted Farminson.

Silence filled the room, broken finally by the President. "And that's what Lucifer's going to be using?"

"Through Black, of course," said Sparrow.

"I must say, gentlemen, I'm beginning to lean toward postponement even more strongly."

"Then the explosives will be used someplace else and

we won't have the advantage of knowing when or where," countered Sparrow.

"All the same, there will be three thousand people in that building on Oscar night. You can't expect me to use them all as bait."

"To prevent Isosceles from being launched, I'm afraid I do."

"What do you suppose their strategy will be?" Farminson asked Sparrow.

"To begin with, they'll use as few people as possible —Black himself and maybe a couple others. The *plastique* will have already been molded into the proper shape and will be present inside the building, conceivably in plain view. I'd guess the trigger will run off some type of sensor, either microwave or ultrasonic, to be activated by one or two hand-held detonators, and Black will undoubtedly have one of these."

"You seem to know Renaldo Black quite well," said Triesdale.

"I understand him, if that's what you mean. To continue, the explosives will be set off at a predetermined time during the awards ceremony, with no warning whatsoever. People within a square mile in any direction will feel like a nuclear bomb or an earthquake has struck the city."

Paul Quinn leaned forward. "Mr. President, if I may . . ."

"Please, Paul."

"Sir, it seems to me our strategy is obvious. We let the Oscars go on as planned so that Lucifer will follow through with their attack. I'm assuming here that whatever they mold the plastics into will have to be inside the building well in advance. So everything with the awards goes as scheduled . . . until the first limousine arrives. Then we cancel the whole event on the assumption that Lucifer has committed themselves, in that they've more or less handed the explosives over to us."

"A worthy proposal, Mr. Quinn," Sparrow complimented him, "except that you're placing too much emphasis on the explosives themselves; Lucifer can always get more of those. It's Black we should concentrate on. He's the key and he *will* be there, but not if we cancel the Oscars at *any* time. If we get him, we destroy Isosceles. Lucifer wouldn't risk trying to find a replacement or triggering it on their own. It defeats their purpose. It's Black's expertise in terror that's taken them this far, and if we get him it'll be as far as they go."

"And while we search the building, a hundred fifty pounds of Prometheus explosives just might go off," mulled the President.

"That's a chance we'll have to take."

"You mean I'll have to take, don't you? This whole mess is going to fall on my shoulders one way or another. We're talking about three thousand people who control one of the most powerful industries in the country, not to mention the percentage of these whose faces get plastered across magazine covers on a regular basis. Lucifer picked the right target, that much is for sure. Americans worship entertainers and spend two billion dollars a year at the movies. Ninety million of them will be watching the Academy Awards on live prime-time television. Hollywood is something that touches everyone's life. A terrorist attack at the Oscars would be the greatest disaster in our history. The outcry would be loud enough to shatter glass in the White House. They'll want to hang me from the Washington Monument, and they'll have every right to."

"And if we let the trigger slip from our grasp and sometime in the next six months Isosceles is launched, where will they want to hang you from then? You see, we can't take that chance. Those missing jets of yours give Lucifer the trump card it needs. With F-16s in their possession, limitations that might have otherwise applied are lifted. Lucifer no longer has to worry about distance between targets and launching points. The quick-strike concept can achieve maximum efficiency. The three legs of the triangle can work independently of each other yet simultaneously. Target choice is expanded. Options are considered that ordinarily would be out of the question."

"Target options?"

Sparrow nodded. "Including my first choice when Isosceles was initially conceived, ruled out because of tactical implausibilities no longer present." He paused. "The North Schwerin region of the Soviet Union—the center for international terrorist training, planning, and expansion; the home of Department V."

"Russia?" blared the President. "Lucifer is planning to attack Russia?"

"That is now certainly within their reach, yes."

"But the repercussions from even the kind of minor, conventional strike we're talking about will be severe. All of Europe will be thrown into jeopardy."

"Triple jeopardy. Isosceles has three legs."

"Even so, the Russian limb is all they need. The whole world will be plunged into chaos."

"That might be exactly what they want. Imagine the

power an organization like Lucifer would have in a world of total chaos."

"I'd rather not. . . ."

"The alternative," Sparrow went on, "is to find those planes, or at the very least neutralize Black at the Oscars."

"I think I can be of some help there," began Thames Farminson. "I can have teams of agents monitor the Los Angeles Music Center twenty-four hours a day. That way, we'll be there when Lucifer delivers the explosives. We'll be able to get them out *and* let the ceremony go on as planned."

"Unless Lucifer or Black realizes their moves are being monitored," the President pointed out.

"I'll make sure they don't," Farminson promised. "We'll use strictly our top people, maybe even borrow a few from Bart here."

"And finding Dan Lennagin might not be a bad idea while you're at it," Sparrow suggested.

"The President swung toward Quinn. "Paul?"

"Our efforts in that respect aren't proceeding very well, sir. We came up empty in Zurich. However, an arms dealer Lennagin read about in Bathgate's file has been killed."

"Are you implying that Lennagin is now a murderer?"

"Not at all. But he might be traveling with someone who is and not realize it."

"Explain."

"The thing of it is that Lennagin has left bodies wherever he's been, three to be exact. The killing of that arms dealer named Lutz was crass and amateurish, but the other two were different matters entirely. A body was found inside a Providence bus station repair garage an hour after the boy left for Logan Airport— a known Lucifer operative who had the misfortune of having a stiletto driven through his heart. Remarkable shot for a boy whose file lists no prior experience with any weapon of the sort. A second body turned up on the plane he took to Washington. Natural causes were suspected at first, but a detailed autopsy turned up a small pinprick evidently made by some kind of syringe at the base of the neck. The residue of a fast-acting poison was found in the man's system. Another known Lucifer operative."

"You're not saying Lennagin killed these two agents?"

"More likely they were planning to kill him, sir. Somebody stopped them—permanently. And whoever he is, he's damned good."

"You think the boy's traveling with him?"

"One way or another. He just might not be aware of it. But whoever this phantom is, he seems determined to keep the boy alive, which is all well and good for us considering we can't even find him."

"Hmmmmmm," from the President.

Sparrow leaned forward. "If Mr. Quinn's assumptions are correct, this phantom must have a very good reason for its actions. Whoever this person is, he or she doesn't work for you or for Lucifer, which means a third party must be involved with a stake in the Isosceles Project themselves and, in some respects, they're working on our side. But for an unknown reason they remain in the shadows, probably using Lennagin to do their bidding, which means he's important to them, which makes him important to us.

That makes it all the more imperative that we find him."

Here, Paul Quinn flapped a travel packet in the air. "I leave for Zurich this afternoon to pick up his trail. It's as good a place to start as any. I'll find him," he added determinedly.

The President sighed. "Paul, I'm still not convinced you're the right man for the job."

"I'm the *only* man for the job."

"Except you've got no field experience."

Quinn had started to object when Sparrow's voice drowned him out. "Let's send Felix with him. He knows the field better than anyone."

"And I know Lennagin," Quinn followed, grateful.

"Your man wouldn't object?" the President asked Sparrow.

"On the contrary, he'd welcome the opportunity. I'm afraid he hasn't taken an immediate liking to your country."

The President nodded. "Well, I have to admit that if anyone can insure Quinn's safety, it's that giant. And I would like to have Lennagin brought in at all reasonable costs *without* involving anyone else directly. The boy might be the only person outside this room who can help us unravel this mess."

"There's another," said Sparrow. "The head of Lucifer."

Bart Triesdale would have chuckled if he remembered how. "Except his identity might as well be insured by Lloyds of London."

"I still have contacts in Lucifer. I still know the right buttons to push, calls to make." The end of Sparrow's words trailed off to a sigh. Fatigue and pressure swept across his face. He looked profoundly weary.

"I'd recommend resting up before you start," the President suggested.

"I plan to." Sparrow's gaze was empty, far away. "But I have family here in Washington. I think it's time I paid them a visit."

TWENTY-FIVE

Renaldo Black was not a happy man. A perfect plan
had gone to waste in Washington. He had been beaten
by bad luck, nothing more. Sparrow had come out of
the explosion unharmed.

Sparrow, the famous Israeli terrorist hunter, the
Lion of the Night, was after him. Something had
passed between them and Black couldn't fathom what
it might be. He had seen rage blazing from the old
man's eyes at the airport, the rage of vengeance, which
told him Sparrow meant to kill him at all costs. Simply
stated, he had to kill the Lion of the Night first. It
shouldn't be hard, by all rights. Sparrow was nearing
sixty, with a bad leg to boot. But Black knew neither of
these amounted to much when it came to a death
match. The motions of the body were nothing compared to those of the mind, and here Sparrow was as
quick and sharp as anyone. Black had seldom been
graced with so worthy a challenge. He was already
looking forward to returning to it from four thousand
miles away in Spain.

It was hot in Madrid and he cursed himself for
choosing a taxi that lacked air-conditioning. Open
windows did little to quell the heat, especially when

most of the trip from the airport into the city had been spent at a crawl or dead stop.

"Sorry, señor," the driver said repeatedly, fearfully checking his passenger in the rearview mirror. The gesture was unnecessary. People often made unnecessary gestures when around Renaldo Black.

The cab swung a left, then a right. Spanish youngsters were playing ball on the street. The cab slid between them. Black watched their motions, aroused. He'd find himself one after his business here was finished.

The cab drew to a halt outside a small gift shop in Madrid's commercial center. Black paid the driver, entered, and approached the counter.

"May I help—" a female clerk started, stopping when a spark of recognition filled her eyes, becoming a flame. "I'll get Mr. Gaxiola."

Black did not bother to thank her.

"Good to see you again, my friend," bellowed a husky voice before the man attached to it emerged fully from the back room. "Shall we go upstairs?" he asked with a smile.

Black nodded and allowed him to lead the way toward the steps. The second floor of the gift shop served as a safe house for the Spanish wing of the international terrorist network, ETA-Militar. They turned right at the top of the stairs and entered the office of Juan-José Gaxiola, one of its chiefs. Certain matters remained to be finalized. Gaxiola locked the door behind them.

"Your trip was good, *amigo?*" the Spaniard asked. He was a flab-filled man just out of his thirties. His jowls had started to droop and his body was rapidly taking on the shape of a bowling pin.

Black suppressed a sigh. There was no accounting for how people let themselves degenerate. "Good enough," he said simply. "You know why I'm here, of course."

"I can guess, *amigo*. You are here to check up on the Spanish leg of your plan."

"You're right. How goes it?"

"Smooth, *amigo,* very smooth. The jet has been stored at a secret airfield in the northeastern province of Catalonia near the town of Cassa. From that position, it lies a scant seven hundred fifty miles from its target inside France."

"Excellent," grinned Black. "Now go over the plan one more time for me from your end."

Gaxiola seated himself behind his desk. He lit a cigar and shook the match out, not bothering to offer one to the still standing Black because he knew he didn't smoke. "In the early morning hours of next Tuesday, I will receive a call from America with the words 'The trigger has been pulled.' At that point, I will make a call to Catalonia to a pay phone where a man will be waiting and repeat the message for him."

"You know this man?"

"I've worked with him before. Most efficient and reliable."

"He's the only one besides you who knows about the plan?"

Gaxiola pulled the cigar from his mouth, looking shocked. "No, señor, of course not. He knows only *his part* of the plan. The rest does not concern him. He knows only what he has to. But, yes, he is the only besides myself who knows anything."

"And what do you know?"

"Only what you have told me. The plan is brilliant. ETA-Militar is proud to be a part of it."

"But only through you."

"Just as you requested, Señor Black, yes."

"You alone can contact the man in Catalonia."

"Yes. For security reasons, I have elected not to choose a backup."

Black nodded, apparently pleased. "Your precautions impress me. Still, we must arrange for a backup in the event that you die before Tuesday."

Gaxiola laughed. "I plan to be bursting with life on the appointed day."

"Death sometimes comes at the least expected times."

Gaxiola's expression dulled and sombered. "You want me to choose someone?"

"I'll handle it from my end. That way, you won't have to worry. The responsibility is mine."

"I appreciate that, *amigo.*" Gaxiola rested his cigar on the sill of the ashtray and pulled a black book from his top desk drawer. "I'll get you the number. The line has been checked and cleared, of course."

"Of course. And I assume the plane's cargo arrived safely."

"Already loaded," said Gaxiola, now with pen in hand.

"You've done well," Black told him.

"The cause suits me." He finished writing the number and ripped the page off his pad. "There." He started to hand it across the desk to Black with a friendly smile.

"Death sometimes comes at the least expected times," the blond man said.

It was then that Gaxiola saw the pistol in Black's hand. He was still smiling when the muzzle erupted.

Black stayed in Spain only long enough to make two phone calls, the first to Munich.

"Hello," from a woman.

"I will hold off saying it's good to hear your voice, Gabriele, till I hear what that voice has to tell me."

"The news is not good on either count. To begin with, Lennagin knows about Code Oscar."

"He knows what it is?"

"Not specifically. But he relayed it along with a phrase linking it to Isosceles to the FBI. Certainly they have figured it out by now."

"Perhaps," said Black diffidently.

"And of course the fact that Lucifer is behind everything must be obvious to them as well."

"Which matters not in the least to us."

Gabriele hesitated. Her report should have bothered Black but it didn't. His tone was indifferent, cagey. Why?

"What of Lennagin's guardian angel?" he asked her.

"I've felt his presence since I linked up with the boy in Zurich. I'm certain he's still around."

"But you haven't seen him."

"It doesn't matter."

"You're right. It doesn't matter because he can no longer do us any harm and neither can Lennagin."

"I—I don't understand."

"Nor should you. The mission has entered its second phase. It is time for Lennagin's guardian angel to watch him die."

"But I haven't learned everything yet," Gabriele

protested, searching for a way to keep the boy alive.

"You've learned enough. His execution will take place tonight outside Der Vergnügen as planned. I will meet you inside an hour after. Your role in the murder is as follows. . . ."

When he finished explaining the plan to her, Black hung up immediately and dialed an American exchange. A series of beeps sounded, after which he held a small cylindrical object against the receiver and pressed out a similar series. His call would now be routed in America through an untraceable exchange. The man he spoke to would have no idea he was actually calling from Spain.

"Yes," responded the man from Houston.

"This is Black."

"What is your report?"

"Lennagin relayed nothing that can harm us to the FBI. The trigger is safe."

"Then Code Oscar is a definite go."

"The Americans are still in the dark about its existence. The explosives are in Los Angeles and will be in place on schedule."

"Very good."

"I'm running a check now on all launching points of the F-16s to assure maximum efficiency. No problems yet."

"Get back to me when you're finished."

"My pleasure," said Black.

"Please sit down," said the President.

Sparrow did, facing him.

"I didn't ask you to come here for a social visit."

"I know."

The President hesitated. "I had you followed after our meeting this afternoon broke up. That means I know where you went . . . and why you've really come here."

"I want Black."

The President said nothing.

"And when this matter is resolved, I expect you to give him to me no matter the cost."

"I can't promise that."

"I suggest you do. You need me and I want Black. A fair trade, wouldn't you say?"

"Only you have nothing else to offer from your end."

Sparrow held his next words back briefly to heighten their effect. "Except the head of Lucifer. I've known who he is all along."

"Still the Lion of the Night, aren't you?"

Sparrow's gaze was distant. "But the night's gotten darker."

TWENTY-SIX

The wind was blowing chill and damp air from the sea over the Reeperbahn in the St. Pauli quarter of Hamburg, the city's red-light district. The night was cold and crisp, and the two figures huddled at the alley front had to blow onto their hands to keep the circulation going for want of gloves. Around them the city of sin was bursting with its forbidden pleasures. They stood at the edge of the Herbertstrasse, a pedestrian-only mall presently lined with prostitutes displaying their wares through flimsy or skin-tight clothes that concealed nothing. Men or women, boys or girls, all were available on the Reeperbahn for a price, and a not too exorbitant one at that. Gluts of human meat kept the costs down. Often supply would dwindle slightly when a woman, girl, or boy left with a mark and was not seen again until their body was pulled from the Elbe. It made little difference. The glut remained.

The brilliantly lighted bars and clubs sat on the main drag of the Reeperbahn directly in front of the two figures in the alley. One of these—the largest, in fact—commanded their attention: Der Vergnügen, its name showcased in huge, blood-red letters.

Fitting, thought Dan Lennagin.

Gabriele Lafontaine wasn't thinking of the letters at all or of the fact that in English Der Vergnügen meant "the pleasure." She checked her watch: eight fifty-five. In five minutes a black car would appear at the head of the street just within her line of sight. It would flash its lights. She would lure Lennagin out from cover and keep him there as it edged near. The windows would open, black barrels emerging from the shadows, unseeable to anyone not looking for them. The boy would not be looking.

Eight fifty-six . . .

"When we going in?" he asked her.

"Soon. When it fills up a little more. Patience, college boy." Her guise of Jill Levine was wearing thin. She hoped he wouldn't notice. She hated Jill Levine almost as much as she hated herself.

Eight fifty-seven . . .

The boy had made her see so much in herself these past few days. It was easy to kill from a distance, either physical or emotional. It was much harder from this close. She knew she didn't love Dan Lennagin because she wasn't capable of loving anyone. That ability had been burned out of her long ago when all those she had loved had been killed and she had embarked on her present path.

Eight fifty-eight . . .

But Dan Lennagin wasn't a politician or a capitalist or a symbol of tyranny for the oppressed. He was just a person who'd been tossed into an arena with walls of death closing in around him. He didn't understand the forces he was fighting or those he was indirectly working for. Just a person. . . . His death was senseless. At least the others she'd participated in over the years had had meaning, purpose. Or at least the lie had come easier back then. Symbols were easy to slay. They bled when you shot or knifed them but their blood was cold and lifeless even before it spilled. People were different.

Eight fifty-nine . . .

Things suddenly seemed so complicated in her life. Where once order had resided, chaos was taking over, all because of this boy she had to kill. There was no choice, just as for her there never had been. She was committed.

Nine . . .

Up ahead to her right a traffic light glowed red. A black car in the lead of the approaching bunch flashed its lights. The pole lamp changed to green. The black car edged forward, stopped to allow a car taking a left to swing in front of it, then started again. Seventy yards away. Windows closed.

"We better get going," she said to Dan.

"Three minutes ago it was too soon."

"I get impatient too, college boy. There's just the right number of people inside for cover." She bit her lip, forced back the empty feeling pressing to enter.

The black car rolled on. It was less than fifty yards away now, windows opening.

The two shapes emerged from the alley, one an extension of the other. Gabriele looked at the car, then back at Dan. His eyes were glued to Der Vergnügen. The kill would be fast and easy. Black would be pleased.

The empty feeling found her stomach, held it in a chain-mail grip, a reminder of the misery behind and ahead.

The black car was twenty-five yards away, windows opened all the way. Barrels rested on the sills, shadowy figures behind them.

Dan Lennagin was moving across the street into their path. Gabriele lagged one step behind and then another. The bullets were not hers. A dive to the ground, a flash of fire, the car would pick her up and it would be over. So easy. So simple and uncomplicated. Just get out of the way and let it happen.

The car was close enough to spit on when she leaped, the timing of the move as perfect as it could have been. But her fall found flesh, not pavement, which surprised her as much as it did the men in the car. They fired, but hitting a diving figure from a moving car is nearly impossible for even the best marksman.

Dan Lennagin felt her crash hard into him and take him with her to the ground. A series of soft spits followed, and chewed-up tar coughed into his face. He was stunned and scraped. No bullets, though, had found him.

The black car sped away.

Gabriele Lafontaine helped him to his feet. "Welcoming committee," she said, because that was the way Jill Levine would have put it.

"I'll say," came the shaken mutter from beside her.

But it had not been Jill Levine who'd saved the boy's life. It had been Gabriele Lafontaine, the action unconscious and irresistible. She had saved a life that for no good reason was about to be taken.

The men in the car, though, wouldn't see it that way. They would make out a report detailing her actions. Cries of shock would follow, but not for long. Her actions dictated theirs. They had no choice, just as she hadn't. A chance leap that took place within a fraction of a second had changed everything in her life. She had broken one commitment while finding another, far more perilous one. The machine in her switched off. She had acted independently of the action they had imposed on her. It felt good, refreshing in a clean sort of way, though she didn't expect the feeling to last very long.

Dan felt the change in her but couldn't grasp it. He steadied himself and she smiled at him. Her eyes betrayed the change, warm for the first time, but somehow dull.

"They know we're here," he said flatly.

"We better get inside."

And together they walked across the street toward Der Vergnügen.

Once inside, the next order of business was to get upstairs.

They stood in an anteroom waiting for someone to lead them to a table in the smoke-filled bar. It was about half-full, mostly couples who had come together only after entering separately. There was music but it was soft and from their position virtually indiscernible. The lounge area looked distinctly smaller than it did from the outside, an illusion really, because the floor was partitioned into several different rooms, each a step higher than the one before it. You worked your way up, in a manner of speaking.

To the far left of the main room stood a door painted the same scarlet color as the showcase front. Black letters spelling out the word "lounge" in English and German jumped from it, signaling the entrance to the downstairs area, something there for everyone.

After a few minutes of standing, they realized that no one was going to seat them and chose a table by themselves. Flimsily dressed waitresses glided across the room with drink trays balanced in their hands. None stopped at the table where the strangely dressed young man and woman had sat down.

Dan looked around him. "The office section must be up there." His eyes pointed to a flight of carpeted stairs all but hidden in an alcove situated in the room's far right corner. A man stood subserviently at the bottom, arms crossed, fronted by the same kind of velvet fence ushers hide behind in cinemas. "That's where I have to go."

"And how do you plan to get by the guy with the swivel jaw?" she challenged.

"I plan to be escorted up by the manager. I'm here to purchase merchandise, remember?"

"Slipped my mind. Anyway, I thought we were in this together. All of a sudden, though, you're making all the decisions."

"And all of a sudden, you're the voice of diplomacy." He looked at her calmly. "I can take care of myself."

"That's what you keep telling me."

"Any better ideas?"

"Yeah. If we're lucky enough to get the manager over here, let me do the talking."

Dan shook his head. "Won't work."

"Enlighten me, college boy."

"Look around you, Jill. The women in this room haven't got brains anywhere else but below the neck. They're whores and that's probably putting it nicely. They smile, dance, and screw, not necessarily in that order. The manager won't like hearing anything from a woman, never mind doing business with one."

"So I just sit here and smile."

"Dancing and screwing might be overdoing it a bit."

His eyes darted beyond their table. "Unless you want to check out the other rooms."

"No thanks. I'd rather watch you try and talk your way upstairs. Entertainmentwise, it should be better."

"It's a start."

"Sure."

When the waitress finally came over, Dan slid a twenty mark note into her hand and asked her to get the manager. Gabriele watched his motions with refined interest. They were steady, unhesitant. The boy was learning, which made her feel sad for him. There were some lessons that never went away. She had learned them all and he was picking up many. She looked across the table and grasped his eyes. They were cold and hard, reminding her of the eyes she saw every time she faced a mirror.

The manager appeared at the table. "Something I can do for you?" he asked in poor, German-dominated English.

"Maybe," Dan said, pulling out the extra chair and offering it toward him. "And maybe there's something I can do for you."

"Like what?" the manager asked suspiciously. He was a heavy-set man with a poorly fitting toupée that shone in the dim light.

"I make movies," Dan told him.

"That is supposed to interest me?"

"I'm looking for Wolfgang Bauer. I understand he represents the kind of actors I require."

"I know no one by that name."

Dan leaned closer to the toupéed man and lowered his voice. "Let me explain. The kind of movies I make aren't shown in theaters. They're sold privately for great sums of money to people whose cinematic interests are a bit hard to meet. The actors are very seldom around to do sequels. Strictly one-option deals, so the money their agent receives for their services is expectedly high. Half for their skin and half to keep his mouth shut. Am I making myself clear?"

"That depends."

"On what?"

"On what person in your industry gave you the name of this Wolfgang Bauer."

"Stettner Lutz." Dan watched Jill cringe at mention of the dead man's name.

The manager's eyebrows flickered. His toupée hugged his scalp like a cap. "Dead contacts are, of course, difficult to check."

"I was afraid Wolfgang might meet a similar fate before we had a chance to do business. That's why I made my move now."

The manager thought for a few moments. "I know no man named Bauer, but there is someone else I know who might be willing to do business with you. But he's very expensive."

"It's all deductible."

The manager eyed him strangely. "He might be willing to see you."

"What does it depend on?"

"A healthy word from me would go a long way."

"What's the going rate on your word?"

"Five hundred marks."

Dan dug into his pocket and came out with the bills. Surprise covered the manager's face. "Expected me to talk you down, didn't you?" Dan asked him. "Why bother? Money isn't the problem. My clients pay very well for the pictures I film for them. You and I, we're both middlemen. Middlemen must look out for each other."

The manager smiled and edged the five hundred marks into his jacket pocket. "I'll see what I can do."

He left the table and moved toward the forbidden alcove, greeted the guard perfunctorily, and disappeared up the stairs.

"Not bad, eh?"

"Think you're fooling them, college boy?" Gabriele asked.

"Any reason why I shouldn't?"

"'Bout a thousand, not the least of which is that they could be fooling you at the same time, and they make a living at it."

"How will I know?"

"You won't. Baader-Meinhof is famous for a bullet in the back of the head."

Dan leaned back uneasily. "Maybe I should take your pistol."

"Ever shoot one before?"

"My brother's a cop back home. I've been to the range a few times."

"People are a little different than cardboard. Besides, they'll search you before you get in to see Bauer. A gun might make them nervous."

"I get the point."

"Then get this, college boy. If I get the feeling anything's wrong, I'll come running. We'll be okay so long as there aren't more than six of the bad guys. I don't fancy the idea of having to reload."

The toupéed manager returned to their table. A taller man with a pencil-thin head and thick sideburns stood by his side. "This is Hoffer. He will see you upstairs. I will keep your woman company while you speak to my employer."

The manager smiled, his message obvious. Jill was a hostage. If anything went wrong upstairs, she would die. Dan rose unhesitantly, not worried. She could take care of herself, he thought. At that moment, Gabriele was wondering whether the same could be said for him.

The tall guard led Dan up the stairs. The fact that he was positioned behind the bigger man made him breathe more easily. A man can do extraordinarily little to you from the front. From behind, his options are limitless.

On the second floor, they walked slowly down a plushly padded hallway in direct contrast to the unfinished shabbiness of the lower level. The people of Baader-Meinhof obviously knew how to take care of themselves. They approached a door that had three locks on it, while all the others possessed but one. Dan gave in to instinct and stopped at it. The gap widened between him and Hoffer. His fingers found the knob at the very instant the bigger man whirled and lunged in the same rapid motion, lacing his fingers around Dan's wrist. The grasp struck a pressure point. Dan shrank away, his whole arm trembling under the grip.

"If this was your throat, you'd be dead already," the guard assured him. "Keep your hands away from places they don't belong."

Dan said nothing. They walked on, side by side now. The bigger man's eyes never left him. The element of trust was gone, sacrificed. It had been worth it, for he'd found the room he wanted and his fingers had been on the knob long enough to determine that, incredibly, it was unlocked.

The guard opened the door to a small office down

the hall and around one corner. He beckoned Dan to enter, watched him doubtfully for a moment, and then searched him thoroughly. Gabriele had been right. Dan felt certain that if he'd taken a gun, Hoffer would have killed him there and then.

"Herr Bauer will be with you shortly," he said and the door shut behind him.

Dan listened for a click. There was none. Hoffer hadn't locked him in. He put his ear against the wood and strained to hear footsteps. If there were any, they escaped him. But the door was thick and hard. Hoffer might have walked away without Dan's picking up the sound of his soles striking the thick carpet. Then again, he could be waiting right outside the door or down the hall a bit, anticipating Dan's emergence, in which case he'd have reason to spring his awesome grip into use again. Dan pushed that thought aside, knowing he had come too far to turn back now or not go on.

He lowered his hand to the knob and started to turn, keeping his ear pinned to the wood, though it clearly did him no good. The catch gave. He pushed the door slowly open, careful not to let the hinges squeak. His heart raced against the possibility that the grinning face of the powerful German would be there when he slipped through.

It wasn't. Dan closed the door as softly as he had opened it, heard a click and returned his hand to the knob. It wouldn't budge. Somehow he had locked it. There could be no turning back now. Stealthily, he glided down fifteen feet of carpet to the edge of the corridor, pressed his back against the wallpaper and tried desperately to become a part of it. Because he heard footsteps. Heavy yet soft with a slight squeak added for measure. Hoffer's footsteps. . . .

They seemed to be moving toward and away from him at the same time, the carpet distorting their direction. They grew louder, coming toward him, surely. He lowered his hands to his sides and prepared himself to leap when Hoffer turned the corner. On equal terms he knew he was no match for the bigger man, but if he could take him by surprise. . . . Hoffer's rhythmic footsteps scraped still closer. Dan held his breath, melted into the wall.

"Hoffer!" came a voice from the bottom of the stairs.

The footsteps stopped, turned, headed away. Dan's breath left him in a soft rush. He struggled to get it back. Where there had been little time, there was now none. Hoffer would be back and soon. He'd check the office where he'd left Dan and, finding it empty, would go immediately to the triple-lock door. That fact quickened Dan's strategy but didn't alter it. He *had* to get inside that room, though he was totally uncertain of what he might find. This was a safe house for Baader-Meinhof. Its leader was linked to Renaldo Black and thus perhaps to Isosceles. Inside the room might be nothing or anything. He had to check. His instinct told him to and instinct was all he had left. Escape would follow through a yet undetermined route. As for Jill, well, he'd cross that bridge when he came to it unless it was blown out from under him.

Dan's eyes led him around the corner and he shuffled quickly to the triple-lock door, then was inside with little pause for precaution and no eye toward the stairs.

The room was large, at least twice the size of the one Hoffer had put him in. Maps covered the walls, mostly of selected areas of Germany. Parts were outlined in red or black, dates penciled nearby—all in the future.

This was more than a safe house, it was a planning center.

Dan crept over a worn patch of the same color carpet that covered the corridor toward a large wood desk with a single chair in front of it. There were numerous other chairs in the room, as well as three folding steel tables cluttered with papers. Only the chair before the desk, though, had arms and a leather hide.

Dan reached the desk and saw the blotter had been obliterated by a map that at one time or another had hung on the wall, judging by the holes in each corner made by tacks or nails. The map was of northern West Germany and was dominated by the North Sea and dotted by a chain of islands called the East Frisians. One of these, the furthest east almost directly above the city of Wilhelmshaven, had a black cross on it. Dan looked closer. It wasn't a cross at all, but a triangle.

An isosceles triangle!

Dan felt a tremor pass through him. For the first time since he'd embarked on this desperate trek, he had found a link to the Isosceles Project—an island in the North Sea. What did it mean? Something that would lead him to the other two legs perhaps, the island in the East Frisian chain being the first. He moved behind the desk and began to rummage around.

He heard the voices an instant before the footsteps. His initial thought was of Hoffer, but the footsteps grazed the carpet comfortably, more than one set, and the voices were soft, muted. Of course! The door had been unlocked because someone had vacated the room only for a few moments.

Dan remembered a closet in the back of the room and rushed toward it, pulling the knob behind him just as the triple-lock door swung open. The two sets of feet scraped across the rug, the voices temporarily silent. Dan shrank back against the wall of coats he found himself near, fearful one of the intruders would open the closet to withdraw or deposit something. But the footsteps moved away in the direction of the desk. He breathed easier, but not much, and would have preferred not to breathe at all.

"I hope coming up the back way was not inconvenient for you," one said to the other.

"I appreciate the precaution, Herr Bauer," the other returned. "It is not a convenient time for me to be recognized by anyone."

"Is it ever?"

"Especially not in Germany. You forget perhaps that this is my home country, though never my home."

The voice was cold and chillingly even, precise. Every syllable fit where it belonged. One word blended easily into the next, like the text of a prepared speech. Dan's spine quivered, though it wasn't the voice that did it. He was remembering something from Bathgate's envelope.

"So I've heard," Bauer was saying. "Come to check up on me?"

"Confirm," the smooth voice assured him, "not check up."

"It amounts to much the same thing."

"Not with me."

"I've heard that too, Herr Black."

Dan lost his breath in surprise and had to fight to regain it. Renaldo Black! The man he sought was standing in this very room, not twenty feet away! Bathgate's file had mentioned he was of German extraction. Now only a closed door separated them.

288

Dan moved his hand to the knob. But his fingers were shaking too much to grasp anything, and he had to ask himself why he'd bothered reaching for it in the first place. Black was undoubtedly armed, while he wasn't. Lennagin settled himself in the closet and strained to listen.

"Where is the jet?" Black asked.

"Here," replied Bauer, and Dan imagined his index finger landing on the island in the North Sea, the one marked with the Isosceles triangle. "We maintain an airstrip on the island that none of the authorities know about. Until now, we've only used it to transport equipment and personnel, but I'm sure it will more than do for your needs. The runway is well paved and plenty long."

"And the cargo?"

"Already loaded as per your instructions. I must ask, though—"

"You must ask nothing."

Bauer mumbled something Dan couldn't decipher.

"Repeat the itinerary for me one more time," Black told him.

"This meeting could just as easily have been conducted over the phone," Bauer said suspiciously.

"An operation of this magnitude requires a more personal touch, don't you agree?"

"Perhaps."

"Then would you be so kind, now that we are face to face, to dictate the itinerary."

Bauer was silent for a moment. Then, "At approximately eight next Tuesday morning, I will receive a call from a man who will utter the words 'The trigger has been pulled.' I will then immediately call my man on the island and repeat the message for him. The jet will be in the air just a few hours later toward its target, the choice of which I must—"

Bauer cut his own words off. Black had said nothing to make him. Dan remembered the terrorist's picture from Bathgate's file, recalled he didn't have to speak to make a point. Lennagin pressed his ear closer against the closet door. Isosceles was being revealed to him. A hidden jet ready to launch toward a secret target after a code was given. But that was only one leg. What about the other two? He could only hope Black would mention them.

"Who is your backup?" Black asked.

"I was not authorized to have one."

"You are now. Give me the number of the man on the island."

"Do you think that's . . . necessary?"

"If you are unable to make the call on Tuesday morning for whatever reason, where would that leave us?"

"I understand."

Silence filled the room. Dan used the time to contemplate what his next move should be. He thought of Hoffer. Minutes had passed since the call had come for him from the bottom of the stairs. If he still intended to check the room where he had left Dan, he would sooner or later end up here. The door was locked now, his employer busy inside. He wouldn't interrupt. He might even think Bauer was in conference with the person he was assigned to watch over. So long as Bauer and Black continued their meeting, Dan decided he had a chance. Black, though, wasn't the kind of man who stayed in one place very long. He would leave. Hoffer would realize the truth. What then? Dan went over the floor plan of the room searching for a possible escape route. There was none. He felt stuffy and confined. The congestion of jackets in the closet made it impossible for him to stand fully erect. His back ached, muscles cramping. If he had to move fast now, the motion might be denied him.

"Here it is," Bauer said and the sound of paper being torn across a pad followed his words. "The number but not the name of the man."

A pause followed, long enough for Black to reach across the desk and accept it. "You've done your job well," he complimented.

"Baader-Meinhof is happy to be of service to you. We trust your operation will end up being of service to us. I look forward to seeing its results."

"Don't look too far. . . ."

"WHA—"

Dan caught the unfinished cry and the spit that followed it. There was a sound of something slipping and a thud when Bauer toppled to the floor. Dan pressed himself back hard against the coats, straightening his spine involuntarily. Jackets plunged to the floor. Hangers plunged after them. The racket stung his ears. He froze, listening for Black's footsteps, fully expecting them to be racing toward the closet. He thought about bursting out now, perhaps taking the terrorist by surprise. His hand felt for the knob, then pulled away quickly.

Because a crashing sound had greeted his ears. It came from the left, the area of the triple-lock door. Another soft spit fluttered through the room followed by the thump of two bodies crunching against each other. Somewhere glass shattered. There were gasps of pain and muted wails.

Hoffer, thought Dan. The pencil-headed guard had

realized his employer was in trouble and had broken in on Black, taking him by surprise. Black had gotten one shot off, no more. Their continuing struggle indicated it had done little damage, if any.

There was no more time to waste. Dan decided to use the fight as an opportunity to escape. Remaining here was ludicrous. He was the prize for the victorious party. Both knew someone was in the closet and neither could let that someone live. He was a witness as well as a trespasser. The winner of the fight would kill him for one reason or the other. He reached for the knob again, started to turn it.

It went nowhere. The door had locked from the outside!

There was a loud bang, seeming to come from far away. A second, then a third. His ears pinned them to the downstairs bar. Jill! The volley of gunfire had to be hers. As of yet, it had not been returned. What was happening? Dan strained his eyes, as though they could show him the scene taking place beyond walls and doors. Frustration gnawed at him, the feeling of being helpless . . . and trapped.

The light sneaking under the closet door dimmed, virtually extinguished. In the room beyond, there was a resounding snap followed almost immediately by a hideous gurgle. A body lurched to the floor. One of the men was dead. But which? He had to get out. But how?

He crashed his shoulder against the closet door. The wood, though, was thick, and even if it hadn't been there was no way he could gather sufficient momentum in the small confines to make so much as a dent in it. His instincts told him the room beyond was empty now, save for the two corpses. That left either Hoffer or Black still alive, but where? No footsteps had passed him. Might the victor be hiding somewhere in the office?

Then there *were* footsteps, not leaving the room but entering it in a rush. They paused briefly, as though to take in the scene, and moved closer to him, just outside the closet door now. The lock was turning. Dan braced himself, forced his body as far back against the jackets as possible, ready to spring when the latch gave.

It did. He hesitated, froze. The door swung open. Dan mounted a charge that got no further than the heart thundering forward in his chest.

Jill Levine stood before him gun in hand, eyes blazing with hot, desperate resolve.

"Let's get the hell out of here!"

TWENTY-SEVEN

She pulled him from the closet.

"Quick! This way!" she managed between heavy breaths. "Follow me!"

Then she moved unexpectedly toward the rear of the office instead of back for the door. Dan had to step over the broken body of Hoffer on the way, his dead eyes staring blankly into space. So Black had been the winner. Bauer's body was face-down on the carpet next to his chair. Black had killed them both.

Dan watched Jill go behind the desk to the wall where a map had been ripped down exposing a section of rich wood paneling. She felt along its edges and pushed. The paneling gave, became a revolving door.

"Come on!" she instructed and Dan followed her through. The hidden door locked back into place.

They found themselves in a damp, musty corridor. The air was stale and thick, drenched in darkness.

"What the hell happened in there?" she demanded, as they felt their way down the blackened corridor that turned and twisted like a funhouse. Their pace was much too fast considering the obstacles. A single slip would send both reeling headlong into a wall, or worse.

"Black killed those two men," Dan muttered.

"Black was there?"

"And he must've gotten out the same way we are. I didn't hear him leave the room."

She hesitated. Dan heard her take a deep breath. "We've got to hurry. They'll find the panel before too long."

"I heard your gun."

She was in the lead, feeling about the walls for direction, pulling Dan along behind her.

"Good ears, college boy. Three bullets. Three kills."

"Why?"

"The manager and his friends heard the noise upstairs. They didn't seem too happy. I figured you were in trouble. I didn't bring the gun with me to keep my pocket warm."

They snailed on. The going became tougher. First there was a steep incline and then a drop-off. They negotiated both with surprising calm, only slightly varying their pace. With light, the trip would've been hard. Without it, it was brutal. There was no end in sight.

"How did you know about the panel?" Dan asked suddenly.

"All terrorist offices have a secret way out, college boy. They aren't the kind of people who trust front doors."

"But you knew exactly where it was. I saw you."

He was pressing her and she knew it. "The map was down. I took a chance."

"You went to it first; no doubt, no hesitation," he persisted.

"You're learning, Lennagin, but not too well. Your instincts got you stuck in a closet. Mine found us a door. Better read some more books."

He was silenced but not for long. He was too damn clever for her to keep this ruse going. She'd have to tell him the truth soon, tell him that Jill Levine had never existed and that Gabriele Lafontaine had been sent here to kill him. He wouldn't understand. How could he be expected to when she didn't understand herself? She might lose him and right now he was the only thing she had. She wished she could see his eyes. They'd tell her what he was thinking. The darkness made it impossible. She saw nothing, felt much. They crawled on.

"I know what Isosceles is," he told her. "Bauer was a part of it. Black killed him."

"Doesn't make much sense."

"I know. But there are planes and targets and secret codes and—"

"Tell me about them later. Right now let's worry about getting out of here."

That matter was suddenly complicated by the sound of shoes racing behind them. They glanced toward the noise, saw brief glimpses of light. Their pursuers hadn't found the light switch either, or perhaps they preferred to leave their quarries in the dark while they followed with flashlights or lanterns. That way they could maintain a distinct edge. The footsteps sounded closer. At least four men were following, with more undoubtedly behind them.

"Run!" Gabriele screamed and let go of Dan's hand.

The darkness swallowed their fleeing figures. Dan dragged his left hand across the wall as guide, keeping pace with her. She moved like a cat in the blackness, graceful and quick, as though she'd traveled these corridors before. His feet gained confidence, starting to lift higher off the ground, strides easier and less taxing.

The confidence betrayed him. He lost concentration for just an instant, which was long enough for him to lose touch with the wall. When he tried to regain the feel, it was gone. His hand clawed the air desperately. His head smashed into a wall and then his knees. He went down stunned, lost, unsure of which direction was correct. The corridor had become a labyrinth. He crawled toward a wall and fought for his bearings. They eluded him. Pencil-thin beams of light found his eyes. He was facing the direction his pursuers were coming from. He turned on his hands and knees and moved away tentatively, each motion a task in itself. His breathing came hard, dismal. He wanted to call for Jill but knew a shout would forfeit his position as well as hers. He struggled to his feet and found the guide wall. More light struck him. Bauer's men were closing. He doubted any of them had known Black had been in the office. They'd think he was the killer of both their employer and Hoffer.

He placed both his hands on the wall and slid along it, as if walking on a ledge. He shuffled his feet, didn't step with them. Bauer's men closed further. Only the curves and corners of the darkened labyrinth were saving him. He looked back at the flickering lights and collided with another wall that rose out of nowhere. He started to go down, righted himself, and found the abutment. He slapped it with both palms, slid deliberately across. His exaggerated motion made it seem endless. Finally he was back in the corridor and a cold hand gripped his arm. He started to scream but a palm covered his mouth.

"Just a little further," Jill told him.

"You shouldn't have come back."

"You're probably right," she said, leading him now.

"But the girl scout in me always wins out."

They reached a protrusion in the darkness, a grayish silhouette cast against the dark shadows. Gabriele led into it with her shoulders. Another hidden door gave. The smell of the city flooded their nostrils. They were moving up a steep incline, almost climbing. There was light up ahead, straining through a series of jagged holes cut out of something above them. They felt like trapped insects, given only a few vents in the top of their jar through which to breathe.

Dan watched Jill reach for a ladder that had appeared before them. She started climbing. He followed.

The secret cover gave easily, lending them passage into a section of Hamburg's sewer. The light, although dim, stung Dan's eyes. He lifted an arm to shield them and withdrew it gradually. Jill was heading for another ladder amidst the dripping filth. The stink forced Dan to hold his breath and pray he could keep down the bile. Traces of the aroma had been present in the escape maze, but it was much stronger here at the source.

Jill went up the second ladder. Dan let his breath out and kept his hands just below her feet. She pried a manhole cover off, exposing the city. Bright lights filtered in. The smell of concrete and exhaust replaced the sewer stink. Horns honked. Tires screeched. Dan pulled himself up the final rungs of the ladder. One last heave and he joined Jill on the pavement. She jammed the manhole cover back into position and moved from the gutter onto the sidewalk. People looked at her and Dan quizzically, shook their heads, and then moved on. This was, after all, the Reeperbahn section of Hamburg. Little came as a surprise, even less as a shock.

Dan wiped the filth and grime from his clothes, hating the gritty sensation passing over his hands. He judged them to be about halfway down the main street, just out of sight of Der Vergnügen, a good quarter-mile from the traffic-free Herbertstrasse. As yet their pursuers had not emerged from below. The jammed cover would hopefully detain them long enough. Dan and Gabriele walked on, keeping a frantic pace through bodies both in motion and stationary.

Suddenly she froze. Dan drew even with her. Directly in front of them, motionless in the bustling crowd, stood a tall blond man with steely eyes. A spark of recognition filled them. His hand went for his pocket.

Renaldo Black! Dan recognized him from the picture in Bathgate's file. There was no mistaking that face. The terrorist's eyes still glowed with recognition. A half-smile crossed his lips. His hand was emerging from his pocket.

Jill Levine made no motion for her gun. Dan spun her around away from Black.

The manhole cover popped off. One hand appeared and then another. Now it was Dan who took the lead, grasping Jill's arm and pulling.

"Come on!"

A body was lifting itself from the sewer. Renaldo Black was moving for them. Something bounced up against the sides of Dan's consciousness and he shoved it aside. He pulled Jill into the center of traffic, adding a third threat to their predicament. Brakes squealed around them. Tires mashed against asphalt. Steel met steel as fenders crumbled.

The traffic flow moving west was easier. They skirted between it without causing a single accident and only a minor squeal or two of brakes.

Behind them, Renaldo Black made use of the confusion by tumbling Bauer's man back down the sewer and resealing the cover, which would trap the rest of the troops long enough to make it impossible for them to give further chase. Black wasted no time and set out for his quarries. Gabriele had deceived him. The boy was supposed to die in Hamburg. He had arranged everything. Yet Lennagin was still alive and Black knew it was because of her. She had not followed his orders. Pity. Now they would both have to die. He could see their fleeing figures sprinting down the sidewalk, heading for the Herbertstrasse. Black ran in their trail.

Dan realized the strategy of running was wrong too late to alter it. They had already risen above the crowd, stood out, and no sense could be made of slowing down now. They ran in single file, strides in perfect rhythm, Gabriele following in the path Dan plowed. His mind had conjured up the shadow of a plan. Reach the Herbertstrasse. That was it. The pedestrian mall was jammed with people buying and selling. It must have been close to eleven o'clock. Peak hours. He ran on, fully aware that Black was gaining, but not daring to slow down enough to check how much.

A hundred yards before the packed Herbertstrasse, Black pulled his pistol, an eight-shot Browning 9-millimeter. He had used one bullet on Bauer and one on his thug, which left him six; more than enough. He held the Browning low by his side as he ran, not caring if anyone noticed and concerned even less about the police. In Hamburg they patrolled the streets with blinders on and arrived purposely late to calls in this district. His work would be finished before they bothered to show up at the scene.

Black quickened his pace, charging through the crowd like a wild stallion. People dived out of his way in fear. Some screamed at the sight of the gun but the screams were lost in the general banter of the mall. Others shrugged off the sight or laughed at it.

His quarries' strategy was suddenly clear to him: Reach the Herbertstrasse and they might be able to disappear into a sea of people. Lennagin would certainly believe they could, even Gabriele perhaps. All the better, Black thought.

They'd be playing right into his hands.

"Give me your gun!" Dan commanded when they reached the mall.

"No!"

"You had a chance to use it back there and you didn't!"

"There were too many people around him."

"Not for you."

"Dan—"

"I don't want explanations, I want the damned gun!"

When she still hesitated, he stripped the thick-barreled magnum from her jacket. She didn't resist. They moved onto the Herbertstrasse and were swallowed by the sea of people around them, absorbed into it. Dan looked back. Black was nowhere to be seen. They moved further into the crowd. Dan stopped, checked the gun.

"You can't go after him," Gabriele pleaded. The guise of Jill Levine slipped and fell. She didn't have the strength to retrieve it. Seeing Black had faced her all at once with the reality of what she had done tonight, what she had committed herself to. There was no going back. One mistake was the same thing as a hundred.

She wanted very much to be the person she had pretended to be for so long. It was so much easier that way. Dan Lennagin had complicated things brilliantly. She should have let him die. It wasn't the same thing as killing him. Yet when it had come down to it, she couldn't kill Black either. Too much a mirror image of herself. Too much like self-destruction.

"Why?" Dan challenged her.

"Because he'll kill you."

"Not if I see him first."

"You won't, Dan. This is his world."

"What happened to 'college boy'?"

"Black wants you to go after him. You'll be playing right into his hands."

"You seem to know him very well."

She ignored the insinuation. "He'll kill you."

"Because you didn't kill him when you had the chance."

He started to move away. Her hand came round in a blur of movement and stung his wrist. The gun went flying, landed yards away, was immediately covered by churning feet.

"Now we have no gun," Dan snapped angrily, eyes ablaze.

"That might be the only thing that keeps you alive."

They were slicing through the crowd together, away from where they thought Black would be. Dan's motions were slow, reluctant. He was uncomfortable with the woman who had saved his life three days before. She had changed, or maybe he had, both perhaps. Their eyes scanned the perimeter. The prostitutes were out in force on the Herbertstrasse, flaunting the law that restricted them to showcasing their wares through windows, since there was no one around to enforce it. Dan and Gabriele moved past a flowing fountain that spilled brownish water in irregular spurts into a wading pool. Young boys with long hair sat on the edge in leather or denim, their pants tight—smiles tighter.

Renaldo Black forced his gaze away from them as he pulled the Browning from his belt and lowered it to his hip. No one noticed the motion and from this position no one would associate him with the shots, either. People expect guns to be held high. Hold them low and you can fire at will.

Black held the Browning low, muzzle pointing up from thigh level. He would shoot Gabriele first. The amateur Lennagin would freeze. The second killing, usually the harder, would come with ease. The two figures kept walking, approaching the fountain. Black adjusted his aim.

He regretted having to kill Gabriele. She had done well for him, provided him with the cover of a constant companion—the greatest camouflage of all in a crowded airport. He'd replace her, as he had replaced others.

He saw the boy's eyes swing about him, watched them find nothing. He stepped up his pace, angled for a clear shot. At last he had it. The girl first.

Black started to squeeze the trigger.

The tip of his finger had just completed its curl when the broad man lurched drunkenly into him, his muttered apology lost in the gun's cry as the bullet tore a harmless path upwards. Black shoved him aside, caught his face and memorized it.

Gray hair and a thick black mustache, somehow familiar. There was no time to give the matter further consideration.

People ahead of him were screaming, running, swallowing his targets. He ran into the mass prying, searching. They were gone. He sped on, neared the fountain. Black thought fast. The crowd had to be scattered. He fired twice, half-randomly. There was a scream and a prostitute went down. One of the boys seated on the pool's edge collapsed into it.

Shrieks and cries filled the Herbertstrasse. People rushed for cover or just rushed. Black flew on, searching for his targets. He couldn't find them amidst the hysteria, not yet, so he ran down the center of the mall, confident they had chosen the same route.

They had. Dan struggled to keep up with Gabriele. His body smashed against a man on his right, then a woman on his left. He slithered and darted at full speed, all the time tensing his muscles against the expected entry of one of Black's bullets. A man with orange hair shoved Gabriele. She stumbled. Dan righted her, helped her on. They had broken out of the pack's mainstream, committed totally to their present direction. There was no place to stop or hide so they just kept going. They were out of Black's sight for the moment and they had to make that moment count.

There was another gunshot and the screaming intensified wildly again, the unfamiliar wail of sirens not far behind.

Doors and lights flew past Dan and Gabriele. Scantily clad prostitutes left their customers to press eager eyes against windows. None undid any bolts. The result was to make the Herbertstrasse seem a hideous tunnel with no escape from either side. There was only forward.

But Black was gaining. Two shots left. All he would need.

Dan glanced to his rear, saw a fissure spreading through the crowd's center as a huge shape barreled on, coming into range. Dan's breath left him, his will following rapidly. He wanted to stop, to tell the girl at his side he was finished and that if Black wanted him he could have him but not without a fight, however futile.

An open door flapping to their right below ground level grabbed his eye and he peeled toward it, Gabriele in tow. They were inside a split second before Black emerged from the crowd, gun raised and ready, aimed at targets no longer there.

TWENTY-EIGHT

Dan closed the door behind them and made sure the latch caught. They were in a darkened cellar lit only by whatever beams could creep through the windows from the mall. It was filthy and dank, littered with crates and old furniture, a small latrine in the rear.

Dan's eyes locked onto Gabriele's. He was across the room in a flash of movement upon her, grasping her shoulders and forcing her against a wall. A sliver of light grabbed her face and illuminated the fear in her eyes.

"It wasn't me he recognized back on the street!" Lennagin charged in a stifled scream. "It was you! Black knew who you were! *He knows you,* goddammit, and I don't!"

"You do!" she insisted.

"Who are you?" He shook her hard. "Tell me who you are!" he demanded loudly, oblivious to the fact that Black could have been right outside the door.

Gabriele said nothing. Dan shook her again, jammed her shoulders against the rotting plaster.

"Come on, Miss Jill Levine, crusader searching for the killers of her parents, tell me about Alexandria, Virginia. Tell me what color hair your brother had. Tell

me what your father's job was with the government.
You can't, can you? Because it's all bullshit! *You're* all
bullshit!"

"No!"

"You had a chance to kill Black back there and you
didn't. You could have used the damn gun you're so
good with *but you didn't!* He knows you and you know
him. You've been in this together against me the whole
time!"

"It's not like that," she sobbed.

"Then tell me what it is like!"

Silence.

Dan slapped her.

More silence.

He slapped her again.

The blows would have been nothing for Gabriele to
deflect. She could disable him easily. The boy's rage
could not match her coldly seasoned training. But she
kept her hands by her sides, as though the pain she felt
with each slap might somehow alleviate the agony that
tore at her insides and ripped them away.

"Who are you?" Lennagin demanded once more.
"How did you know the layout of Der Vergnügen so
well? What happened to cold-as-ice Jill Levine and her
blood quest for the murderers of forty children in
Virginia?"

"I am one of the murderers."

Dan's fingers fell from her shoulders, hung limply in
the air. He looked at her, through her to the wall. His
eyes lost their rage, lost everything. He was a blank, a
portrait outline waiting to be filled in. He backed away
shaking his head slowly, wondering if there were tears
swelling in his eyes or whether he had lost the capacity
to shed them.

"No," he muttered. "No. . . ."

"You've known me all along," Gabriele continued, "ever since you read Bathgate's file."

"Gabriele Lafontaine. . . ."

"You get an 'A' for the course, college boy."

"But the picture, it wasn't you."

"Describe it."

"You were wearing army dress. Your hair was short and dark."

Gabriele almost laughed. "Taken six years ago. In this business, you have to change your appearance as often as your attitude."

Dan looked at her dumbstruck, his face an empty mask. Then something happened. It started as a chill in his spine and thundered toward his head. His features grew taut, angry, red. The pressure spilled over. He stormed forward and slammed Gabriele hard against the wall, stunning her.

"You're a fucking murderer! You're a lousy killer! Renaldo Black's whore with a gun in one hand and your tits in the other!"

"No," she pleaded. "He wants me dead now, too!"

"You killed forty children!" He shook her again. *"Forty kids!"*

"I *had* to."

"Did you have to fuck me?"

"I had to kill you. Tonight. I didn't." A pause. "I knew about the car. I—I—I couldn't let them kill you. I made a choice."

"Sorry, I can't be grateful."

"Just don't hate me," she sobbed. "People have hated me all my life for what I was and what I wasn't."

"You're breaking my heart."

"You're the first person I almost let myself . . . love

in ten years. I guess I made a mistake."

"Right," Dan told her, his grip still strong.

"You hate me?"

"I hate what you are."

"Then get a knife. Slit my throat. I won't resist. I don't care. I'll even show you the proper way to do it. Kill me. If you don't, Black will."

"That won't kill what you are."

"Good, Lennagin, very good," she said, tears of anger mixing with those of depression. "Two weeks ago you got pulled out of your little Wonderland away from your books and friends and beer, and got shown how lovely things can be away from the hallowed halls of an Ivy League institution. You've seen people die. Well, people kill each other every day. When they don't have good reasons, they make them up, and when they can't make them up they use their guns anyway. We thrive on hate, not love. There's no love left anymore, if there really ever was any in the first place. A thousand kids die of starvation every single day, college boy. We only killed forty in Virginia. I hated every minute of it, but it was necessary. The media called it Bloody Saturday. Well, what about Bloody Monday, and Tuesday, and Wednesday? The world shits. Face it."

He looked her right in the eye. "I think I am."

She lunged at him, flailing away with both fists. The blows were random, poorly aimed, all her training forgotten. They struck his face, his arms, his chest before his hands locked on her wrists and pinned them to the wall. She snarled. He shook her hard, pulled her away from the wall and then slammed her back into the plaster. It felt good. Before him was all the horror and pain of the past two weeks. They had to be slain.

The plaster gave again. Gabriele's eyes went glassy.

Dan's body functioned outside of his mind, totally apart from it. The action wasn't conscious. It barely qualified as an action. He pummeled her against the wall a fourth time. Blood bubbled from her nose. The sight made him stop suddenly and let go his grasp. Gabriele slid toward the floor, a line of blood trailing her head. She landed in a half-squat, hands flapping helplessly by the sides of her jeans. Her eyes were empty, almost as empty as his.

"What have I done?" Dan muttered distantly. "What have I done?"

"Come on, college boy," she mumbled, straining to look up at him. "Finish me off. Find a piece of pipe or something sharp. I'm not good at waiting."

"I . . . can't." He covered his face with his hands.

"What's the matter? Can't you finish what you start? Kill me. Finish me off." She started to push herself back up the wall.

"Leave me alone," he sighed. "Just leave me alone."

She looked at him blankly. "I'd like to, I'd really like to. But it's too late for that. The funny thing is that I signed my own death warrant when I saved your life tonight, you see. Not that it matters, because I really died fourteen years ago, but I didn't know enough to lie down." She paused. "Let me tell you a story, college boy, one those books of yours probably missed. Once upon a time about fourteen years ago, a young German girl was sitting home with her mother and younger brother. Her father was an anarchist, a revolutionary, a vocal opponent of the government. He chaired meetings, led protest committees and formed movements. Twice he was beaten up. Once they broke both his arms. That didn't change or stop him. They tried to kill him and failed. He disappeared. Then one night his wife opened the door and three men in masks barged in. They demanded to know where they could find her husband, while her son and daughter hid in the closet. The boy and girl went there every time the doorbell rang, you see. Wonderful way to live. Anyway the woman told the three men nothing so they strapped her to a chair and made good use of a red-hot poker from the fireplace. They started with her breasts and progressed rapidly to her face. Her screaming was awful until they stuffed a rag in her mouth. Still she refused to talk. One of them moved the poker toward her eyes. Her son, eleven at the time, sprang from the closet and charged at the man holding it. The struggle didn't last long. When the son turned around, a knife was stuck in his stomach. Another man shot the mother through the head. The daughter was frozen by shock and fear. She didn't leave or make a sound. The men left the house. She stepped out of the closet to find her mother's face splattered across the walls and her brother still alive enough to be crying in his own blood. He died when she lifted his head to her lap. I don't have to tell you who that girl was, do I?"

"No."

"Then maybe you can understand."

"I'm . . . trying to."

Gabriele looked away, wiped the blood from her face. "So am I." She looked back at him. "I didn't want those kids in Virginia to die, and I didn't want my brother to die, either. But they all did, because they had to. I spent my most formative years with anarchists who took in a homeless orphan whose dead father—yes, they got him too—had been a great man. And when the foul-smelling men weren't raping me, they were usually talking to me about causes and about how important it was to believe in something, to fight for it like my father had. Only they weren't there to see what the fight had done to my mother and brother. So the only thing I learned from them was that you were best off believing in nothing and fighting only for yourself. I learned to hate, college boy, and I got pretty damn good at it because it was the only thing that kept me going when every man with a union card in Germany was sticking his prick into me. The beautiful daughter of their dead leader. Made quite an item, I suppose. When I turned seventeen, I ran away and hooked up with some terrorists who made hate a profession in the Baader-Meinhof gang. I liked the way they looked at things. There was something to be said for their philosophy, and their guns gave me a vent for the hate that had been building in me since that night when my mother and brother fell victim to the betterment of the state. Killing really isn't so bad once you get used to it. But then ten years down the road I meet you, innocent, redeemable Dan Lennagin, who had qualities that made me think of the little girl before that night and the not-so-little girl after. You made me look at myself a little differently, and I hated what I saw."

"I'm sorry," Dan said, fighting back the thickness in his throat. "I really am sorry."

"Save it. I don't need your pity, college boy. I lost my virginity when I was twelve and I've done my best to lose everything else since. I've been running a long time looking for a reason to be someone else and someone else to be."

"That's where we differ," Dan told her. "I want to get back to just being the person I was two weeks ago. But I know I'll never be able to. I used to be a college student. I drank a lot of beer, had a lot of laughs, and I was even president of a fraternity. But I don't remember any of that because that fellow's gone, dead I guess, and he's never gonna be back. And I want to cry for him but I can't, because I've forgotten even how to do that. Get it, Jill or Gabriele or whatever you want me to call you? You want to be somebody else and I just want to be what I used to be. But neither of us is going to succeed. That's where we're the same."

"You've got no right to compare your life with mine, college boy. You've—"

"Maybe I don't. After all, your father got killed because of a cause he believed in. Mine got killed because the first vacation of his miserable life happened to coincide with a terrorist hijacking. That's all right, though, because the American Legion sent an honor guard to his funeral, except they had to leave early to make another across town. I've always pictured a different person behind the gun that killed him and right now I see you cocking the rifle. It wasn't you, but it might as well have been, because you're all the same. You ruined a good part of my life. You took something from an eleven-year-old kid that nobody could ever give back. That's why I can't shed any tears for you. I haven't got any left. They ran out before I even had a chance to cry for myself."

Gabriele looked across the floor at him, her flow of tears free again. She had revealed herself, stripped her spirit naked. The last two weeks of hate, fear and loneliness for him were a microcosm of her entire life. He hated her for what she was because he was evolving into the coldly precisioned professional she was trying not to be. And yet both of them had had a chunk of their lives torn away at a young age, the ensuing years a continuing battle to fill the hole. Dan felt himself moving toward her. Then they were together, embracing, Dan holding her tighter than he had ever held anyone before.

"Dan . . . Dan. . . ." Her whimpers barely reached his ear.

He stroked her hair, moved her gently away, still holding tight. There was no going back to the world he had come from and no use in trying. He saw that now and the realization made things easier, though no less painful.

"Where do we go from here?" he asked softly.

"I don't know," she muttered. "I just don't know anymore."

The manager of the Baur au Lac looked up from the picture of Dan Lennagin that had been thrust across his desk.

"I know he was in this hotel," Paul Quinn charged. "And I want to know where he was headed when he left this morning."

"Your FBI has no authority here, monsieur," the manager said firmly.

The knot in Paul Quinn's stomach tightened. He was out of his element in such an environment. Clearly he didn't belong. But every time the urge came to board a plane home and accept failure, the memory of Dan Lennagin sitting in front of his desk returned to him. He owed the kid something and running away was no way to pay off. He'd been running too long now, ever since law school and mostly from himself. It was time to stop.

"Look," he began in a softer tone, "I've got no authority, but I do have a conscience. And a good measure of the blame for Dan Lennagin's being here in the first place rests with me. I haven't slept in more than a day and I've tracked him halfway around the world." A pause. "All I'm asking you is to help me help him."

The manager played with his mustache, thinking only briefly. "Hamburg, monsieur. I sent him on his way to Hamburg."

"Thank you."

"Please don't bother," the manager sighed. "I know the men he is running from. No one can help him. Save your time. Return to your country. The young man is dead."

"What did he say, friend Quinn?" Felix asked when the FBI man returned to their car.

"The kid's on his way to Hamburg, but he thinks we're wasting our time."

Felix chuckled briefly. "Time cannot be wasted. In Zen they say seconds pass only for those who watch them."

"Except the hotel manager says Lennagin's already dead."

"If it was his karma to die from this, he would have left his corpse in America."

"Good point."

"Hamburg, friend Quinn?"

"Hamburg."

It took ninety minutes the next morning for Dan and Gabriele to reach the main Hamburg train station on the opposite side of the city from the Reeperbahn. Gabriele's route made use mostly of the U-bahn, the city's subway. They crisscrossed Hamburg in no regular pattern, getting off at one street only to pick the U-bahn up again two streets later. They arrived at the station confident they hadn't been followed or seen.

Both were tired. The night before Gabriele had rigged a trap over the door of their cellar room for anyone who might have ventured inside while they slept, which turned out to be superfluous, since she spent the measure of the dark hours washing the grime and stench from their clothes in the small corner sink, using a stale fragment of soap as detergent. Dan, meanwhile, found sleep only in short, uneven spurts. The strain of the chase had brought the pain back to his ribs, so each minor toss or turn shook him rudely awake. Eventually he gave up and stared dimly at the ceiling in the neon-shrouded darkness.

Once at the station, they chose a train to Amsterdam with many stops along the way. The choice held several advantages. Besides being heavily crowded, the main stations the train paused at on its route offered possible refuge points should things not go as planned. If they did, Dan and Gabriele would find passage to London once they got to Amsterdam. Next they would make contact with the American embassy and tell their story. Dan had what he'd come to Europe for: a piece of specific knowledge concerning Lucifer in the form of evidence of Isosceles's existence. He'd tell the American officials about a secret runway on an island in the East Frisian chain. The rest would fall into place. Isosceles would be uncovered, destroyed. Lucifer would be revealed for what it was. He would be safe. Officials would believe him now because he had proof.

And he had Gabriele.

Theirs was a relationship based on convenience and

desperate necessity, nothing more. There could be no love, and Dan wondered seriously if there could even be trust, in spite of what she had done for him in the face of her own peril. She had stopped him from dying; she had *not* saved his life. There was a difference, slight perhaps, but definable nonetheless in the complicated world he found himself embroiled in.

He wanted to live. She wanted to live.

They shared that much. And it was all they needed at this point.

The train began to roll with them uneasily cooped up in a private compartment, alone with their thoughts.

"All aboard!"

The last man to heed the conductor's call had run a long way to catch this train, but he wasn't even winded. No strain or exertion showed on his face beyond a few beads of sweat dropping from his strong brow to a heavy, black mustache.

The man smoothed his silvery hair back into place and headed for his compartment.

TWENTY-NINE

Halfway across the world in the Oval Office, the President and his ad-hoc task force turned their attentions to Monday night's Academy Awards ceremony.

"Thames," the chief executive began, "how are we proceeding at the Los Angeles Music Center?"

Farminson stirred in his chair. "We've had the building under surveillance since our meeting on Tuesday. All reports are negative now. The Prometheus *plastique* just isn't inside yet, nor has anyone made an attempt to bring it in. When they do, we'll be there."

"Have you made a list of the possible planting points?"

"We've tried. But because of Prometheus's adaptability to almost any shape, the list is endless. Besides, the whole Dorothy Chandler Pavilion inside the Music Center gets done over for the Oscars. People have been lugging crates of decorations and scenery in all week. My agents tell me they've got thirteen different sets for the entertainment portions of the telecast alone. Rehearsals are becoming a problem. Entertainers are in and out all day. It's virtually impossible to keep track of all of them. And things promise to get even worse on Sunday when the television crews start to move in and a full dress rehearsal takes place. So long as my agents are restricted in number by the covert nature of this operation, I can't keep track of everything and everyone."

"You'll be able to use as many as you want on Monday."

"By then it might be too late."

"Unless your surveillance maintains its effectiveness."

"Not really, because we don't know what we're looking for. My agents have got their eyes trained for something that weighs in the vicinity of a hundred fifty pounds—the amount of Prometheus we believe Black obtained for the trigger. If someone's smuggling it in piece by piece or bit by bit, there's little I can do short of going through every inch of the building every hour with electronic sniffers, and we're damn close to doing that right now."

"Then where does that leave us?"

"To begin with," said Farminson, "under no circumstances can I guarantee the safety of those in attendance at the ceremony once things get under way."

"Unless we find the explosives before then," Sparrow reminded him. "I might be able to point you in a better direction."

"Specifically . . ."

"Let's look at things from Black's and Lucifer's standpoint. They want their trigger to receive maximum exposure. Since Prometheus can achieve its maximum explosive potential when arranged at optimum spread, this rules out its placement anywhere else but somewhere in the audience or damn close to it."

"We've been proceeding on that assumption from the beginning," interjected Farminson.

"Then you've no doubt catalogued all the possible points the *plastique* could be comfortably hidden in the audience. Seat cushions, chair arms, carpeting, and the like."

"Of course. They're all clean right now."

"So we keep checking on a day-to-day or hour-to-hour basis. Sooner or later something might turn up."

"And if it's later?" lamented Bart Triesdale.

"That's a chance we have to take. We know the limitations of Prometheus. We must make them work for us."

"Except," countered the President, "we seem to be equally aware of our own limitations. The Music Center is going to be a madhouse on Monday, and I can't see turning it into a slaughterhouse as well. If we don't find the explosives by show time, I'm afraid I'll have no alternative but to cancel the ceremony."

"Let's just keep our options open until then," Sparrow suggested.

"Oh, we will," Farminson assured him. "I've assigned twenty additional agents to the area at considerable risk of exposure. If those plastics come in before Monday night at six P.M. Los Angeles time, we'll find them."

"Which raises an interesting point." The President turned back toward Sparrow. "Assuming the explosives have been split up into something like seat cushions, how can they still be detonated together by the means you mentioned before?"

"Ultrasonic sound, most likely, because we can't jam the signal. A box the size of a portable radio would do quite nicely."

"Easily concealable in a pocket, then."

"Absolutely. Black's plan, I'm sure, depends on it."

"Then how will he get out once the explosives are triggered?"

"A timing device could give him upwards of a minute once the button is pushed."

The President swung in Thames Farminson's direction. "And what about Dan Lennagin?"

"Quinn's on his way to Hamburg with Felix. He's picked up a lead."

"I suggest we order him not to follow it," said General MaCammon suddenly.

"Why?" from the President and Farminson in unison.

MaCammon shifted uneasily in his chair. "We have to consider the practicalities of the situation. If we are successful in putting down the threat posed by Lucifer, we'll want to keep the whole matter under a tight seal. No publicity, no leaks. It's the only way, I'm sure you agree. But this boy knows, or knew, *everything.*"

"We could keep him quiet," suggested Farminson.

"And live with the threat of his opening his mouth looming perpetually over our heads? I think not."

"So you propose that we feed him to the wolves," concluded the President.

"No. He's already fed himself to the wolves. I propose we merely let them have him."

"Amounts to the same thing, doesn't it?"

"That depends on which way you look at it."

"Well," said the President sternly, "the way I look at it, General, you're asking all of us to become accessories to murder."

"Hardly, sir. I'm merely—"

"Don't bother explaining yourself, General. Your intentions are quite clear, so I'll make mine clear as well. I don't care what Lennagin knows or doesn't know, but if he's still alive I want him found and brought in safely. I don't care how many men it takes or what the costs are." The President paused. "We may be dealing with wolves here, but we don't have to become a pack ourselves. That would mean this country's finally going to hell."

"It may," said MaCammon, "already be there, sir."

THIRTY

Dan Lennagin and Gabriele Lafontaine sat in the quiet confines of their private compartment as the train rolled over the German countryside toward the Netherlands. The compartment had cost three times the price of regular seats, but the privacy and security it offered were priceless.

"We could stay in Amsterdam and relay our message from there," Gabriele suggested.

"No chance," Dan snapped. "I don't trust any country where English isn't the primary language."

"London is not exactly an American satellite, you know."

"No, but it's swarming with American diplomats, and MI6 and the CIA are still buddy-buddy. I read that in a book."

"You trust books?"

"More than I do people. You included, unless you lay everything on the line for me."

"I have."

"Then tell me why you bothered with the elaborate deception of Jill Levine. Why didn't Black just have me killed?"

"Because someone else has been helping you. He

eliminated two Lucifer people assigned to do the same to you. We had to find out who he was, how he connected to the plan."

"So all of a sudden I've got a protector. . . ."

"The idea was to flush him out, only no matter what we did he wouldn't show. Black got impatient. You knew a helluva lot more than he thought and he was afraid you might make contact with someone in America who had patient ears. And there was more."

"What?"

"Well, all of a sudden he didn't care anymore about the man who'd been protecting you. A major concern became nothing—just like that. He ordered your death knowing it would eliminate any chance we had of determining the identity of the third party."

"Did you know Black was going to be in Hamburg?"

Gabriele nodded, just once. "But I didn't know he planned to kill Bauer or that he would show up at Der Vergnügen so early. We were supposed to meet later. Of course, he had no reason to believe you weren't dead. You overheard a conversation that was important enough for him to risk everything by chasing us down the Reeperbahn."

"Where was he before Hamburg?"

"Spain. Madrid, I think. Why?"

"Just thinking. If Isosceles has three legs, the first being that East Frisian island, then maybe the second is somewhere in Spain."

"And the third?"

"Spain was Black's first stop when he left America?"

"Yes."

"Then he hasn't gotten to the third yet. But for some reason he's killing off his contacts. Bauer in Germany, someone else in Spain, and a third still to come."

Gabriele shrank backwards. "I pray you're wrong."

"I didn't think you were the praying kind."

She scorned him with her eyes, then her stare softened, becoming distant.

"You look scared," Dan said.

"I'm scared of what these killings might mean. The victims are obviously middlemen set up by Black for Lucifer. You see, the plan all the time was to make select terrorist groups think that Isosceles was a plan devised by the international terror hierarchy utilizing their combined resources. A symbol of unification. By killing the middlemen, Black not only takes the terrorists out of the game, he also takes Lucifer out. The game becomes his own. It explains why he lost concern for your guardian angel. Finding out who he was didn't matter any longer, because he posed a threat only to Lucifer. Black couldn't have cared less, because he's on his own. Yes, that must be it. All the time he was working for them, he had something else planned. They thought they were using him, but he was using them."

"For what?"

"I don't know. But consider the ramifications of what we're talking about. For any change or cancellation of plans, Lucifer had three people to contact. Black is now in the process of exterminating them. From what you've told me, that makes him the only person who knows where all the planes are."

"Except for us. One of them anyway."

"But Isosceles has three legs. We've got to find the other two." Gabriele paused. "I still can't figure out what Black has to gain from all this. Why take over the project when Lucifer put him in charge of it in the first place?"

Dan shrugged. "I'm going to London. It's time to let the professionals take over."

"There's a warrant out for my arrest in London. We shot two airport security men during a hijacking at Heathrow two years ago."

"But if you offer to help, they'll—they'll . . ."

"They'll what, college boy? Commute my sentence to life? They still have the death penalty over there, and I'm sure they'd like nothing better than to use it on an international terrorist. Might as well make it a public hanging."

"They'll understand."

"Sure, they'll understand that I can't tell them anything you can't and they've got no reason at all to make any deals with me. I'll be in irons before we hear Big Ben strike a second time."

"People *do* change."

Gabriele smiled. "But if I can't convince you, think what fun I'll have convincing them. No, college boy, I can't go to London now that I've got another choice."

"Choice?"

"Isosceles has three legs, right? So if it's really a triangle, I'll bet leg number three is somewhere in the Mideast. Black must be headed there right now. Tell you what, let's flip a coin. Heads we both go to England and I get hanged. Tails we're off to the Mideast to collect two bullets with our names on them."

Her unexpected levity brought life back to Dan's dull eyes. "What do you say we take a walk to the dining car first? No sense deciding our fates on empty stomachs," he said in grim amusement.

They ate well and comfortably. On the way back to the compartment, Dan fought down an urge to take her hand or arm. Somehow he felt safe now. They had escaped Black. Amsterdam was only a few short hours away. From there, London.

Dan unlocked the compartment doors, slid them apart, and stepped inside with Gabriele right behind him.

He heard a slight whistling sound an instant before something crunched into the back of his neck. He tried to maintain his balance and turn but it was already gone and he was falling, eyes dimming. Before he struck the floor, he reasoned it was a hand strike that had felled him, and an extremely professional one at that.

Amazing how much he had learned.

When he finally came to, his head felt three times larger. His temples were pounding and the back of his neck might have had a twenty-pound weight on it. His vision cleared to reveal an overcoated figure sitting on the berth across from him.

The man had gray hair and a jet black mustache. Dan had only seen him twice, but he recognized him instantly. He shuddered, tried to move his arms, and realized they were tied behind his back. By his side, Gabriele was stirring, eyes flickering to life, her hands tied similarly.

"I apologize for the rope, young Lennagin," the man said. "But I felt it necessary until I had a chance to explain who I am. Otherwise, you and your lady friend might be tempted to rush me and I'd be forced to hurt both of you again." His English was slightly laced by a foreign accent. Dan knew it but couldn't pin it down.

"I assume if you planned to kill us, we'd already be dead."

The man chuckled. "Oh, most certainly."

"Then what do you want?"

The chuckle grew into a laugh. "Merely to save your life once again. This is the fourth time, you know: Providence, Washington, the Herbertstrasse, and now today."

"Today?"

"Black has people waiting in Amsterdam."

Dan's eyes bulged with surprise, then confusion. It made no sense. "You're my guardian angel!"

"In a manner of speaking, I suppose."

"Who are you?"

"Colonel Stephan Ivanovitch Koralski," the overcoated figure announced proudly, rising to his feet.

"'Colonel'?"

Koralski nodded and started to untie Dan's hands. "Of the KGB. Department V. I bring greetings from the Soviet Union."

"We better talk," Dan said after a pause that seemed longer than it was, rubbing the cramped muscles of his arms.

"And we will, once we are off this train." Koralski moved toward the still silent Gabriele and leaned over to release her bonds. She pulled away. "We are on the same side now, Miss Lafontaine. There is no reason to offer resistance, nor is there any time." Gabriele relaxed enough for Koralski to free her. She glared at him with the eyes of a cat about to strike. "You see," Koralski went on, "if I found the two of you, you can guess how easy it was for Black to do the same." Lennagin started to say something. "Don't worry, he's not on this train, nor is he in Amsterdam. He has other matters to attend to. It's my guess he'll have somebody waiting to board in Wassel, though. Your friend with the steel arm perhaps, young Lennagin."

Dan felt a chill creep through his spine. "You know him?"

"Our paths have crossed. He is known only as Tungsten."

"Then what do we do?"

"Get off at Oldenberg, of course."

"The train doesn't stop at Oldenberg."

"It does now."

The train rolled to a halt minutes later in the town of Oldenberg. There was no one present to meet it because no one was expecting its arrival. Only two trains stopped daily in the town, one going east and another west. Koralski led Dan and Gabriele off the train and into the back of a waiting van, careful to keep his body between them and the freedom promised by the adjacent hills. He closed the doors behind them.

"Where to now?" Dan asked.

"An airfield my people use frequently for missions to the West. Its precise location does not concern you."

The van was done over in rich carpeting and vinyl seats that looked like couches facing each other in a rectangle. Against one wall were a refrigerator, two cupboards, and a locked cabinet. Koralski moved to the refrigerator and withdrew a container of fruit juice, then three glasses from one of the cupboards.

Gabriele whispered something into Dan's ear.

"I do not think the girl trusts me, young Lennagin," Koralski noted, looking back in their direction without pouring the drinks.

"Any reason why I should?" Gabriele challenged.

"I am your only hope to be alive two days from now. Is that reason enough?"

"I've done all right by myself for ten years, thank you."

"Ah, but the Isosceles Project is reaching its endgame and your friend Black will be most interested in removing you from the field."

"Unless I remove him first."

"A noble fantasy. May I ask, though, all things considered, is there any reason why you should not accept my help?"

"You're too mysterious for my blood," Gabriele told him plainly. "Appearing out of nowhere in time to rescue us in Hamburg and then again today, so we conveniently trust you. Quite a coincidence."

"Oh, there was nothing coincidental about it. With a few exceptions, I've been following young Lennagin here since he left Providence . . . and, accordingly, you, Miss Lafontaine."

"So you know who I am."

"That is my business."

"Only the KGB Department V seldom hands out cards."

Koralski smiled, the tips of his heavy mustache rising toward his cheeks. With his overcoat off, his frame had the shape of a perfect six-foot V, all muscle and bone.

"Don't be so short, Miss Lafontaine. We are, after all, in the same business, at least we were. In fact, my department has probably been responsible for funding some of your operations."

Department V . . . Dan recalled reading about that branch of the Soviet KGB designed to immobilize Western nations during times of international crisis.

Koralski's presence here, helping them, was a total anomaly. If anything, he should have been on Black's side.

"Your people had you follow me," Dan said. "Why?"

"It is a long story, young Lennagin, and very complicated. I will start at the beginning. Stop me when things get too confusing." Koralski shifted his muscular frame slightly so he was facing Dan and Gabriele simultaneously. "Let me start by saying there are forces in my country—people, that is—who greatly desire a Third World War, preferably nuclear. The reason? Simple really; right now we have three times the supremacy over America and the NATO nations combined. We are at our strongest. But the advantage will not last long. We do not build as well as you do, we merely build more. Your technology surpassed ours some years ago, and soon your productivity will, as well. We will be back to where we started at the opening of the Cold War. For some Soviet officials, this is unthinkable. They urge that we should strike now while we have the strength and the capacity."

"An unprovoked attack?"

"No. A reason was needed. It had to look like America made the first move, whether directly or indirectly."

"What do you mean?"

"The term 'first strike' had to be avoided at all costs. Other means to justify the war we now could win were required."

"Renaldo Black and the Isosceles Project. . . ."

"Very good, young Lennagin. You have learned your lessons well. Lucifer contacted Black and Black contacted us. Not Department V specifically; we were too small for what he had in mind. He went right to the

331

top of the armed forces who, along with the war-mongers on the Presidium, crave thermonuclear conflict above all else, or at least the threat of it."

"What's the difference?"

"Quite a bit. The more sober minds in my country who have spent their lives analyzing your country's moves claim that America at this point will avoid a nuclear confrontation at all, at *any,* costs. Since your government is made up of somewhat rational minds, they know they cannot win a nuclear war—nor really can anyone. So they will give in, and that will make us the victors symbolically and assure us of the supreme voice for the next generation or so."

"I don't believe it."

"I'm not saying it would happen that way for sure, but under either scenario, I'm afraid, your country will be the loser. The problem for Moscow was to bring the conflict to that point, of no return, I guess you would say. Then Black appeared. He had a plan, but to carry it out he required certain materials. His contacts in the Kremlin agreed to supply them."

"What kind of materials?"

"That does not concern you, nor hopefully will it ever. That is why I am here."

"At last we get to that," Gabriele muttered under her breath.

"You see," Koralski resumed, "there are still enough reasonable minds in Moscow to see that the course Black and the warmongers advocated was wrong. They covertly set up an attempt to realize their goals, so we covertly set up our own strategy to stop them."

"Sounds strange coming from a colonel in the KGB," Dan noted.

"Not really. We are not in the business of war."

"No, just terror. *Organized* war."

"Ah, young Lennagin, you have struck the key word: organized. Under the vision held by our enemies in the Kremlin, the world would not be fit for any organization at all. Believe it or not, a code of ethics exists between rivals in our profession. A brotherhood, you might call it. We spy on them and pilfer their secrets; they spy on us and pilfer ours. A game, that's all. We seek to beat them but if we destroyed them, we'd also destroy our own reason for being. This business of people undertaking hazardous missions into foreign countries is the product of fiction. We know who they are, they know who we are. We go about our business and do our jobs. We are not butchers."

"The people you employ are."

"Sometimes. We seek to maintain a delicate balance between our way of life and yours. Once in a while, we go too far to make sure we go far enough. Do you follow?"

"Not really. But I'd like to know where I come in."

"You have Major Bathgate to thank for that. He decided to set you up as bait for the people his man The Doctor had discovered were responsible for Bloody Saturday. Of course, he had no way of knowing it was Lucifer until it was too late and they had dispatched Tungsten to kill him."

"I think he started to suspect."

"By then, the cards had already been dealt."

"You were in Providence?"

"Yes. Keeping tabs on Bathgate and his efforts to track down Black. They killed him before those efforts ever got under way. That left us with only you. You alone had Bathgate's envelope and knowledge of Isosceles."

"I didn't know what it was, though. I still don't."

"Neither did we for sure at that point, nor did we have the ability to find out without exposing our intentions to our enemies in the Kremlin. Those intentions would have been squashed, the people behind them murdered in most painful ways. Our only alternative was to lay low, as you say, and continue Bathgate's strategy of using you."

"It seems I've been used a lot lately and I haven't even known it."

"That was the whole point. You became our unwitting agent. Your assignment was to put the pieces together for us and perhaps throw a scare into Renaldo Black. My assignment was to keep you alive for as long as it took."

"And how have we done?"

"Far better than anyone had reason to expect. I made sure you got to Washington safely, and both Lucifer and Black got nervous, especially Black. If this mysterious third party, represented by me, got hold of the truth and exposed it, he and Isosceles in the new format he had created for it would be finished." Koralski's eyes focused on Gabriele. "So he ordered your female friend there to keep tabs on you while he set out to eliminate the middlemen he had retained for Lucifer. That way, he stripped the organization of any control it may have had over Isosceles."

"But you said you had no idea what Isosceles was."

"We didn't . . . until I borrowed the envelope you had with you on the plane. We broke Bathgate's simple code and did some checking. It didn't take long to discover that Isosceles in its original form was a retaliatory plot to strike at three major terrorist centers in the wake of a major assault."

Dan settled back. It all made sense. Three jets, one of which was in Germany. Three targets. The riddle of Isosceles had been solved.

"Wait," he said abruptly, "terrorists killing terrorists? That doesn't seem to wash."

"Until you consider that Black was actually in the employ of Lucifer and acting in their interests."

"'Was'?"

"Now we come to the real problem. All the time Isosceles remained their plan in theory, Black was redesigning it according to specifications laid out by the warmongers in Moscow. These specifications maintain the basics of Isosceles, meaning there are still three targets. Black killed a man in Madrid before coming to Hamburg. That gives us Spain and Germany as two of the launching legs. He's on his way to the third now, in Cairo, we believe, because his contact there has made sudden arrangements to return from Amman. We have agents in Egypt waiting for Black."

"He'll spot them," snarled Gabriele.

Koralski shook his head. "I am more worried about his slipping out unnoticed. That is where you come in, young Lennagin."

"I figured we'd get to this sooner or later. . . ."

"An obvious ploy, isn't it? We merely keep using you as bait. Black wants you dead more than anyone else because in his mind you are the only person alive outside of a select circle who knows part of the truth about Isosceles. You can become far more than a slight embarrassment to him now. He'll go out of his way to eliminate you, take risks that will put him in a compromising position."

"Like what?"

"Like leading us to the third launching leg."

"Don't think he's a fool because you are," snapped Gabriele suddenly.

"You misunderstand me, Miss Lafontaine. The identity of his Mideastern contact whom he is about to kill means nothing. It is the information Black makes him pass on prior to the murder that interests me." Koralski turned back to Dan. "Tell me, was anything exchanged between Bauer and Black while you were in the closet?"

"A sheet of paper."

"With a number on it, perhaps?"

"As a matter of fact, yes."

Koralski nodded, satisfied. "There you have it. Black obtains the number of each contact point before he slays the man he has set up for Lucifer. That eliminates the middle. He becomes the only man who can trigger Isosceles. Quite a responsibility. Foolishly carried out, I might add."

"You plan on killing him?" Gabriele asked incredulously.

"Eventually."

"Hah! Black would make mincemeat out of your Russian hide and spit it out."

Koralski smiled. "I was chosen for this assignment for a very good reason. You are obviously unaware of my reputation and my abilities. No matter. You are supposed to be. My assignments seldom receive publicity, even in your circles." A pause. "Yes, I will kill Black, but not before I have obtained the locations of the three F-16s to be launched three days from now. Killing Black before that information is in my possession would make it impossible to trigger them but it would do nothing about the threat they might someday present again. Department V wishes them disposed of once and for all so that embarrassment is spared my country."

"And where does that leave us when all this is over?" Dan asked uneasily.

"My orders are explicit: You are both to die."

Dan started to stand up. A sledgehammer went off in his head and forced him back down.

"Relax, young Lennagin," Koralski soothed. "Orders mean nothing to me. I obey only the ones I choose to obey. I have no thoughts at all of killing you and when I'm finished with Black I plan to do everything in my power to see you safely back to your country."

"With no fear of what I might say?"

"I leave such considerations to the politicians."

"And what about her?" Dan asked looking at Gabriele.

"My orders actually were to kill her as soon as I made contact with you. But the two of you had grown closer than I had expected. Sparing your terrorist friend was the least I could do for all I've put you through."

"You?"

"Young Lennagin, the phone call you made after you so professionally disposed of the man in your Washington hotel room—it was me you spoke to. I *made* you go to Europe, flee to Europe. We couldn't have you associating with the FBI because they would have put you underground, just as we couldn't let you give them that envelope Bathgate left you because it would have confirmed your story immediately. We wanted you working for us, not them."

"You made me think Quinn was one of the bad guys."

"I put you on your own. You couldn't go home because there was apparently no one to go back to, which was exactly the way we wanted it. We needed you in Europe working for us by forcing Black's hand and following the leads Bathgate had uncovered. Measures had to be taken, I'm sure you understand."

Dan did, all too well. "You're not a very honorable man, Colonel."

"These are not very honorable times, young Lennagin, as you have seen these past few weeks."

Silence filled the van, except for the drone of the engine. Dan had forgotten they were moving.

"How can you find out the locations of the F-16s before killing Black?"

"The three contact numbers. If Black is foolish enough to trust them to memory, I have tortures even he won't be able to resist. I am quite an expert, you see. More likely, though, Black will trust the numbers to his physical prowess, which means they will always be somewhere on his person. The numbers will be traced, Isosceles destroyed."

"As simple as that?"

"As simple as that."

THIRTY-ONE

Paul Quinn shivered against the Hamburg cold. The wind sliced into him, turning his flesh raw. He couldn't stop his teeth from chattering and wondered if it was the cold or the uncertainty. When he had insisted upon going out after Lennagin, his resolve had been so total that everything else had paled by comparison. Now, standing on a corner in a foreign city with his confidence gone and his nerve rapidly following, the reality of the situation struck him as sharply as the air. Who was he kidding? He knew how to arrange surveillance and fit all requested information between the required lines of reports. Take him away from his desk, though, and he was lost, a ship adrift without anchor.

Three prostitutes walked past him on the Reeperbahn, tilting their eyes seductively. A man followed in their wake, stopped to light a match, then moved on.

The signal . . . the man was the CIA's operative in Hamburg. Quinn walked just fast enough to catch him at the corner.

"You Quinn?"

"Yeah. You—"

"Just leave my name out of this and keep walking.

339

You domestics got no right messin' on our turf."

"Spare me the bullshit."

The CIA man took a menacing step forward. He was big and dark. "It comes with the territory, but you can just get your ass outta here. My section chief says we don't talk to you 'cause you haven't got proper authorization."

Quinn had expected that. Proper authorization was impossible to obtain because it would have meant going through channels the White House didn't want alerted. So he'd planned for the eventuality.

"Felix," he said simply.

Moving like a cat, the giant had crept up almost equal to them without the CIA man's even knowing. In fact, he didn't become aware of Felix till a massive hand snaked between his legs and closed on his testicles.

"What the fu—"

The CIA man's breath was choked away when Felix heaved upward till his shoes clapped against each other in the air.

"Jesus Christ, put me down!" the man rasped.

The giant obliged. "The name is Felix and next time, friend, I hang you from a street lamp."

The half-doubled-over CIA agent cupped his hands over his groin and regarded Felix fearfully. "Okay, okay," he managed, struggling for breath. "Screw procedure. I'll play ball with you." He made it upright with a taut grimace and looked at Quinn. "Your boy was here."

"When?"

"Someone fitting his description entered a bar near the Herbertstrasse last night. Nobody ever saw him leave. That's the last we heard."

Quinn swallowed hard, eyed Felix. "Dead?"

"Doubtful. They carried a half-dozen bodies from the bar a few hours later and his wasn't among them."

"You sure?"

"Look, asshole—" The CIA man's eyes found the giant again. "Yeah, I'm sure."

"Nothing else?"

"That's it. The trail's cold. If I were you I'd go back to the home front with the rest of the domestics."

"What about Renaldo Black?"

"Nobody knows a damn thing. Contact of his we've been watching just hightailed it back to Cairo, though."

"Cairo," Quinn repeated to Felix, knowing at once the trail wasn't cold at all. "What's his name?"

"Abdul Habash." The CIA man smirked. "You're out of your league here, asshole. When they send you home, it'll be in a pine box."

"Don't count your nails yet."

"You don't trust Koralski, do you?" Dan asked Gabriele.

She studied him briefly from her bed in Cairo's Nile Hilton Hotel located in bustling Tahir Square. Her eyes returned to the ceiling. "I don't like him, if that's what you mean."

"It's not."

"Well, I don't know much about trust. It's never been an important part of my life. But since he's let the two of us live this long, I guess you can take him at his word."

"He needs us."

"You, not me. He could have left me dead in Germany and nobody would've been the worse for it.

But he didn't. I guess that counts for something."

"And you still don't trust him."

She looked at him finally. "You know, Dan, instead of asking me if I trust Koralski, ask yourself if he trusts us. If he did, why would he leave those two gorillas outside our door? Anyway, it's not Koralski I distrust or dislike, just what he represents. I've lived with his kind longer than I try to remember. Most people call them survivors. They're not; they just exist, moving from country to country, drawing blood and living off it."

"You might be describing yourself."

"Maybe that's the problem."

Dan nervously checked the room's electric clock, saw eight o'clock had just passed. Outside, night had fallen over Cairo. They had flown here from Frankfurt. Koralski had left as soon as they reached the hotel and had now been gone almost three hours. The colonel was proceeding on the assumption that Abdul Habash was the man responsible for the third leg of Isosceles, the third link to be severed. Black had called him back to Cairo to learn the final trigger number, after which the Egyptian would meet the same fate as Bauer in Germany and Gaxiola in Spain. Black had met the others on their home territory and the same methodology employed here meant that the meeting would be held at the Abdel-Aziz, Habash's restaurant a scant mile or so from the hotel.

Dan looked toward Gabriele who was staring intently again at the ceiling. She had been strangely silent and distant the whole trip here, ever since Colonel Koralski had appeared on the train.

She seemed to read his thoughts. "For a few minutes in Germany, we had something. You know that?"

"You're talking in the past tense."

"Maybe I shouldn't be talking at all. It was probably just my imagination back there wanting to believe in something like the future. I was wrong."

"About the future?"

"Yeah. There is none . . . for either one of us."

"You can't know that."

She smiled faintly. "You're new at this, Dan. You haven't learned the Golden Rule yet: Think and dream, but never hope, because there isn't any hope, not on the road we're stuck on."

"We'll get off it," Dan insisted halfheartedly, rising to his feet. "We'll get off it just as soon as Koralski finishes with Black."

"You really think it's that simple? Look, Dan, even if Koralski kills Black and gets us out of this, it won't last long. We're pariahs to both the good guys and the bad guys. It'll be a race to see who finds us first, since neither side'll want us alive."

Dan searched for words to refute her, was about to speak when he realized it was pointless.

A key turned in the door. Koralski stepped inside and threw off his overcoat, settling himself into a chair. "I hate the Arab countries. The people are so unreliable."

"The information was wrong?" Dan asked.

"About Black's Egyptian contact? No, it was quite correct. From what I can gather, Black is meeting with Habash tonight at the Abdel-Aziz, as I suspected. It's just that the two Arabs who passed the information on to me insisted on an elaborate system of codes and security measures and then showed up forty minutes late for our meeting."

"But Black *will* be seeing Habash tonight."

"We know where and approximately when."

"It's not like Black to be so careless," Gabriele warned. "You may, Colonel, be walking into a trap."

"Ah, Miss Lafontaine, your sudden concern for my safety pleases me no end."

She looked at Dan. "It's his safety I'm worried about. A trap for you is likewise a trap for him."

Koralski stroked his mustache, studying her. "You've not considered all the circumstances. For instance, that Black came to Europe expecting no complications and has found many, even without being aware of my emergence onto the scene. I have an entire intelligence network at my disposal and plan to utilize it. You would like to hear the details perhaps?"

"Yes," said Dan.

Gabriele remained silent.

Koralski spoke to him, ignoring her. "Peak hours in the restaurant tonight will be between nine and eleven. At ten o'clock sharp, Abdul Habash will retire to his office to eat in private, as is his custom. Only tonight dinner will be for two. Black will be joining him and Habash will be dead before dessert but not before he hands the third trigger contact number over."

"And you'll be inside waiting?"

"No, young Lennagin, you will."

Dan's face fell into a mask of surprise.

"Habash's people will be all over the restaurant," Koralski told him. "I'm afraid my face is too easily recognizable in these parts. Disguise is unnecessary and superfluous to the design of my plan." Koralski paused, went back to tinkering with his heavy black mustache. "We will go to the restaurant together. A reservation has been made for you. Single patrons

344

often cause suspicion, but you are an American tourist wishing to sample some of Cairo's finest cuisine. We will go there at nine o'clock. If Black arrives earlier, I will receive a call here at the hotel. I'm not expecting him to. Nine forty-five is the most realistic time, nine-thirty at the outside. Five minutes after he enters, you will follow and be seated at a table close to the door and facing the staircase, which leads to the second floor and Habash's office."

"But—"

"It has all been arranged. Department V is not without friends in Cairo. The building has no rear exit, just the front and two sides and to use any of these you must go down the staircase. When Black comes down after killing Habash, he will see you. You will leave the restaurant immediately and move toward an alley where I will be hidden with three of my best men in similar perches. Black will undoubtedly follow you. The rest will be left to us."

"You'll kill him?"

"But not before the three numbers I need to destroy Isosceles are in my possession."

"One problem, Colonel," Gabriele began. "I know Black. When he sees Dan, he'll leave that restaurant shooting.

"The possibility had crossed my mind."

"It's not a possibility, it's what's going to happen," she insisted.

"Not if young Lennagin here moves as I tell him."

"I won't let you jeopardize his life like this. Let me go with him. A couple sitting at a table will be far less noticeable than a single person."

"I thought of that but ruled the possibility out."

"Because my face is too well-known, like yours?"

"Because I'm still not sure I can trust you, Miss Lafontaine."

"But I trust her," said Dan.

"Leave this to me, young Lennagin."

"We're talking about my life, Colonel. I haven't stayed alive this long to set myself up as a duck tonight for Black."

"Let him catch a fleeting glimpse of you, nothing more, before you leave. He'll have no time to draw his gun, no less fire it. Once outside you'll move quickly to my position. My men and I will be spaced so it will be impossible for Black to get us all before we get him."

Dan considered the Russian's words. "It doesn't sound like you need me at all."

Koralski smiled the way a teacher might to an unknowing student. "Ah, young Lennagin, you are not well schooled in these matters. You do not understand people like Black and myself, how we have managed to stay alive so long against the concerted efforts of enemies who wish us dead. Our guards are always up. Our feelings guide our eyes and ears. If I try to take Black myself tonight, he will feel my presence as soon as he steps out the door. The best I can hope for under those circumstances is a stalemate, a double-kill, perhaps. I am better than Black, but he is more desperate. Neither of us can leave anything for chance. You are the ace I hold up my sleeve. In following you from the restaurant, he will let his guard down long enough for my team and me to finish him. I cannot afford to let him kill me as well. This is my operation and on the KGB books it does not exist. Hence, there can be no replacement. Success or failure lies solely with me—and now, young Lennagin, with you."

"I understand," Dan muttered distantly.

Gabriele stood up and stormed forward, locking her eyes with the Russian's as she spoke. "He's going to sacrifice you, Dan. He'll kill Black just as Black kills you. A bullet for a bullet. A life for a life. In his mind it's a fair trade."

Koralski's face paled. The tips of his mustache seemed to dip toward his chin.

"She's right, isn't she?" Dan asked him.

"Only as a last resort. If you do exactly as I say, it won't come to that."

"Are you going to tell him how to dodge bullets, Colonel?" Gabriele challenged.

"If the bullets don't come tonight, they will come another time. I am young Lennagin's—and your—only hope to avoid them altogether." He turned toward Dan. "There is risk in helping me tonight. I won't deny that."

"And if I refuse?"

"Will I force you, do you mean?" Koralski shook his head slowly, the muscles in his huge neck tensing. "No. The choice is yours. If necessary, I will go alone. Both of you will be free to leave the hotel and go your own way. But keep in mind, young Lennagin, that if I fail tonight, your corpses will be buried alongside my own. I am your only chance, but I need you as well."

"My presence tonight is that important?"

"We are dealing with intangibles, my young friend, and with men of the level of Black and myself, intangibles are often the only things that matter." Koralski checked his watch. "I must be going now . . . with or without you."

Dan's stare held Gabriele's for a long instant. "With,"

he said.

Colonel Koralski smiled almost sadly.

At nine-thirty they were standing across the street from the Abdel-Aziz restaurant, shielded by the black of the Egyptian night. The city of Cairo was a paradox, staid ancient buildings clashing anachronistically with modern structures not unlike those in a typical American city.

The Abdel-Aziz was located on a street of the same name in the most modern, fashionable district of the city. The road before it was black with freshly rolled tar and the sidewalks were in various stages of reconstruction. Occasionally a bus would pass by with people hanging everywhere, evidence of Cairo's failure to grow with its population.

The traffic noises and city smell soothed Dan, made him feel at home and more within his element, though he was desperately out of it. It was a busy time of night, as evidenced by two lanes of cars screeching by in both directions. The Abdel-Aziz had only a softly lit sign over its entrance. Dan had to strain to make out the letters. Exclusive restaurants seldom had to advertise themselves.

They had left the hotel thirty minutes earlier. Two of Koralski's five-man team stayed behind to "watch" Gabriele. The other three accompanied them to the street and had already taken up their positions. Dan tried but couldn't recall their faces. He remembered only their bearlike frames and mechanical eyes. A KGB hit squad, Koralski explained to him, an elite corps of professional killers.

The minutes ticked on.

"You're sure Black will use the front door?" Dan asked Koralski.

"He hasn't got a choice. I know the layout. No convenient secret passages like in Bauer's bar."

Dan hesitated. "You really don't trust Gabriele?"

The Russian looked at him compassionately. "You love her, young Lennagin?"

"I . . . don't know."

"Try not to. There is no future in it. But in answer to your question, I don't trust her abilities. She had a chance to kill Black on the Reeperbahn and didn't even draw her gun. The same mistake tonight could cost both of us our lives. The two men I left outside her door will make sure she does not jeopardize our plan."

"Colonel, I—I think I do love her."

Koralski smiled. "The folly of youth, young Lennagin. She is something to hold on to in the world of fear and hopelessness you have stumbled into. She is not something to love. But if you have made up your mind, then I suppose I'll have to see you both to safety. We may even find a priest along the way," the colonel laughed.

Dan smiled with him, though his heart was not in it. He liked the Russian. Looking at him now, it would have been easy to equate him with Renaldo Black. They were the same in so many ways, yet different in a few crucial ones. Koralski possessed the capacity to temper his coldness; Black did not. The colonel accepted his dark world of death; Black cherished it.

"There is another possibility, young Lennagin," Koralski told him. "When this is over, you could stay with me, join my network of agents. You've learned much already. I can teach you the rest."

"I've never fancied myself as a Russian spy."

"You'd be surprised how often we fight the same enemies as you Americans. Intelligence people are professionals above all else. Some of the men who are supposed to be my most dire enemies are my closest acquaintances precisely because I know what to expect from them. The bickering goes on far above those of us at the soldier level. Usually we ignore it and do our jobs with friendly, competitive rivalry."

"Strange way of looking at things."

"And what about what your eyes see? They don't belong to a frightened boy anymore, nor to any boy. I've looked into them and can promise you that. You have lost something you can never get back and there is no worth in trying. Better to accept and embrace the life you have found."

"I don't think I could live it."

The right side of Koralski's mustache curled upwards. "You already are."

"How poetic."

"Not really, but nonetheless true. To describe the way we live as a way of life isn't very accurate. Hours often feel like days; days like weeks; weeks like years. The result—for those of us who survive—is an incredible amount of living packed into an incredibly short period of time. You learn to appreciate moments of peace only as interludes. The real life occurs at times like these when every breath is precious and every step must be sure. Any motion can conceivably be your last so you cherish and appreciate them all. An alluring kind of existence, which in many ways is attractive and in all ways impossible to escape from."

"Because it's addicting?"

"More or less. I've known agents who've tried to retire before their time. The results are always the same. Deep depression. Dependence on drugs or alcohol. Perhaps a desperate request to undertake a suicide mission or a more banal bullet in the head."

"You're talking about men with years of experience," Dan argued.

"The years are inconsequential. It's the experience that matters. A week, young Lennagin, is all it takes. You hate what you're doing and what you think it's doing to you. But then when it's over, you crave more because you realize that only in the moments when your life was truly in danger did you feel truly alive."

"Then you're not afraid of death."

"Of course I am. It gives the moments meaning and value. I merely choose to look death in the face. He has yet to look back."

"I'd rather close my eyes."

"Now perhaps. If you are fortunate enough to survive this adventure, though, everything else will seem humdrum by comparison. Your perspective will have changed thoroughly. The things you once valued will be as foreign to you as toy soldiers are to a teenage boy. You'll want the danger back again, feel like you'll burst if you don't get it. The process perpetuates itself. The circle never ends."

"Until you die."

Renaldo Black stepped out of a taxi across the street. Dan felt the colonel's hand grasp him at the bicep and draw him further into the darkness between the two buildings. Black's eyes swept the area, found nothing. He walked through the front door.

Koralski kept his eyes locked on that target as he led Dan down the street. They passed one building and then another. An alley appeared, black and without end. Koralski backed into it.

"Lead Black in this direction, young Lennagin," he said simply. "We will do the rest."

Dan looked around him. "I can't see your men."

"Neither will Black."

Dan studied the distance between the Abdel-Aziz and the alley, about forty yards. "It's a long way."

"Not really. You'll have a headstart and the flow of traffic will prevent Black from firing his gun too soon."

"That didn't stop him in Hamburg."

"This is Cairo, my young friend. Things are different here."

Dan shrugged.

Koralski patted him on the shoulder. "Better get going."

A few minutes later Dan was inside the stunningly appointed Abdel-Aziz. The maître d' showed him to his table, which was, as promised, in full view of the staircase that rose toward the second floor where private functions were held and Abdul Habash maintained his Cairo office. He assumed Black was already upstairs with the PLO man. He might be joining him for dinner, which meant the wait could be a long one.

The waiters of the Abdel-Aziz all wore tuxedos and were required to speak Arabic and English and preferably a third language. One of them glided over and handed Dan a menu, saying in English he'd be returning shortly. Dan held the menu before him but his eyes stayed locked on the staircase. Koralski had already told him what to order. There was no need for further scrutiny. The waiter returned and Dan recited Koralski's words to him. The man nodded a few times, eyeing him, and jotted down the order. The next time he returned it was with a decanter of wine and a tray of hors d'oeuvres. The waiter poured a glass of wine and promised to return with the next course in minutes. Dan picked at the hors d'oeuvres, unsure of what he was eating but hungry nevertheless, and sipped some of the wine. Never did his eyes part from the staircase.

The minutes passed, each one longer than the one before it. The fearsome reality that any time now Renaldo Black would appear on the stairway struck him all at once. The urge to flee rose but he quickly suppressed it. Koralski's way was right, the danger present but necessary. There were risks, but there was quite a bit to gain as well.

Dan's eyes wandered to the grandfather clock against the far wall. Twelve minutes had passed since he had sat down, which meant Black had been inside for twenty. Was he having dinner? Koralski had warned him about a possible delay, but he wasn't prepared to wait long. Around him the Abdel-Aziz was filling up. Well-dressed couples with flashing jewelry pecked at their food and their conversation. A wine cork exploded, sounding like a gunshot. Dan's heart raced, then settled. At the table nearest him, a bearded man was handing an unsatisfactory dish back to the waiter who muttered a polite apology and was quickly on his way back toward the kitchen.

Dan's waiter arrived with the second course, a rich seafood bisque with reddish crackers served as an accompaniment. Nearly a half-hour had gone by now. Where was Black? Could Koralski have been wrong about there not being a rear exit? Something felt very wrong. He wanted to bolt for the door and it took every ounce of self-control he possessed to keep himself pinned to the chair.

Footsteps pounded the carpeted staircase. The guests of a private party were descending, all grace and smiles. Perfect camouflage for Black. Dan's eyes examined the crowd, ruling one out after another. Might Black have donned a disguise upstairs? No. There was no reason. He could leave the restaurant without fear, because according to routine Habash would not finish his dinner till eleven. Nothing was yet out of place.

The crowd of party-goers filed swiftly out of the Abdel-Aziz. Black was not among them. Dan checked the throng one final time, careful to give the tallest men who might have passed for Black a third and fourth glance. Satisfied that none of them were, he turned back to the staircase.

Renaldo Black was standing there in the middle, eyes and frame frozen. Dan's knees shook, went wobbly. His bowels turned to ice water. Black descended two steps, then a third. Dan forced himself to rise and backed toward the door. Black went for his gun. Dan crashed into the street.

He was running even before his feet found the pavement. He cut directly across the flow of traffic and left maddening horns and burnt rubber in his wake. He rushed on, afraid to look back because he knew Black would be there stalking him. He waited for a gunshot, hoping very much he would hear it, because that would mean he was still alive.

Stay with the plan! Stay with the plan!

The voice rose from deep inside him. He barely heard it in time to veer toward Koralski's alley. By now, the colonel would certainly have spotted Black behind him. His three Russian bears would be preparing to catch him in their cross fire. Dan had to keep the terrorist in the open for a clear shot. A hail of bullets and it would all be over. The alley came into view.

354

Kill him! Dan heard himself think. *Kill him!*

But the bullets didn't come. Dan kept his eyes before him. Almost at the alley and still no bullets. Then he reached it.

"Colonel Koral—"

The alley was deserted. Koralski was nowhere to be seen. Dan spun quickly, eyes searching. Black was gone. Or was he just choosing his moment to strike? There was no trace of Koralski's KGB executioners. Where were they? What had happened?

Dan thought fast, instinct taking over. He turned out of the alley and started running again, dodging pedestrians, not looking back, keeping his body pressed as close to buildings as possible to make a bullet's path more difficult. But his strategy was rushed, wrong. He had to consider the ramifications of this sudden turn of events, had to find direction and reason where none presently existed. He had to think.

Dan slowed his pace. Up ahead, the sidewalk dropped off against a row of apartment buildings, providing access to below street-level rooms. He took the first set of downward steps in two bounds, angling his body to the side to check for possible pursuers. He reached the bottom of the black stoop off balance.

And that was when a cold hand jarred his shoulder.

THIRTY-TWO

Colonel Koralski stayed on his feet only long enough to pull Dan down to a squatting position. Lennagin felt the chill of his hand even through the jacket. And when he saw the Russian he knew why.

Koralski sat in a widening pool of his own blood, one hand supporting his frame, the other clutched over his stomach as if to hold its contents in. Bathgate had been mortally wounded in the same manner but the Russian was even worse off. The right side of his face and head formed a continuous mass of bloody pulp. Dan couldn't tell whether the eye was closed or missing. Koralski's right shoulder was twisted in an absurd position, the arm attached only by the sinews of a few muscles and tendons. The left half of his muscular neck had a large tear in it just under the jugular. Blood sped from it with each of his labored breaths. The throat itself looked strangely shrunken and small. Dan couldn't believe the man was still alive.

"Things did not go as I planned, young Lennagin," Koralski whispered because that was all he could manage.

"Your team! What happened to your team?"

"The steel man killed them all. He caught me from

behind when I had just realized and left me for dead. But I do not die so easy. I got away and made it here." Koralski coughed. Blood oozed from the corners of his mouth. "He will be after you."

"Don't try to talk," Dan said lamely, shuddering at the possibility of confronting the black giant who had just murdered three KGB assassins with ease.

"Why not? I am going to die anyway, my young friend, and there are things—" Koralski coughed again, deeper this time, and oozed more blood. "—I must tell you. It's up to you now, all of it."

"No! I can't! I—I ...."

"You are better than you think you are, better than *they* think you are. You and I, we both fled to the same stoop. Two professionals." Koralski coughed and spit blood again, starting to slump down. Dan lifted him back up and held him against the brick. "I knew you would come, young Lennagin. I know how you think because I know how I think. You must finish my work, relay the message."

"What message?"

Koralski turned away. The blood was coming from his nose now as well. His face was totally white, his eyes lifeless. "Go back to the hotel," he rasped painfully. "Get your girl. She is good at what she does. She will help. If you die, it will be together, not alone like an old Russian like me." Koralski started to smile. The smile fell into a cough. He had little breath left now. "You must return to America, my young friend. Sparrow is there and he is the only one you can trust."

"Sparrow?"

The name chilled Dan. The only other time he had heard it mentioned was from Bathgate's dying lips, and now Koralski was dying too and he would soon be alone again.

Koralski tried to nod but the slight motion was denied him. "Sparrow only one you can trust now," he repeated. "Tell him the . . . secret. The secret of . . . Isosceles."

"What secret?"

Koralski lost his air, started to cough but couldn't complete it. His eyes were dull, listless. They didn't blink.

Dan grasped him by the shoulders and pulled him forward. "What is the secret of Isosceles?"

With his last breath, the Russian told him.

Dan shuddered. Everything made sense now.

He looked down. Koralski was dead. He had kept himself alive only long enough to deliver the message. A bulge protruded from the left side of his jacket, evidence of a gun Tungsten had not given him time to use. Dan held his breath against the sickening touch of warm blood and reached inside. His fingers emerged with a square pistol, its handle soaked in red, and pocketed it.

Shoes ground against the cement above him. Dan looked up. Tungsten grinned, started down the steps.

Dan fumbled for Koralski's gun in his pocket, couldn't find it, and ran up the opposite side.

Tungsten was extraordinarily quick for a man his size, especially at the start, and the start was all he needed to cover the length of the stoop and dive. His hands clawed for the churning ankles just above him, found them but gained no purchase.

Dan tore free and sped up the stoop onto the street.

He never broke stride, running haphazardly through the strange streets, propelled by instinct, finally to rest behind a family of garbage cans. The smell was awful but well worth the cover. He listened for Tungsten, heard only the pulsing of his own heart. He held his position, fingering Koralski's pistol the whole time.

The secret of Isosceles. . . .

America . . . he had to reach America. The secret of Isosceles had to be relayed to Sparrow. Such was the intent of Koralski's dying words. There was no choice now but to follow them. But how to reach America?

Gabriele would know. They would go there together.

He rose from his hiding place, holding his breath against the possibility Tungsten had been hovering over him the whole time. He breathed easier. He shared the night with no one except one of Cairo's innumerable cats. He moved toward the lights and traffic he saw on an avenue nearby, walking until he found the most congested street of all, which gave him a reasonable feeling of security.

A new awareness filled his being. He looked at people he passed or who passed him and read their thoughts, determining from their eyes whether they knew him or not. He found that in walking, he could accurately gauge the precise number of steps separating him from the person immediately behind him and could sense any variance in their stride. The ability was instinctive to all men but ordinarily lay buried in the layers of contemporary consciousness, which no longer required it. Dan had dug it out.

He walked on, thinking of Koralski, of the fight he must have put up against the giant Tungsten. A regular man would have been dead a dozen times over but the Russian had refused to die until his final message had been delivered. Koralski had retained his will when he had nothing else left. There were lessons to take from that and Dan wanted to learn them.

He kept his fingers poised on the gun in his pocket and turned his thoughts to Gabriele. She would teach him the rest of what he had to know. But first he had to reach her, had to get back to the hotel. He was in her world now and though he didn't embrace it, he accepted things for what they were and determined to make the best of them. He had to return to the hotel careful not to let anyone follow. His route would be random, irregular. The enemy would be hard pressed to keep up with his twists and turns without exposing himself. Satisfied, Dan picked up his pace and had walked more than a quarter-mile when he stopped dead.

They weren't following him; they had no reason to because they knew exactly where he was headed. The hotel was his only possible refuge point, Gabriele his only ally. They'd know that and beat him there. His mind acted swiftly, came up with a compromise. He entered the anteroom of a bar for the sole purpose of making a phone call. The Egyptian coins jangled down. He dialed the hotel and gave the room number.

"Hello." Gabriele's voice.

Dan sighed in relief. "It's me. Something went wrong. They got Koralski."

"Are you all right?" Her voice was fearful.

"For the moment. How about you?"

"Nervous."

"We've got to get out of the city," he said weakly. "We've got to get back to the States."

"They'll cover our every route of escape. Our only hope will be the port district of Alexandria. I know people there."

"I'll be back at the hotel in twenty minutes."

"I'll be ready." Suddenly Dan felt breathless panic

360

coming over the line. *"Dan, they're here! Don't come—"*

"Gabriele? . . . *Gabriele!"*

The line clicked off.

And Dan felt panic again, this time his own.

Koralski was dead. They had Gabriele.

He was alone.

He dropped the receiver and scanned the area. Clear. He left the phone booth and walked slowly away, careful to seem casual but certain the thundering of his heart would betray him. After a block, he eased into a steady pace. If they were still around, he'd be dead already. No, they had expected him to return to the hotel so there had been no reason to dragnet the area. He was safe, for now.

He quickened his pace, confident now that he wasn't being followed. The enemy had badly misjudged him or perhaps hadn't judged him at all, which was clearly to his advantage. Something else going in his favor was the last bit of information Gabriele had passed on to him. She had given him a destination, a means of escape.

Our only hope will be the port district of Alexandria.

But the men in the room would've heard the words. They'd know where Dan was headed. They'd be waiting for him there. But he was out of options. Alexandria was his only choice. He'd take his chances there of finding a boat to get him safely out of Egypt and begin his journey home.

Home . . . How far away it was, how long ago it seemed he had left.

Dan hopped in the first cab he saw and listened to the driver balk in broken English at the 125 mile trek from Cairo, warning the price would be steep. Dan told him money was no problem.

He collapsed in the backseat, realized he was trembling horribly. Tears forced their way into his eyes and he let them fall. Guilt ripped at him. He had left Gabriele at the hotel, left her there for Black. Maybe he should have rushed back after their phone call and attempted a rescue. He owed her that much, didn't he?

No, that would have been suicide, an amateur's desperate response, not what Koralski would have done.

He wrapped his arms around himself to ease his trembling. Black had Gabriele now and would make her pay a terrible price for crossing him before letting her die.

If I had listened to her, this never would've happened, Dan reflected bitterly. *It's my fault. . . .*

That thought made him feel even more alone and isolated. He might have given in to the pain, given up, but he couldn't. There was a mission to finish.

Koralski's last words, the secret of Isosceles . . . it could not remain a secret.

He had to pass it on.

THIRTY-THREE

Admiral Magnum Ridgestone stepped out of his limousine as always at nine A.M. sharp. Before him, on South Post Oaks in the center of Houston's Magic Circle, rose the thirty-story steel and glass structure that bore his name. The building was the centerpiece of the city's second downtown, a masterwork of contemporary design in silver and black.

Ridgestone adjusted the patch that covered his left eye and entered. He always used the main entrance, though a private one was available as well. He enjoyed the wide-mouthed greetings his employees gave him, eyes bulging with surprise that he had descended to their level. In fact, he took his lunch hour at the same time they did to afford them still another glimpse. While they dined at the local deli or Burger King, though, he took his meal at the exclusive University Club overlooking the Galleria shopping mall. Ridgestone enjoyed their adulation. He thrived on his power and position, neither to be taken lightly but both to be enjoyed.

Passing toward the central elevator so he could grant some of his followers a close-up look, Ridgestone had to fight down an urge to raise his hand into saluting position. Old habits died hard. He'd been a navy man for twenty-two years, right up until the strategic disaster historians called the Korean War. Ridgestone, when he talked about it at all, called it a mess. In World War II, he had distinguished himself at the battle of Midway and a dozen others. Great things were predicted. MacArthur made him the architect of his naval strategy against Japan. Then the Korean conflict came and more great things were predicted. Before he was finished, Ridgestone would have an admiralty and a carrier to bear his name.

He got neither.

When MacArthur went down, Ridgestone went with him. Not out of loyalty—the admiral never believed staying with a sinking ship was sound military strategy. He was just aligned too closely with the great general and when it came time to clean MacArthur's house, he happened to occupy a primary floor. They buried him in an office job, gave him a pencil sharpener instead of his admiral's stars.

Well, Ridgestone had enjoyed the last laugh. He had left the service of his country and joined the service of self. He had seen enough top secret future defense plans to know a fortune lay in microcomputers. Ridgestone Industries was born. A private citizen now, he took the liberty of promoting himself to admiral, and almost everyone assumed the title was legitimate. He always felt his most important command was yet to come, and when it finally came there was no one to take it away from him. He never got his carrier but his building more than made up for it.

Three years past seventy now, the admiral looked none the worse for wear. He strolled with back straight and erect, gait proud and regular. His hair was the same silvery shade it had been twenty years before and not more than a handful of strands had been lost during that period. He had fourteen custom-tailored admiral's uniforms and he rotated them religiously, collar starched and tie tightly knotted. He had lost his left eye in a training camp accident a dozen years before Pearl Harbor and had chosen the eye patch for effect. Legend had it that a Jap bayonet had been the culprit instead of a thrown fork in a South Carolina mess hall.

Admiral Ridgestone rode the elevator to the top floor, drinking in the gaping stares of the employees around him. His good eye stayed fixed surlily before him. His left upper lip curled toward his black patch. It wasn't until the elevator slid open on the thirtieth floor that Ridgestone realized he had been alone for the last eight.

"Good morning, Admiral," his secretary greeted him, handing him his morning cup of heavily sugared coffee as he stepped out of the compartment.

"Any messages?"

"A dozen. All on your desk."

Ridgestone walked as though a hundred eyes were upon him and entered his office. The first thing he noticed when he closed the door was that his swivel desk chair was facing the rear wall, which was strange because he never left it in that position and the cleaning men came only on Wednesdays. A coldness gripped his insides and his next step logically should have been back toward the outer office, because he sensed the presence of the intruder clearly now. Instead, he let his coffee slip to the rug and started across the room. He was quite fast for a man past seventy and his gun was palmed before the man in the chair swung in his direction.

"You were never a very good shot, Admiral."

Sparrow held Ridgestone's eyes. The admiral's face was uncharacteristically pale. He held his pistol unsurely.

"Put it away," Sparrow advised him. "You'd be dead before you fired a second shot."

"How did you get in here?" Ridgestone demanded, trying to appear steady.

"Wrong question, Admiral. You're supposed to ask what am I doing here. My entry is already a foregone conclusion."

"You asked the question. Why don't you answer it?"

"I came to visit an old friend. It's good to see you keep office hours on Saturday."

"Get out!" Ridgestone showed the gun higher.

"Is that an order, Admiral?"

Ridgestone lunged back toward the door, stopped when he heard it lock electronically. Sparrow lifted his finger from a panel contained in the top desk drawer.

"My secretary will call security," he insisted.

"Your secretary never does anything unless it's on your orders. You're in no position to give any at this point and personal initiative was never something you fostered in your employees."

Ridgestone realized if he had meant to use the gun, he'd have done so already. So, fingers trembling slightly, he returned it to his holster. Sparrow looked older than he, more worn, but he possessed no illusions over who was the better man.

"Make it fast, Sparrow. I'm a busy man."

"I intend to. I came to do you a favor."

Ridgestone moved toward the desk. "I thought you were in Israel," he said innocuously. "Called it quits just when I joined the executive committee."

Sparrow started to scowl, then found himself smiling humorlessly. "It was your executive committee that forced me to quit."

"Retirement either way."

"Thanks to you, I've decided to come out of it."

"Oh?"

"I won't bother listening to you deny that you've tried to kill me four times in the past two weeks. I haven't got the spare minutes. When I left Lucifer in the hands of people like you, I always feared it would come to this sooner or later. Too much power for any small group of men to wield. It was built into the system and required a man devoid of politics and prejudices and ambitions at the helm. You are a man obsessed with all three, Admiral, even more than the men who preceded you in this job after I was forced to step down. But if Isosceles was ever to become active again, I should have known it would have been by your lead."

Ridgestone took a seat before his own desk. "Well said, Sparrow. Of course, I won't bother denying any of it. So now here we are, face to face. You, with no chance of getting out of this building alive if I so choose; and me, with very little chance of getting out of this room alive if you so choose. A stalemate."

"Not from where I'm sitting."

Ridgestone was livid. "I've got the gun, Sparrow," he said, inching toward the holster again. "You seem to be forgetting that."

"Your gun against my hands is a fair fight anytime. But I wasn't talking about that. I came here to put an end to Isosceles. I won't leave until I have."

The admiral's hand was back by his side. "And you expect me to abandon the operation just like that?"

"I suppose I could appeal to your common sense and

remind you that since the US government is aware of your plans, carrying them out will lead only to Lucifer's destruction. Or I could appeal to your sense of reason and remind you that you have corrupted the forces you were charged with leading. I will do neither."

Ridgestone snickered. "You merely plan to politely ask me to give up Isosceles, then."

"In a manner of speaking."

"You've just sealed your fate, Sparrow. Even lions grow old. No matter what happens to me in this room, you will not leave this building alive. Without your constant menace, Isosceles will go off as planned."

Sparrow stood up and moved to the window. "Beautiful day, isn't it, Admiral? And I understand the forecast is for a beautiful weekend. Good time for your annual spring barbecue down on the Texas ranch with your entire family, children and grandchildren included, gathered together. A lot of them have arrived already."

Ridgestone leaned forward, eyes wide. "You're not saying—"

"I knew your own life was a relatively inconsequential matter. Other means were called for. Unless I call a certain number in a half-hour, an F-4 will take off from the air force base in Galveston. A cover story for the tragedy has already been arranged, something to do with a terrorist attack on a major industrialist. Why, they might even call a Lucifer alert."

"You can't be serious."

"Unfortunately, I am."

"You're talking about innocent people," Ridgestone pleaded.

Sparrow gritted his teeth. "No less innocent than those children in Virginia."

Ridgestone didn't bother denying it. "That was necessary. A price of war."

"War?"

"That's what terrorism is and you know it, and the whole human race are the soldiers. You're the last person I should have to explain these facts to. You created Lucifer and you developed Isosceles."

"Neither toward the ends you are striving for."

"And are those ends so bad? The end of organized terrorism on an international basis . . . that's what Isosceles will accomplish. It will draw terrorists out into the open, strip their cover away. They'll be on our turf then and won't stand a chance. A year from now the international terror network will be in shambles, a chain without links, but only if Isosceles is allowed to go on. If not, well, did you really think the timing of the project was random? It's not. Next Tuesday in Paris twenty-four terrorist leaders are gathering together for a conference. An *open* conference, *goddammit,* with all the fanfare of a major summit. Don't you see what that means? Terrorism is gaining legitimacy, and with that legitimacy comes organization. If Tuesday's summit is successful, we'll never be able to keep pace with them again. A united terrorist front would command the attention of a first-rate world power. They'll be the winners, while Lucifer *and* Israel—*Israel,* Sparrow—will be the losers."

"Launch Isosceles and we'll all be the losers."

"It's not that simple. Do you know what one of the topics on their agenda is? Lucifer, Sparrow, *us!* Not specifically, of course, they wouldn't dare. They plan to deliver a joint speech calling for the abolition of a free world terrorist organization that has forced them to maintain arms to protect themselves. They're blaming us, can you believe it? So a hotshot congressman with an eye on the White House gets ahold of that and all of a sudden there's a congressional hearing. The existence of Lucifer comes out. We'd be able to bury most of the truth but we can't bury ourselves. Exposure would destroy us. We can't function with our people on the covers of *Time* and *Newsweek* or being subjected to the same kind of scrutiny CIA personnel went through a few years ago. Hell, the Company still hasn't recovered from that yet. The point is, we'd be finished. Every subscriber to the ACLU newsletter would be screaming fascism because they don't understand that we're the only thing separating them from something much worse. They don't understand terrorism because they've never been exposed to it."

"But Bloody Saturday changed all that," Sparrow said bitterly.

"Dammit, Sparrow, I'm talking about survival here!"

"Then to survive, Admiral, you've had to become the very thing you're supposed to stand against. If you're telling me that's what you have to do to keep going, I say Lucifer is better off coming to an end. But I don't think it has to be that way. Terrorist groups have been trying to formally unite for ten years and have never gotten beyond shouting at each other and counting their money behind closed doors. At this summit, the shouting will merely be louder and the counting more extensive. As for exposure, I think you can stand up to it and survive; at least you could have until Bloody Saturday. If it comes out Lucifer was behind that, cause and country notwithstanding the organization would be finished. But it wasn't the organization that gave the kill order, it was you. And the organization didn't retain the services of Renaldo Black, Admiral, you did."

"That's right, Sparrow, because desperate times require desperate measures."

"To be taken by desperate men. . . ."

Ridgestone forced a chuckle. His silvery hair was matted down to his forehead. "Is that supposed to hurt my feelings? It doesn't, because I know I'm desperate; we're all desperate, thanks to a perpetual climate of fear fostered by international terrorism. Lucifer is the only force holding it reasonably in check. But even we can't keep up with the terror network's global expansion, especially with our hands tied behind our backs."

"So you hired Black to keep the ropes off, to do your dirty work for you. It would have been a brilliant scenario from your point of view, one which left Lucifer right where you wanted it to be. Except that Bathgate's man caught wind of the trigger portion of the plan while in Los Angeles: the murder of three thousand people before one hundred million witnesses. Lucifer would be able to blow up the world with that as a reason. You'd never have to answer to anyone again. Your power would be absolute."

"Lucifer's power, that is."

"Unfortunately, they're one and the same."

Ridgestone's features sank. "Wait, how did you know about the trigger?"

"From Bathgate through Lennagin."

"But Black told me Lennagin knew nothing about it," the admiral said unsurely, "that everything could go on as scheduled."

Sparrow's eyes flashed like a computer after reaching the solution to a problem. "Black lied," was all he said, something suddenly clear to him.

"An oversight perhaps."

"I don't think so." Yes, very clear. "What would you have done if Black had reported the truth, that we knew everything?"

"I don't know."

"Cancel Isosceles?"

"At least postpone it. Maybe search for a new trigger. To do otherwise would defeat our own purpose."

"As it does now."

"Not necessarily."

Sparrow smiled, though he plainly had no reason to if his latest suspicions were founded in fact. "The disposal and dispersion of the F-16s was handled by Black?"

"Yes."

"He alone knows their locations?"

"But I alone can trigger their launchings."

"How?"

"Three phone numbers."

"Which Black provided you."

"And which have been checked and double-checked."

"But you were his only contact inside Lucifer."

Ridgestone nodded. "For security reasons."

"And you left the Academy Award trigger phase of the plan totally in his hands, to his discretion."

"Again, security reasons."

Sparrow lunged forward and thrust the phone receiver from the desk in Ridgestone's face. For a long instant, an empty dial tone filled the room. "Call the numbers."

Ridgestone accepted the phone reluctantly. "It's only over for now, you know."

"I don't think it is." Sparrow's tone was tautly reflective.

Ridgestone pulled a small black notebook from his jacket, turned it to the middle, and started dialing. The receiver seemed an extension of his ear. Strands of his silver hair might have sprouted from it. The veins near his temple started throbbing. He hung up the phone slowly, retrieved it, and dialed the same number again.

He looked at Sparrow with barren eyes. "The line is dead," he reported, feeling like a man who stores his cash in his hip pocket only to find a hole in it.

"Try another number."

The call went through quickly to Hamburg, Germany, but reached no one. The receiver slipped from Ridgestone's hand. Sparrow gave it back to him.

"And the third."

The results were the same.

"Oh my God," the admiral muttered. "You knew, Sparrow. I saw it in your eyes; you knew."

"Black used you, Admiral. He was never working for anyone other than himself. And now he's got the F-16s and can send them anywhere he damn well pleases."

"No," Ridgestone insisted grimly, pulling on his eye patch as though he expected the empty socket to reveal some unseen answer. "Their targets have been preprogrammed into the auto-pilot along with the attack times. The only variable factor was the launching points. Even the pilots are ours."

"Black could replace them."

"You don't understand. Precautions were taken, *technical* precautions. Our pilots are the only ones who can make those jets fly. Something to do with keys. Even then, any deviation from the target or attack time would force the armaments system into an automatic shutoff."

"What are they carrying?"

"Conventional Capricorn missiles modernized for exceptional accuracy with computer chips made by my company." Ridgestone looked up hopelessly at Sparrow. His lips quivered. "The strikes are going to occur simultaneously on Tuesday."

"What are the targets?"

Ridgestone tried to swallow. The motion was denied him. The only similar feeling he had ever experienced was the recall from Korea and loss of a potential admiralty. That made him mad. This frightened him. He started to speak.

"The open terrorist conference in Paris. A logical choice, don't you think?"

"Go on."

"Seven terrorist training camps in Libya in addition to Tripoli, and . . ."

"What? Where is the third target?"

"Russia."

"The North Schwerin terrorist training centers?"

Ridgestone shook his head and managed a smile as cold as death. "The plan was to go after the generals of terrorism, not the soldiers. To strike deep in the heart of the most threatening force in the world. Very deep. That's what we needed the F-16s for." A pause. "The source, Sparrow, we wanted to hit them at the source! The jets gave us the ability." Ridgestone took a deep breath. "Headquarters of the KGB and Department V. . . . The third target is Moscow."

THIRTY-FOUR

"So where does that leave us?" the President asked when Sparrow finished his report.

"With no choice other than to let the Academy Awards go on as planned," the Lion of the Night said firmly. "Black is the only one who can trigger Isosceles. He wouldn't trust the code phrase to anyone else any more than he would pass on the responsibility for detonating the Prometheus *plastique*. So capturing . . . or killing him at the ceremony is the only sure way we have to prevent the launch order from being given."

"One thing bothers me about that," challenged the President. "Black undoubtedly knows we're onto him, so why should he bother with the trigger at all when he could still give the launch order at the proper time without it?"

Sparrow's eyes flickered knowingly. "Maybe because he has no way of knowing we've reached Ridgestone and therefore wants to keep everything as it was planned for as long as possible. Maybe because he can't give up an opportunity to murder three thousand people on live television. But most likely because continuing with the trigger is something he promised to whomever he's working with now."

"I thought you said he was working for himself."

"Not entirely. There are too many inconsistencies, too many unanswered questions. Why has he taken Isosceles over? What could he possibly have to gain from such a maneuver unless he feared Lucifer might have found out something that would've led to the project's cancellation? Black killed three of his own people to block Lucifer out of Isosceles because he knew we were getting close. He'd have no reason to do that unless he was hiding something."

"I'm not sure I follow you."

"Consider this, then: Renaldo Black, a notorious international terrorist, has taken over an operation that will do irreparable harm to the face of international terrorism. It makes no sense until you look at it from another angle. Who else might have something to gain from the bombings of Moscow, Libya, and the terrorist conference in Paris?"

"Besides us?" quipped Triesdale dryly.

"Russia," muttered General MaCammon.

The President scoffed at the remark.

Sparrow didn't. "Precisely. They could blame the strikes on us with little difficulty, saying we lashed out at them falsely in response to the tragedy at the Academy Awards. It would give them a free shot at us or Western Europe, a big enough shot perhaps for them to obtain the food they need from their enemies forcefully."

"I don't buy it," persisted the President.

"I'm not finished yet," Sparrow went on. "The picture gets even worse, if that's possible. If my theory was correct in itself, the Russians would've had no reason to pull Black from the original plan or link up with him to start with. They obviously wanted more."

"More?"

The Lion of the Night nodded. "Isosceles in its original form didn't quite suit the Soviets' purpose. Modifications were required. And they needed Lucifer out of the way to accomplish them. Then they'd have their free shot at the West toward gaining undisputed global supremacy."

"And if we resisted?" the President posed hesitantly.

"World War III," muttered Thames Farminson.

"There you have it," Sparrow concluded. "Isosceles is no longer what Lucifer set it up to be. But we can still put a stop to it by finding those F-16s."

"We've been through this before," Bart Triesdale reminded him helplessly.

"But thanks to Admiral Ridgestone, we've narrowed the problem down to three countries: Spain, Germany, and Egypt. Ridgestone had a contact number in each to call when it was time for the jets to launch."

"Numbers which are meaningless now."

"Maybe not. From what I can gather, Black set up a middleman in each of the three countries to arrange all the details. Then he passed their numbers in to Ridgestone to provide the impression that Lucifer could trigger Isosceles or call it off. Before he killed them, then, Black must have obtained the numbers through which to relay the trigger phrase that would activate the final stage of the operation."

"What are you getting at?"

"Simply this: Each of the middlemen must have given Black a number they had undoubtedly called prior to their final meeting. Checks had to be made, receipt of equipment and personnel confirmed. I doubt they handled everything in person."

"And the point?"

"That if we can get a list of all phone calls, long distance at the very least, made from the three disconnected numbers that Ridgestone so graciously provided us with, we'll have a clue to the locations of the planes. Transfer each number into an address and check them all and our missing jets will almost surely turn up."

"You make it sound simple," moaned Triesdale.

"Just logical under the circumstances."

"But not under the time scheme," the CIA man resumed. "Spain, Germany, and Egypt aren't exactly being breastfed by Ma Bell. Getting those lists won't be easy and tracing the numbers will be all but impossible, within the next forty-eight hours, anyway."

Sparrow considered the argument. "According to Ridgestone, Black initiated this phase of Isosceles eleven days ago, so concern yourself with phone calls made between the eighth and the nineteenth. You might also focus your attention first on numbers that were called more than once during that period, perhaps even on a regular basis."

"I'd feel a lot better about all this if we found the explosives," advanced the President.

"They have to be in the building before we can find them," Thames Farminson said briskly. "And right now they're not, nor will they get by us prior to the ceremony."

"Unless Black's considered something that we've totally overlooked," Sparrow offered.

"Not possible," from Farminson.

"And what about Paul Quinn in Europe?" the President asked.

Farminson's eyes left Sparrow's. "No trace of Lennagin. Paul's following one last lead but I doubt it will go anywhere. We must assume the boy is dead. Not that it matters so far as Isosceles is concerned, because I can see no way he could be of any service to us now."

"Hell of an epitaph you've written for him, Thames."

"It might well end up as an epitaph for all of us."

Suppressing a smile, a man in blue work overalls stepped out of the Los Angeles Music Center. He passed under the newly erected canopy, swung by the van he had arrived in regularly for the last six days, and entered a phone booth.

"What is your message?" asked the voice on the other end.

"The trigger is in place," the man reported. "All is ready."

THIRTY-FIVE

"You better let me do the talking here, friend Quinn."

Felix led the FBI man down the main pier of the port of Alexandria.

"I've done pretty well myself so far," Quinn pointed out.

"Things are different here, much different. Information does not come easy and often not at all. This is my territory. It calls for a different brand of persuasion." With that, Felix tucked his sheepskin vest under the hilt of his samurai sword. "Besides, I don't remember you mentioning anything about speaking Arabic."

They continued down the pier, soles wet from the high waters, approaching a weatherbeaten watchtower.

"You expect to find something here?" Quinn asked.

"Some*one*. A harbormaster of sorts. A busybody who sees all that transpires on the docks. If your boy left Egypt from here, he'll know about it."

"But will he tell us?"

Felix just smiled.

The giant opened the door to the watchtower without knocking. It squeaked awfully and nearly fell off its hinges. Boards had been nailed everywhere to serve as patches until now it looked like there was no place left to nail them.

"Who the hell are you?" the Egyptian charged, thrusting a thick revolver at them. The shack was lit by a single kerosene lamp that cast dark shadows over his already dark, beard-stubbled face. His face was thin and wild. He wore only a white T-shirt and stained khaki pants. There was a half-emptied bottle of cheap whiskey on the table he sat in front of.

"I said who the hell are you?"

Quinn followed Felix in and closed his nostrils against the bitter stink of stale sweat.

"We mean you no harm, friend," Felix comforted the Egyptian. "We come only in search of a few simple answers."

The man held his pistol higher, regarded Felix curiously with his head tilted over to one side. "I don't know you. I'm sure I don't."

"But you have information we seek. The night is cold, friend. Another bottle or two would help you see it through well. Help us and I will—"

"I don't need your goddamn charity!" The Egyptian cocked his pistol. "I could blow both your brains out and nobody would know the difference. I don't know you and I don't owe you nothin'. These are *my* docks. Nobody—"

The next instant was a blur before Quinn's eyes. Felix moved—Quinn had never seen anybody move so fast—and there was a whistling through the air. Quinn saw something glimmer and then realized the giant had drawn his sword, the realization coming an instant after the blade's flat edge had smashed down on the Egyptian's wrist and his gun had gone flying. Before the man was able to move again, the razor edge of

Felix's sword was pressed against his throat so that the slightest motion would tear it.

"You know who I am now, friend?"

"Yes. Felix," the man whispered, afraid even to speak any louder with the cold steel against his jugular.

"You might die tonight, friend. But I am in a charitable mood and will spare your life if you answer my questions. Understood?"

The man started to swallow, then stopped. He managed the semblance of a nod.

"Good. There was a boy on the docks tonight, an American in his early twenties, seeking passage out of Egypt. Do you recall him?"

"Yes."

"And did he find the passage he sought?"

"Yes." The Egyptian's eyes locked on the blade at his throat. The water mark across its very edge stood out in its dullness. "Word arrived before him."

"What word?"

The Egyptian hesitated and Felix pushed the blade a fraction closer.

"Pleasssssse . . ." The man's eyes bulged. "Word of a hefty price on the boy's head. Dead or alive."

"Oh my God," Paul Quinn muttered.

"And the captain who accepted his passage?" Felix continued.

"A rat and a scoundrel who makes his living off blood money."

"How long ago did they leave, friend?"

"Two hours, three maybe."

"In what direction?"

"Northwest. Toward Greece."

"You can arrange for us a boat fast enough to catch them?"

The Egyptian relaxed a bit, feeling for the first time Felix was going to let him live. He nodded.

"Of course, friend, you know the penalty for lying to us or planning a double-cross. I'm going to let you live tonight, but there is no place on earth you can hide where I won't be able to find you if I choose. Remember that, remember it always."

Quinn could tell by the Egyptian's eyes that he would.

The boat rode the choppy seas easily, its captain steering it with the waves or between them. Dan Lennagin stood on the deck shivering from the cold night breeze, alone with his thoughts but seeking to be rid of them. A mist poured in, rising from nowhere. Dan felt its damp touch and shuddered against it, shrinking back though there was clearly no place to shrink to. The cold brought the throbbing back to his bruised ribs. Perhaps the warmth of Monday's approaching Mediterranean dawn would bring him some relief. By then, with luck the boat would have reached Greece.

Time had long since ceased having any meaning for him. He'd lost all frames through which to judge its passing. He was exhausted, but afraid to sleep; lonely, but afraid to reach out. He missed Gabriele. He had told Koralski that he thought he loved her. Truth was that he didn't know and guessed he never would. She was in Black's hands now, dead or soon to be. A coldness rose in him coming not from the mist or the wind but from the depths of his own being.

He wanted to kill Renaldo Black. In the confusing mess his life had turned into, that desire fed him purpose. His mind centered around, fantasized about, inevitably came back to that goal. He placed his hands on the damp deck railing and looked into the distance. No land was in sight, Alexandria far in the past as was everywhere else.

Alexandria.

The drive had taken longer and cost more than he'd expected. The man behind the wheel claimed he'd taken many men on this route with the common goal of exiting Egypt fast. He knew captains in the port city who would be more than happy to complete the journey providing sufficient padding was added to their pockets. Dan was receptive, though not too much so. The driver shrugged and brought the subject up again later. This time the amount of padding was decreased. Dan accepted his help.

The port district of Alexandria was cheerful and lively even at the relatively late hour they arrived. The driver led him down one of the many endless docks toward a pleasure craft called the *Renaissance*. A burly, balding, bull-shouldered man with a heavy beard was mopping the decks. The driver addressed him as "captain."

Ten minutes later the deal had been consummated. The captain would get him to Greece, after which Dan would have to fend for himself. And since most of the journey would take place at night, the cost had to be inflated accordingly. Dan didn't bicker; bargaining takes time and he had none to spare. He handed over almost three-quarters of his remaining funds, the bills, of different shapes, sizes, and foreign denominations, amounting to roughly fifteen hundred dollars. They were under way within a half-hour.

Suddenly the boat chopped against a wave and

shook. The engine sputtered, died.

"Shit!" came a roar in English from the bridge. The captain pressed the starter button. The motor flickered back to life, then faded again. Three more attempts to revive it followed, all unsuccessful.

"Shit!" bellowed the captain once more as he descended the ladder from the bridge. Dan felt for Koralski's pistol and watched him pull up a hatch in the center of the deck and lower himself into the guts of the boat, a flashlight's narrow beam providing the only break in darkness.

"We have a problem," the captain reported. "Gears are stripped. We may be here a while."

Dan leaned over the hatch.

"Well, Americano, it's a good thing we're ahead of schedule. I have a long job ahead of me."

The captain shifted positions. Dan heard something clang and leaned further over the opening.

He heard the boat chain a second before it wrapped around his neck and yanked him downward into the hole. His feet fought for the ladder's rungs but found only air. His hands struck the cold, hard wood an instant before his face did. The smell of oil and gas filled his nostrils. He felt sick.

The bull-shouldered captain stood over him smiling, holding the chain like a dog's leash. He started to twist, stripping Dan of his breath. Dan's hand pawed frantically for Koralski's gun, found it, fired blindly into the hulking shape before him as the steel started to tear into his flesh. The captain gasped and let go of the chain. Dan propelled himself backwards, still square on the deck, unraveled the chain and caught his breath.

The captain rushed at him. Dan fired again. The impact shook the bull-shouldered man, sent him reeling against the crankshaft. Dan struggled toward the ladder, had passed three rungs when a set of callused fingers grabbed his ankle. The captain pulled with all his strength. Dan held out against it. The grip weakened. Dan aimed the gun downward and squeezed. The bullet ricocheted harmlessly. He jerked free, slipped, lifted himself to the main deck.

The captain was right behind him, his powerful arms preventing Dan from closing the hatch. Dan forced his weight against it. The captain mounted a sudden thrust upward. Dan went flying, looked up when he landed. The bull-shouldered man was rising to his feet, chain dangling by his side, two red holes glistening in his black shirt, his eyes ablaze with fury but somehow distant and unknowing. He staggered forward, a dark shadow swallowed by the swirling mist on deck, silhouetted against the night. A fourth squeeze on the trigger brought only a click. The gun was empty.

Dan started to rise, slipping on the wet surface as the chain swirled at him in a blur. He lurched back from its jagged end but not far enough. The sharp grappling hook grazed his thigh. The captain jerked it free and took a piece of flesh along with it.

Dan screamed in pain, lost his balance. The hook whirled for his head. He ducked away but it tore into his shoulder and sent him careening to the deck. He struck the surface hard with nothing to brace the fall. He tried to push back up with his good arm but it slid across the wood, denied purchase. He looked up to see the captain struggling to free the grappling hook from the cabin door where it had lodged.

Dan's shoulder was numb. Blood pulsed through the wound in his leg.

The captain almost had the hook free.

Dan slid back against the gunwale and tried to rise, only to have his feet slip out from under him. The captain yanked the sharp hook from the splintered wood, started forward. Dan shrank back further, dimly conscious of motion and rumbling in the waters behind him.

The captain held the chain over his head and began to twirl it.

Dan closed his eyes, grimacing, then opened them when he heard something crash onto the deck, to find a giant, bearded figure lunging forward in the captain's path. Too late, though. The hook had already begun its deadly journey forward.

The giant snatched it out of midair, closing his fingers around the chain just below the honed edge. The captain tried to pull back and Dan watched the giant let him, thrusting his other hand forward till it grasped the bull-shouldered man's neck. The giant lifted him off the deck. The captain's eyes bulged, then glazed.

The giant let him crumble to the wood, as another figure swung itself onto the deck.

"My God, am I glad to see you!"

Dan looked up into the wide eyes of Paul Quinn, tongue-tied with relief.

"Talk to me, kid."

"Isosceles," Dan muttered through blue, quivering lips.

Quinn was kneeling next to him. "Jesus Christ, we better get you patched up."

"The secret of Isosceles. Must tell . . . Sparrow . . . the secret. Koralski knew. Koralski—"

"Sparrow? Hey, what are you talking about? What secret?"

Dan faded.

Quinn grasped him at the shoulders. "Dan, what secret!"

"Hydrogen bombs. The three jets are carrying hydrogen bombs. . . ."

V

BLOODY MONDAY

THIRTY-SIX

"Ladies and gentlemen, live from the Dorothy Chandler Pavilion in the Los Angeles Music Center, it's the fifty-seventh annual Academy Awards. . . ."

The announcer's rich voice blared through the Los Angeles Music Center and into sixty million homes across America.

"And now, here's tonight's host . . . *Johnny Carson!*"

Thunderous applause shook the pavilion. The festivities had begun.

Sparrow, strained in the confines of his tuxedo, looked out from his perch just off the right side of the stage and watched a graying entertainer stroll regally into the center of the bright lights to a mark drawn in chalk. Sparrow never watched TV and went to the movies on a yearly basis at best, so the man was unfamiliar to him, as were the hundreds of other celebrities in attendance. His only interest in them lay with the fact that they were all potential victims. He turned to his right and saw that Felix had returned to his side.

"It will be soon you think, Israeli?"

"I don't know. Where's Farminson?"

"With some of his men in that closet they call a command post. He sent me to get you."

"I'd rather stay here."

Felix started to back away. "I'll tell him."

"No. I better see what he wants."

"Whatever you say, Israeli."

Felix had flown out to meet him in Los Angeles immediately after getting Quinn and Dan on their way to a hospital in Tel Aviv. The giant had had almost no sleep in three days but it didn't seem to faze him. He was back in his element, in appearance anyway. He wore a leather vest he had modified to hold his daggers. Two pistols protruded from his belt. He had hidden the samurai sword as best he could but the lower half of its scabbard still stuck halfway out his belt. One of his monstrous hands curled the tips of his beard as he walked.

Sparrow limped along to keep up with him, his bad leg all the worse from the extra strain and tension the day had brought with it. Usually his handicap bothered him in public. Today there were more important things to consider.

"There you are," Thames Farminson greeted him as Felix led him through a door usually reserved for a dressing room. The only furniture inside now was a series of tables placed against the walls. Television monitors fought for space on them with transmitting equipment and sonar specially designed to pick up the hum of a trigger mechanism once activated. The sonar screen fluttered in regular blips, thankfully finding nothing. Wires ran from the TV monitors connecting them to computer terminals where wide-eyed men maintained their vigil over the IDENT system. "Thought I'd fill you in on where we stand now,"

Farminson continued. Felix closed the door. "I think we're in pretty damn good shape. This place is wired for everything. If Black did make it through our security screen, we'll know it if he picks his nose."

"Triggering the explosives wouldn't take that much of a motion," Sparrow warned.

"Well, I don't think it will come to that anyway. The last check with the sniffers was made ten minutes before the doors opened. They found nothing."

"What about the set scenery that was delivered today?"

"Checked and double-checked. All clean. There are no explosives in this building," Farminson said confidently.

Sparrow eyed him with skepticism. "Black's found something we haven't considered."

"Then we'll have to find Black." The FBI chief beckoned toward a row of twenty television monitors. "Seventeen of the cameras belong to ABC. We added three more of our own to handle sweeps of the upper balconies. They give us full view of everything going on in the pavilion at any given time. We were able luckily to tie in the IDENT system to all of the cameras. Amazing how it works really. We've programmed the computer with every known and assumed physical fact about Black from the angle of his nose to the distance between his eyes. IDENT stores all this material and searches for match. A buzzer goes off if it finds a potential one and the screen automatically freezes. So far no buzzer."

"That doesn't mean he isn't here."

"With that in mind, we've intensified our sweep. But to insure accuracy, this sort of thing takes time."

"We may not have much left."

The computers remained silent.

At that moment, nine of the screens were sweeping the crowd. Four had different views of Johnny Carson and two were panning the sides of the stage. One caught the area Sparrow had just left. An agent or two sat huddled over each screen searching for something out of place or sync even before the IDENT system picked out Black.

"Of course," Farminson was saying, "all of this couldn't have been done without ABC's help. They got pretty curious when our people arrived in force late this morning without disguises or covers, but fortunately the entertainment division's handling this. If it was the news department, we'd have had a helluva headache to go with the one we've already got."

"You sound confident. Aspirin?"

"Experience. This is the smoothest, cleanest operation I've seen since I came to the Bureau. My men have been nothing short of fantastic. They've done everything possible to keep this building in one piece, and frankly I think we're gonna succeed."

"Unless Black is better than they are."

"We're talking about the *entire* FBI."

"I know."

Farminson checked his watch. "I make a routine call to all my agents stationed in and around the auditorium every ten minutes. Heightens my sense of security."

"Can't say I blame you."

Farminson moved to one of the tables and stretched a headpiece around his head. "Fifteen units in all, two men in each always in sight of each other," he explained to Sparrow and then lowered the microphone portion. "Eagle one, report."

"Eagle one, rear balcony. Clear."

"Eagle two, report."

"Eagle two, side exit A. Clear."

"Eagle three, report."

"Eagle three, side exit B. Clear."

Sparrow felt his mind wander away from Farminson's security check. He was vaguely aware of the gray-haired comedian warming up the crowd with a well-received monologue. He could tell by its tone and intonation that the man named Carson was almost finished.

"Eagle nine, report."

"Eagle nine, rear quarter A. Clear."

"Eagle ten, report."

"Eagle ten, rear quarter B. Clear."

Farminson's strategy meant nothing to Sparrow. His men, no matter how able, well-trained and strong in number, wouldn't be able to find something or someone in time unless they knew precisely who or what they were looking for. Unfortunately, that was not the case here. Sparrow knew Black. The presence of a federal army would have meant little to him. The contingency would have been planned for, even expected. Where, then, were the explosives? Farminson said they were nowhere in the Music Center. The Lion of the Night knew better. The remaining questions were: where? And how?

"Eagle fourteen, report."

"Eagle fourteen, right stage scaffold. Clear."

"Eagle fifteen, report."

"Eagle fifteen, rear stage area. Clear."

Tungsten lowered the microphone from his lips and smiled. The backup detonator rested comfortably in his right pocket.

Sparrow emerged from the monitor room and found himself standing next to Johnny Carson.

"I blew the line about Charlton Heston," the host told him.

Sparrow shrugged.

"Well," Carson resumed, "no matter how much you prepare something, there's no way of being sure it'll come out right."

On stage, the president of the Motion Picture Committee for the Arts and Sciences was explaining the balloting procedures and the total secrecy surrounding the identities of the winners.

The words never reached Sparrow. His mind had journeyed back to that afternoon, when an Academy official named Friede had gone over tonight's layout with him, Felix, and Farminson.

"All the nominees," Friede had explained, "are seated in the first tier. This allows for the least possible delay between the time the winners are announced and they make it to the stage, and it also makes matters far simpler for the television people who must follow their ascent onto camera."

"What happens after they collect their trophies?" Farminson asked.

"After they've made their acceptance speeches, you mean?" The four men had been standing directly in center stage, the approximate position from which the winners would speak. "Come this way, gentlemen," Friede beckoned. He was a slight, balding man with glasses. He led them off the stage to the right. "Down here are a series of annex rooms that will be filled with refreshments and news people. After the winners make their speeches they are requi—, er, asked to make a brief round through the press rooms where they can be captured at the peak of the exciting moment, so to speak. Afterwards, they return to their seats."

Friede had shown the men some of the reception rooms, which were already adorned and decorated, lacking only refreshments and the constant fluttering of camera shutters. Rostrums had been set up in the front from which the winners could conveniently speak.

"I'll have a team on each of these doors tonight," Farminson had assured Sparrow on the way back to the main staging area.

Everything here seemed ready to go, as well. Center stage was a stately portrait of silver and white, dominated by a huge white dais—a stage upon a stage—with steps leading up to and down from it. The dais possessed two wings with two sets of staircases, each descending from the off-stage area. In addition, the structure's rear and front were formed of steps. The group of men had climbed up, the extra five feet feeling like five hundred to Sparrow.

"This allows presenters to appear from a variety of angles," Friede had explained. "Eliminates viewer boredom and the routine if all presenters approached from the exact same place. You'd be surprised how much of the telecast is taken up with precisely that."

"Will all the entertainment segments take place here?" Sparrow had asked, checking the footing.

"Yes," Friede responded. "But this round pedestal can be changed into a half-dozen other shapes, including a square, with the touch of a button. The front half is mobile, you see. The sets and scenery, meanwhile, are moved about much the same way they are on Broadway, mostly from above." Friede pointed above him toward the rafters. Workmen were busy rigging cables to massive montages that would fall and rise or float across the stage effortlessly that evening. "We try to provide the illusion for the television audience that actually more than one stage is in use. The people who choreograph these kinds of performances are true masters. They work with what they have like magicians. Things appear and disappear out of nowhere. The camera is most cooperative in that respect."

"And back there?" Sparrow had asked, gesturing toward a black lace curtain that only partially obscured three levels of chairs and tables.

"The orchestra," Friede said matter-of-factly. He snapped his fingers. "Sometimes you see them and sometimes you don't."

"And behind the far wall?"

"Why, the backstage area, of course. But we don't use it anymore, except for storage. It's turned into an unnecessary bit of space, since all technical matters, lighting and such, have come to be directed from above."

"I'd like to see what goes on up there in the scaffolding, as well as backstage."

"As I said, nothing goes on backstage."

"I'd like to see it anyway."

Friede had obliged, leading Sparrow, Farminson, and Felix through the left staging area into a narrow corridor that connected directly with the dead space behind the orchestra section of the main stage. It was cramped with wires and cords, offering no view whatsoever of the festivities soon to be taking place, a graveyard for discarded and disowned equipment. Old lighting poles were stacked up against the wall, their bulbs never to flash again. Scaffolding rose five levels up, a piece missing here and there, the entire structure on the verge of tumbling to a dusty demise.

"As I mentioned," Friede had reminded them by way of explanation, "we don't use this area anymore."

"I'll have a team stationed back here anyway," Farminson said.

"Is there anything else I can do for you?" Friede offered.

Farminson looked at Sparrow. His expression was blank. "I think that will be all for now," the FBI chief said. "I trust you'll be available to us tonight."

"Certainly," Friede said.

"If anything at all unusual comes up, you'll contact us immediately."

"Of course," Friede had promised and took his leave.

Farminson was still looking at Sparrow. "You don't seem satisfied."

"With the tour? Oh, I'm satisfied that there are no hidden doorways, secret passages, or alcoves. There are just too many holes, too many things that can go wrong. Consider, for instance, the number of people who'll be malingering backstage."

"We can handle them. Besides, our number one priority remains the explosives, and as of this moment they are not present in this building."

"There's still Black to think about."

"And we hold a major advantage over him because we know the precise timing of everything that will take place tonight down to the last second, thanks to yesterday's dress rehearsal. They ran through it all, from the arrivals to the entertainment segments to the presentations, with everything except the envelopes. I had men here studying every possible angle."

"And how do you know Black wasn't here as well?"

That was six hours ago, and now Sparrow was

struck by the strongest feeling that the Prometheus *plastique* was in fact planted and set to go off. What's more, he could feel the presence of Renaldo Black. He was somewhere in the building, in the audience Sparrow assumed, where he had the shield of more than three thousand faces. The IDENT computers were supposed to be flawless. But a man who knew how the machine worked could circumvent its effectiveness. Black would know. He'd have come ready for IDENT.

Johnny Carson was standing in front of his glass podium again. "Now, to present the award for best actor in a supporting role, here are two of Hollywood's finest talents. . . ."

The surety of Black's presence inside the Music Center set Sparrow onto another track. The terrorist wasn't the kind to blow himself up in the midst of his greatest moment. Moreover, the rest of Isosceles depended on him. Obviously, then, he planned to be out of the building before the explosives went off. But how could he expect to accomplish this in full awareness that the FBI had the building blanketed? What was he using for a disguise? What final card was he holding?

Sparrow gazed out from his perch on the left side of the stage. It was much quieter here than on the right. On stage, the applause died down as male and female presenters completed their glide down the silver stairway and reached the podium.

"In the category of best actor in a supporting role, the nominees are. . . ."

Sparrow felt a gnawing inside him, rising out of his stomach toward his chest. With all he knew, he was still utterly helpless. He had argued vehemently that this ceremony should be allowed to go on, confident of his ability to keep pace with his opponent and eventually outdistance him. But Black had stayed a length ahead the whole time, and now Sparrow felt as though he had let the Americans down. They had placed their trust in him and he hadn't proved up to the task. Black was better than he was; he had to face that. What was he missing? Black planned to trigger the explosives and then disappear. How? The Prometheus explosives were in the building, yet the FBI hadn't found them. Again how? And where?

"And the winner is. . . ."

Enthusiastic applause caused a tremor in the hall. Sparrow lost a breath, thinking for a split second that the explosives had been triggered. He settled himself down.

An actor still in or barely out of his teens was jogging toward the stage, taking the steps in two effortless bounds. The female presenter handed him a gold statue, which he raised triumphantly over his head, revealing its green felt bottom. The audience quieted, as though on cue. The young actor leaned forward over the glass podium, still clutching the statue tightly in his hands.

"I'd like to thank. . . ."

The whine of feedback blared from the hidden speakers.

Sparrow moved two steps forward, almost on stage now.

"Oh my God . . ."

There it was, right before him. So obvious that he hadn't seen or picked it up.

". . . who gave me this chance and stuck by me when things weren't going very well. And most of all, I'd like to thank my father, who always offered me inspiration and. . . ."

Sparrow looked across the stage, his heart thundering. Thames Farminson stood directly before him in the right wing, taking in the festivities like an interested fan. Sparrow had to reach him fast. Time was running out, if there was any left at all. His next course of action might not have been the professional thing to do but it was mandated by the situation.

"Thank you all once again." With one final gesture of gleeful triumph, the young winner moved gracefully off the stage.

Sparrow hobbled in his shadow, his bad leg cramped with tension. For a brief moment, his image flashed across sixty million television screens throughout America.

Farminson caught sight of him when he was halfway across the stage and could sense the desperation in his stride.

"What's going on?"

"Get Friede!" Sparrow commanded.

"Why?"

"Just get him. There's no time to explain."

"I left him in the control room a few minutes ago. He's probably still there."

When they reached the command center, Friede was just closing the door behind him. "Quite an efficient operation you gentlemen—"

Sparrow cut him off. "Tell me about the Oscar statues!"

"What would you like to know?"

"When were they delivered here?"

"This afternoon."

"What time?"

"They were signed for at two P.M."

"How did they arrive?"

"I don't understand what—"

"How were they packed?"

402

"In special cartons, twelve in each."

"How many in all?"

"A hundred seventy-four."

Sparrow drew back against the wall. Thames Farminson looked at him, confused.

"We did check them all," he offered lamely.

"Each carton?"

"Each *statue.*"

"With the same equipment you checked the rest of the building with?"

"Of course. But—"

"We've got to get those statues out of here!"

"I told you, they're clean."

Sparrow swung back toward Friede, eyes raging. "What happens after they're given out?"

"After the brief press conferences, most winners elect to bring them back to their seats. Until the final number, of course."

"What final number?"

"The winners all file back on stage together, statues and all, to sing 'God Bless America' as the final credits roll. It's something new this year."

Sparrow's face was ashen. "That's when Black'll make his move." Then to Farminson, "We've got to get those statues out of this building *now!*"

"I keep telling you, they're clean," Farminson insisted. "Our equipment confirmed that, and it's made to sniff through plate gold."

"And what about lead?"

"Lead?"

"Because that's what the surface of those statues is made of. Just enough to protect the *plastique* Black has molded into the shape of our friends named Oscar: one hundred seventy-four of them!"

"Oh my Christ . . ."

THIRTY-SEVEN

Thames Farminson dabbed nervously at his sweat-soaked brow as he approached Sparrow in the corridor.

"We got them all," he reported. "Packed them away in a specially sealed truck for the lab. I was in Korea and came damn close to losing my life a dozen times, but it was nothing like handling those boxes, knowing they could blow me into a million fragments at any second."

"Did you check them?"

"The statues? For what?"

"To make sure my hunch was correct."

"I've got faith in your judgment. Besides, it would have taken too long. I thought I'd let the lab boys handle the confirmation." Farminson checked his watch. "By now the truck is out of range of any triggering mechanism on the market. How do you think Black planned to set the explosives off?"

"High-frequency sound most likely."

"And blow himself up?"

"No. There'd be a delay on the trigger, a minute or thereabouts. That doesn't explain how Black expected to make his exit in full view of the agents he knew damn well would be here, of course."

"The whole plan seems chancy."

"Technologically it depends on the expertise of the wiz behind it. You can bet Black got the best."

"Doesn't matter, I guess. A trigger isn't much use when there's nothing to trigger. We can breathe a little easier now."

"We still have to find Black."

"I've thrown a dragnet around the entire building," Farminson told him. "I've got men at every exit, every door, every goddamn crack in the floor. Black may have gotten in, but he's sure as hell not getting out."

"What do your computers tell you?"

"That he's not in the building."

"I wouldn't take that to heart."

"Don't worry. There are some things men can do much better than machines."

Sparrow glanced out at the stage where the ceremony was moving along right on schedule. A quick cover story was made up to explain the absence of the Oscar statues. It seems they had strangely disappeared, blocks of formica placed in the crates in their place. New material was written on the spot for Johnny Carson's apparently impromptu announcement, which was held up for two awards while the boxes of statues were loaded onto the truck. Farminson didn't want to give Black a chance to set the explosives off in desperation. This way he found out with everyone else, too late for it to matter.

"There's no reason for him to stay in the building now. He might try to take off on us during the ceremony," suggested the FBI chief.

"And lose his cover during the frenzy when it finishes up? I don't think so."

"All the same, I've got my men focusing now on anybody who leaves their seat suddenly for no apparent reason. If someone in the audience rises to go to the bathroom, we'll be with them until they pull their pants back up."

"Black'll have an escape route mapped out. He wouldn't leave a contingency like this to chance."

"But if he plans to use a door or window, my men will snatch him. His disguise can't be that good."

"It's been good enough to fool the computers."

Sparrow looked out on the stage. Another winner was making an acceptance speech. "How long before the lab tests the statues?"

"I should get the preliminary results within fifteen minutes. Why, you nervous?"

"Just concerned."

"Don't be. The use of the statues explains why our equipment never picked anything up. Though I'm damned if I can figure out how Black got to them and replaced them with his own."

"That's what's bothering me," Sparrow said.

"Don't forget that Black engineered the theft of three of our F-16s."

"I'm not."

"Then why should a few hundred pounds of golden statues worry you?"

Sparrow shrugged. "I don't know. Just nerves, maybe."

"Or withdrawal symptoms. Look, we've spent a lot of time with this. Sometimes it's hard to let go. But our job's been done, most of it anyway. The ball's in Bart Triesdale's court now. He's got to find those jets. . . . Wanna join me in the command center?"

"I think I'll have a look around the building."

"How 'bout I wire you in case you find something?"

Sparrow tapped his bad leg. "This restricts my movement plenty by itself."

Farminson nodded diffidently. "Well, if you need me. . . ."

"I know where to find you."

Farminson moved away. Sparrow looked toward Felix. The giant studied his eyes.

"Something is still bothering you, Israeli."

Sparrow shrugged. "Farminson might be right about it being withdrawals."

"He might be wrong."

"Keep an eye out, Felix, a sharp one."

"My eyes know no other way. And you, Israeli?"

"I'm going to take a tour of the premises."

Sparrow tugged on the vest of his tuxedo and headed toward a door that opened on the far right side of the pavilion facing the rear. He descended the steps lightly, wanting least of all to draw any attention to himself. Black knew he was here; there was no doubt about that. But that didn't mean he had to know exactly where.

The Lion of the Night found himself in an aisle that divided the main body of seats from a small section of four in each row against the wall. Aisles were plentiful in the Dorothy Chandler Pavilion to facilitate the rapid approach of winners to the stage. Few took notice of Sparrow, for he'd chosen a strategic moment to move; some of the more glamorous awards were about to be given out and the audience's attention was riveted forward.

One man, bearded and dark with olive skin and glasses, stole a glance at the ascending figure and recognized it immediately. Black had seen Sparrow dart across the stage after the first award was handed out. Then the statues were suddenly unaccounted for, and Black smiled at the way the Lion of the Night had put things together and come up with the wrong answer. An unfamiliar flutter of fear raced through him as Sparrow passed his aisle. Recognition now would forfeit everything. Of course, none of this would have been necessary if the Russians hadn't insisted on following through with this stage of the plot as planned. Black couldn't risk antagonizing them. Besides, they had arranged for a high-powered jet for him to leave the country in once this was finished, though he would still be cutting the final stage awfully close. Black dabbed at his brow, careful not to disturb the heavy plastic makeup that changed his face totally. Just another ten minutes was all the disguise had to hold out for.

Sparrow reached the back of the first tier and centered himself beneath the balcony. The vantage point was poor, his view severely restricted. He found a richly carpeted staircase and climbed to the second level. Even standing in the back he had a decent view of the festivities. He moved forward to his right toward a fixed camera position where a casually dressed man was bringing a silver monster about in a wide arc. A camera would have the best possible angle from up here. He placed himself behind its operator and looked down. The man swung angrily to his rear, then saw the badge pinned to Sparrow's lapel and went back to work.

Where are you, Black? Where are you?

Sparrow swept the crowd with his eyes, mimicking the motion of the camera, searching for something that didn't seem right or someone who caused a spark of recognition to flare in him.

Nothing on either count.

He felt frustrated, unsatisfied. Why? What did he feel? The discovery of the explosives should have set him at ease. It hadn't.

Another man in casual dress brushed by him and moved to the man operating the camera, tapping him on the shoulder. The operator took his headset off and leaned over.

"Boss says your lens is off," the new arrival in the balcony told him.

"Boss is full of shit."

"You wanna tell him that?"

"I already did over these goddamn earmuffs. That's why he sent you up."

"He told me to check your lens."

"It's fucking fine, I tell you. I've already checked it myself three times. Nothing's wrong. It's the goddamn lighting that sucks. Don't blame me because the fucking chandelier casts shadows."

"It didn't during the test shots last week."

"I wasn't here for the test shots."

Sparrow felt something cold rumble through him. It started as confusion, progressed to uncertainty, and in a second had hardened into fear. He looked up.

The lights of the chandelier flickered and winked at him.

He strained his eyes and looked closer. The thing seemed alive, with its dazzling crystals hanging free and twinkling apparently at will. What might have been huge, oblong pearls hung between the crystals, reflecting the lights' sparkle and radiating their brilliance. Hundreds of pearllike objects. Thousands maybe.

"In the category of best foreign film, the nominees are. . . ."

409

Sparrow rushed down the staircase, holding his heart in his mouth with a scream trapped behind his lips.

"Don't blame me because the fucking chandelier casts shadows."

"It didn't during the test shots last week."

He stopped at the bottom of the steps, glanced up at the stage where the list of nominees was being read. How could he have been so wrong? Perhaps he was just overreacting now, looking for something that wasn't really there.

The chandelier twinkled at him. One hundred fifty pounds of Prometheus *plastique* dispersed over a thirty-five-foot radius. . . . It would bring the entire ceiling down.

The fear stayed with him but now it was hot, steamy. Sweat caked his brow. It was impossible. Farminson had said everything had been checked. Did that, though, include the chandelier?

"And the winner is. . . ."

Sparrow could stand the fear no longer. He gave in to it and bolted down the center aisle at the top speed he could muster. The name of the winner was read. A few cameras caught him, reacting to the timing of his rush, then quickly turned away toward the approach of the real winner.

Sparrow never broke stride. He climbed the center steps that fifty winners had already climbed before him, passed before the eyes of ninety million Americans, and rushed on. Johnny Carson looked at him dumbfounded. The Lion of the Night didn't look back.

Thames Farminson, seeing the havoc break out on one of his monitors, met him just off the stage. The crowd was still buzzing. The producer of the victorious

Belgian film was just reaching the podium.

"What the hell's going on?" Farminson demanded.

"You've got to evacuate the building!"

"What are you talking about?"

"It wasn't the statues."

"But you—"

"I was wrong. The explosives are packed into that chandelier, and unless we do something fast the whole damn roof is gonna come crashing down on everyone in this building."

"Oh Jesus . . ."

Farminson had started to raise a walkie-talkie to his mouth when a breathless agent in shirtsleeves slammed to a halt next to him.

"Sir, the lab just called. The statues are clean!"

Sparrow and Farminson exchanged empty glances. The FBI chief had the walkie-talkie at his lips when it beeped twice.

"I've lost contact with Eagle fifteen, rear stage area," a nervous voice reported.

A heavy hand clamped down on Sparrow's shoulder. "I'll handle it, Israeli," Felix said and he moved away.

On stage a bearded man, producer of the winning foreign film, was praising America and her penchant for free expression. Something about the heavily accented voice made Sparrow turn. He caught the winner's profile. The Belgian turned a quarter more. Their eyes met briefly and with a shudder Sparrow realized he was looking at Renaldo Black. He saw the terrorist's hand drop into his pocket and stay there.

"It's Code Nero," Farminson was saying into his walkie-talkie, giving the signal for evacuation. "Repeat, we have Code Nero." Then to Sparrow, "We'll try to do this as orderly as possible."

411

But the Israeli had already reached across him and pressed the fire alarm.

"What the hell . . ."

Sparrow darted onto the stage before Farminson had finished his sentence. The fire alarm was wailing in raspy screeches that alternated each second with silence.

"Cut the cameras! Cut the cameras!" Farminson screamed into the leather mouthpiece at his lips.

And on stage Renaldo Black's hand was emerging from his pocket with something in it. Sparrow crashed a shoulder into him and the big man went reeling sideways. Sparrow seized the moment. He was on Black again immediately, whipping a sizzling kick toward the hand that was gripping the detonator. He guessed it would set off a timing fuse that would allow Black sufficient seconds to duck backstage, bypass the press rooms, and make his escape. Yes, that must have been Black's plan all along. He must have been right about the explosives' being set off by high-frequency sound. Otherwise, Black would have been able to activate them from his pocket.

The kick landed square in the terrorist's fingers, crunching them. Something dark and square went flying. Black dived for it. Sparrow cut him off, toppled him over with the force of all his weight. They were alone amidst the crowd, the chaos on stage precluding the intervention of any FBI agents, even if they had been aware of the struggle amidst the evacuation.

The fire alarm kept screeching. Felix hurried toward the backstage area. Tungsten readied his backup detonator.

Stunned, Black still managed a powerful blow to Sparrow's stomach that stripped him of a measure of his wind. Another blow headed for the throat was right on target, but the Israeli twisted his shoulders at the last instant and the strike found only air. He had position on Black as they struggled on the floor and had to take advantage of it. The terrorist, though, deflected one powerful strike and a second barely grazed his ear. Then Sparrow felt a rigid hand ram into his groin. He gasped, felt himself being pushed away. He reached out but Black was free. His eyes sought the gray detonator.

Black's didn't. He pulled back his sleeve and aimed the dart launcher. Sparrow caught the hint of movement, so when Black flicked his wrist he was able to spin from the dart's path.

Instead of readying another dart, Black rushed Sparrow as he completed his twist and struck him with a palm-heel to the face. Sparrow felt blood dribble into his throat from his nasal cavity and two streams erupt from his nostrils. He staggered backwards, blinded for a second, which was long enough for Black to lash out with a dizzying kick to his face that sent him sprawling. He teetered on the edge of the stage for an instant before tumbling over.

Black readied another dart, closed for the kill.

Sparrow started to draw his .45 even as he was in midair.

Black grasped the flash of steel with his eyes. His darts took two seconds to immobilize their victim, another three to kill—plenty of time for the Lion of the Night to get off at least one shot.

Sparrow steadied the gun, started to squeeze the trigger.

Black shrank back amidst the panicked crowd on the stage.

Sparrow pulled his finger away when he perceived

one of his bullets was about to rocket toward one of the female stage ushers. He struggled to his feet against the protests of his racked body, climbed back up the steps, and pushed his way in the direction he had seen Black disappearing. He drifted into a sea of black tuxedos, one man distinguishable from the next in the rush for the exits only by his height and hair. Black could conceivably have been any of half of them.

Sparrow pressed on, feeling the tight fingers of failure grasp his insides, knotting them with frustration. He had had Black and had lost him. Again. A shudder moved through his spine. What about the detonator? A fair portion of the crowd was still in the building. Had Black triggered the *plastique?* Sparrow struggled back through an opening in the crowd toward the front of the stage. His eyes swept the floor through the tide of churning feet. If one of them struck the button. . . .

He fought to remember which direction the detonator had jumped in when he had separated it from Black. He aimed his gaze to the far right, the sight of the dark box scraping across the floor suddenly fresh in his mind. A shape appeared on the shiny granite surface near the white dais, kicked by one man and then another. Sparrow shouldered his way desperately for it. He lost the box for a second, recovered it, and lost it again. Then it was there, just below him, sharp in his sights. A shoe was rising over a red button in the box's center, descending now in line with it. In Sparrow's mind the issue had already been decided. But his body acted separately, darting between two frames and sweeping a hand across the floor. It passed so close to the descending shoe that the heel actually scraped his knuckles as he retrieved the detonator and grasped it tightly in his hand.

Miraculously, the red button remained elevated, unpressed. The *plastique* had not been triggered by this box. But there had to be a backup unit. A plan of such intricate timing would require one to insure effectiveness against the slightest slipup. But where was it? And where was Felix?

Felix crept down the backstage corridor. The dim light rendered his sharp eyes almost useless, while the panicked screaming along with the alarm neutralized his ears as well. The giant had only his feelings to guide him and they warned him he was not alone.

He kept his right side pressed against the wall as he moved. To his left was five thousand square feet of outdated lighting and other equipment, a maze of steel and cable that somewhere hid the holder of the second box.

Tungsten stood huddled behind two thick lighting poles. His left hand held a detonator identical to Black's. His orders had been explicit. When the winner of the best foreign film was announced, he was to wait for Black to make the acceptance speech. If for any reason Black didn't, he was to detonate the explosives immediately. Now Tungsten was confused. He had heard Black speak all right, but only briefly, and then the alarm and sounds of panic had drowned everything out. Something had gone wrong. Tungsten waited one minute and then decided to use his detonator.

The huge hulk of the man he remembered from the airport in Washington slithered by, ignorant of his presence. Tungsten held the detonator tightly in his flesh hand and edged backwards.

His heel struck a piece of twisted cable.

Felix caught the slight sound and whipped his pistol toward it. He got off one shot, which would have been a direct hit had Tungsten not shifted to the side and spun forward. Felix saw the black blur of motion whirl before him and resteadied the gun. A gloved hand flashed in front of him, its motion subtle and swift. There was a crash on his wrist, like meeting a tree branch, and the gun was gone.

Tungsten lunged for the kill. He never saw Felix's second pistol.

Felix managed one shot, a damn good one just a little low in the chest, before the gloved tree branch pounded the side of his head and he was airborne, feeling himself smash hard to the floor.

Blood eased from the black giant's chest but he seemed unfazed by it. His normal hand started to close around a gray box.

Felix drew a dagger from his vest and flung it. Its hilt struck the fleshy fingers square on. The detonator went flying. Then the other dagger was in his hand and he flung that too, a chest shot, because he knew that the head or heart were the only useful targets against this opponent.

The dagger sped forward, slicing the air, in perfect line with its target. At the last possible instant, Tungsten threw up his steel arm in an eclipse of motion and deflected the blade upward.

Felix was already back on his feet, whisking his sword from its scabbard in a low-to-high draw designed for narrow confines and approaching for an overhead cut. His wrists snapped forward and the blade whistled straight down through the air to the black giant's head where neither bone nor muscle could stop its blinding assault.

Steel was another matter.

Tungsten threw up his right arm as the blade glistened downward. A thud and soft clang followed. The sword broke in two. Felix jabbed the ragged half he still held by the hilt for the thorax before him, but Tungsten was equal to this task as well. He lowered his steel arm fast and hard, gloved palm down. At impact Felix felt the bones of his forearm vibrate madly, the heavy muscle around them not enough to shield the blow. Then the gloved hand was whirling toward him in a backlash. But he ducked under the blow, deflected it slightly, and rammed his shoulder into the black giant's ribs like a linebacker heading off a running back. He felt something give, heard air escape from the mouth above him, and shoved the black hulk backwards.

Tungsten went with the move, allowing Felix to take him while he regrouped his strategy. His steel arm had been pinned for a moment, but now it was free again. And as he was being propelled backwards, he slammed it down on the bearded man's back.

Felix felt everything inside him shake, the trembling extending all the way to his fingers. His knees hit something, and it took him a second to realize that it was the floor and that the black giant was unleashing a thunderous overhead strike for his skull. Felix met the blow the only way that could have stopped it, with his hands locked over each other in an X-pattern. He took the impact squarely on his wrists. Only by raising his arms and intercepting the strike before it gained momentum did he save his bones from certain breaking.

Tungsten pulled back for another blow but Felix was

on his feet again by this time and dodged it effortlessly. The black giant's jacket was drenched in red now. He was weakening; he had to be. His blows were still powerful, though not as quick. Felix sidestepped another and snapped a lightning kick out in retaliation. It hammered home. Then a punch to the black giant's solar plexus, and his knuckles came out red. Felix felt the tide turn. He had him.

Until he let his guard down for the briefest of seconds. It wasn't so much negligence on his part as expertise on Tungsten's. The black giant drew him in with a vicious strike with his gloved hand, caught his eyes, then lashed out with his normal hand for Felix's jaw. The blow took Felix totally by surprise. Oh, he saw it at the last instant before it smashed under his chin, but the best he could do was tense his muscles and turn with it. His head was snapped back. His shoulders crashed into a pair of light stands.

The steel fingers stretched for his throat, so close the hairs of his beard prickled on end. One squeeze and it would be over. Felix could not allow Tungsten that squeeze. He managed to get an arm out in an attempt to deflect the angled steel coming for him. He shrank his neck back from the hand almost upon it and pushed against the glove. Tungsten changed his motion almost imperceptibly to meet the challenge. In that instant, Felix shifted his push to a pull, adding to the black giant's momentum and taking him in the direction he was weakest. Felix pulled the gloved hand past his face and then drove it forward. Glass shattered. Tungsten's steel arm was imbedded in a light fixture up to his elbow. Felix spun for the kill.

But Tungsten was too fast for him. Instead of trying

to extract the hand, he yanked down with it on the light stand. The whole assembly came crashing down, covering Felix with steel, glass, and cable. Tungsten pulled his arm free, moved for the detonator. With all his strength, Felix heaved the stand off him. He was halfway to his feet when Tungsten stung him with a kick. Then the steel arm was swinging down. He turned and took the blow square on his shoulder, felt bone and cartilage crack, powerless to stop his pitch sideways toward the scaffolding. He struck it hard, felt it give, and knew five levels would now be tumbling toward him. He was able to right his position in time to avoid direct impact, but the move cost him his balance and he struck the floor hard, chin first.

Tungsten had the detonator in his hand now. His finger edged for the red button. Felix sprang from the floor in an incredible blur, swept his sword handle off the rough surface without slowing his motion. Tungsten swirled his steel arm around in the most powerful sweep yet. But Felix was already inside it, close enough to the black giant to smell the blood draining from him and to neutralize the effectiveness of his greatest weapon.

Tungsten reached for him with his gloved fingers.

Felix drove the broken edge of the blade forward and up, both hands tight around the silk-wrapped hilt. The edge ripped into the front of Tungsten's throat and tore through the back of his neck. His eyes bulged but he held his ground, kept reaching with his steel fingers. Felix twisted the blade sharply, was showered in scarlet. Tungsten's arm slipped to his side. His mouth hung open but all breath and sounds were choked off by the blood pouring from the jagged tear in his throat where the sword handle still protruded. He keeled over backwards, eyes grasping death with shock and surprise.

The detonator slid from his fingers. Felix reached for it.

The button had been pushed!

The fire alarm was still blaring, making it impossible for his ears to tell him if anyone was left inside. He thought of running back to the stage to issue a final warning but there was no time. He had at best thirty seconds to escape himself.

Actually it was fifteen. The blast came just after he had slammed the emergency exit behind him, projecting him headlong into the night air. He was too stunned to brace for impact and didn't even realize he had landed until his torn fingers pressed asphalt beneath them.

"Get these people back! Get these people back!"

Thames Farminson ran along the front line of police and FBI personnel fighting against a crowd of celebrity seekers eager to catch a glimpse of their favorite star fleeing the building.

"Move them!" the FBI chief screamed. *"Move them!"*

The crowd retreated but not much, certainly not enough to take them out of range of the blast that came seconds later.

The front of the Los Angeles Music Center seemed to go first, rupturing from within and scattering wood and cement fragments a full city block. The bleachers lining the building's front, which spectators had been filling since dawn, splintered into thousands of deadly projectiles. Those bystanders lucky enough to avoid them were propelled backwards, slammed against walls or through windows. The Music Center's remains rained down, falling from the blackened sky. They landed with the volume of gunshots and for those beneath them the effect was far worse.

There was another blast from somewhere inside the building that was actually the sound of the structure breaking apart as the roof caved in and plummeted toward the now empty seats. Flames pushed out, swelled, then stretched for the sky. More of the building's walls tumbled, to be swallowed by the inferno. What remained after only seconds was a ragged shell, indistinguishable from what it had been at the start of the evening.

The red carpet leading to the main entrance had been totally obliterated, liquified splotches of it seeming to spread over the street and sidewalks from bodies that writhed horribly or writhed no more.

Police and FBI officials struggled to pull the wounded off the road and gather them together for the ambulances. The carnage was sickening. The initial force of the explosion together with its rumbling aftermath had severed arms, legs and heads—a hideous combination of which now lay strewn on the pavement, not necessarily close to the bodies they had once been attached to.

Sparrow searched for Thames Farminson amidst the horror, his stomach reeling against the sight of the dead and dying. He had no idea how much of the audience in the upper tiers had been stuck inside when the blast came. Even discounting these, the toll of casualties promised to be high. Ambulances were already screeching to the scene along with a horde of fire engines, six battalions in all. For them, the succeeding hours would be endless. The night had turned deathly quiet, broken only by the roar of sirens, the whimpering of the wounded and the crackling of the frames over what had been the Los Angeles Music Center. Bodies lay everywhere, the sight not unlike that of a battlefield's bloody dawn.

Just ahead, Sparrow saw three FBI agents huddled anguishedly over someone. He knew who it was well before he reached the fading eyes of Thames Farminson.

"How . . . many?" the FBI director muttered between trembling lips.

"A lot less than three thousand."

Two men in white laid a stretcher next to Farminson on the pavement.

"You . . . get . . . Black?"

"I will."

Farminson tried to smile as they carried him away.

"You must give me a piece of him too, Israeli."

Sparrow turned to see Felix leaning against a severed lamppost, his face scratched and bleeding. One arm dangled uselessly by his side.

"When we find him," Sparrow promised. "When we find him. . . ."

And two blocks away Renaldo Black dialed his first overseas number.

"The trigger has been pulled," he announced simply and moved on to the second.

THIRTY-EIGHT

The President hung up the phone and faced Bart Triesdale and General Bob MaCammon.

"Sparrow's on his way in." He sighed grimly. "Thames is still in critical condition. Doctors are doing the best they can to save his leg but it doesn't look good."

"Damn," muttered Triesdale.

"And as for the rest of Los Angeles," the President continued, watching the luminous dial of his digital clock move past midnight, "the death toll's up to three hundred, while the number injured stretches into the thousands. And since we didn't catch Black, we've got to move on the assumption that the final stage of Isosceles has been activated. Bob, if Lennagin is right about the bombs, what kind of destruction are we looking at?"

MaCammon didn't even have to think. "Even combined, the Capricorn missiles we believed were going to be used couldn't be measured in the megaton range. The three hydrogen bombs pack something close to a hundred fifty megatons."

"Oh my God . . ."

"It gets even worse when you consider the long-term

effects of the accompanying radiation. You can't hide in your cellar from fifty megatons of hydrogen bomb, and even if you could, it wouldn't be safe to come out again for another hundred years or so."

"At this point," interjected Bart Triesdale, "we stand a pretty good chance it won't come to that. We know the jets are somewhere in Spain, Germany, and Egypt, so I've got special assault teams on alert in each. One phone call and the teams scramble within ten minutes, no more than two and a half hours from any conceivable takeoff point. Quinn said Lennagin was mumbling something about the East Frisian Islands before he passed out, so we're concentrating our search in that area for the German leg of Isosceles. The computer should be spitting out a batch of phone numbers and corresponding addresses any minute." The CIA man shrugged. "Let's just hope Sparrow's suggestion is on target."

The President nodded reflectively, his stare surprisingly passive. "Find those jets, Bart. Just find them."

It was two hours later into a sleepless night when Triesdale returned to the Oval Office to find the President in the same position he had left him.

"We found them," he pronounced.

The President felt a cold wave of relief sweep through him. "Thank God. . . . Where?"

"Three small, unlisted airfields. Germany came in first, just as we suspected on an island in the East Frisian chain. Funny thing about the phone number there was that it was a brand-new listing—operators didn't have it yet. I cross-checked that clue with our

Spanish and Egyptian lists and came up with the other two. The Spanish field is located in Cassa, the Egyptian field on the Nile, just north of Thebes. Our teams will be closing in on all three in just over an hour. I chose a simultaneous strike for security reasons."

"Good judgment on your part." The President leaned back almost comfortably. "Sparrow will be arriving here any minute. It'll be nice to have good news to tell him for a change."

But the news, as it turned out, was not good.

"Bart, what are you saying?" demanded the President.

"Simply that when our assault team reached the airfield north of Thebes in Egypt, they found nothing. We recovered two bombs and two jets but the third of each, I'm afraid, is unaccounted for."

"And could be anywhere in the world. . . ."

"Not quite," interrupted Sparrow. "We know the target must still be Libya. That was fixed by Lucifer, in addition to the attack time. The only changeable factor was the launching point, and Black has taken full advantage of that. But with the target still Libya his options are cut down considerably, probably to one: Israel."

"Israel?" the President quizzed skeptically.

"My country may be small areawise, but she's got more hidden airfields from the Haganah days than the rest of the Middle East combined. Besides, the cover's perfect. Israel and Egypt have been conducting joint air force exercises this week in recognition of the new strategic treaty. American-built jets have been buzzing the skies for days now. So all Black has to do is change the markings of his a bit and it would have free reign of airspace right up to the Libyan border."

"I assume there's more," advanced General MaCammon.

"Indeed. Black's got two options now and both of them are deadly. If things go as planned, the F-16 will take off for Libya on schedule. If they don't . . . he'll use the hydrogen bomb on Israel."

Shock replaced Sparrow's voice in the room.

"He'll detonate it at ground level if he even suspects we're closing in on him," the Israeli continued. "And he'll have taken plenty of precautions to let him know."

"It doesn't make any sense," Bart Triesdale argued.

"Militarily," countered General MaCammon, "I'm inclined to disagree."

"Indeed," said Sparrow. "Consider first that Black's been using Lucifer the whole time, with the help of powerful forces inside Russia. All along, though, the possibility existed that his scheme would be uncovered. What then? Simple: If all three of Isosceles's nuclear legs couldn't be preserved, at least one could by relocating it under Black's supervision. But which one? Certainly not Moscow—too much of a sacrifice, and I doubt it was ever really threatened in the first place, more of a smoke screen than anything else. And the obliteration of Paris wouldn't go anywhere toward provoking the threat of war from the Soviets' standpoint. That left the Libyan leg. As a last resort to accomplish his and the Soviets' purpose, Black could launch the jet from Israel—"

"—and give the world the impression that Jerusalem was responsible for the destruction of Tripoli," com-

426

pleted the President.

"In which case, what would the Soviet Union's reaction be?"

The President didn't hesitate. "Kaddafi's their puppet and Libya represents their only real stronghold in the Mideast. They wouldn't take it lying down, I can tell you that much. If they were looking for war, an apparent Israeli strike on Libya would give them a damn good reason to mobilize. Then we either sit back and watch them destroy Israel or mobilize ourselves. Makes sense, doesn't it?"

"All too much."

"And if we close in on Black before he can launch," resumed the President, "he blows up the bomb on the spot and we lose *our* stronghold in the Mideast, allowing the Russians to move in as they please . . . unless we choose to stop them."

"Which is exactly what they'd want."

"It's a no-win situation under either scenario."

"That's the point."

"So we're damned if we do and damned if we don't."

"Unless we let Black launch his jet and take our chances of finding it in the air," Sparrow suggested. "We could ground all other air force traffic to make it stick out."

"Our chances still wouldn't be any better than fifty-fifty."

"Also no worse."

"I don't know," muttered the President. "We're talking about buttons and bombs here. It all strikes pretty close to home."

Sparrow settled back in his chair, seized by a chill. Suddenly the way Renaldo Black thought and acted was clear to him. There were a thousand potential airfields inside Israel, but only one the terrorist would use.

"Have you got a plane that can get me to Tel Aviv in six hours?" he asked abruptly.

The President glanced at General MaCammon, who nodded. "Yes," he said, "but what good can you do over there?"

"Find Black and deliver the third leg of Isosceles to you."

"You know where he is?"

"Yes."

"Then tell us, for God's sake," the President pleaded. "Let me contact Israel and have a team sent in now."

"Black would know they were coming before they got within five miles. He'd blow up the country while they loaded their rifles. The operation has to be mine and mine alone. And if I fail, you'll still have fifteen minutes to scramble fighters and catch the jet before it enters Libyan airspace."

"That is, if your failure doesn't mean Israel gets blown to hell. We're playing with the deaths of millions of people here."

"Or preserving their lives. We play the endgame my way or you find the airfield yourselves."

The President hesitated, realizing Sparrow's voice had taken on the same grimness it had when they'd discussed the death of his family a few days before. He wasn't bluffing. "You and that giant of yours plan to handle this alone?"

"No." A pause. "I'm going to give you a list of seven commandos who are on constant call in Israel for situations like this. Contact them and have them meet me in Tel Aviv."

"Seven men? That's all?"

"With these, that's all it'll take. Besides, any more and we run the risk of alerting Black to the raid." Sparrow thought briefly. "And I'd like that Lennagin boy to meet me in Tel Aviv as well."

"Good God, you're not planning to take him along too?"

"I'm planning to let him make that decision for himself. He deserves the opportunity."

The President's eyes blazed across his desk. "You're pushing things, Sparrow."

"I haven't even begun to push yet."

The President nodded deliberately.

Sparrow knew he had won and might have smiled but his thoughts precluded that gesture and all others. He was going back to an abandoned airfield he had used as a Haganah freedom fighter forty years before, modified into a kibbutz so he could live out the present with the past and its memories never far away. Going back for a third crack at the terrorist he wanted to kill more than anything else in the world. Going back to the last place on Earth Renaldo Black would expect him to look for a missing F-16 and hydrogen bomb.

The Lion of the Night was going home.

THIRTY-NINE

"So what do we do now?" Dan asked Quinn when they reached an isolated, restricted section of Ben-Gurion Airport in Tel Aviv.

"We wait. As ordered."

"And what are your orders concerning me?"

Dan's left arm was held in a sling, his shoulder pieced back together by tape and bandages. He could move the arm only with substantial discomfort. The sling kept it restricted. His leg wasn't much better. The doctor had recommended crutches as they were about to leave the hospital. Dan had left them in the lobby.

"Stick to you like glue," Quinn told him, "and make sure you arrive back in Washington safely for debriefing. Might take a year with all you've uncovered."

"And then?"

Quinn looked away. "That's not my field."

"Neither was rescuing me on the Mediterranean."

Quinn looked back at Dan. "Look, I've been with the Bureau for going on fifeen years and I've started each day with the resolve to keep my nose in my paperwork and not try to smell out anything else. But sometimes you can't help it. Sometimes you see how the real pros operate."

"So?"

"So you asked me what's going to happen to you after they're finished. The answer is that they're never going to finish. You know too goddamn much. You've seen too goddamn much. You're what real pros call a high-level security risk. Not because of what you've done—hell, you're a hero for that. It's because of the harm you could do if you fell into the wrong hands."

"Fell?"

"Or got pushed. Same thing basically, and from the pros' standpoint there's no difference at all. They'll probably treat you real nice at first. Keep you in a pleasant house in the country for a couple weeks while they ask you a zillion questions they expect you to have answers for. And then they'll let you go."

"Just like that?"

"Not quite, because you'll never be rid of them. They'll always be around the corner or down the street. They'll know who you see and what you say to them. Then one day if they decide you said too much and they can't control you any longer, out comes a man with a poison pen or umbrella or dart and the next time you wake up Koralski and Bathgate will be beside you."

"Do I have a choice in all this?"

Quinn tightened his features. "No, but I do, *goddammit!* It's a crowded airport, kid. I could tell them you slipped away from me in the confusion. They may buy it, they may not."

"Your job's finished either way."

"Private practice is looking better all the time." Quinn looked at Dan pleadingly. "Split from me here and hop on a plane. You risked your life for these fuckers and they'd just as soon hang you out to dry. Get out of it while you still have the chance."

431

Dan smiled faintly. "I can't."

"I hope you got a good reason why."

"Not really. I just know I can't run. I've been running for the last two weeks, scared out of my wits and forced to do and say things I thought somebody else must've been responsible for. But you know something, Paul? At least the whole time I was after *some*thing, trying to get *some*where. You're telling me I should run, not *to* anything or anywhere, just run. I can't. Not now, not ever. No way. Koralski said this sort of life gets to be addicting, like drugs or cigarettes. I don't know if he was right, but I do know the only place I can go is wherever Sparrow takes us."

"Cigarettes aren't exactly good for your health either, kid."

In Washington, the minutes were speeding by.

"It might be time to let the Russians in on what's happened and what might be about to," the President told the two men facing him. "Bring everything out into the open, eyeball to eyeball."

"And hope the Russians blink," completed MaCammon.

"Otherwise," began Triesdale, "we're totally dependent on one man."

"Whose stake in this stretches far beyond even ours."

"Sounds like you know something we don't, Mr. President."

"If I told you, you'd understand."

"We're listening," from MaCammon.

Dan Lennagin watched the graying man limp toward

Paul Quinn right from the only gate in the restricted terminal. By his side walked the bearded giant named Felix who had saved Dan's life in the Mediterranean. He was carrying a duffel bag.

The graying man advanced ahead of the giant. So this was Sparrow. . . . Somehow he didn't measure up to Dan's expectations. An old, hobbled man in a world of violence and death. It just didn't fit, not at all, that is until Dan saw his eyes; cold, deep-set, and hard. They were Koralski's eyes, Gabriele's eyes, Black's eyes. And then Dan knew.

"We meet again," Sparrow greeted Quinn.

"Yeah, just like old home week."

Sparrow's eyes found Dan's. Something unspoken passed between them. Quinn had the feeling he was trapped in the middle of two magnets pulling fiercely toward each other. It was as though the aging Israeli and the boy were being reunited instead of introduced. There was definitely a bond there, subtle and beneath the surface, but tight, nonetheless. Here were two souls that felt as one, strangers and yet not strangers.

"Excuse me," Quinn managed. "This is—"

"Dan Lennagin," Sparrow completed and stepped toward him. Dan felt a shudder pass deep within him. The Israeli extended a warm hand. "I've heard a lot about you."

"Likewise," Dan forced lamely.

"You'll be coming with us this afternoon?"

Dan just nodded, half looking at Quinn.

Sparrow eyed him knowingly. "I thought as much." The pull between them returned, like a highly charged energy field. Sparrow broke it by turning back to the man from the FBI. "Has my team arrived?"

"They're waiting outside."

Sparrow checked his watch. It was five o'clock exactly. "We've got forty-five minutes to reach our destination. I'll have Felix brief them on the way."

"That's cutting things a little close," Quinn cautioned.

"That's the idea."

They spoke only briefly, as time would allow and necessity mandated, while Felix and Quinn picked up the truck.

"I read your file again on the flight over here," Sparrow said.

Dan smiled inwardly. "Thank you."

"For what?"

"For not saying what a wonder it is I'm still alive, like everyone else has."

"Because it isn't a wonder. My friend Felix passes everything off to fate, to karma. People are what they're meant to be, he says, and nothing else. The book is written; all we do is turn the pages. I'm beginning to think he might be right."

"What does that have to do with me?"

"Everything and nothing. Fortune guided you in the beginning, but skill took over after you left Hamburg. There's a very fine line that separates the professional from the amateur, not so much a state of being as a state of mind. The professional acts, the amateur questions."

"I still question."

"Do you? Or do you merely consider your options and choose the cleanest? For the amateur, each task is an end in itself. For the professional, there are only means. You tell me, Dan, which describes you better?"

Dan looked away, confused. "I don't know."

"Nor should you. You've crossed the line but the evolution continues, as it always will. The professional never stops growing. The amateur never begins."

"You make it sound attractive, like Koralski did."

"I don't mean to. Because with the growing come the lies, and the lies never stop either. That's what this kind of life is centered around, you know—lying. Any way you look at it, the truth is the rarest commodity of all. Men like myself—and Koralski—learn to be proficient in every weapon imaginable. We learn codes and forging; we learn about sterile lines and controls and moles and clearance and scramblers and plants; we learn how to kill and how to live. But most of all we learn how to lie to ourselves and others. There's never any trust, just convenient cooperation. And once in a while men like myself try and run from the lies, but they always seem to catch up to us and we end up just about the same place we started."

"Why are you telling me all this?"

"Because you've crossed the line and I'm hoping against hope there might be a way to push you back. I doubt it, though. Everything changes on this side. The other becomes a vacuum. There's no going back. You retreat there and the lies follow you, return you to the other side. But it depends on how far you've come across, on how much of you has. When this is over, I'm going to try and push you back. I want you to know that."

"It seems futile."

"Except that the lies haven't begun for you yet. Until they do, there may be a chance."

"And if there isn't?"

"Then I'll find some other means to keep the lies away," Sparrow assured him. "There might be no escape, but there is hope. I know how the lies have affected my life, and given it to do all over again, I should know how to avoid them and still survive; become the master of them instead of letting them become the master of me."

"And what about the truth?"

"There isn't any, not for us."

"There is one. . . ."

Their eyes met, stares becoming one. They might have been the same body, the same spirit, so much so that when the next words were spoken it was difficult to tell which of the two they came from.

"We've got to kill Renaldo Black."

"You can come back in now, gentlemen."

Bart Triesdale and General MaCammon rose from their seats just beyond the door to the Oval Office and moved inside. The President had asked them to step out while he completed his call to the Soviet Union. Now, after closing the door behind his advisors, he shuffled to the large bay window, fingers quivering near his temples, and looked out dimly into the fresh morning light.

"The Russians were not very receptive," he reported.

"You didn't get anywhere at all?" Triesdale asked.

"Far enough to be told that they would not allow one of their allies to fall victim to a carefully orchestrated capitalist plot to attain supremacy in the Middle East, and that if I thought I could escape blame by trying to pin it on somebody else in advance, I was failing to consider some rather severe ramifications."

"Sounds like a concealed threat," noted MaCammon.

"Oh, there was nothing concealed about it. They closed by saying that if our plane launches a successful strike on Libya, in retaliation they will . . . destroy Israel."

"We can't let them get away with that, sir," insisted the general after a brief but foreboding pause.

The President nodded, a mask of emptiness drawn over his features. "No, I suppose we can't." He moved to his desk and reached for a phone that linked him directly to SAC mission control. "This is the President. We're going to Condition Red. . . ."

FORTY

They drove southeast out of Ben-Gurion Airport on a secondary road that left barely enough room for vehicles to approach from the opposite direction. The bright warmth of the afternoon was gone, replaced by a cool breeze that formed the leading edge of the coming dusk. Their destination was an isolated kibbutz between the villages of Gizmo and Mero Modri. The road would grow from bad to worse, then disappear altogether.

Their vehicle, hardly suited for the terrain, was a modified produce truck, full of squeaks and rickets, but also a sight that would draw a minimum of attention. Sparrow drove. Quinn sat up front with him. Dan was in the back with the seven-man commando team and Felix, who stayed poised near the tailgate, ready to spring out every time the truck's brakes came on. The giant's right arm had swollen through an ace bandage he had tied uneasily around it. He moved the arm awkwardly and as little as possible, never so much as flinching. The pain was there, Dan knew. Felix just ignored it.

The other seven men in the truck were, after Felix, the toughest Dan had ever laid eyes on. Weapons hung from their belts and broad shoulders as naturally as fruit from a vine. An air of indestructibility enveloped them. Almost like the battle had already been won; all that remained was to fight it.

Dan's own role in the assault on the refuge of the final F-16 and its deadly cargo had never been defined or elaborated on, at least not verbally. His instructions came from Sparrow's eyes: The choice was his alone. He could stay in the truck if he pleased, or, similarly, he could remain with the group every step of the way. His decision had already been made, and he had removed the sling from his arm in preparation for carrying it through.

The truck squealed to a slow halt. Sparrow touched the horn lightly once. Felix pulled back the tailgate, prepared to lower himself from the truck.

Sparrow had seen the Arab standing on the opposite side of the road from quite a distance; a hitchhiker not interested in a ride, the first of Black's lookouts.

"Excuse me," Sparrow yelled out the window.

The man pretended as though he didn't hear.

"Slikhá," Sparrow repeated louder in Hebrew. That caught the man's attention. "I'm afraid I'm lost. *Tukhál la-a-zór li?"* He switched back to English. "Could you possibly help me with directions?"

The man hesitated, then moved impatiently across the road to Sparrow's window. Agreeing to help would be the quickest way to be rid of the menace. The man's senses were on alert. His hand felt for the pistol concealed beneath his shirt. He switched his walkie-talkie off to avoid its suspicious crackle. No one would take him off guard.

"Where are you headed?" he asked routinely.

"Ramallah," Sparrow told him.

"Well, that explains it. You're heading in the wrong direction."

"Oh no."

"What you've got to do is—"

The man proved no match for Felix. He never heard the giant glide around behind him. A quick, sure strike to the base of the skull and the Arab went down. Felix lifted him effortlessly into the back of the truck where he was bound, gagged, and tucked in a corner. The truck started on its route again.

There were six lookouts in all, so the process had to be repeated five more times. The men had no concrete reason to doubt the authenticity of the produce truck because their orders were to watch for an armed convoy or anything that smelled of official government envoy and report accordingly. The truck smelled only of rich Israeli oranges. There was nothing to report. Nor would the lack of their regular reports mean much now. Black would have other things on his mind these final thirty minutes, the possibility of a still imminent attack not even considered, and the lookouts thus superfluous. It was too late; it had to be. Such was the basis of Sparrow's complex timing.

The Lion of the Night checked his watch: five thirty-six. They were right on schedule. He swung the truck off the main road onto an unmarked dirt route. His stomach fluttered with the familiar scent and feeling of home.

But it was not his home today.

The truck rode the dirt and rocks uneasily, too heavy and poorly balanced for the terrain. Men crashed against each other in the back. Dan's shoulder jammed against the frame and pain exploded right down to his fingers. He swallowed it like a bad piece of fruit, keeping his face empty of expression. He looked up and saw Felix smiling at him.

The big bastard can read my mind, Dan thought.

Sparrow did the best he could to keep the truck steady. It wavered a bit with his concentration when he passed another similarly unmarked road that led to the abandoned airfield he had turned into a kibbutz and private heaven from the hell of the world. Only the hell had caught up with him. He drove on, nearly half a mile, until the access road was totally shielded from sight. Felix met him just outside his door. The seven handpicked commandos gathered at the rear of the truck.

"How many did you make back there, Israeli?"

"Two."

"One in the tree and one behind the rocks?"

"Exactly."

The giant smiled. "Our eyes see alike."

"I guess we'll have to take those guards out," said Quinn, who'd joined them. "And it'll have to be done quietly or we might as well walk right up to Black and invite ourselves to dinner."

"Don't worry," Sparrow assured him.

Felix pulled the duffel bag from his shoulder and unzipped it, exposing a crossbow and an armory of tight-pointed arrows.

"If they scream," the giant said, "it will be heard only in hell."

"What's the plan from here?" Quinn asked.

"After we take out the two guards at the roadside, Felix and I will move on ahead, say a hundred yards beyond you and the team. We'll handle anyone or any*thing* else along the way. When we reach the kibbutz, we'll wait for you to catch up. The rest is all timing. We'll be able to see the airstrip from the road, and we won't make our move until they tow the F-16 out of the barn I too used as a hangar more than forty years ago."

"Why wait?"

Sparrow checked his watch. "Because once the jet is out of the barn, there'll be no way Black can explode the nuclear device at ground level. The ground-based detonation hookups must be deactivated before the jet can be moved. That means our only concern will be preventing it from taking off, and that task belongs to Felix and myself. You and the commandos are responsible for keeping Black's forces off us until we've disabled the jet."

"Disabled?" Quinn posed tentatively.

"Blown up. Don't worry, the bomb's fail-safe mechanism will prevent it from going off. Now, we better get started. Give Felix and me a few hundred yards' headstart before you follow with the team."

The giant slung the bag back over his shoulder. It was obviously quite heavy, evidence that something besides a simple crossbow was contained inside. Together, the two men set off, Sparrow's limp suddenly less pronounced.

What about me? Dan wanted to shout. But he didn't, because he knew his place now was with Quinn. Whatever happened later would happen. He would trust his feelings and respond to them.

Sparrow and Felix crept along the side of the road, out of sight of anyone who did not directly pass them. They reached a small clearing twenty yards away from the access road entrance, both men sensing that so much as one more step would bring them into the view of the two hidden guards. Felix raised a set of binoculars to his eyes.

"Still there?" Sparrow asked him.

"Haven't moved an inch, Israeli."

Felix lowered the binoculars and reached for his crossbow. Each motion was sure, betraying neither his shattered arm nor the fact that he was well aware of the difficulty of the task he was about to attempt. To keep the guards silent, he'd have to aim the arrows for their throats, leaving him no margin for error at all. Bad enough to have to hit one, but two, within seconds of each other? For anyone else, the charge would have been impossible.

As things were, it promised to be little easier for Felix. The one in the tree was a pretty clean shot. The one behind the rocks was unreachable at this point, in the throat anyway, and that was the only target that mattered. Felix's strategy dictated itself. He would nail the one in the tree first and hope that the other would rise from the rocks in the shock of the moment. That would give him the clear shot he needed. Sparrow guessed each man had a panic button rigged into his walkie-talkie, which left absolutely no room for anything but perfect hits. Felix didn't even think of the delay in reloading the bow. So many things could go wrong, there was no sense in considering any of them.

He fit the first arrow in the center slot grooved for its precise shape. Then, holding the second arrow between his front teeth, he aimed the bow through the sight on its tip. The tree guard's throat appeared. Felix froze his motion, squeezed the trigger, held the bow steady just long enough to make sure the arrow was on its way, and reached for the second.

The man in the tree lurched suddenly on his branch, starting to slip when his jacket latched onto some protruding bark, and his body hung suspended between the sky and ground.

The guard in the rocks caught the sound of fabric tearing and what might have been a soft gasp. He turned toward his fellow, rising slightly—too slightly for Felix to make an accurate shot.

He aimed the crossbow.

The man was dropping a finger toward a black protrusion in his belt.

Felix fired, at the back of the man's neck instead of his far more desirable throat.

The arrow split the vertebrae and creased through the soft flesh of the guard's windpipe. He threw a hand instinctively upward, touched the pulpy head jutting from his throat, and toppled over. He was dead before he hit the ground . . . and before he could hit the panic button on the communicator laced to his belt.

Sparrow checked his watch: five forty-five.

"Good shot," he complimented Felix. The bow was already back in Felix's bag, covering another weapon he'd be using soon, if all went as planned.

They broke into a run and then slackened their pace when they reached the road. Sixty yards on the right was the entrance to the home Sparrow had deserted two weeks before. For him, the nightmare was ending in the very place it had begun.

Both men walked on the road's edge, what would have been its shoulder had it ever been paved. Felix kept his eyes peeled above for the presence of possible cameras. Sparrow kept his focused below, looking for wire strung tight across the road that when struck would trip an alarm in the main house alerting Black to the presence of intruders. Felix never looked down, Sparrow never up. Together they saw everything.

One of Sparrow's hands on his chest stopped Felix in his tracks. He glanced down for the first time. The wire was almost invisible, camouflaged by air and dirt, thin and gnarled. Sparrow's foot rested just under it. Another quarter-step and the secrecy of their assault would be forfeit. Holding his breath, the Israeli reached into his pocket and came out with a pair of wire cutters. A quick slice would cause only a fleeting blip on the screen. It would fade swiftly, as though the wind were responsible. Certainly not something worthy of being investigated.

Sparrow probed the wire cutters down through the air, pulled them back slightly to resteady his hand. If the cut wasn't clean, the blip wouldn't fade. He lowered the instrument again in a line straight as a ruler, centering the wire between the two pincers.

CLIP!

The sound seemed much louder than it actually was. The wire slipped harmlessly to the ground. Sparrow turned long enough to catch his breath and exchange smiles with Felix. Then they were on their way again.

Five forty-nine . . . Eleven minutes to go. . . .

Sparrow guessed there would be two more of the wires before they reached the kibbutz entrance, and he was right. It would have been far simpler merely to step over them, but the entire reason that he and Felix had gone ahead of the commandos was to clear the way for them. They were all tough and seasoned men, superbly trained. Not one of them, though, would have picked out the wire. Sparrow felt certain of that.

There was one man poised at the front gate of the kibbutz, pacing regularly back and forth. Felix reached for the crossbow, but Sparrow shook him off. They couldn't down the man as he stood; he could be seen too clearly from the house and the land around it. Sparrow heard Quinn and the commandos rummaging to his rear, their arrival only seconds away. He thought fast and acted faster, tossing one stone against another. Felix slithered away, in tune with the plan. Sparrow hugged the ground, kept just enough of his frame visible so the guard would investigate.

The man at the gate leveled his rifle and squinted his eyes. He thought he saw something rustling in the brush up ahead but he wasn't sure. Probably just his imagination or a field mouse. He wouldn't know until he checked.

The guard had reached the conclusion that it was a man in the brush when a massive hand closed over his mouth and something sharp bit into his back tearing through his heart. He arched spasmodically and lost his scream in the fingers that shut off his mouth.

Felix pulled his dagger out and slipped the corpse into the bushes. The fact that the guard was no longer at his post wouldn't remain unnoticed for long. They had to act fast.

Five fifty-two . . .

Sparrow and Felix hurried to the gate, keeping their bodies low and just out of view of anyone who might be watching from a reasonable distance. Quinn, the commandos, and Dan approached in single file at near trotting speed and huddled behind the cover of thick bushes, peeking out at the land beyond.

Five fifty-three . . .

Sparrow felt suddenly queasy, a lump in his throat sliding for his stomach. He was home, but it was home only in appearance. He saw the buildings in the foreground and the orchards set behind them, the fields in front; the barn that had once been and was again an airplane hangar; the far field in front of it, now plowed and flattened so it once more assumed the appearance of a runway. The rocks and slopes would make taking off hazardous at best. But plenty of Haganah planes had managed it in the name of freedom, and now one jet was about to try in the name of death.

Five fifty-five . . .

The barn doors swung open. A motor grumbled and sprang to life. Sparrow's newest tractor edged into view, engine revving high, but little ground being made. Chains rattled. The explanation followed. The tip of the silver F-16, its markings changed to match Israel's, moved out from the barn. The doors were just wide enough to accommodate its wingspan, and now those wings eased gracefully forward, the tail of the jet following in their wake.

"Just a little further," Sparrow whispered to himself.

The jet seemed to hear him. The final feet of its sleek body cleared the barn doors, the glistening bird looking like a hostage in chains. The tractor angled slightly to the right to center the F-16 in the makeshift runway.

It was out in the open. The bomb could no longer be set off at ground level.

Five fifty-eight . . .

It was time.

Felix had already pulled what looked to be a shrunken-down bazooka from his duffel bag. In reality, it was a miniature rocket launcher known as the SAM-7, capable of bringing even an airborne craft down. A heat-seeking rocket not more than sixteen inches long and four in diameter at its widest point followed the SAM-7 out of the bag. Felix popped open a rear hatch, slid the rocket in, and closed the latch behind it. He tightened two knobs, slid a bolt back, and held the SAM-7 comfortably by his side, respecting its potential for incredible devastation.

"Ready, Israeli," he announced softly.

Sparrow turned toward Quinn. "Felix and I are going to rush the jet. When you hear the first burst of gunfire, lead the commandos over the fence and keep Black's forces at bay." He whipped an Uzi from the duffel bag, slid back the bolt, and held it out.

"Huh?" Quinn managed, swallowing hard.

Sparrow smiled at him. "Maybe you should guard the front gate and watch our rear."

"That's better," sighed Quinn, taking the Uzi from Sparrow's outstretched hand and feeling immediately uneasy holding it.

Sparrow and Felix crawled away.

Dan looked toward the barn. Renaldo Black stepped into the sun, moving back for the house and signaling the now detached tractor to follow him. Dan felt his muscles tense and his flesh crawl. Before him was the man who had killed Gabriele. He felt in his pocket for the pistol Sparrow had given him.

The Lion of the Night was about to make his rush when his eyes caught something. The ground up ahead immediately beyond the fence to about ten yards back looked as though it had been turned and tilled. But he had never farmed this portion of his land, and unless Renaldo Black had suddenly taken up agriculture there was no explanation for the oddity except. . . .

Sparrow led Felix back away from the gate just as the giant was about to take his first step inside.

"Land mines," he whispered. "The whole area's booby trapped."

"That changes things, Israeli."

"Can you hit the jet from here?"

"Not without luck and a strong wind. And there won't be time for a second shot."

"Then we'll have to circle around."

The F-16's engines kicked on and started revving. The shape of the pilot was all but indiscernible behind the darkened glass.

"Too late," said Felix. He thought quickly. "I can get through the field as it is. Mines do not bother me. I've experienced this type of situation before. I could do it blindfolded, Israeli."

Sparrow acknowledged acceptance with his eyes, not doubting for a second that Felix could accomplish the apparently impossible task.

"Once you're past the mine field," he said, "I'll blast the suckers and we'll follow you in to provide cover."

The thought of shooting out the mines before Felix made his rush crossed his mind but he quickly dismissed it. The explosions would bring all of Black's forces down upon the gate. Felix would never be able to make it through with enough time left over to fire the SAM-7. This was the only way.

The jet engines revved higher, a few scant moments away from takeoff level.

Dan Lennagin was more interested in the sound of the tractor. The driver was still atop it and the engine was still roaring. Renaldo Black emerged from the main house pulling something behind him. Dan sharpened his focus and saw it was actually a some*one*.

"Oh God . . ."

It was Gabriele, alive yes, but not as he remembered her. Her face was purple with bruises and swelling. One eye was totally closed, the other halfway. Her ravishing hair seemed to be shaved in irregular patches all over her scalp, evidence of a particularly awful torture Dan remembered reading about in one of his books. Gabriele had survived it, an amazing feat in itself, and now what was left of her struggled against Black's grasp. Where was he taking her?

Lennagin glanced back at the tractor and the answer became clear. Its grass-cutting blades had been lowered. Black planned to run her over with them! Dan began to rise slowly, saw a man run from the house toward Black who was now dragging Gabriele across the ground by the strap lacing her wrists together. Then a powerful hand belonging to one of the commandos yanked him back down and held him firm.

Black smiled. He had saved this until the last possible moment. He would nail Gabriele's hands and feet into the hard ground with heavy spikes and watch the tractor's mowing blades slice her to bits. It promised to be an excruciating and slow death, fitting for someone who'd betrayed him. Still she resisted. He slapped her hard, drew a few drops of the blood still left in her swollen mouth. He'd enjoyed trying to break her, knowing she would never give in and didn't have anything worth telling him in the first place, performing the torture just for the sport.

He heard the jet's engines screaming now, making final preparations for takeoff. He stole a glance toward the runway and then went back to dragging Gabriele. He might miss the takeoff, but he would not miss her final, agonizing death throes as the machine tore her literally apart. His mouth was dry with anticipation.

He had planned this final leg of Isosceles this way from the start as a contingency wholly supported, even preferred, by the Russians. The damn Lion of the Night had ruined his brilliant plan at the Academy

Awards, but he'd repay him by using his former home as the site from which the world's end would begin. Black prided himself on never running out of cards to play, and this was his final trump. He wondered once again what lay behind Sparrow's constant, obsessive stalking of him, quickly dismissing the thoughts, because all that was over. Libya would go first, then Israel. The rest of the world would tumble like dominoes.

It was all arranged. Fate had spoken and he was its instrument.

And Gabriele Lafontaine was going to die.

A glorious day.

Suddenly the radio man was standing by his side, breathless. "I've lost contact with all the guards! All the lookouts!"

"What!"

Black's cascading thoughts came to an abrupt halt and collided. His precautions, all of them, hadn't been enough. It was the damn Lion of the Night, he felt certain of it, haunting him still, refusing to let him complete his work. He glanced at the jet angling on the runway and cursed himself because detonation of the bomb at ground level was no longer possible.

"Go!" Sparrow screamed.

Felix danced through the mine field, sliding his massive body one way only to shift it all at once back the other. His feet tapped out a bizarrely irregular pattern. He glided effortlessly, never out of step, seeming to float through the air.

"Now, Israeli, now!" he yelled the moment he cleared the field.

Sparrow jammed his finger on the trigger and held it. The mines coughed funnels of dirt into the air, gaping holes left behind them. Sparrow fired in a horizontal plane, clearing the final obstacle between himself and Black, raising the barrel slightly after each pass to strike the next row. The resulting explosions stung his ears. The whole process took exactly seven seconds.

Dan Lennagin vaulted into the field of fire after five, gun drawn and leveled, running toward the downed Gabriele and never feeling the agony that seared through his bandaged shoulder and leg from the strain. Dirt spit into his face, blinding him. He heard his name being screamed from behind but didn't heed the call. Then the calls stopped because the men shouting them had joined him on the other side of the fence, diving, rolling, spinning. Rifles ready and eyes sure, grenades hurled strategically, the commandos fanned out for maximum spread and optimum angle.

More dirt sprayed into Dan's face. He cleared it from his eyes, but their watering had blinded him. The bitter stench of cordite found his nostrils and burned his breath. He ran in the direction he remembered Gabriele to be, while the terrorists who sprang out to defend against the assault from the commandos did so from another direction altogether, saving him from the relentless barrage of bullets that would otherwise have felled him. His eyes finally cleared.

Black was gone. No sign of Gabriele, either. The pistol trembled in his fingers. It was small caliber for easy handling and practicality. Limitations, Sparrow had told him, always be aware of your limitations and respect them.

The F-16 started to dance slowly down the runway.

Felix had aimed the SAM-7 dead on with it when the heat ripped into his lower back, pitching him forward. The launcher fell just ahead and he struggled to reach it. But his fingers balked at the simple commands. Everything became slow, drawn out. His eyes tried to close. He kept them open. His hands, though, were gone. He saw them but couldn't feel or move them. The early evening light was dimming, as though someone was drawing a curtain before him. He disappeared behind it.

The F-16 was gliding now, charging its engines for a final run.

Dan saw the giant go down, saw the blood erupt in a stream from his back, and turned in the direction the shot had come from.

Renaldo Black stood poised behind the tractor, holding Gabriele by the strap in one hand, a long-barreled revolver in the other. He started to squeeze off a second shot to finish the giant off.

Lennagin raised his pistol and fired in a single motion. His aim was off badly, the bullet clanging into the steel of the tractor and becoming lost in its gears. But it struck close enough to Black to stun him so that his shot went wide of its mark. He spun alertly in the direction the bullet had originated from and found himself face to face with the college boy who'd escaped his bullet in Hamburg.

Dan switched his stance to a classic combat style, his left hand steadying his right through the pain in his shoulder. He stood right out in the open, no cover available and none sought. His eyes locked with Black's.

Dan saw a mixture of surprise and uncertainty.

Black saw nothing.

Then the terrorist pulled Gabriele further in front of him and aimed the magnum over her right shoulder. Lennagin fought for a fix on Black's head. It was denied him. He couldn't make himself chance a shot, not with Gabriele so close. He held his ground because he had nothing else to hold.

Black jerked Gabriele one final time, the magnum bulging from her shoulder, straight and steady now. Black started the trigger backwards. Gabriele twisted and pulled, using the leash restraining her as a weapon. Black felt her dip behind him and saw the leather strap climb over his face. He got his left arm up just in time and shifted his shoulders. Gabriele escaped his eyes but she could not escape his gun.

The magnum angled over his shoulder and he fired it blindly into her. The bullet entered just under her nose, shattering what remained of her once-beautiful face. Black heard her gasp and tumble, knew he had killed her, and swung the gun around again.

Dan had moved ten yards closer, right in line with him. Black reckoned he felt the heat of the first bullet an instant before it burned into his shoulder, driving him backwards. The second rammed into the pit of his stomach. Blood spurted, not denying the terrorist his senses. He reasoned the bullets must have been of low caliber, .22 even, which meant he wasn't mortally wounded. Not even close. As Dan closed for the kill, he vaulted up and over the tractor, pushing off with his hands and swinging his legs like a gymnast. A line of blood stained the air in his wake.

Dan lost the precisioned certainty of the moment. Cold reality poured into him, sent his next two shots flying errantly away. He took careful aim at the figure of Black fleeing toward the main house. The steadiness, though, was gone, and so was the resolve. He glanced down at the shapeless mass that had once been Gabriele, felt bile rise in his throat, and looked away.

The bile left a hot, chalky sensation all the way down his insides. To have her back only to lose her again, for good. The hopelessness of it all was utterly revealed. He wondered where the tears were.

Beyond him the F-16 was roaring down the final stretch of runway, its tires ready to embrace the air after being delayed considerably by the rut-filled field. Dan sped toward Felix, not thinking of the jet until he saw the thick tubular weapon lying just in front of him. The giant's dimming eyes beckoned him to take it. Dan lifted the SAM-7, judged its weight, pulled its sight to his eye. The weapon felt rear heavy, hard to balance.

The F-16 touched the ground one last time. Its nose angled upward, lifting the bird sharply into the air.

Dan adjusted the SAM-7's barrel to rise with it, watched the jet rapidly ascending out of range. In his mind it was too far alway already and he could never have hit it with so unfamiliar a weapon even if it had been stationary. The SAM-7 was too bulky. It shook in his hands. His torn shoulder throbbed madly from the pressure.

The F-16 banked toward the clouds.

Dan pulled back on the heavy trigger. The recoil slammed the SAM-7 into his chest. He toppled backwards, head landing first. His eyes met the sky, caught a whirl of motion rising after the jet for the clouds. At first, it seemed the small missile was hopelessly off target. But suddenly its sensors caught the F-16's exhaust fumes and sent it rising sharply toward their source. The gap narrowed. The F-16 became a speck; the SAM-7 rocket vanished altogether.

Dan felt the emptiness of despair, of failure, of futility.

Until the sky blazed fiery orange. The blast felt like it

sprang from a dream. A horrific roar and then there was nothing besides tiny fragments of silvery metal dancing and darting in the wind. A cloud rolled forward and even these vanished.

"Good shooting, boy," Felix muttered.

To their right, the handpicked commandos were still engaging Black's forces. They were outmanned, but the enemy's superior numbers did little for their organization. They moved as individuals, not a unit. The seven expertly trained specialists had learned long ago that maneuvers won battles, not bullets. And they used them all, conveying the impression that there were far more than just seven of them. Each time the terrorists tried a rush, they were cut down in their tracks, from the rear as well as the front, two members of the crack team having managed to slither through their lines to the rear flank. They were more than neutralizing Black's men; they were destroying them.

Dan searched for Sparrow in the midst of the battle, but his eyes came up empty. The old Israeli was nowhere to be seen. He had been the first to rush through the shattered mine field. Might one of the terrorists have picked him off? There were so many bodies now; just no way to tell. Dan stayed pinned to the turf, holding his jacket against the wound in Felix's back to slow the giant's blood loss.

Renaldo Black had crashed through the front door of the main house, his entire body an inferno of pain from the searing wounds in his stomach and shoulder. He tripped on a cord and went down hard, struggled to his feet and slid to the window. The F-16 was tearing for the clouds, a semblance of victory. Then the blast came and it was gone.

He had lost. It was over. The battle in the front was

still raging, which left the rear clear. He'd make his escape in that direction, cross into Jordan and build himself back to life. He needed medical attention. But he'd traveled much farther with more severe wounds than this. The two small caliber bullets in his flesh wouldn't even slow him down. Later he would seek revenge, find another Isosceles a thousand times more effective. The thought spurred him on.

But not very far.

He heard the click of a pistol's hammer being pulled back because Sparrow wanted him to know what was coming. The first shot spun him violently around, the magnum flying from his hand. The second thumped into his chest. Black felt his breastbone shatter and his breath escape in a rush. His head crashed into something and he realized with cold fear that it was the floor, which meant his senses were gone and death was coming.

The magnum was just beyond his grasp. He strained to reach it.

Sparrow's .45 appeared in his path, its muzzle on line with his face. Black's eyes locked onto his expression, grim yet placid. The Israeli had chased him halfway around the world and back again. Now he had finally won, but no glint of victory sparkled in his eyes.

"Why?" Black rasped. "Why?"

The Lion of the Night regarded him distantly. "Because Jason Levine was my grandson."

Black lunged for the magnum.

Sparrow pulled the .45's trigger.

EPILOGUE

It was a week later when Sparrow met the President for lunch before returning to Israel.

"Is there anything we can take out of this?" the chief executive asked him as they strolled together through the Rose Garden.

"Not unless you count the hope that it will never happen again."

"I don't." The President shook his head reflectively. "The irony of it all is that in theory the original Lucifer Directive makes a great deal of sense."

"I wasn't talking about Lucifer, not specifically anyway. There are dozens of other organizations all across the world that fit a similar but smaller mold. They don't have the power and resources Lucifer has, but that's not saying they won't someday."

"So what should we do, disband them all?"

"That's not the answer, either. You're right in stating there's purpose in their existence; if nothing else, at least to keep a balance between murderers and those who seek vengeance for their senseless acts. Take them away and the balance tips too far in the direction of Renaldo Black and his kind. We have to maintain a system of checks."

"On terrorism or ourselves?"

"Both."

"Then maybe the system's wrong."

"Maybe. But you can't have it both ways. Without organizations like Lucifer, terrorism would open its floodgates and pour freely everywhere. With them, well, we've witnessed the ramifications of that now, too."

"Any ideas on how to eliminate the catch?"

"Redesign the system, don't abolish it. The way things are right now, we need Lucifer more than ever. But not the kind of Lucifer that can take matters into its own hands."

"Sounds like you're offering your services."

Sparrow smiled, hedging. "I come from a different age. I'm not sure my kind of thinking would be very well accepted these days."

"On the other hand, it might be just what we need. You helped build the original Lucifer. Now I'm asking you to *rebuild* it."

Sparrow's eyes found the President's. "I'll give the offer some thought."

"I'd appreciate it."

The two men started walking again and took seats at a neatly set table beneath a canopy. The spring air felt warm and crisp, laced with a hint of summer. Sparrow eased his bad leg next to his good one. The pain was at its least bothersome.

"How's Felix?" the President inquired.

"Doctors pulled a bullet out of his spine and said he'd never walk again. He's already trotting down the corridors."

"Amazing man."

"Yes."

The President poured two glasses of iced tea and passed one across the table. "And what of Lennagin? I mean, we can't expect him to just pick up his diploma and go on his merry way after what he's been through."

"I suppose not."

The President leaned forward. "Of course, if you went back into Lucifer, you could take him with you. We've already seen what he's capable of. And Lucifer would be the perfect channel for him to utilize his newfound abilities . . . and knowledge, under your guidance."

Sparrow fingered his chin. "I hadn't thought of that. . . ."

"Like the idea?"

"It certainly has possibilities," the Lion of the Night said, and somewhere deep he buried a smile.

On the steps of the J. Edgar Hoover Building, one figure climbed gingerly toward another waiting near the entrance.

"I guess this is good-bye, Paul," Dan said, extending his hand toward Quinn when he reached him.

The FBI man looked hurt and confused. "You only just got here."

"I'd like to get back to Providence."

Dan's wounds had healed well. His leg pained him only when he climbed steps and he had discarded the sling two days ago, though his range of motion with his left arm was still quite limited. Quinn studied him briefly, making the inevitable comparisons with the youth who'd walked into his office on a Saturday three weeks earlier. Lennagin's eyes then had been fearful and uncertain. Today the uncertainty remained but the fear was gone, replaced by a stone-cold emptiness that rose from deep within, looking almost like the eyes of a man who has seen the film he's watching too many times before.

"How'd the briefing go?" Quinn asked.

"It was thorough and exhausting, but they kept me comfortable. They seemed satisfied I wasn't holding anything back."

"You got the treatment usually reserved for defecting spies."

"They also took care of my debts to the university and my fraternity. I guess I should feel grateful." Dan hesitated. "By the way, I'm surprised you're not cleaning out your desk by now. What happened to private practice?"

"I don't have the guts to make a career change at this point. Besides, I just got a promotion and a fat raise to go with it. I know too much for them to let me slip away. In that sense, you and I are pretty much alike. So call the new office and extra bucks bribery if you want, but I'm not complaining. At least I won't be piloting a desk anymore."

"I never really got a chance to thank you," Dan offered lamely.

"Forget it, kid. I headed over to Europe because I knew I was the only one you knew and might trust, and I figured I owed you. But if I'd known in advance that bringing you back home would mean going through a couple machine gun clips and putting my balls on the line, I'd have applied for early retirement and hung up my legal sheepskin then and there. Hell, up until a week ago, the only people I'd shot were made of cardboard and had black circles drawn on their chests." Quinn paused. "You going back to Providence for good?"

"My diploma will be waiting in June whether I do or not. They told me I could have any degree I wanted. Not that it matters, because I can't see myself plunging into the job market at this point anyway."

"What's the alternative?"

"Lucifer."

"Lucifer?"

Dan nodded. "Sparrow told me the President asked him to rebuild it and suggested he take me along."

"When did he tell you that?"

"Two days ago."

Quinn looked puzzled. "That's funny, because he's meeting with the President right now for the first time since this whole mess ended. But I guess they could have spoken about it before today."

"Sure," Dan said, but somehow he knew otherwise.

"Is that what you want, kid, to go into Lucifer?"

"I don't know, Paul." Dan turned away briefly so Quinn wouldn't see the uncertainty in his eyes. "I don't know what I want. In Cairo, Koralski said that once you've experienced this sort of life you can never go back to anything ordinary. I'm starting to understand what he was talking about. I mean, there were times during the last few weeks when I never felt more alive."

"Considering you came close to getting yourself splattered all over Europe, that's a pretty strange feeling."

"Managed to get myself back, though," Dan said hopefully.

Quinn regarded him with a sad smile. "Maybe, kid. Maybe."